# DAVID HAIR

# The King

## THE RETURN OF RAVANA
### Book IV

Jo Fletcher
BOOKS

First published in Great Britain in 2019 by

Jo Fletcher Books
an imprint of
Quercus Editions Ltd
Carmelite House
50 Victoria Embankment
London EC4Y 0DZ

An Hachette UK company

A CIP catalogue record for this book is available
from the British Library

PB ISBN 978 0 85705 363 3
EBOOK ISBN 978 1 78429 083 2

This book is a work of fiction. Names, characters,
businesses, organizations, places and events are
either the product of the author's imagination
or used fictitiously. Any resemblance to
actual persons, living or dead, events or
locales is entirely coincidental.

10 9 8 7 6 5 4 3 2 1

Typeset by CC Book Production

Printed and bound in Great Britain by Clays Ltd, Elcograf S.p.A.

*This book is dedicated to Jo Fletcher;*
*my editor and guide in bringing most of my books to life —*
*I'm very, very lucky to get to work with the best.*

# CONTENTS

## PART TWO: TO REIGN IN LANKA

# PROLOGUE

# THE PHOTOGRAPHER

*Harappa, Punjab, April 1947*

'Mister Tim — Tim-sahib! Chai? Chai?'

The shrill cry jolted the white man beneath the straw hat from his daydream. He looked down from his vantage point, a stone platform at the highest point of the excavations, and waved to the little chai-wallah below. Sweat had plastered his shirt to his back and standing up for too long in this heat was dizzying. The grit filling the air had itched its way into the corners of his eyes and dried the roof of his mouth. It was only April — what would the height of summer be like here? Realising that he was really thirsty, he waved again and called, 'Yes, please, Ramesh. Make it a big one. I'll come down!'

'No—no, Tim-sahib, I climb! I climb!' The little urchin — he was no more than eleven — swarmed up the rocks like one of the brown monkeys that infested the site, grinning through uneven white teeth. 'See? I climb.' The boy's limited English was definitely improving. In seconds he was crouched beside the Englishman in the shade of the pinnacle and peering around, delighted to be so high up. 'Like ants,' he grinned, pointing down at the dozens of men labouring below.

Tim Southby smiled back. 'Just like ants,' he agreed.

The boy poured a cup of sweet, spicy tea, and handed it to the Englishman with hero worship in his eyes. To them he was a war hero, a fighter pilot who'd won the DFC and Bar at the Battle of Britain. Those surreal, harrowing days had ended when an ME-109 got him in its sights and blasted his right leg off below the knee, so now he was just a photographer with a wooden leg. But everyone here insisted on treating him like some kind of minor deity. It wasn't something he enjoyed.

History and photography had been his twin passions growing up, and when the war was over he'd needed little persuasion to leave battered, miserable England behind to join an old school chum here in the Punjab, especially after his sweetheart Annie had made it abundantly clear that a one-legged man – even a hero – could offer her nothing. Within weeks of dumping him, unable to bear his 'repulsive scars', she'd latched on to one of his squadron mates, so when his ship left Southampton, he'd been on the foredeck looking determinedly ahead.

Ramesh drew his attention back, fishing into a pocket and pulling out a little metal disc. 'Money,' he said, in an awed voice. 'Old people money.' He showed it to Southby, who took it thoughtfully.

'Look,' he said, showing the boy the etched figure of a seated man in profile. 'It's another one showing a king.'

'King?' The boy tried out the word.

'Your word is "Raja",' Southby told him, returning the coin – they were common enough here that he could turn a blind eye to it disappearing back into a grubby pocket instead of being handed over to the site supervisor. Together, they sipped the chai and gazed over the dig, which extended hundreds of yards in every direction. All around them were trenches and walkways bridging holes and walls as the shape of the buried city slowly emerged from the earth like dinosaur bones.

'This place may be the most significant archaeological dig of the era,' Southby said, more to himself than the boy, who wouldn't understand most of what he was saying. 'Hammond believes these Indus Valley sites may predate Egypt or Sumeria: this may be the very place where man first evolved civilisation. There are drains and watercourses, walls, streets . . . it's *magnificent*. All the stone blocks are regular, precisely placed and fitted. And there is no obvious royal or religious ostentation, either – the society here must have been far more egalitarian than later cultures. Before the warlords and priests got their grip on the people,' he added vehemently, thinking of generals and priests he'd known in the war, men who thought only in terms of 'acceptable attrition' and 'sacrifice for the greater good'.

'This place must have been a relative paradise, an island of culture in a sea of primitive barbarism.'

'Baa-baa . . .' Ramesh echoed, giggling at the word.

'Bar-bar-ism.' Southby grinned. 'Actually, the word does come from "baa-baa" – the noise the Romans heard when the Germanic tribes spoke.' He grunted. 'Damned Germans, still causing trouble.' He finished his tea and was about to rise when a movement below caught his eye. 'Hey, who's your friend?'

'Friend?' Ramesh puzzled over the word as he peered into the shadows. 'Oh, it's Kamila – *Kamila!*' He waved a hand and a plump girl of about his age slunk from behind a rock and stared up at them.

'Hello!' Southby called down.

The girl shrank back. Ramesh called to her in his rapid-fire Punjabi and she answered tentatively. 'Kamila is scared of you,' Ramesh reported.

'I won't bite her.'

'Bite!' Ramesh chortled, snapping his teeth. 'Bite-bite-bite!' He called something teasing to the girl in his own tongue, and she took fright and fled. 'Heh-heh. I say to her, "Sahib will bite you!"'

'For shame, Ramesh. She'll be scared of me for the rest of her life, now.'

The boy grinned mischievously until an impatient voice shouted in Punjabi. Ramesh shouted back, reclaimed Southby's empty cup and with a wave, he was gone, bouncing back down the pile of stones.

Ramesh was soon replaced by the foreman, Anand Gupta, a plump fellow who always smelled like he needed a bath. His moustaches were always immaculate, though. 'Good evening, Southby-sahib,' he greeted the Englishman. 'Is it a good day for pictures? Is the light good today?' he asked politely, although he had little knowledge of the arcane arts of photography.

Southby shook his head. 'The air is very hazy today,

Anand. Not good for photography, only for pretty sunsets. There's a lot of smoke coming from the cities. More even than during the winter.' He thought about that. 'Is there trouble there, Anand?'

Anand Gupta frowned. 'There is always trouble these days, Southby-sahib. Ever since Jinnah won the right for this new "Pakistan", this Muslim state. My people are worried. They say Muslims are killing Sikhs and Hindus here in Western Punjab, and Sikhs and Hindus are killing Muslims in Hindustan. It is not good.'

'It isn't good,' Southby agreed, scanning the hazy horizons. Most of the early workers had come from the nearby town of Harappa – well, it was little more than a village, really – until the need for labour had increased; now it was a pretty mixed crew, from all over the region. There had already been trouble between the Muslims and Hindus, fuelled by the rumours. But Southby was just the camera-jockey. The workers were Gupta and Hammond's problem.

'They say the Muslim National Guard are going from village to village,' Gupta added. 'The Guard have been declared illegal, but the army does nothing – you Britishers, you do nothing,' he added sullenly.

Southby said apologetically, 'Welcome to independence. You have to solve your own problems when you're independent.'

'You British *caused* most of those problems,' Gupta snapped back, then bit his tongue. 'I am sorry, Southby-sahib. I know it is not your fault personally. I am talking from worry only.' He hung his head. 'I am talking too much.'

Southby inclined his head sympathetically. Gupta wasn't

a bad old stick, and he must be worried for his family and himself, a Hindu stuck here in what would soon be the territory of Pakistan.

'We have been given guarantees from those men who will form the new administration in Islamabad,' he reminded the foreman. 'You and your people will be safe here.'

Gupta looked at him with troubled eyes. 'I am thinking you are very naïve, Southby-sahib.'

Southby woke to find a gun jammed viciously into his cheek. The man wielding it looked like an Afghani tribesman, but he wore a deep green overcoat and the crescent badge of the outlawed Muslim National Guard. His lean, scarred face was buried in a spade-like beard; his eyes were sunken pits. The skin on his hands and face was blotched and pitted all over, as if he'd been scalded by boiling water as a child.

'Get up, English,' the man snarled, poking him with the gun muzzle, and now Southby could see two smaller men behind him, dressed in the same uniform, with rifles levelled at him.

Southby slowly lifted his hands. He was unsurprised to find himself calm; any fear of death had been burned away in the skies above England, exorcised by the sounds of shredding fuselage and the pumping guns of the Messerschmitt. 'What is going on here?' he asked levelly.

'You are leaving, English,' the big man told him. 'This is not your land any more. Get dressed, gather your belongings.'

'Where's Hammond?' Southby demanded. One of the men behind his captor snarled and snapped something. The scarred man barked back, and the other man subsided.

'Mister Hammond is being packed away also. Now get up, Mister Southby, before I ask my friends here to help you.'

The two riflemen grinned wolfishly at him, stroking their weapons.

After the humiliation of having to strap on his artificial lower leg under the sneering eyes of these men, Southby quickly gathered his gear before working up the nerve to ask the scar-faced spokesman, 'Who are you?' He wasn't really expecting a reply.

'My name is Mehtan Ali,' the man replied. 'I am a commander of the Guard.' He was leafing through the photographs with surprising interest. 'These are fascinating, are they not?' He examined a shot Southby had taken of Mohenjo-Daro to the south, for comparison purposes to this site. 'These sites are all from the same period?'

'We think so,' Southby responded coolly, jamming his clothes into his battered suitcase. 'Are you a scholar, Mehtan Ali?'

'I have been many things,' Mehtan replied. 'What are you Britishers calling these places?'

'Harappan, named for this site,' Southby replied. 'Look, we have permits and—'

'Your permits mean nothing, Mister Southby. I am moving you for your own protection.' Mehtan Ali opened a drawer before Southby could reach it and removed Southby's revolver. 'I do not think you will be needing this,' he said mildly, thrusting the gun into his own belt. 'My soldiers would take it amiss if they saw it.'

'What about the workers here?' Southby asked, failing to keep anxiety from his voice.

Mehtan Ali scowled and the thin veneer of civility vanished. 'This is *Pakistan* now, Mister Southby: an *Islamic* state.'

'Not until June.'

'It has *always* been Muslim, Mister Southby — even before the Ghori crushed that pig Prithviraj Chauhan, this region bowed to Allah. But it needs to be purified anew.' He looked at Southby's suitcase and the bags containing his photographic equipment. 'Is that all? Then come.'

Southby hefted his gear and walked outside. Dawn had not yet broken, but in the dim light he could see fierce green-clad irregulars everywhere, all of them brandishing rifles and vicious-looking knives. He could see Gupta, standing amongst a huddled group of workmen; with a chill he realised they were all Hindu. The Muslim workers appeared to be walking freely among the fighting men, although they too looked frightened.

Southby turned back to Mehtan Ali. 'Now, see here—' he began, but his words were choked off when Mehtan casually grabbed his throat in a vice-like grip.

'You will be *silent*, Mister Southby.' He released his hold, leaving Southby doubled over, fighting for breath, his neck throbbing.

Southby's cases were taken and loaded onto a Jeep, but he himself was led to a vantage point overlooking the dig. Hammond was there too, his cheek bleeding and his eye puffing up.

'Southby!' the archaeologist exclaimed. 'Thank God — are you all right?'

'I'm—'

But Southby's intended words were silenced by a sudden volley of gunfire. He spun round, looking for the Hindu workmen, but they had already been reduced to a bloody tangle of bodies. Riflemen poked through the fallen, laughing and calling to each other as they bayoneted anyone unfortunate enough to still be breathing.

He turned to Mehtan Ali. 'By all that's decent, man, what are you doing? That's *barbaric*!'

The Muslim captain's face held little expression in the half-light. He ignored Southby's tirade completely. 'Harappa. Mohenjo-Daro. I have always been drawn to these places. We knew they were there, long before you British "discovered" them. Sometimes I feel that they call to me . . .'

'The workers . . . your men have . . .' Hammond stared, wide-eyed.

Mehtan Ali's eyes remained unfocused, as if he were looking into the past. 'This was the cradle of civilisation,' he said softly, 'a great Bronze Age civilisation, the equal of anything in your *Iliad*s and *Odyssey*s. This was a place of legend.' He turned to them slowly, his voice reverent. 'This is the birthplace of India. Imagine that.'

Hammond looked fearfully at Southby. *Do not provoke him*, Southby tried to convey with his eyes; *he's clearly dangerously insane*. Southby turned away – and saw something else that sucked away his breath.

Two bodies were swinging from a gallows made of tent poles: Ramesh and his friend Kamila had been hanged, then spitted through the belly with spears. The corpses swung slowly in the dawn breeze. Their eyes were open, their mouths frozen in soundless screams.

Mehtan Ali followed his gaze. 'Ah, yes,' he said, with immense satisfaction. 'It is a momentous day. A day of great victories.'

# PART ONE
# IN SEARCH OF LANKA

# CHAPTER ONE

# A SECRET WEDDING, AND AFTER

*Pushkar, Rajasthan, March 2011*

Amanjit Singh Bajaj rode a white horse, wearing a heavy white sherwani and a red turban. He carried a gold-hilted scimitar. About him, a small group of family and friends danced and sang with the band, a loose gaggle of trumpeters, cymbal-bangers, drummers and fire-eaters, as they clamoured through the streets of Pushkar. Before them was the final climb to the Brahma temple, where his beloved awaited him. They had a Sikh giani and a Hindu pandit, for this ceremony was going to be a weird blend of Sikh and Hindu traditions – one to make the traditionalists wince, not that he cared. He grinned down at his mother Kiran, clad in her widow's garb, looking torn between tears and happiness. He smirked at his brother Bishin, who was dancing with an impossibly lovely local girl in a pale yellow sari. He tossed money to the musicians to keep them playing hard, all the while laughing for such joy that he could almost ignore the strangeness of it all.

For this wasn't Pushkar at all — not the *real* Pushkar, anyway. This was a *secret* Pushkar, a Pushkar few could find — but he and Vikram Khandavani, his soul-brother, could. Vikram was his stepbrother too, son of his mother's dead husband. Vikram was flanking the procession; it was he who'd brought the families from *real* Pushkar to this other place so they could bear witness as Amanjit married his beloved Deepika. They'd told the guests it was an exclusive theme park, for in this hidden Pushkar, the town was still mediaeval, with no electricity, no cars, no reception for their mobiles. There were horses on the streets, and far fewer people. If they'd looked closely enough, they might even have been able to discern that the moon was not a lump of inert rock orbiting the Earth, but a silver chariot driven by a god. *This* Pushkar was *truly* legendary: one of those rare spots where belief had generated a *different* place right around the corner from reality.

So far, none of his family had noticed the lack of power lines or vehicles in the streets, or the out-of-time locals; they were admiring the *costumes*, pointing at the armoured swordsmen on the streets and laughingly keeping an eye out for demons — all just part of the entertainment, something to marvel at while drinking and partying. *Very Punjabi*, he thought, smiling.

He looked over at Vikram, who was shadowing the procession, holding a bow and poised for action. Vikram was no longer the skinny, short-sighted young man he'd first met. He'd never be tall, but he was all toned, lean muscle. His hair had grown and was now caught back in a ponytail. He had an erect bearing and an air of grace and command about him; his eyes, filled with knowledge and old sorrow, made him look older than his years. In a way, he was: Vikram could remember all his past lives, and perform feats far beyond normal men. He was Amanjit's closest friend, and when he married Amanjit's sister Rasita, they would truly be brothers.

His smile faltered when he thought of Ras. *Where is she? Is she safe?*

It was hard to ignore such burning questions, but he was resolved to, for Deepika's sake. With a prayer, he pushed Ras' image to the back of his mind; this wasn't the day to dwell on such things. He waved at Vikram, then nudged his horse around the final bend and looked up, seeking his bride.

There she was! At the top of the stairs Deepika waited for him, shining like an angel in the midst of bewildered-looking girlfriends, cousins and parents. She was wrapped in a scarlet wedding sari stiff with embroidery and decoration and glittering with gems and sequins. Her lovely face peered out from between the folds of the pallu. When she met his eyes, his heart sped.

Today, finally, they were going to marry.

He looked back at Vikram, who gave a taut smile. *Be happy, Amanjit-bhai*, his eyes said, then he looked away and Amanjit guessed he was thinking of Rasita too.

*We'll get her back, brother. Have faith.*

Then his eyes went forward again, and all he could think of was how his heart might burst before he was married, it was hammering so hard.

\*

A week after the wedding found Vikram in the courtyard of the Brahma temple, bare-chested, going through a sword drill . . . *again*. Apart from an ancient man in orange robes with dreadlocks past his knees, he was alone. Somewhere in the raja's palace, Amanjit and Deepika were also alone, but together, laughing, joking, holding hands – being in love. *Being married*. They were two halves of a whole and it was beautiful to see, even if that was denied him, for now at least.

Memories of the wedding flooded back: the love, the laughter, the singing, the music, the dancing – all night, like dervishes! Even he had been able to put all his fears aside for a while.

'Focus, Chand,' Sage Vishwamitra warned again. He had called Vikram 'Chand' over many lifetimes; he was too old to change now, he said.

Vikram stopped and refocused, centring his balance and flexing. 'Sorry, Guru-ji.'

'A poorly executed drill cheats only yourself,' Vishwamitra told him for the third time that morning. 'Again – and perfect, this time, please.'

This time Vikram threw himself into the routine, sending the blade flashing about him, each movement graceful and as good as it could be. He wasn't as blindingly fast or powerful as Amanjit, but he was still pretty damn good, and by the time he'd finished, he was breathing hard and sweating.

He gulped down some water, then sat with the sage and gazed out through the gates towards the lake. Sunshine glittered distantly on water. In the real world, an inept de-silting operation had left the lake all but dried up, but in this legend-place it was full – it still had fish and even crocodiles in it. Vikram had been told that in the real world, worshippers long ago used to allow themselves to be eaten by the crocodiles – it was said to be good luck, although presumably in their next life!

*Good luck for the crocodile, anyway . . .*

After the wedding, Vikram had taken the guests, who all believed they had been in some beautiful mediaeval theme park near Pushkar, back to the real world. This was the last day of Amanjit and Deepika's brief honeymoon; tomorrow they too would resume training – they couldn't afford to set aside any more time for pleasure, not with so much at stake. The wedding had been important and necessary, but now it was time to refocus on an ages-old conflict that appeared to be coming to a head.

'Have you formulated a plan?' Vishwamitra asked.

'Tentatively, Guru-ji,' Vikram replied, 'but I haven't talked it through with Amanjit and Dee yet, so nothing is set in stone.' He ticked off the points on his fingers as he explained. 'So, here's the basic idea: we're guessing Ravindra has taken Rasita to "Lanka", which we presume is actually "Sri Lanka", as the *Ramayana* tells. When Ravindra set up the ritual in Mandore, he needed to kill each of the queens while they were wearing their heart-stones, and that went wrong when Padma, who's now Ras, gave her brother Shastri, or Amanjit, her heart-stone to give to me, and I – as Aram Dhoop, obviously – rescued Dee, or Darya, as she was. So he doesn't have everything he needs. He's got Ras, but not her heart-stone. He has Deepika's heart-stone, but not Dee – and he thinks she's dead. And he seems to need to kill me, which he hasn't done either.' His face clouded. 'Yet.'

The sage put a hand on his arm. 'In the *Ramayana*, Ravana tries to *seduce* Sita; he does not use violence against her. So she should be physically safe, and I am quite sure you can count on her loyalty. She will not be seduced. You *know* that.'

Vikram didn't feel so sure; his past lives had told him that flesh and will could sometimes be weak, even in the strongest person. 'In the *Ramayana*, yes – but we don't know why a lot of what we do appears to be mirroring the *Ramayana*, or why sometimes it doesn't. Like Deepika and what happened to her: she transforms into the Goddess Kali when she loses her temper – but Kali isn't part of the *Ramayana*, is she? So even now, we don't know the rules! We don't know *anything* for sure. How do we know that in this life, Ravindra has to seduce her at all? Maybe he'll just kill her? Or rape her? He might have already . . . and we've done nothing.' He hung his head, distraught at his helplessness.

Vishwamitra put a hand on his shoulder. 'Chand, this delay has been unavoidable. For a start, you all needed rest – your last encounters with the enemy left you all on the verge of collapse. And now Amanjit has made the breakthrough and can use the astras, he must be trained: you know this. Deepika too has work to do: she must learn to control and channel her fury, and to mask herself so that she is not revealed to Ravindra.'

Vikram nodded gloomily. 'And just to make life more interesting, we also have to prevent Uncle Charanpreet from getting all Amanjit's mum's money, and Tanita from getting all Dad's money. And we have to find Sue Parker. And clear our names over Sunita's death.' He sighed wearily. 'I barely know where to start.'

Vishwamitra grinned through broken teeth. 'Yes, you do have a few things to focus on – but I will give you this advice: don't let the magnitude of your tasks overwhelm you. Great journeys are made up of small steps, Chand, and small steps are always achievable.'

Vikram smiled. 'You're right as usual, Guru-ji.' He stood up and stretched, then picked up a bow and strung it. 'I'd better get back to my drills.' He grinned mischievously. 'Is there anything you'd like demolished?'

They set up a broken wagon in a field outside the town. Mythic Pushkar was eerily devoid of humanity, and perhaps all the better for it – there were no roads or refuse-pits, no continual rumbling traffic or constantly smoking fires. This was still a pristine place of gentle breezes and clean streams, plentiful birds and wildlife. Snakes coiled on rocks; lizards basked. Foxes would steal past, and deer gambolled in the glades. It would be an easy place to live.

But Vikram knew he'd have no peace until he saved Rasita and slew his Enemy. *Maybe when all this is done, I'll live here in the myth-lands, happily ever after* . . . But he couldn't picture such a time. In life after life, he'd failed – why should this one be any different?

He readied his bow, drew it and awaited Vishwamitra's command.

'Aindra-astra!' the old sage shouted.

Vikram muttered the incantation and fired, and his arrow burst apart as it flew, becoming a vast shower of shafts that arced and then slammed into the wagon and the area about it. He'd split it into at least four dozen arrows.

'Focus, Chand!' cried Vishwamitra; Vikram knew it was at best a moderate effort – he'd achieved more. 'Agniyastra!'

This time the arrow burst into flames as it flew, striking the wagon like a rocket, blasting a hole in its side and setting it alight.

'Varuna-astra!' the sage yelled, barely giving him time to examine the results, and the next arrow became a torrent of water that extinguished the flames.

Vikram was panting a little more now, as each arrow drew something from him. Legend said that the astras were gifts of the gods, but to Vikram, the vital energy that empowered his astras had always come from within; he'd never sensed any divine presence when using them. They left him tired, hollowed out inside, as if the marrow of his bones had been sucked out.

'Naga-astra!'

His next shaft became a snake, a common brown, that struck a pole beside the wagon and wrapped itself around, biting the pole, then slithering down it and wriggling away. In a few minutes, it would be an arrow again, lying in the dirt, twisted and unusable.

'Nagapastra!'

This time the arrow split into a host of snakes that hammered against the wagon and lay there stunned, then twisted into a pile of wood shavings.

'Vavayastra!'

The arrow vanished, but a vicious gust of wind slammed against the wagon and flipped it over and over before dissipating.

'Suryastra!'

A brilliant light that outshone the sun lit the field like a flare, and both men had to shield their eyes.

'Good, Chand, good!' the sage called. 'Now the vajra!'

Vikram fired the arrow straight up and it exploded far above into a bolt of lightning that blasted the wagon in a dazzling flash that looked like a tear in the fabric of the world. His hair stood on end as the current earthed, and when he could open his eyes again, what was left of the wagon was gently smouldering, although sparks were still leaping on the metal parts.

Vishwamitra laughed aloud. His dreadlocks had lifted about him from the static charge, looking like rays of a grimy sun. The old guru muttered a word and earthed the current through his wooden staff, causing his locks to flop back down about his face. He chuckled merrily. 'You are a shocking pupil, Chand,' he joked, as he always did at this point in the routine. 'Now – the mohini!' He gestured, and a gaudy bipedal reptile, human-sized and brandishing a sword, appeared a hundred yards away, roared and sprinted at Vikram.

The mohini arrow sliced through the illusory being and immediately sucked the magic into itself. Having destroyed the spell, the shaft hung in the air, crackling, then twisted and burned to ash.

'And finally, the parvata-astra!'

Vikram took his last arrow from the quiver and fired. The arrowhead grew as it flashed towards the charred remains of the wagon, becoming a rock the size of a boulder. It shattered the remnants into splinters and tangled metal. He panted, feeling a little woozy.

Vishwamitra patted him on the shoulder. 'Well done, Chand, well done. Come, let us return home and rest. And you can tell me of other astras you know on the way back.'

It was in the 1140s that Chand, as he was named in that life, had first come to the gurukul; it was there the guru Vishwamitra had discovered that he was one of a tiny number of warriors who could summon the astras. He'd been trained under intense secrecy, but he had left the ashram before completing that training, for he wouldn't be parted from his best friend, Prithviraj Chauhan.

After recovering his past-life memories in later lives in the thirteenth and fourteenth centuries, he had returned to finish his training – then the gurukul had vanished and he'd not found it again . . . until, just a few weeks ago, while hunting Rasita's heart-stone, he'd chanced upon Master Vishwamitra again, here in Pushkar.

Vishwamitra claimed he'd adopted the name of the legendary sage who'd taught Rama in the *Ramayana*, but as he dwelt more and more in the myth-lands, he barely aged.

In almost all his lives since Chand Bardai, Vikram had used astras in secret, when it was necessary; he had even invented some of his own. But this time his past-life memories were still patchy, so it was good to have this time with his guru, to be reminded of things he had genuinely forgotten, and to polish his technique.

'The other legendary astras are these, Guruji,' he said now as he walked beside the spry old man. 'The twashtar confuses a body of men, disorientating and stunning them, making them see friends as enemies for a time, or setting them wandering aimlessly. It's useful against unsuspecting enemies, but not in battle, where the reality of the situation will quickly refocus the mind.'

'Correct. And you told me you used the sammohana, the sleep arrow, recently?'

'Yes, Guru-ji – but it's only really useful against people who are already drowsy. It doesn't do any lasting harm, but the victim can be woken easily, so the sammohana is not useful in combat, only in situations requiring stealth.'

'And you have invented some astras of your own?'

'Yes, Guruji. A musafir. It's a traveller arrow; you hang on to it, or ride it; you can fly through the air for miles and miles. Then there's a seeker arrow that can usually find a person you know by pointing towards them. And a shielding arrow, which operates like a missile defence system, shooting down incoming fire, even lots of arrows, although it doesn't work so well if the incoming arrow is also an astra. You need a mohini then.'

'Well done. You must show me these new innovations. We're never too old to learn new tricks, eh?' He chuckled to himself. 'But what of the three Greater Astras, Chand – the Trimurti astras?'

'No,' Vikram admitted, 'I've never been able to work them out, Guruji. For me, the power and energy of my astras come from myself, so if I empower too many arrows, I get tired out really fast. But the Greater Astras – in legend, they're a boon of the greater gods. The Trimurti astras are supposed to come from Brahma, Shiva and Vishnu, and you once told me that a man can only summon each of them once, and they are unstoppable and all-powerful – but I don't know how. You've never told me and I've never been able to figure it out.'

Vishwamitra looked thoughtful. 'We are made of energy, Chand — all things are. Our bodies are billions of particles zooming about each other, each unaware of the whole, all bound together by energy. That is a great source of power. But when you expend energy, you deplete yourself.'

Vikram already knew this, but he listened patiently as he explained, 'The world about you is also made of energy and you can draw on that too — in fact, learn to do that, and you will be able to fire astras tirelessly. Only when you have made this connection will you be able to draw upon the power of the Trimurti arrows.'

'But the gods—'

'I cannot speak for the gods. I have known men who needed faith and prayer to invoke these astras, and others who didn't. You'll find your own path to them. Energies of creation, preservation and destruction surround us. Whether they are personalised forces — gods — or impersonal energies that we have imagined as godlike personas is irrelevant for our purpose. What matters is that these energies are *real*. Draw on them, and your astras will go from being the small combat weapons they are now to major forces of destruction. The Brahmastra of Brahma, the Pashupatastra of Shiva and the Vaishnava-astra of Vishnu never miss, and are said to be able to kill a god or destroy an army. If you can draw on the energies that flow around you instead of taking only from within, these weapons will be open to you. And remember, in the *Ramayana*, it is a Brahmastra that slays Ravana. It may be that only such a weapon can truly kill Ravindra-Raj forever and break this cycle you are trapped in.'

Vikram stared thoughtfully at the ground as they trudged on in silence. There was little comfort in the guru's words. He had really been hoping he was ready to face Ravindra, but Vishwamitra was clearly suggesting he wasn't.

He gritted his teeth and set his jaw. *I have to learn more. I have no choice.*

That evening, Amanjit and Deepika joined Vikram and Vishwamitra for dinner. The newlyweds sat together and touched each other constantly, leaning into each other, sharing intimate looks and knowing smiles.

Past lives whispered to him, reminding Vikram of what they had and all he'd lost: as Chand, married to Kamla; as Doc, dancing with Crazy Jane; as Mark Mutlow with Emily before the bottle took him. Other lives flashed before him, other names, other women, and his thoughts went to Sue Parker, who was missing, possibly even dead. It had been confusing, even frightening, being with her, but she was his reincarnated ex-wife and he still cared for her.

*And I cannot think of you at all, Rasita, without all my fears overwhelming me.*

As if they sensed his sadness, Deepika and Amanjit moved fractionally apart and turned their attention to him. They discussed his plans and agreed that Sri Lanka was their obvious destination, then moved onto ideas of how they would counter Uncle Charanpreet's malicious lawsuit against Amanjit's mother before tossing around increasingly crazy ideas on how to clear their names of the Bollywood murder of the century — for who would believe a centuries-old demon had killed Sunita Ashoka?

Vikram's eyes kept returning to the incense brazier, imagining he could see Rasita's face there. He stroked the heart-stone in his breast pocket and sent her his love.

# CHAPTER TWO

# ISLE OF THE DEMON-KING

*Lanka, March 2011*

Some days, it was as if Vikram were beside her, holding her hand, keeping her strong.

Other days, Rasita wanted to strangle him. Her trust in him had been fractured by a handful of photographs of him kissing Sue Parker on a shadowy balcony that looked like a hotel in Udaipur. They were grainy and blurred, but he and Sue were unmistakeable.

*Did it go further between them? Did they go inside that hotel room and—* '

*Please, no!*

Such thoughts had driven her from her bed to the balcony, where she sat wrapped in a blanket against the pre-dawn chill, her legs hugged to her chest as she watched the dawn slowly bloom. The stars, looking so bright and close, were fading as the sky changed from indigo to a silvery blue-grey and the eastern horizon brightened to rosy gold. Here, every day was exactly like the one before: the perfect golden sun

– if you squinted, you could make out the chariot of Surya and his horses – rose, and the marble and gilt palace awoke. With each day that passed, it was harder to remember her past life.

Noises from inside told her that her maid, Kaineskeya, had arrived. The girl looked about fourteen, and was pretty if you discounted her budding deer-antlers and back-jointed legs.

Kaineskeya peered around the curtains and brightly wished her good morning.

There was nothing good about the morning, to Ras' mind. Her skin was itching; she had only the small basin to wash from because she refused to use the communal baths below. Her hair felt greasy and her body was beginning to make her own nose wrinkle.

'I want to wash,' she told Kaineskeya. 'Properly, I mean – I want a bath.'

'Then you must come to the bathing pools, mistress,' Kaineskeya replied. The girl was never less than cheerful, even when Rasita screeched at her, which she'd done many times since her arrival, sick with fear and dreading that at any moment Ravindra would arrive, drag her to the bedroom and take what he wanted.

'I want to wash here!' she demanded.

'I'm sorry, mistress, but we all wash in the bathing pools. They are under the women's palace, on the west side. It isn't far.'

'I'm not going to bathe in front of all you *animals*,' Ras snarled.

'We're not actually animals,' Kaineskeya replied cheerfully, as if instructing an ignorant child. 'We asuras are people, just like you. And there are actually human slaves here too, in Lower Town.'

'*Slaves?*' Ras was appalled. 'You keep human slaves?'

'Oh yes, it's quite normal. Because they live here, they don't age. Some have been with us for centuries and won their freedom. And the pens are quite well-kept, you know—'

'Pens?' Ras pulled a face. 'Go away to your duties.'

Kaineskeya curtseyed, smiled her irritatingly happy smile and vanished back into the apartment, and Ras went back to brooding as the palace and the city below woke.

She'd lost count of the days she'd been here – although it couldn't have been more than a couple of weeks since Ravindra – or 'the Ravan', as everyone called him here – had clasped her to him and borne her on the back of a naga, a giant winged snake, to this fantastical island fortress. He hadn't come near her since; perhaps he thought she just needed time to get over the horror of seeing him kill Deepika? Perhaps it was the first phase of a campaign to win her over. She didn't care. She hated him, and that would never change.

It was days before she could stop crying. Her last sight of Deepika haunted her: the girl transfigured into a black-skinned being that looked a lot like the goddess Kali. Ravindra had almost slashed her to pieces before sending her tumbling into the well at Panchavati, then the ground had collapsed about her, leaving her buried in the soil. She would always hate Ravindra for taking Deepika's life.

But it was hard to focus on hatred and revenge when

she was so alone, in this weirdly tranquil place. At first she refused to eat, but she couldn't sustain that, and when she relented, she found the fruits and breads succulent and wholesome. And the wine which her horned servant girl brought in the evening was *divine*: unearthly, and dangerously heady.

The palace was set within a walled city on an island, but an island so large that the sea was only visible to the southwest, some miles away. It was richly forested, dark verdant trees fringing the plain where the city stood. The stream disappeared beneath the city into a vast underground drainage system. The fortress, the city and the island were called Lanka.

Ras was being housed in a tower in the citadel. Facing north, from her balcony, she could see the lower town below her, where thousands of demon and human residents lived. She wasn't sure if 'demon' was the right word any more; the asuras didn't seem so unearthly and evil when she watched them from up here going about their normal everyday tasks like any human would. The word 'asura' might be synonymous with 'demon' at home, but here it was just a name, with no connotations of demons or evil.

The citadel was where the rakshasa, the asura lords, lived; if she'd understood Kaineskeya, the rakshasa were capable of using magic. From her tower, the city had an orderly, precise look to it. Farms all around the city provided for the inhabitants, but the asuras sometimes raided the human world for conveniences, Kaineskeya had told her.

The little maid poked her nose through the balcony

curtains again. 'Breakfast is here, Lady,' she called. 'Fresh eggs, poached as you like them. Shall I bring your plate out?'

Ras scowled miserably, but nodded. Kaineskeya fussed over her, placing a tray and pouring freshly squeezed orange juice, and making a great show of grinding pepper over the eggs.

Yawning, Ras tucked in.

'Did you sleep well, Lady?' Kaineskeya asked, as she did every morning.

Ras flinched. 'No.'

She feared the night-time the most. Lying alone in her bed, she flinched at every sound, afraid it might be Ravindra, about to burst through her door. When she did doze off, she was beset by bad dreams, always the same, and vividly frightening: in them she was a ghost, lost and hungry, stalking a strange forest. Mewling with thirst and longing, she snatched eggs from nests, only for them to crumble to dust in her bony hands. These visions scared her hugely, because she knew they weren't true dreams, but the thoughts of her other self – the ghost of Padma, a lost part of her fractured soul. Padma was seeking her, and she had an implacable hunger.

She finished her breakfast, then sat scratching her head glumly. *I stink*, she realised. *My armpits stink and the hair is growing and my legs need shaving and my crotch is smelly and I hate myself.*

It occurred to her that she'd been subconsciously trying to make herself repulsive so that Ravindra wouldn't come near her, but she couldn't take it any more, all that itching and scratching and rubbing and wallowing in misery.

'All right,' she snapped abruptly, pushing away the tray, 'take me to the baths.'

Kaineskeya clapped her hands as if this were a truly happy event. 'I'll show you the way,' she chirped, and Ras left her apartment for the first time in weeks. The little servant led her through a maze of corridors and down grand staircases to a huge chamber of marble pools deep beneath the women's wing. At the door, she stopped and stared at the naked demon-women swimming, frolicking or gathered together chattering. The combinations of animal and human forms made them look very alien, in some cases downright hideous, to Rasita's eyes, especially those who were closer to beast than human — although none could have been taken for normal. There were human bodies with the heads of cows or pigs or wolves; one female torso was topped by a thick python head. Some had lovely bodies and an alien beauty, even with their beastly features. It took Rasita a moment to realise that none of them were old, and there were no children.

As she entered, the room fell silent and the asuras all turned to watch. Their eyes were as varied as their bodies, many slit-pupiled, some fiery, or pure black, like holes in space. They tittered as Ras disrobed and closed in, circling about her. A few bared teeth as Ras lowered herself into the warm water, trying to hide her terror. She was determined to do this.

Kaineskeya was already in the water. She stroked Rasita's shoulder soothingly. 'They won't harm you, mistress. They are your subjects.'

'Don't touch me,' Ras snapped, then she added, 'Make them go away. Don't let them look at me.'

'But you must get used to them, and they to you,' Kaineskeya told her calmly. 'You will learn to love them as they learn to love you.'

Ras looked at the grotesque bodies and faces with their chilling eyes and pressed herself against the wall of the pool. 'Make them go away,' she said, her voice breaking.

Kaineskeya clapped her hands. 'Look at you!' she told the gathered she-demons. 'Look at you, scaring the queen! She is your new mother – give her privacy and your respect!' She followed that with a torrent of words in her own tongue and to Ras' surprise, they listened and started backing away.

'Just another queen,' hissed one in Hindi, as she moved away. 'Another cruel queen.'

'My mistress is not like the Shadow Queens,' Kaineskeya replied, lifting her head possessively. 'She is a true queen. She will heal our Lord: she will make him strong and good again.'

The asuras muttered sourly, but moved to the far recesses of the baths, giving Ras space.

*I'm not their queen*, Ras thought. *I'm the only normal person in a freak asylum.* She turned away and tried to wrap herself in solitude as she scrubbed the filth away, but Kaineskeya stayed beside her. Rasita had to admit that her skinny, girlish body was almost normal – if you disregarded her claw-like fingernails, backward-hinged furry legs and the budding antlers on her brow.

None of the women spoke to Rasita, but they bombarded Kaineskeya with a barrage of questions in their own language. She answered most, though some she waved away scornfully.

'What are they saying to you?' Rasita asked reluctantly when there was a pause.

'They are saying that you are very beautiful, mistress.'

Rasita snorted. No one had ever called her beautiful – she was too skinny, too sickly and pinch-faced to be thought of as pretty. But she was vaguely aware that this was changing; since her spirit had joined with Sunita Ashoka, her health had definitely improved, and she had begun to develop the curves of a mature woman. Her face was losing its normal hollow, gaunt aspect and as she washed it now, she realised her hair was no longer straggly and limp. These changes might have pleased her at another time, but here and now, they felt horribly dangerous, as though she were no longer fully herself.

The asura women went back to plying Kaineskeya with questions and the maid told Ras, 'They are asking if you dance – if you sing. And they want to know many other things,' she added.

She could tell Kaineskeya was sheltering her; some of the comments had been accompanied by expressions that suggested they were lewd or antagonistic. She averted her eyes from the demon-women again, not wanting to keep looking at such an array of strange flesh, alien faces and piercing eyes. 'I'm clean now. Let's go.'

As she rose from the pool, water streaming down her body, she was acutely aware of her nakedness, and was grateful to wrap herself in the towel Kaineskeya handed her. When she was dry, the asura handed her a fresh silk robe. 'Your old clothes are filthy and silly-looking,' she sniffed. 'Shall I have them burned?'

Ras looked shocked. 'No, don't burn them!' They felt like a lifeline to her own world: a reminder that she hadn't always been in this strange place. 'I want them washed and mended.'

She tried to remember the route as they returned, but there were so many twisting corridors . . .

While Kaineskeya cleaned the apartment, Rasita went up to her roof garden and sat beneath a pagoda, staring out over the city of the demons, which was gleaming in the sunlight with a soft creamy-golden hue. Beyond the walls, the green plains ended in lush forests. She looked mostly to the southwest, where there was a distant sea view; sometimes it was full, other times it receded some distance, but very gently, not like an ocean with big waves. The wind from that quarter smelled as much of silt and mud as it did of salt.

The city was not at all what she would have thought a city of demons might be like. She'd pictured torture chambers and grim battlements with heads on spikes, but this place was more like some Mediterranean resort in a travel brochure, with blue swimming pools and colourful gardens full of bright flowers. But fierce beast-faced asura warriors patrolled the walls, and the little bat-faced baital circled above at night.

*I am alone here. There is no one like me in all the fortress.*
*No one but Him.*

'Call me Keke,' Kaineskeya told her. 'Everyone else does.'

Rasita tried to ignore the girl; she didn't want to like her, but she was the only company she had, and in truth, she was sweetness itself. As the days passed, a routine was established; Kaineskeya took Ras' tantrums and weeping storms and gave back sympathy. She protected Rasita from the other asura women. She played chess or cards with her when she was asked. She brought treats from the kitchen and arranged musicians to entertain her. She wore Rasita down with kindness.

In this fragile normality, Ras began to hope that maybe Ravindra had forgotten about her. She started to sleep better, not always dreaming the ghost-dreams, and as she awakened refreshed, the face in the mirror grew softer in outline and the darkness beneath the eyes faded. Her hair looked lustrous.

'Keke,' she asked one morning as the girl mopped, moving as if to unheard music, 'how old are you?'

Kaineskeya paused, frowning. 'I don't know, mistress. A few hundred years, I think.'

*A few hundred years!*

'How can you not know?'

'We don't count time here, mistress. And sometimes, it's as if we all sleep.'

Rasita puzzled over this. 'What do you mean?'

Keke shrugged. 'Lanka without the King is like a clock with no battery. Everything stops.'

Ras didn't like this reminder of Ravindra or his powers; she hadn't seen him since that awful night when Deepika had fallen down the well, and she had no wish to. 'Everything stops?' she echoed doubtfully.

'Well, we don't actually stop. It's just that without him there is no direction, no purpose. But he is back now, and everything is waking up again,' Keke enthused. 'His sons are returning — Lord Indrajit is coming back, they say.'

Rasita recognised the name: in the *Ramayana*, Indrajit was the greatest of the demon-warriors apart from Ravana himself — he nearly killed Rama and Lakshmana. *But he'd been killed, hadn't he? Why was he supposedly alive, here? Why were any of these beings alive?*

'Keke, do you know the tale of the *Ramayana*?'

'Of course. It's mostly just a fable, but there are some true things in it.'

'In the *Ramayana*, Ravana dies,' Rasita said, watching her carefully for her reaction. 'So do Indrajit and all his captains. So how are they here now?'

Keke frowned and was silent for so long that Ras wondered if maybe she'd asked a forbidden question. But eventually she responded, her voice more measured than usual, 'The old ones say that after the great war, Vibhishana the traitor, Ravana's younger brother, was left here as King of Lanka. For a time it was hard for him, but he won over the people. Then, after many lives of men, the rakshasa lords were reborn, as part of the cycle of rebirth. They took Vibhishana away and he was never seen again. It made the asura sad, because the new masters were harsh and cruel.'

'What about Ravana?' Rasita asked eagerly.

Keke shrugged. 'We always knew that one day he would return, because his soul is on the wheel of rebirth. And now he has — now, everything is going to work out!' She spoke so brightly that Ras could scarcely credit they were talking about the same thing.

'Keke, you're talking about a man who has abducted me——'

'You will come to love him,' Keke replied, her face radiating infuriating happiness.

'Never! Don't you realise that the *Ramayana* is re-enacting itself? Vikram and Amanjit are going to kill him, and I'll dance on his grave.'

'No, not this time,' the maid responded brightly. 'This time will be different. The wrongs will be righted and you will give your love to the Ravan and he will be restored. We all know this.' She spoke as if speaking of some ancient prophecy in a fairy story.

Her blind faith made Rasita shudder. 'Leave: I wish to be alone,' she snapped, sick to the stomach suddenly.

'Mistress, why do you resist?' Kaineskeya asked. 'The king is a mighty lover and a great man. He will heal you and make you whole. Then you will reign here for all eternity, in joy and fulfilment. It is written.'

Rasita straightened. '*Go — get out*,' she shrieked, in sudden fury. 'Get out *get out get out!*'

'Poor Keke,' purred a darkly melodious voice behind her, some hours later. 'She is quite tearful today.'

Rasita whirled in sudden fright. She'd been standing at the edge of her rooftop garden, wondering if she should just jump and end it all. It was only the hope that Vikram would come soon that kept her here.

She faced her abductor, trying not to let him see how badly she was trembling.

Ravindra still inhabited the body of the Mumbai detective, Majid Khan: beautiful, sensual, familiar and frightening. He wore a moustache now, a flowing one above a clean-shaven chin. His eyes were golden and his hair flowed to his shoulders. He wore an open-fronted shirt, and his torso rippled with muscle: he looked like a male model from a magazine. His muscular legs were sheathed in golden pantaloons, and he had a curved dagger tucked in a waist-belt.

Golden armlets and earrings glittered, but her eyes went straight to his throat, to the four smoky crystals hanging from a gold chain: the heart-stones of the surviving queens of Mandore – except her own. Two had been destroyed in Mumbai, and hers remained hidden – or with Vikram, she hoped fervently.

She backed to the edge of the rooftop as he glided closer. *Is this it? Is he going to—?*

'Stay away from me!' she cried. 'Stay away, or I'll jump—'

He put a hand on a curved marble pillar and gave her a calm, quizzical look. 'Why?'

'Why?' She spluttered. 'Because I'm not going to let you get your filthy hands on me, not ever, you stinking, kidnapping murderer!'

She expected mockery or anger, but instead he replied calmly, 'I will not lay a finger on you without your permission, Rasita.'

'Then let me go, because that will be *never.*'

He was shaking his head as he said, 'I can't just let you go, Rasita. I need you here. But I swear that you have the freedom of Lanka, and the allegiance of all who dwell within it.'

'I don't want their damned allegiance – I don't want yours, *demon.*'

'"Demon?" What is a demon? You know the word "demonised", I take it? It means to besmirch the reputation of someone so that they are considered evil, subhuman – which is precisely what Valmiki and his poison-penned poets did to me when they wrote the *Ramayana*.'

She stared at him. She wanted to rage at this glib response, but the part of her that was far older than her teenage years – the Sunita part of her, the inherited soul inside – told her to wait. *To think*.

'You expect me to accept that? That you're just misunderstood, that you never meant to hunt down and kill my friends in life after life? That you're not a killer now?' Her voice came out hoarse and shaky, at the edge of breaking.

'I don't deny anything I've done in the past,' he replied. 'But just as you have been learning in this life, so have I. I'm finding this place as strange as you are, Rasita. A kingdom which thinks I'm their king. I'm learning that I've made awful mistakes in my past lives. I'm discovering things that have eluded me for centuries. *For millennia*. But I'm resolved to be the king I was born to be.'

*Can I credit that?* she wondered. *Or is it just more lies?*

'What part does holding me a prisoner play in that?' she demanded. 'What is it you want from me?'

'To be my queen,' he answered immediately. 'Willingly and joyously.'

*Impossible.* 'You will never have that,' she told him.

'Rasita, I know it seems that way to you now, but there's more to learn. You were born to be my queen, as you once were, so many lives ago. You don't remember, but I'll help you.'

Again, she swallowed the urge to shriek at him that she would *never* be his queen. Sunita inside told her that she could reject what he said, and could still be regal about it. *Shame him, and his lies*, the former Queen of Bollywood told her.

'I don't care what you want,' she said icily. 'I thank you for the "mercy" of not ravishing me, but if you expect gratitude, you're mistaken.'

Ravindra sighed wryly, as if this were to be expected. 'I merely came to enquire after your comfort. Have you been well cared for? Is there anything you need? Do you wish for company beyond Keke? Several of the young women have asked permission to attend upon you, to talk with you.'

'I don't want anyone's company.'

'Then what of creature comforts? Is there anything of your old life you need?'

*Very well*, she thought, *let's test the limits*.

'I want a television set and a radio. And a mobile phone.'

'I am afraid electronic goods do not function well here,' he told her, sounding genuinely apologetic. 'It's the nature of this place.'

'Then I want books.'

He bowed. 'At last, something I can provide. Give Keke a list.'

'I want a copy of the *Ramayana*,' she demanded truculently, interested to see how he reacted.

Ravindra smiled maddeningly. 'Of course.'

'And is there a shrine? I want to pray . . . to Rama. And Vishnu.'

He laughed aloud. 'I'm sorry, this is not a Hindu society.

In fact, we are pagan.'

That stopped her in mid-flow. 'But the legends say Ravana was an acolyte of Shiva.' She frowned, interested despite herself.

'Then the legends must be wrong again, my dear.'

'I'm not your "dear",' she snapped. 'Don't call me that.'

'As you wish.'

She glared at him. 'How are you even real?'

'Ah. I heard you'd asked this question. Be patient and I am sure all will come clear.'

She turned away, hoping he would get bored and leave, but he remained.

After a moment he started, 'Listen, Rasita; there is something serious I must talk to you about. As we now know, when you died without your heart-stone in your previous life in Mandore, your soul divided into three. Two parts — you and Sunita Ashoka — have been reunited, but what is left is the ghost of Queen Padma. Keke says you have nightmares of Padma's ghost, and that tells me you are in imminent danger from it.'

She lifted her head defiantly. 'What danger could be worse than my current plight?'

Ravindra frowned. 'You have seen my queens: would you truly want to become one of them? Rasita, in all your lives since Mandore, the ghost of Padma was either blind to you, or more afraid of you than you of it — but not any longer. It is seeking you now, and you are sensing its approach. In these myth-lands, a ghost is far more formidable and complex to deal with than in your world. Only the person the ghost is haunting can bring it peace — and no force known can stop it or turn it aside.'

She stared at him, trying to read his face. Was this true, or just half-truths and lies? *What did he want?* 'In Jodhpur I stabbed it with silver and made it go away,' she told him.

He bowed his head. 'That was in your world. Now you're here.'

'Then take me back.'

He shook his head, half-amused. 'Impossible, and futile. In your world it will still hunt you, and in any case, it cannot be destroyed. Nothing would be resolved. This situation must end, Rasita. The ghost suffers and only you can lay it to rest. But you could also die, be swallowed up by it, and if that were to happen you would become like Halika and my other queens: a living-dead thing, until I can find your heart-stone and Darya's ghost and complete the Mandore ritual.'

She shuddered at this dismal prospect. It offered no escape, and no hope.

'Alternatively, if you deal with Padma's spectre, it will complete your rehabilitation: you will finally have normal health. You will be whole.'

Put like that, it sounded like she had no choice. 'So what do I have to do?'

'Face it, and take it into you,' Ravindra replied. 'But be warned: it will destroy you unless you accept protection.'

'What sort of protection?'

He gave her an appraising look, as if measuring her resolve – or maybe her gullibility, for all she knew. 'You have to understand that Padma wants to be whole, but she has been alone for centuries. She knows what she is, and she hates it – hates herself, her very existence, a thing she doesn't know how to end. She doesn't care who "wins" as long as she gains oblivion, and the only way she knows for that to happen is for you to submit to me and let me complete the Mandore Ritual.'

Ras felt her heart sink. His words had the ring of truth. 'You're saying your walls can't keep her out, your people can't keep her out, that you can't keep her out, and she wants you to have me in your vile ritual? I'd rather die!'

'That's the thing – you won't. You'll be consumed and become as she is, I'll never complete the Ritual and this eternal cycle of rebirth and revenge will go on for all eternity.'

She closed her eyes, bowed her head. *Dear gods, why are you doing this to me?* 'Then what hope is there?'

'You must convince her that you too desire the ritual to be completed, so that she will gain oblivion.'

'How?'

'When you encounter her – as you inevitably will – only one thing will appease her, allow you to overcome her hostility so you can take her into yourself and become whole. That is a token, truly worn, that you will submit to me.'

'*Submit?* What do you mean?' Her breathing became ragged; she was horribly afraid that she knew exactly what he meant.

'Simply this: agree to a betrothal, and accept my ring as a sign of that: Padma's ghost will see you not as someone to overcome, but to join with, making you whole, removing all of your health issues for ever, and giving her the means to gain final oblivion.'

She stared. 'Weren't you listening? I will *never* marry you.'

He raised a hand. 'I did not say, "marry", Rasita, I said "betrothal". *Engaged*. Become my fiancée, *sincerely*, and it will enter you peacefully. If you are dissembling – if you refuse, or are insincere – it will know, and it will destroy you.'

*Can I believe this?* 'This feels like a game you're playing. I have only your word about any of this.' *But it does feel true*, she acknowledged silently to herself.

'I don't blame your mistrust, Rasita. But I'm not lying.'

'No, I refuse,' she said. 'Let it kill me – I don't care.'

He was beside her suddenly, in a frightening blur of movement. 'Rasita, you do care.' He gestured to the balcony railing. 'You don't desire death – you could have leaped from this balcony at any time since your arrival, had you truly wished. You mistrust my explanation of the ghost; I understand that. Believe me, I've thought long and hard about to how to appease it. There truly is no other way. As it comes closer and your dreams worsen, you will understand.'

Ras stared up at him, trembling. 'Get away from me, or I *will* jump.'

'Don't make claims you don't mean, Rasita. It only makes you look foolish.'

'If I've not jumped it is only because I *know* that Vikram and Amanjit are coming to save me.'

'Of course.' He bowed mockingly. 'Consider what I said, Rasita. Padma's spectre will be here soon.'

She struggled for a caustic response, but by the time it was formed, she was alone.

It wasn't long before Rasita received an even more

unwelcome guest. She was standing at a window, gazing out into the night, feeling melancholy and slightly drunk. She only realised she wasn't alone when a chill wave of air washed through the room. She half-turned – and froze.

Halika, Ravindra's chief wife and accomplice down the centuries, was leaning against a pillar, staring at her with gloating eyes. Tall, curvaceous and sultry, Halika blended the cold arrogance of royalty with the sensual pout of a street-girl.

'Get out,' Ras snapped at once, but Halika just snickered, picked up Ras' wine glass and drained it.

The implication of the act took a few seconds to register: Halika had not just lifted an inanimate object, but she had consumed the fluid. Rasita caught her breath. *Is she still just a ghost?*

'Keke,' she called out, trying to keep the fear from her voice.

'I sent your maid away.' Halika poured herself more wine from the decanter and swirled it thoughtfully, savouring the smell. 'Ahhh . . . you have no idea how good it feels to finally be able to drink more than just blood.' She pulled a face. 'Blood is so very nourishing, but variety is nice.'

Ras felt herself shudder. 'Wh-what do you want?'

'Why, we wanted to see you, of course, sister.' Halika half-turned and called, 'Come in, you two.'

Out of the shadows two more of the ghostly queens emerged; they too looked more solid, although not so tangible as Halika. They exuded a palpable cold that made Rasita's skin prickle.

The taller of the two lesser queens had a lean, hungry

look to her, and grey hair fanning about her face weirdly, as if moved by unseen winds. Jyoti, Rasita remembered – a Padma memory. Spaced-out, spooky Jyoti, who in Mandore had been so addicted to the opiates they gave her that she barely spoke. Beside her was needy little Aruna, a short, plump, earthy lump who'd been, after Halika, Ravindra's most enthusiastic consort. The lesser queens stared at Ras as if she were food.

'Go away—' Rasita tried to sound calm, but her voice almost gave out.

Halika ignored her. 'Of course, your Vikram killed the other two in Mumbai by destroying their heart-stones. Pretty little Rakhi and silly Meena are dead, their memories and souls gone into Darya – but Darya is dead now too, which means her ghost is out there somewhere. The Master has summoned it and someday soon she will come creeping over the walls with blood on her lips. She'll be just like us.'

The thought of Deepika so transformed sucked the strength from Rasita's limbs. 'Please,' she begged, 'leave me alone.'

'When she comes, all we will need to complete the ritual is your heart-stone.'

'Vikram will destroy it,' Ras asserted.

'Impossible,' Halika asserted. 'And even if he could, it would kill you – he knows that.'

'Better dead than here,' she countered, and she meant it.

'Really? It's not so bad, my dear. And all you need to do is give our lord what he wants. Give him your body and your heart and he will heal all your pain. He will elevate us all and we will reign here together for ever.'

'Why would I even want that?' she said scornfully. 'To rule over monsters in a backwards world like this? You don't even have hot running water or electricity.'

Halika glared at her. 'Foolish girl – what have you to look forward to in your own pathetic world but pain and ageing and death? Here, you can have bliss eternal. Just give the king what he wants.'

She conquered the reflex to scream. *Be regal*, she reminded herself. 'Never.'

Halika sighed as if Ras were a recalcitrant schoolgirl. 'Sister, you will learn.' She crossed the distance between them in an eye-blink, making Ras flinch, and caught her in icy hands. 'You are just a silly little virgin who doesn't know what she's rejecting. But we have eternity to show you.' Her icy carrion-breath washed over Rasita's face. 'Have you ever even been kissed, little virgin?' She bent Ras over backwards effortlessly and Ras thought for a second that the ghost-queen was going to kiss her . . . or bite her . . . or throw her from the window . . .

'Get away from me,' she pleaded in vain, squirming in the dead queen's frigid grip.

Halika's fingers slid the strap of Ras' dress from her shoulder and she chuckled lewdly. 'Haven't you grown,' she purred.

Jyoti and Aruna hovered closer, tittering and licking their lips, and Ras shuddered. There was only one thing she could think of to do, although she hated it.

'Ravindra—' she shouted desperately.

Halika flinched as the other queens cringed and pulled back.

In seconds, Ravindra was stepping into the room. 'I was already on my way – Keke told me you had visitors.' He glared at Halika. 'You were commanded to stay away from here, wife.'

Halika tipped her head defiantly, but she removed her hands from Ras, who clutched at the railing. 'I am a queen – I may go anywhere—'

'And I am your king – get out, all of you.'

The dead queens hissed, but they backed into the darkness and were gone.

Rasita clung to the rail, shaking and trying to catch her breath. Halika's fingers had left a pink hand shape on her bared shoulder, but it was slowly fading. She pulled up her strap, feeling ashamed to have been reduced to calling on Ravindra for protection, but terrified of what Halika might have done if she hadn't.

'Go away,' she whispered, but there was no reply.

Ravindra was already gone.

# CHAPTER THREE

## READINESS

*Pushkar, Rajasthan, April 2011*

Every night Vikram and Amanjit asked each other, 'Are we ready?'

Only when they both answered honestly, 'Yes!' did they pack for the journey.

For Vikram, April had been all intense revision: he drilled with sword and bow with single-minded determination. He refused to believe that Rasita would ever succumb to Ravindra's threats or wiles, so they had as much time as they needed to gird themselves for war . . . But not too long . . .

He'd thought there was nothing new to learn, but he made unexpected breakthroughs: as he stood in the field, shooting with single-minded determination at a battered target a hundred paces away, he suddenly realised that he'd fired more astras in one session than ever before. When he wiped the sweat from his eyes and looked about him, he saw the grass at his feet was dead and littered with lifeless bugs, and the corpse of a sparrow was lying not far away.

The air was unnaturally cold, too, and he shivered, feeling sick: he had actually sucked the energy from the grass, the bugs, the bird, even the air itself, to fuel his weapons: just as Vishwamitra had spoken of.

Then he thought of Ravindra, picturing his heart as the target, and carried on.

Most days Amanjit worked with Vishwamitra. His sword-work had always been good, but as he packed on muscle, it became brilliant. He was learning how to manipulate magical energy too – by using the forces of gravity and momentum, he could leap as if he were a wire-suspended samurai in a martial arts movie, and he relearned skills he hadn't used since his life as Prithviraj Chauhan: he could manage most of the basic astras now, especially the destructive ones, and he'd remastered the art of shooting by sound alone. For the first time in any of his lives, he was a voracious student, more focused than Vikram had ever seen him. And in the evenings, when training ended, Amanjit was able to put everything aside and relax with Deepika.

But Vishwamitra spent most time with the Delhi girl. 'She's much prettier than you two,' the old sage joked – but they all knew the real reason; she *had* to master her powers or she would be at Ravindra's mercy. In some of her past lives, Deepika had channelled a fierce and brutal energy that fed on blind rage and manifested like Kali, the feared and revered avatar of the great goddess. In Hindu myth, Durga, the Queen of the Gods, had fought a battle against the demons, but they were too many for her, so in desperation she had gone deeper into herself and literally gone berserk, becoming Kali, a persona of pure destruction. As Kali, she had slain the demons, but she had left her rational self so far behind that she had become a danger to the whole universe. Only Shiva, her husband, was able to calm her by lying prone at her feet; his helpless submission brought the goddess back to sanity.

Somehow, Deepika was able to draw on that same furious energy, but even in that state, she hadn't been able to stop Ravindra kidnapping Rasita. She knew that if she hadn't fallen down the well-shaft at Panchavati she would have been captured herself, or killed. And now Ravindra had her heart-stone. Knowing she needed to learn to control her powers and conceal her existence, or he would be able to use it to capture her, she threw herself into the training with all of her being.

But after her secret lessons with the guru, she too was able to put the day behind her and return happily to her husband's arms. *Husband* . . . The word was like a magic spell, she told Vikram one night.

It was hard for Vikram to watch their happiness. All he could do throughout those long, lonely nights was to hold the Padma heart-stone, sending Rasita his love and longing through it, and hope.

The challenge lay not in lighting the fire; that was easy. It was putting the flames out that she found impossible.

Now Deepika shaped her hand, struggling to caress the orange tongue on the candle gently, when all she really wanted to do was RIP RAVINDRA LIMB FROM LIMB FOR WHAT HE—

The candle exploded, scorching the wall behind it, and Vishwamitra tutted impatiently.

She bit her lip. 'Sorry, Guru-ji,' she muttered. 'I just . . .'

The old sage said, 'I know, this is difficult. You have a power that you can only draw on when you are angry, but to control it you need to be calm, and as soon as you try to calm yourself, you lose hold of the power. If you retain your rage, you lose control. A dilemma indeed.'

She hung her head.

'Then we are approaching this the wrong way.' He tapped her on the knee. 'You must access your powers without resorting to anger.'

'But I can't,' she told him.

'Of course you can, my dear. Remember, Deepika, there are many paths to power. Let yours be the desire to *protect*, not to harm, and you will be stronger.' He tapped his heart. 'Anger and destruction are how you have manifested your power until now, but you are more than this: just as Kali is only a part of the goddess, not the whole.'

'But all I do is destroy things,' she replied despondently. 'It's the only thing I'm good at.'

'There is much more to you, my dear. Think of the times you have manifested power: yes, there was anger, but it was anger roused in protecting you and yours. You have a strong spirit, a *protective* spirit. Kali is just a part of the great goddess. We must reach the Durga-spirit in you.'

After that, his instructions changed as he focused on protection. He lit a taper and made her try to extinguish it with a thought before it burned her fingers; at first she could only make it explode. Her hand became a blistered bundle of pain, but the guru refused to treat it and forbade the boys from helping her, even to alleviate the burning. Some nights she couldn't sleep, even lying beside Amanjit as he snored contentedly.

Some days she wanted to thrash the old man for his cruel lessons.

But pain is a teacher and after a week of failure, she managed to stop the flame, not by dousing it, but by forcing it away, back to the already consumed part of the taper, so that it burned itself out. It wasn't perfect, but it was a beginning, and after that, breakthroughs came daily. She learned tiny skills and subtle tricks until the world about her felt like an extension of her fingertips. She learned ways to fool people into thinking she wasn't there, and to manipulate the elements. Initially her efforts were crude and basic, but the more she practised, the more sophisticated they became.

It took many weeks until she finally felt ready to play her part. By then she had forgiven the old man for being such a hard teacher – but only after she had worked out how to heal her own hand.

'Are you ready?' Vikram asked as usual, but this time Amanjit nodded briskly.

'Too damn right.'

They both looked at Deepika, and for the first time she looked confident. 'Me too,' she said, her voice determined. 'It's been too long. We need to get back out there and sort this mess out.'

Amanjit stroked her shoulder. 'The only thing I don't

like is splitting up. That's what got us into trouble the last time.'

'I don't like it either, believe me,' Deepika agreed. 'But we know it's the right thing this time.'

'Not only are we covering the bases in terms of the *Ramayana* by splitting up, but it makes sense logically,' Vikram said, trying to sound more positive than he really was. 'Not to mention the fact that I won't have to put up with you two canoodling all the time.' He grinned.

Amanjit groaned. 'That's the worst part of the plan. I'm a newly-wed! I have needs!'

'So do I,' Deepika grumped, 'but hopefully it won't be for long. According to the *Ramayana*, Rama and Lakshmana go off to Lanka and rescue Sita. As I'm not in the story, I'm a free agent, but if I go too close to the action, Ravindra will realise I'm around and zap me through the heart-stone. So as I have to stay away from him, I'll deal with the court cases and the police situation. After all, I can now slink around unseen – and unlike you boneheaded sword-swingers, I have some inkling of the law.'

'Huh,' Vikram countered, 'I know *plenty* about the law. I've *written* laws in my day.'

'Not in this lifetime,' she pointed out. 'Whereas I was right alongside that bitch Meenakshi when she was pretending to be our lawyer and *I* did most of the donkey work in pulling our case together. I'll do the sneaky stuff and make sure things work out.'

'It could be dangerous,' Vikram reminded her. 'Ravindra will still have his people watching things, trying to get a lead on what we're doing.'

'I can handle it,' Dee promised, 'and if anyone less than Ravindra himself comes snooping round, they'd better watch out. *Especially* Meenakshi.'

'Be careful,' Amanjit nagged. 'And you'll join us as soon as you can, right?'

'Of course I will.' She nibbled at his ear. 'I won't be able to stay away from you for long, honey-bunny.'

'*Honey-bunny?*' Vikram smirked as Amanjit went red, but Deepika laughed and stroked her husband's cheek.

'My sweet man. You take care of him, Vikram. I want him back in one piece when you're done saving the world.'

'Will it really be that simple, Master?' Vikram asked Vishwamitra as they watched the moon ride across the late-night sky. Amanjit and Deepika had long since gone to bed.

'Simple?' Vishwamitra echoed sceptically.

'Well, you know: go to Sri Lanka, kill Ravindra and rescue Ras? It sounds too . . . well, *clean*.'

'It will have its complications, I am sure. There will be unexpected setbacks and hard choices before the end, of that I have no doubt. But I trust that you will overcome them.'

'Have you ever been to Sri Lanka, Guru-ji?'

The old man shook his dreadlocked head. 'I've never left north India.'

'And Lanka is in Southern India, right? Sri Lanka?'

'We assume so.'

Vikram rubbed his chin. 'In all my other lives, Ravindra has killed us when he could, but in *this* life, which is the closest we've come to duplicating the *Ramayana*, he's been going out of his way to join all the dots – even though in the

*Ramayana*, he loses. It's strange, like he's got a death-wish. Why would he do that?'

'Perhaps he has no choice? Perhaps his actions are compelled.'

'That's insane — that's like saying that we're just actors reading from a script. I could just throw down my weapons at any time and walk away from this, couldn't I? So could he.'

'But you don't, and neither does he, because you both have compelling reasons to continue. Maybe the *Ramayana* itself is forcing your hands, or maybe it's just coincidence. Maybe there are deeper reasons that we have not yet exposed. I'm not saying you should blindly follow the epic, nor trust that it will see you safe. All I ask is that you bear it in mind in your planning.'

'I've been thinking about that,' Vikram replied. 'While I was on the run, after the *Swayamvara Live!* TV show, I made a list of the next events in the epic, and you know what, they all basically happened: Dad dying, Surpanakha betraying us and Ravana kidnapping Sita. So I know we can't ignore it.' He placed a piece of paper on the table. 'Here's the rest of it . . .' On it was a list of the key actions in the latter part of the epic.

1. Rama and Lakshmana meet Hanuman (monkey-god), gains alliance with monkeys.
2. Hanuman locates Sita by flying to Lanka.
3. Vibhishana, demon-prince, defects to Rama's side.
4. Indrajit nearly kills Rama and Lakshmana, who are saved only by Hanuman bringing healing herbs. Lakshmana kills Indrajit.

5. Rama kills Ravana in final duel.
6. Sita rescued, proves fidelity by walking through fire.
7. They return to Ayodhya (origin of Diwali).

'Any thoughts, Guru-ji?' he asked hopefully.

Vishwamitra frowned, tapping the paper. 'The effects of the *Ramayana* on what you do may not always be obvious. Keep your eyes open for unexpected aid. We don't know what was really meant by the 'monkeys' – you mustn't forget that until the Mauryan Empire of 300BC, south India was quite different to the north in terms of language, people and culture. Perhaps "monkeys" was a derogatory reference to a tribe from southern India, or perhaps it really does mean monkeys. Keep an open mind.'

'What about this Vibhishana?'

'Be very, *very* careful. Ravindra has read the *Ramayana* at least as many times as you, I don't doubt. Be prepared for traitors and double agents. Do not expect it to be straightforward.'

'And beware of Indrajit too, I guess.' Vikram sighed. 'What I don't understand is this whole business of the demons: where do they come from? Why do they even exist?'

'It is likely that they exist because they are in the story, just as the "alternate Pushkar" right here exists. If places can be created by belief, then surely so can beings like these rakshasa. That doesn't make them less dangerous – but more so.'

'And what about Sue Parker?' he whispered. 'What about her?'

'If you're asking where she is, I don't know. I've tried to find her with seeking spells, as you have, which means she may be a captive, or dead. Or she might have left India and be beyond our reach.'

Vikram looked despondent, but Vishwamitra tapped him on the knee. 'But if you're asking whether what passed between you two will undermine what you are trying to achieve, I truly don't know. I would guess that depends on what it was, and I'll not ask.' He placed a hand on Vikram's arm. 'I know you worry that Ravindra has always been victorious in your past lives, Chand, but I believe in you, that this time, you will prevail. You need to believe that too.'

# CHAPTER FOUR

# THE BRIDGE OF RAMA

*From Rajasthan to Madurai & Ramanathapuram,*
*Tamil Nadu, April 2011*

'I hate partings,' Deepika said, 'so let's just get this over with, yeah?'

Amanjit stared into her face, trying to imprint it on his brain for ever. He inhaled her scent, the spicy aroma of skin and hair. 'I can't believe I'm letting this happen. These have been the best days of my life and yet I'm just letting you leave? I must be *crazy*.'

All about them resounded the deafening bustle of Ajmer Station, but Amanjit was in his own little world of sadness. Passengers crowded and bumped the couple, but he ignored them. His stomach was churning and his skin was dripping with perspiration. He clung to Deepika and tried to imagine what it would be like to never let her go. Vikram was fretting, but then, Vik always did. This time he could wait.

'I love you,' he whispered for the hundredth time that morning.

'Me too,' Deepika whispered back, pressing herself to him. Her arms were wrapped about him and her lips were so sweet on his that he never wanted to move again.

'Last call, guys,' Vikram nudged them. 'Just get on the freakin' train, Dee.'

Amanjit could feel tears on his cheeks. He hoped they were Deepika's, because he was a kick-ass warrior and kick-ass warriors didn't cry. But if they ever did, now would be the moment. And his eyes really did begin to sting when he finally let her go and stood on the platform while her train pulled away, taking her off to Mumbai and who knew what. They waved until she was out of sight, then they went back to the car park, gunned the engines of their newly purchased Hero Honda motorbikes and began their own journey south, all the way to Sri Lanka.

They wound through slow traffic, dodging potholes, longing for the occasional moments when they could open their throttles and really go for it. The long tiring rides were punctuated with restless nights in overpriced road-stop motels and dodgy meals in tiny dhabas. Leaving Rajasthan behind, they rolled down through Gujarat and Maharashtra into Karnataka, clad in black leathers and wearing reflective glass helmet-visors. Their weapons, wrapped in holdalls, were strapped to the backs of the bikes. Amanjit imagined them as knights of the new age, riding to war.

As they made their way south, the summer heat became more sultry and the foliage lusher, even though the monsoon season was still months away. The road followed the Western Ghats, the mountains forming the spine of the subcontinent, and place names flashed by, quickly forgotten. It felt dream-like, to always be in motion, never arriving, but they reached Bangalore late on the third day and at last they began to feel like they were making progress. They treated themselves to a night in a decent hotel, where they washed and ate a good meal, then took the winding roads south to Madurai. The misery of being apart from Deepika burned in Amanjit, but he put it aside and focused on the task at hand.

The southern Indians had softer, rounder faces, and darker skins than northerners. They had cheery natures too, always quick with a ready smile. Their lands hadn't been as ravaged by war as the north, and there was a gentler pace of life here. Though Hinduism dominated, other religions co-existed; Jain temples were few and Sikh gurdwaras even less common, but there were occasional Christian churches. There were a lot of mosques, too: Islam had spread south by the ancient trade routes.

The Hindu temples, still the most plentiful, were mostly painted in bright colours, with giant domes covered in hundreds of carved and painted images, as if a colourful flock of supernatural beings had decided to fly down and squat on the roof. It was a stark contrast to the more austere temples Amanjit was used to, but he liked it, and wished he could show Deepika. She loved colour, and everything was so bright here.

'So what's the plan, bhai?' he asked Vikram as they wolfed down a thali in a diner near their motel in Madurai. 'Straight on? Do we need visas or something to get to Sri Lanka?'

Vikram looked up from his newspaper, which was full of the latest atrocities – apparently some rebel group had ambushed and murdered a column of soldiers in Bihar, in northern India, the worst of several recent attacks. The media were being kept from the scene of the crime, but it sounded like the military were actually alarmed by the violence.

He laid the paper aside. 'No, we're going to slip into the country uninvited. But we need to give ourselves the chance to meet Hanuman and the monkeys, in whatever form they might take, so I think we'll rest up for a few days here before heading down to the coast.'

'Okay. What's there to do here, then?'

'Here in Madurai? It's just the oldest inhabited city in India and the centre of the old Pandya Empire, that held the south from around 500BC until the thirteenth century. There're quite a few tourist sites.'

'I might leave that to you,' Amanjit said. 'I meant, what's it got to do with the *Ramayana*?'

'Nothing that I can think of,' Vikram admitted. 'Oddly, the *Ramayana* is much less precise about this leg of the story. With all the early northern parts, it's very tied to places like Ayodhya, Panchavati and the like, but down here, things tend to happen in the wilderness. In the story, there're no people and cities, just monkey tribes and caves and mountains, at least until you get to Lanka.'

'I'm worried about Sri Lanka,' Amanjit said. 'At least the war against the Tamil Tigers is over, but it's still a dangerous place, bhai. We really need to get my sister back as soon as we can.' He leaned forward. Dropping his voice, he asked, 'Have you seen any rakshasas on this trip?'

Vikram whispered back, 'A disguised rakshasa shows up

in mirrors and photographs, so I've been checking every-where we go, but I've not seen a single one yet.'

'That's good.' Amanjit paused. 'Isn't it?'

'Well, it either means we're slipping past the enemy's guard, or we're so far off track that there are no defences down here.'

'You're not reassuring me, Vik.'

They stayed in Madurai for almost a week, visiting the holy places: the Meenakshi-Amman temple to Shiva and the Thirumalai Nayakar Palace, even the graceful pink Kazimar mosque. They took dozens of photos and scanned the digital images looking for rakshasas in the crowds, but found none. Vikram looked for gateways into the myth-world, but to their puzzlement, there weren't many, and those they did find were tied to local legends, not the *Ramayana*. It was dispiriting; only the occasional phone calls to Deepika kept Amanjit sane.

They did make one new friend, Kasun, a Sri Lankan Tamil student doctor. Vikram met Kasun, enjoying a post-gradua-tion vacation, and they got talking in a very scholarly way, at one of the temples. He was winding his way through southern India on his way back to his home, a small town in northern Sri Lanka, where his father had his medical prac-tice. That area had been under the control of the infamous Tamil Tigers – the LTTE, Liberation Tigers of Tamil Eelam. He spoke passionately about the sufferings of his people, transplanted by the British into the tea plantations as cheap labour, then so discriminated against by the native Sinhalese that their language had been banned in schools and their rights were almost non-existent.

'One day this LTTE group came to my village,' Kasun told them, 'and I had a gun placed in my hand. "Come and fight with us", they said to me, but I wanted to be a doctor, so I refused. I thought they would beat me, but it turned out they needed medics even more than soldiers.'

'How old were you?' Amanjit said.

'I was fourteen years old and they had me tend their wounded fighters, to prove myself. When they saw that I had the talent, they got me out of the country, into a place in Tamil Nadu where I could learn medicine. But the war ended before I graduated, thank all of heaven. I really didn't want to be a surgeon for terrorists. I don't think they should have turned to such methods; it just gave the international community the excuse to condemn them and ignore the justice of their grievances. And it was just wrong.'

'Is your family still alive?'

'My father drowned in the monsoon floods last year. My brother has kept the surgery, but it's not in use. I really should be hurrying home, but this will be my last chance for holiday for years, I fear. When I get back there will be so much to do.'

Urging them to visit, Kasun left for home the next day, as if the conversation had reminded him of his duties. Amanjit thought he and Vikram were a lot alike, although Kasun was softer, more like old Vikram, not the lean, athletic creature Vikram had become: they had a similar thoughtfulness and intensity.

Their week in Madurai had proved fruitless in unearthing clues, so when Vikram saw a troupe of monkeys making its way southeast down a narrow little alley he turned to

Amanjit and said, 'Hey, shall we treat that as an omen and go south?'

'You bet, bhai. I'm over this place. Let's go down to Lanka and kick some asura butt.'

After a long day of hard riding along the coastal roads of southeast Tamil Nadu, they found themselves on the southeast side of Pamban Island, the furthest they could get by land. They gazed out at a line of little islands and rocks disappearing out into the sea towards Sri Lanka known as the Rama Setu, or Rama's Bridge.

Before them, a spit of sand extended into the water, running for miles, then becoming a line of shoals, dotting the sea in a curved arc that ended at Mannar Island on the Sri Lankan coast. The sunset horizon was lost in a haze, but they were sure they could make out the dark shape of Sri Lanka hunched on the skyline. They had packed and eaten, consigned the motorbikes to storage at a hotel, and Amanjit had phoned Deepika, who was well and creeping about Mumbai trying to pick up the threads of the court case without revealing herself. She'd not seen any rakshasa either. It had been soothing to hear her voice.

They were ready to travel.

They watched and waited as night fell and the last sight-seers finished paddling in the water or sitting in the shade. The surf swished dreamily and the sea air smelled clean and fresh; somehow it didn't feel like they were going to war. It felt more like a holiday.

'The land bridge was passable on foot until the fifteenth century,' Vikram, adopting his 'walking encyclopaedia' persona, told Amanjit. 'Then a big storm ripped a deep channel through it—'

'Whatever,' Amanjit broke in impatiently. He had just patrolled the beach, mirror in hand, trying to spot the enemy, but they were still alone. He was actually keen to see a rakshasa; not knowing what they were up to was beginning to unnerve him. 'Let's go, Vik.'

Vikram stood, pulled out a knife and passed his hand over it, turning the blade into a pale rainbow of light. Vishwamitra had taught him how to open a gateway; he lifted it high and began to carve the air apart. 'There *is* a pocket of myth-land here,' he said, pleased.

Amanjit watched with bated breath as multi-coloured sparks flew from Vikram's knife until the air peeled back like wallpaper and dissolved. A warm, perfume-laden wind swished through the hole and when he peered inside, he could see exactly the same beach, but it was brighter, and lit by a silvery moon. Most thrillingly, there was a structure in the water, a low-slung line of darkness that ran into the sea. He felt a quiver of excitement as, drawing his sword, he stepped through into the myth-lands. The air that enfolded him tasted sweet and clean, as it had in mythic-Pushkar, and he inhaled deeply.

He looked about him, but there was no one there. 'All clear,' said Vikram as he followed him through, then dismissed the gate with a crisp gesture.

They both stared at the Rama Setu. 'This is more like it,' Amanjit breathed.

It certainly looked like they were on the right track now. Even in this light, they could see that the line of darkness was in fact a mighty bridge, upheld by massive fifty-foot-tall stone carved monkeys. The bridge ran out of sight into the darkness beneath a radiant, diamond-studded night sky.

Vikram whistled. 'It's thirty miles long – well, at least it's that far from here to Sri Lanka in our world. And it may be guarded.' He frowned. 'Maybe we should use the musafir-astra?'

Amanjit scoffed. 'Are you kidding? I didn't come all this way to *not* walk the Bridge of Rama!'

They took their time, soaking in the strangeness of it all. The bridge appeared to be made of one piece of beautifully carved reddish-brown sandstone, however impossible that was. Each of the giant monkey carvings bearing the walkway was unique, with different facial expressions or poses or weapons held in their non-bridge-bearing arms.

'Were they carved or petrified?' Amanjit wondered. Either was possible, they were so lifelike. Had some spell turned them to stone, rather than some immense army of masons carving them?

The bridge ran unerringly straight, unlike the Rama Setu in their world, to the distant kingdom of Lanka. The weather was perfect, warm but not oppressive, and they took their time, walking ten miles a day, wary of exhausting themselves before the battle.

The bridge was swarming with real flesh-and-blood monkeys, a massive troop that chattered and skittered about and followed them at a distance. At first they made them laugh, and then they made them nervous. There was no sign of anything resembling monkey food and they weren't fouling the bridge – but perhaps even these wild creatures recognised it as special.

Or perhaps they were Hanuman's people and not ordinary monkeys at all.

Below them the preternaturally clean waters of the Gulf of Mannar met the Palk Strait, the current rushing first north, then south, as if tidally driven. From time to time they saw large dark shapes glide past beneath the waves: fish of unnatural size, completely oblivious to them, caught up in their own world, where the surface was, for them, the roof of all existence.

'Sometimes I think our world is like a drop of water,' Vikram mused. 'We stare at the walls, not even realising there is something outside. It's only when you stumble into places like this that you know there's something outside that droplet.'

'Very deep,' Amanjit snorted. 'Did you bring a stash with you? Have you been smoking ganja?'

'You're just a soulless sword-swinger, bhai.'

'That's me, and happy to be so.'

Gradually, Lanka appeared in the distance, lushly verdant and capped with mountains. They caught a gleam like sunlight on golden turrets. When the far end of the bridge came in sight, the largest of the monkeys came forward and bowed at their feet, then scampered away.

'Aren't the monkeys supposed to help us storm the city?' Amanjit commented.

Vikram threw up his hands theatrically. 'Good point: where's Hanuman? Where's King Sugriva and his quest to wrest back his throne?'

For all his joking, the unspoken question hung in the air: *Have we got this wrong?*

Even at this distance they could see a gateway at the far end of the bridge. It was an awesome sight, thrice the height of the India Gate in Delhi, carved to resemble two massive asuras with horns and teeth, each bearing a cross-beam on their shoulders. The statues were studded with gemstones and painted in bright lacquers. In their free hands each statuary-demon carried a trumpet, and as Vikram and Amanjit approached, the trumpets raised in unison and a deafening brazen blast heralded their arrival.

At once the ramparts of the walls surrounding the gates were filled with rank upon rank of archers and spearmen, capering asuras with beast-heads, their muscular bodies encased in glittering armour. They looked like picture-book figures come to life, but nothing like the asuras they had seen up north; these were watercolour images of how an artist might picture a demon.

Amanjit gave up counting the enemy on the walls and looked at Vikram. 'Now what?' he hissed. 'There are thousands of them—'

But Vikram was slowly shaking his head. 'Something's wrong.'

'Yeah, we're going to be skewered by a zillion demons, and that is clearly wrong . . . so what do we do?'

Vikram opened his mouth to answer, but his words were lost beneath another blast of the trumpets. With a deafening shriek, the gates opened and a massive chariot drove out, bearing a golden-armoured demon holding a white flag aloft.

'Hey, maybe they're surrendering,' Amanjit muttered hopefully.

They drew their bows cautiously as the chariot rolled closer, until they could clearly see the messenger, a twisted, hunched thing with a warthog's head and hooves. But he leaped spryly enough from the chariot, waving his white flag desperately as he cried, 'Parley – a parley, O Great Ones: I bring a message from the king.' He was visibly trembling, as if terrified to be so close to them.

Amanjit eyed Vikram, frowning. 'What are they doing, trying to lull us into a false sense of security or something? Because it's not working.'

Vikram was just as puzzled. He lowered his bow, slackening his draw. 'Speak,' he called to the messenger. 'What's your message?'

The warthog-demon bowed gratefully. Evidently 'shooting the messenger' was still a clear and present danger in these parts.

'Oh Great Lord Rama, and mighty Lord Lakshmana, I thank you for your graciousness.' He stood up as straight as he could and pulled out a scroll, unrolled it ostentatiously and, after clearing his throat, started: 'My Lords, the King of Lanka bids you welcome. He is overjoyed at your return to his realm and sends me to escort you to his palace, where every care will be taken to ensure that your stay here is as pleasurable as can be conceived. We welcome our liberators, our emancipators, the divine heroes to whom our freedom is owed. We bid you cast care aside and dwell with us for as long as it pleases you. We give you our love and adoration and open our arms to you. Let all be as you will it. The king himself trembles with joy at your coming and abases himself before you. Let your path be strewn with flowers; let palanquins of sumptuous comfort bear you; let maidens of surpassing beauty tend you; let—'

'Ahem . . .'

The messenger stopped his flow, and peered at Vikram. 'My Lord? Are you not pleased? Is there a problem?'

'Yeah,' Amanjit put in, 'you can tell Ravindra he can shove—'

Vikram put a warning hand on his shoulder, then turned back to the herald. 'Messenger, we thank your king for his kind greetings. But could you please clarify for us, as we have been out of touch for a long time – who is the present King of Lanka?'

The herald's eyes popped out a little. 'Er, my Lord . . .? You don't know?'

Vikram shook his head apologetically. 'We have been away a very long time – centuries, in fact.'

The herald bowed. 'Of course, my Lord – of course – has it really been so long? Then you will be pleased to know that the throne of Lanka is still held by your great friend and most loyal ally, King Vibhishana . . .'

# CHAPTER FIVE

# THE INVISIBLE GIRL

*Mumbai, Maharashtra, April 2011*

Deepika wasn't really invisible, but she might as well have been. Vishwamitra had taught her how to send out tiny subliminal messages, as much about body language and appearance as magic, so that people subconsciously ignored her. It was about being *unmemorable*, exuding *not-worth-looking-at* vibes. She wore dull clothing, no jewellery, and her lank hair was tied back. She didn't meet anyone's eyes as she walked in a hunched, graceless manner and she talked to no one. A muttered charm every minute or so helped sustain the illusion.

It was working well; days had passed and other than infrequent calls to Amanjit, she'd barely spoken to another soul. She'd rented a room in the Juhu suburb, which was respectable enough to ensure there were reliable security guards on the front doors, and spent her days prowling Nariman Point, where Meenakshi's law firm was situated.

It took a couple of days of lurking before she was able

to approach the woman she needed: Tripti Dharmanshi, the advocate who'd read out Dinesh Khandavani's will and assigned Meenakshi to their case. The woman was not a rakshasa; Deepika had checked that by videoing her on her mobile.

She slid from the shadows one evening when the lawyer was getting into her car and called, 'Ms Dharmanshi?'

The lawyer looked at her warily. 'Miss Choudhary? Is that you?'

Deepika stopped a few feet away, giving the woman some space; there was probably a missing person's report out on her again, maybe even an arrest warrant.

It was six weeks since she'd been attacked by Meenakshi and her fellow demons, Prahasta and Imtakh, on that dreadful evening when so much had gone wrong. The police would surely still be investigating Uma and Tanvir's deaths and wondering where Deepika was, so she knew she had to be very careful. 'Yes, Ms Dharmanshi, it's me.'

'By the gods, girl! I'd heard that you were—' The lawyer looked left and right, clearly afraid. 'What are you doing here?'

'I need to talk to you, in private.'

'Half the police think you're a fugitive from justice, Miss Choudhary.'

'I'm a fugitive, yes – but not from justice. And I didn't kill my friends, I swear it.' She spread her hands, a show of peaceful intentions. 'Please, we have to talk – but not here. I swear I don't mean you any harm.'

Tripti Dharmanshi wavered, then opened her car door. 'I'm going to trust you, Deepika. It's not that I don't believe you capable of violence, but I don't believe you would have harmed Tanvir Allam – I saw for myself that you cared for him. We can talk at my apartment. It isn't far.'

Deepika paused. It was a big step to place herself in the power of another, even if there wasn't much the woman could do to her, at least not physically. But she scurried to the car and slid into the back seat.

The apartment was just a ten-minute drive, a building overlooking the sea near the Gateway of India arch, in a street that looked like it had been built in the days of the British Raj. The interior lobby had a stately, slightly antique feel, with yellowed walls and fussy little touches from another era on the balustrades and pillars, and the lift was old and slow.

'I live alone,' Tripti told her as they entered her apartment. 'My husband divorced me when my career outstripped his. He took the children.' Her voice was flat rather than sad or angry, although it hinted at both. She ushered Deepika into a small but immaculate set of rooms that looked curiously empty, as if she seldom went into them. There were few photographs, just a couple of some children – a girl and a boy – and one of Tripti on a beach holiday with another grey-haired woman, a sister, perhaps.

Tripti poured wine, a French white, and they sat appraising each other silently. The lawyer was silver-haired about the temples; she looked tired, but her eyes were alert. She was dressed in black and grey: western-style professional attire. She wore no make-up, and her jewellery was sober.

'You're wearing a wedding ring, and wedding bangles,' Tripti observed. 'Amanjit Singh Bajaj, I presume?'

Deepika smiled cautiously. 'We married last month, in secret.'

'My congratulations. Does that explain your disappearance? Many of the investigators believe you're dead – they found your blood in the apartment.'

'Sort of,' Deepika replied. 'We were attacked and I was abducted. I managed to escape, and I've been in hiding since. But I don't want my family's affairs to be neglected, so I'm here to ensure that someone is still working on them.'

'Then why not work through your family?'

'They don't really understand legal matters, and I was working closely with Meenakshi Nandita.' It was hard to say that name without feeling her anger surge back to the surface, but she tamped it back down. 'And the police and media are still watching them, so it's dangerous for me to do anything openly. Someone tried to kill me in March.'

Tripti took a deep breath, then exhaled slowly. 'Someone injured Meenakshi too,' she said tentatively, clearly unsure how much she should reveal. 'She's not been back at work since.'

*I bet she hasn't . . . she's probably a real mess . . .* What she'd done to the rakshasa princess' face still slightly appalled Deepika, despite everything the demon was. *I cut her nose off . . . by all the gods, what* happened *to me?* 'Is she still assigned to our case?'

'No – in fact, she's disappeared too. The police initially believed you had both been abducted or murdered. The night you vanished, many people saw or heard some kind of uproar, but when the authorities arrived, a woman fitting Meenakshi's description reassured them and turned them away. The police are now speaking of her as a suspect, but she's vanished.'

The truth, that Meenakshi and the two men were demons who'd tried to kill her, was far too far-fetched, but clearly Tripti believed Meenakshi guilty of something.

'Who's taking our case now?' Deepika asked instead.

'I haven't yet reassigned it. At first I was hoping Meenakshi would come back; more recently, it's been overtaken by other matters.'

'Would you be able to take it on yourself?'

The lawyer pondered. 'Yes. Yes I could,' she replied. 'I'm somewhat intrigued now.'

'I'd like to help, as I did before,' Deepika offered. 'Or at the least, I want to be the family liaison. I'll give you my mobile number. But you need to keep my presence a secret: I don't want to be attacked again.' She knew it was a real risk – if Tripti gave her number to the authorities, she could be traced – but trust had to start somewhere.

'Very well, Miss Choudhary,' Tripti said, and then smiled. 'Or I should say, Mrs Bajaj?'

Deepika felt herself blush with pleasure. 'You know, we haven't even talked about that! I hadn't given it a thought. *Mrs Bajaj* – that's really me!'

The case-work was dull, but it quickly took over Deepika's life and her days drifted into a pastel-grey trudge, so featureless they were instantly forgotten. She still didn't speak to anyone most days, and her increasingly rare calls from Amanjit felt like heaven at the time, then left her in a lonely hell for hours afterwards. Rather than giving her strength, they almost sucked the energy from her – and the last call had frightened her. They were just about to go to the mythlands and cross the Bridge of Rama. And then . . . silence.

Occasionally Tripti called her and they dined together. The Bajaj case might just be one of hundreds Tripti was dealing with, but they were making progress. Finally, as April waned, Tripti gave Deepika a phone number that she knew she needed: one she wasn't supposed to give out. It was an important moment, a sign of trust.

She didn't rush the call. First, she ran through her arguments in her mind with very un-Deepika forethought, and only when she was certain she was ready did she press the numbers into her burner phone.

It was answered almost immediately. 'Hello?' a nervous young male voice quavered.

'Hello, Lalit. May I speak with you, about Vikram Khandavani?' She spoke calmly, quietly; Lalit, Vikram's younger half-brother, had a very nervous disposition.

'Who is this?'

'This is Deepika Choudhary, Lalit. Don't hang up, please.'

There was a long silence.

'Lalit?' she asked anxiously.

'I'm still here,' he whispered.

'Is your mother home?'

'No, it's just me.' He hadn't stopped whispering, though.

'Good. Thank you.' She tried to sound warm and friendly. 'Lalit, can we meet? Please? It could be very important. But it has to be in secret. Just you and me. *Please?*'

There was no reason for him to agree, and no reason she could give him. She was trusting a hunch, and trusting the *Ramayana*, in which Bharata, Rama's younger brother, remained loyal, despite his conniving mother. It was a gamble, but . . .

'Okay,' Lalit said. 'Where and when?'

# CHAPTER SIX

# THE GHOST AT THE CITADEL DOOR

*Lanka, April 2011*

It was April, so Keke told her; the seasons here corresponded to those of the real world and the temperatures were rising daily as the lush green of the distant forests faded to a dirty brown and the brilliant flowers began to look tired. But the rooftop swimming pool of the citadel had become almost tepid, and Rasita couldn't go outside without sunglasses (which mysteriously appeared on her dresser one morning after she'd expressed a need for them).

'Have you worked out how old you are yet, Keke?' she asked one day; she was perplexed by the girl's contradictory childishness and wisdom. Keke was a rakshasa, one of the noble breed, but serving as her maid was an honour, even though it came with menial tasks. Some days she was timelessly wise, others like a young girl.

'I asked around,' Keke responded eagerly, 'and I'm two hundred years old, mistress. We age differently, especially here,' she added, striking a very girlish pose. 'I think I'm like a teenager in your world, now . . .'

'So you've been a teenager for at least a century? That must be awful!'

'You're a teenager too, mistress,' Keke giggled.

Ras didn't feel like one. With her memories of past lives and all she'd gone through, she felt like an old woman. She'd spent the last few weeks swimming, sleeping and reading the days away. She'd gone through the *Ramayana* twice, cover to cover, and thought about it deeply, but no inspiration had come from the tale. She studied the chapters about Sita's time in Lanka especially closely, seeking clues or even just consolation, but she'd gained no great insights.

*Soon Ravindra's going to grow tired of waiting. And the ghost of Padma is nearly here — I can feel it in my dreams.*

Some days she watched the asura warriors drilling at dawn and dusk, their weapons flashing, and Meghanada Indrajit, the general of the rakshasas — a mountainous figure with a bull-head — flawlessly fire burning arrows at targets. Indrajit had sworn a holy pledge to avenge himself against Lakshmana, Keke told her, which made Rasita worry even more, now having to consider that Amanjit might have to face this mighty rakshasa when he and Vikram eventually came to rescue her. That they would come, she didn't doubt, although weeks had passed and there was still no news.

Some days, she just lay on her bed watching the ceiling of her domed bedroom, where the painted figures moved and danced and sang, although she couldn't hear them or their music. The painting was somehow alive, but the figures were leading lives as boring as hers, it seemed to her. Sometimes they watched her, which was a creepy sensation.

But if her days were long, lonely idylls, her nights were all cold sweats and ordeals of terror. She dreamed she was lost in a frozen forest, lurching stiffly from tree to tree, sniffing the air, seeking the one flesh-and-blood being who would satisfy her hunger and need. She was taunted by memories of a life as a queen and driven insane by the relentless slaughter of animals and birds and even people. Lost in the forests, mad for the taste of blood and flesh, filthy and dusty and desperate, and calling the name of the person she sought . . .

'*Rasita—*'

And it was coming ever closer . . .

One night, as she was combing her hair on the balcony, watching the setting sun painting watercolour swathes of crimson across the western skies, the whole citadel reverberated to a sudden crashing sound. She quivered in fright, her mind's eye showing her the palace gates shaking before her sight, as if she had just struck them herself. She knew instantly what it meant.

*Padma's ghost is here—*

Outside in the hall she heard boots thumping, then someone hammered on her doors and a cobra-headed rakshasa in silks glided in. His reptilian features sent a thrill of fear through her, but his hissing voice was thin and anxious. 'My lady, the Ravan requires your presence.'

She stared, heart suddenly pounding. 'Why?'

'He says that you will know why, my lady,' the snake-headed demon responded with a slight inclination of the head, his hood flaring slightly. Keke appeared behind him, her face scared, as a long, piercing shriek, like a bereft seabird, froze Ras where she stood.

The snake-headed rakshasa trembled, his skin slick, as if he were perspiring. 'Please hurry, lady.'

She looked at Keke, who nodded eagerly. It was the last thing she wanted to do, but she was equally frightened to be alone, so she followed the cobra-headed rakshasa out of her suite, down the stairs and through the maze of corridors to an antechamber guarded by half a dozen of the largest asuras she'd yet seen, who peered at her with sullen eyes.

They were admitted into a large throne hall. Ras sucked in her breath. The pillars and arches were carved with all manner of angelic and demonic creatures and the painted ceilings displayed some apocalyptic event, with the skies aflame and the asuras cowering, their faces panicked and beaten, but for one human-looking figure standing alone against the tides of darkness: the Ravan, protector of his people.

Ravindra himself was sitting on an ornate throne of crimson marble surmounted with a carved representation of a naga; his three ghostly queens lounged at his feet. Halika, Jyoti and Aruna looked almost alive now, although nothing could hide the cold menace they exuded. They sat enthroned amidst a court of the most bizarre and frightening figures Rasita had ever seen, more than a hundred male and female figures, some resembling mammals, reptiles or birds, many parodies of humankind. Not all of them were frightening, she realised after looking around; some were just *strange*. They were all dressed like royalty – and they were unarmed, which she thought was probably a good thing, for the air crackled with tension.

As Rasita entered, everyone turned to look at her and fell silent.

Cowering inside, she stopped and swallowed hard, trying to build up her courage.

'Here she is!' snarled a tiger-faced hunchback, whose leathery hide was covered with weeping sores. 'Send her out there – she's no use to us alive—'

Meghanada Indrajit interrupted, belching derisively before saying firmly, 'Syhajeet, you coward: she is our queen and we must protect her.'

Syhajeet, the tiger-faced one, spat on the marble floor. A dangerous purple glow manifested in his right hand. 'You might be prepared to die for her, Meghanada, but I am not, and I daresay most here would agree with me.'

His words were greeted with a surge of approval as many snarled, 'Aye, send her out there.'

Halika leaned forward and hissed at Rasita. She had apparently not noticed that the apple she was holding was rotting in her grasp. 'Send her out to meet it, Lord,' she begged, as her sister ghost-queens giggled malevolently. 'Let her feel what these ages have been to us. Let her endure our condition.'

Ras looked up at Ravindra, whose face was tense, but composed. 'Is the ghost here?'

'Yes. Padma has come.'

'Send her away,' she pleaded. 'Kill her—'

'I can't,' he said. 'I didn't lie to you: only you can deal with the Padma ghost. Anyone who comes between you two will die. Already some of my people have tried and perished. Only the spells woven into the gates and walls currently protect you, and they won't hold it out much longer.'

Another blow on the citadel door shook the entire castle. The courtiers were all quailing; only Ravindra and his queens looked unaffected.

The hunchbacked tiger, Syhajeet, reeking of wet leather and rot, sidled closer. 'Your death comes, lady,' he gloated. 'Your ghost is outside, demanding admittance. You must submit to your destiny and go out to it.'

The decision could be delayed no longer, she realised, although she still wasn't sure if Ravindra had lied to her. *Do I really have to agree to marry him to fool Padma's ghost? Has he told me the truth?*

'Surely you can protect me?' she said to Ravindra, trying but failing to keep her voice steady.

'So: now she unbends – make her beg, my Lord,' a beaked horror with a shaggy hide shrieked at her, and his suggestion was taken up all round the court.

'Go out there and die, you ungrateful wretch!' they roared, almost as one. 'Why should our king protect one who hates him?' They crowded around her, jostling, shoving her towards the doors, shrieking, 'Send her out to face the spectre!'

Ravindra stood and shouted, 'Do not presume to man-handle my queen!'

They stilled, though hostility still burned in their eyes, and their clawed nails still carved the air around her.

Ras, shaking badly, shrank in on herself as Ravindra strode through the crowd of demons, who parted before him.

'Queen Rasita must make her own choice here.'

The hunchback Syhajeet glowered. 'She's no "Queen", Lord – not until she unbends and weds you.' Then he grinned fiendishly. 'Provided she survives this night, of course.'

Ravindra, ignoring him, walked up to Rasita. Putting a hand under her chin, he turned her face up until she met his eyes. His touch made her squirm, but she was frightened to look away. 'You can choose not to believe me,' he said, 'and be taken by the ghost, become another dead thing. Or you can agree to my protection. But you must choose now.'

She was almost too scared to think straight . . . but she had to, if she was going to survive. In truth, she could see no way out. *I have to hang on, I have to stay whole, for Vikram . . .*

'What—' She stopped and swallowed, then took a deep breath, trying to banish the quaver in her voice. 'What rights do you gain over me if I agree to the betrothal?'

The court hissed at her temerity in asking such a question, but Ravindra once again raised his hand for silence and replied evenly, 'You retain your independence and I will demand nothing of you as of right. You continue as you are, except . . .'

She clenched her fists behind her back, but looked up at him, trying to still her fast-beating heart. 'Except . . . what?'

'*Except* you will be my companion, as befitting my betrothed. I have three other queens, so I would expect your company every fourth day.'

'My . . . my *company*? What does that mean?'

'Just that: your company: to sit beside me at table and in court, giving your opinion if asked, providing agreeable companionship in social contexts.' He raised his hands.

'And that's all – nothing intimate, I assure you.' He looked at her intently. 'Rasita, the ghost must truly see sincerity in you, and if not, if it sees that you have no intention of truly being with me, then the token I give you will have no weight. The spectre will not be mollified; it will strike you down and consume you.'

Ras swallowed her rising nausea. 'What are you saying?' she whispered.

'If you accept my token, you are agreeing to marry me – by a set date.'

'*What*—?'

'Because the betrothal must be real for the ghost to perceive it and not attack you. You must be committed, and therefore a finite date is required.'

'What if I break it?'

'I do not know, but I suspect the ghost dwelling inside you will rise up and obliterate you.'

She hung her head, but she had been thinking of little else since he had first told her of her dilemma. Finally, she raised her face to his. 'I will make the pledge and I will keep my word, although I do not expect to need to, for Vikram will come to prevent it,' she told him, marvelling at the certainty she managed to put into her voice. 'But I will live through this night, so that I may become stronger. I will give my pledge to be your engaged companion, and to marry' – she had already worried this out – 'at Dusshera, in September.'

*Take that*, she thought. *Dusshera: the date celebrated for Rama's killing of Ravana in the* Ramayana. *How do like that, 'fiancé'?*

Ravindra didn't show the angry reaction she'd hoped for:

he smiled slightly, recognising the irony of her chosen date.
But she thought there was something like hope in his eyes.

'Then let it be so.'

She closed her eyes, trembling. 'Then let it be so,' she
echoed, choking. 'Let it be so.'

The ceremony was held immediately, and all the while, the
wailing spectre outside the walls pounded on the gates, a
funereal drumbeat. Rasita's skin was so damp with perspiration that the silk she wore felt like an extra layer of skin,
sticking to her and making her feel naked, although she was
sheathed from shoulders to ankles.

There was no shrine in the whole of the citadel, so the
ceremony took place in the throne room, with all those
alien faces crowding about her. The asuras and rakshasas
were once again clad in grotesque finery and only the
dead queens didn't attend, for which Ras was profoundly
grateful – although it was their faces she held in her
mind as the incentive she needed to go through with the
betrothal.

The vows were recited by the cobra-headed rakshasa
who'd brought her here – he was called Lavanasura, another
name she recognised from the *Ramayana*. She repeated the
words after him, line by line. 'I pledge myself to Lord
Ravindra. I pledge companionship. I agree to become his
betrothed. I pledge an intention to marry at Dusshera this
year. I do this of my own free will.' She said it like she meant
it, knowing insincerity might kill her.

But it still made her tremble when Lavanasura spoke the
binding words, first in a rolling tongue she didn't know

and then again in Hindi: 'Let all heaven see that these two are betrothed, and promised one day to wed. Let all the gods mark it. Let all the people see it. Ravan Aeshwaran and Ravani Rasita are pledged to one another, and will marry at Dusshera this year. May every divinity bless their pending union.'

*Aeshwaran*, she noted, the ancient name for Ravana. It gave her a chill to hear it.

Ravindra gave her a diamond ring to wear, larger and more beautiful than any she'd ever seen. To remove it would be to renounce the betrothal, Lavanasura told her. She would have to bear the reminder of her promise everywhere.

But first she had to face a ghost.

Rasita stood alone in the courtyard. Even the guards had fled after those who had tried to assail the ghost had dropped dead before they even reached the spectre. Arrows had no effect, not even an astra shot by Meghanada Indrajit.

She couldn't say they hadn't tried every option, she admitted, looking down at the ring on her left hand, still somewhat in shock. *I've created a timetable for this battle . . . I really am going to have to marry him if Vikram can't save me.*

The air was freezing and her breath steamed as she walked through the gates. The glittering diamond on her finger caught the moonlight, twinkling like a fallen star.

Right in the middle of the road, only a dozen yards away, stood the ghost of Padma: a girl-shaped hole in the living world. Ras had seen her before in Jodhpur and she'd been frightening enough then, but here and now she was *terrifying*. The very earth quailed from her; her tread made the ground dip like fabric. No steamy breath came from her mouth, but she was whispering as she approached.

'*Oh my heart, oh my soul.*'

As she floated towards Ras her features were barely discernible, just a shadowy glimpse of an emaciated face, of teeth too long, eyes too dark, nails too sharp, a tangled veil of hair that carried all of night's darkness in its dusty tresses. Rasita had to force herself not to run.

*She's part of me*, she reminded herself. *She's the missing part of my soul . . .*

The spectre wafted into touching distance, her eyes dark motes, black holes in a pallid face. Ras stared, not daring to move, as Padma reached suddenly and grasped her left hand in a taloned claw. She was painfully icy to the touch, so cold Ras' skin was burned. She whimpered aloud as the ghost bent over the hand, sniffing the ring.

*If she believes me sincere, I live . . .*

*If I lied to myself, I die . . . and become her . . .*

*Was I sincere?*

Her heart was pounding now, a rising tempo that she knew would kill her if she couldn't resolve this. The waiting was going to destroy her if the ghost didn't.

Quailing inside, she reached out, took the ghost's hand and pulled it closer, then embraced it, kissing its cheeks, her warm body against the gelid, gauzy spectre. She felt her body heat drop, and trembling in terror, she inhaled and breathed the ghost into herself. She couldn't have said how she knew what to do, only that it was like drowning, falling into Arctic waters and floating downwards. A flood of horrible memories filled her head: all the longings and lusts of a dead thing forced to consume the living in order to survive; too many, and too ghastly to bear.

She heard herself cry out as darkness swallowed her, filling her mouth and nose and eyes, obliterating her, dragging her down into nothingness.

Rasita woke in her own bed, with Keke at her side, holding her hand. The prints of the ghost's grip still marred the skin on her left hand like an old burn. The ring glittered on her finger.

She'd pledged herself sincerely after all.

And she was alive, and whole.

# CHAPTER SEVEN

# QUID PRO QUO

*Lanka, April 2011*

Rasita's first royal consort duty came four days later. Ravindra sent word that he was inspecting the treasury, so the daylight hours would be her own, but he was expecting her at dinner in the evening.

Keke brought in a glorious silk sari in greens and blues that Ravindra had sent. To put it on felt like a betrayal of all she was, but she'd given her word, and the ghost of Padma was still an unsettling presence inside her, sliding through her subconscious, rearing up unexpectedly at times. While the Sunita part of her was well settled into her psyche, so that they were almost one being, the ghost had still to merge into her. She could feel it stalking the inside of her head, turning over and over that moment when she'd agreed to marry Ravindra. Still assessing whether she'd lied.

But there had been no major trauma since the encounter at the gates and physically, she was feeling fine – better than fine, in truth; she'd never been so healthy.

When Keke led her to the Ravan's private chambers, she felt as nervous as a bride, and terrified that she'd bitten off more than she could possibly chew.

*Please, Vikram . . . you have until Dusshera, and that's only five months, so hurry . . .*

Ravindra had taken some care to ensure that she wasn't made to feel like some kind of exhibit. The only servant present was a dapper little asura whose only discernible animal-trace was the pair of bird-wings folded neatly on his back. There were no other guests. The servant led her to a roof garden overlooking the western walls. The sun was setting, Lord Surya's chariot painting the walls of the fortress a pale orange as it dipped towards the horizon. The distant forest and seas were already turning to shadow.

Ravindra, dressed in black slacks and a white Italian-style shirt, had cut his hair and shaved off his moustache. He looked up at her, took off his sunglasses and smiled as if she were a date he had been anxiously awaiting. 'Rasita – thank you for coming.'

'I didn't have a choice,' she said defiantly. *Be regal*, Sunita reminded her. *Be strong.*

'There is *always* choice in life, Rasita, even here. How do you feel? Are you recovered?'

'I think so,' she admitted. 'The dreams have gone, at least – and she's definitely inside me now . . . sometimes I share her memories, but they aren't pleasant. Mostly, I feel her exploring my past, like I'm a book she's leafing through.' She frowned. 'And I'm definitely healthier: I can feel it when I'm swimming or exercising. I can already do more than I ever could before.'

She didn't tell him about her new dreams, the ones about him. Those had come with the ghost too, and they left her tossing and turning at night, but for entirely different reasons. She had thought herself immune to his dangerous charm. She was wrong.

'Please sit.' He smiled enchantingly. 'I don't doubt you feel trapped and resentful right now, but when you know what's at stake, you'll understand. Please, hear me out.'

The bird-winged servant pulled out a chair and she sat stiffly, wondering if she dared listen to him. *I suppose it's a risk I must take.* 'Then tell me. Help me to understand this bargain we've made.'

He sat opposite and indicated the wine bottle. 'Would you like a drink?'

'No.' She'd made up her mind not to drink tonight.

'That's a shame, when I have a bottle of a very fine French champagne; a Laurent-Perrier.' He frowned. 'You fear intoxication, clearly, but have just one glass – I swear, you will have tasted nothing better, in any life.'

She hesitated, fearing poison, or drugs, but he read her thoughts. 'I don't take advantage of the helpless, Rasita. And in any case, I desire your love freely given, not the ravishing of an inebriated woman.'

*I desire your love . . .* Ras shuddered and sat back, trying to take stock.

This was her sixteenth life. In the first, in Mandore, Ravindra had treated her like a favoured niece: he'd pampered her and left her a virgin while enjoying his other wives – and then he'd had Halika drug her before burning her alive. It was only because she'd given away her heart-stone

– she'd slipped it to her brother, Madan Shastri, and begged him to give it to Aran Dhoop, the court poet she secretly loved, that she'd escaped whatever that ritual was meant to achieve. But the cost had been a fragmented soul and returning through the cycle of life as three entities: a ghost, a madwoman and an invalid. The invalid had never encountered Ravindra before, but the insane woman had, many times.

She lifted her head defiantly. 'You've had me killed in many of my past lives,' she pointed out. 'I've been stoned as a witch and murdered – and suffered even worse. I remember these things now, so how can you have the sheer gall to believe you can win my heart?'

To her amazement, he didn't fly into a rage, but looked at her. 'You're right, of course; entirely right. But there were reasons, Rasita.' He paused, then asked, 'Do you prefer "Rasita"? Or "Sunita", maybe? Or perhaps something in between,' he added archly, 'like "Sita"?'

She didn't dignify that with a reply. Champagne was poured into the king's glass and when she determinedly waved it away, sparkling mineral water into hers. She tried to think about Vikram, but all she could see were those damned photographs of him kissing Sue. She still clung to her faith in him, but it was hard.

The meal was served – the cook had beautifully exploited the natural freshness of the vegetables and the succulence of the meat to produce some of the most delicate, delicious food she could remember. Ravindra ate, clearly enjoying it, in silence, never pressing his betrothal claim on her, nor saying anything untoward.

It felt like one big act designed to make her feel bad, which made her simmer with anger.

As soon as the last dish was cleared, he looked at her appraisingly. 'Do you feel ready to hear of what truly took place, what has led us to this impasse?'

She swallowed the last sip of water, her mind in utter turmoil, petrified to hear what he had to say, although she knew eventually she must. She started to agree – but all at once her nerve failed her and she rose and fled the room.

'Thank you for coming, Rasita.'

She'd spent the last three days brooding, trying to build up her courage again, but she still trembled as she entered his suite, clad in another glorious sari, and sat opposite him again.

'What happened to Sue Parker?' she blurted, because although the American girl might be her rival in love – and Vikram's wife in many of his past lives – she mattered.

'She left India on a flight to Dubai two days after Maricha found you,' Ravindra replied evenly. 'My late uncle let her go. He was a creature of honour, whatever you thought of him.'

Ras remembered the winged rakshasa with a tiger's head and stag antlers. He'd had a strange nobility about him, even though he'd hunted her down implacably.

Deepika had cut Maricha to pieces.

Ras looked down at her hands, clenched in her lap. With the images of those photographs still burning inside her skull, it had taken all her courage to ask that question. That the American had been courageous and selfless in helping Ras get away, albeit temporarily, from Maricha, only made it worse. But she hoped he was telling the truth and Sue was safe – safe, and *gone*.

This time, she accepted champagne. Keke had done her make-up and put her hair into an elaborate pile, taking immense pride in beautifying her charge. Ras didn't want to look attractive for her captor, but she'd finally realised that Keke was being judged on how good she looked, so she'd relented.

As for Ravindra, he looked like a movie star on a yacht in the Mediterranean, the sort of man she'd once fawned over, collected posters and giggled about with classmates at school. Being alone with him was utterly terrifying.

'I don't know what you think to achieve with this,' she told him, once she'd finished her amazing meal. 'I will never, ever, love you. Even if you somehow manage to evade Vikram until Dusshera and marry me, you will never have my love, and you will never be content in your marriage.'

He pulled a rueful face and as he raised his champagne flute to her, the falling sun bathed his face in gold, turning him into the very image of kingliness. 'I wish to tell you a story,' he said. 'Predictably, it's my own story – so that you might understand me.'

She shuddered; she didn't *want* to understand him. But what might his story reveal? *Be regal*, Sunita urged her. 'Then speak,' she said, her voice stony, to mask her fear, because if his actions were explicable, would he still be an enemy? Would Vikram still own her heart?

*Did Sita ever doubt her love for Rama?*

'You have lived – what? Fifteen lives? Sixteen?' he asked. 'I have lived just one life in that time, although I've inhabited more than fifty different bodies. And like you and your Aram

Dhoop, I remember them all, although not always well. I always thought I knew what had to be: kill Aram, reclaim you and Darya . . . but since returning to this place, I've realised that all along I've been *wrong*. I've been like a lion with a thorn in his paw, thrashing about, furious and in pain.'

She stared, then looked away so that his beauty wouldn't distract her from analysing every word.

'My first life was in Mandore – or so I thought,' he went on, 'but recently, I have learned otherwise. I now know there were many, *many* more. Through meditation and incantation here in Lanka, I have finally regained those memories too: I now remember lives *before* Mandore.'

Rasita started; she didn't think Vikram had ever suspected *that*.

But Ravindra was still speaking. 'And there is something that has afflicted me in in life after life after life, every single one, that has driven me insane: the nightmares! In all my pre-Mandore lives, I dreamed of a dreadful event, an apocalyptic trauma: fire in the skies, rivers boiling, forests blasted away, people dying . . . and a woman I loved being torn apart by incomprehensible forces. These nightmares have tormented me in life after life. I didn't understand them, I couldn't stop them and I couldn't endure them. In many lives I killed myself rather than face them. I escaped those dreams only when, as Ravindra, Raja of Mandore, I lost the capacity to sleep.

'Everything changed for me in a life I led in the eighth century in Rajasthan, when I met a guru who claimed to understand dreams. He studied me, taking notes on every aspect of my condition. He found powders and herbs that suppressed the nightmares when I could take no more, and he also helped me to recall the dreams more fully. Through this technique, I found I could remember fragments of the scrolls and ancient symbols that I saw in my visions and we started investigating them. Even then, it was all too much and I hanged myself before we could make more progress.'

When Ravindra paused to sip his champagne, Ras risked a glance at his face. Where before she'd only ever seen malice or a mask of charm, now he wore a grim, haunted aspect. *This is his truth*, she realised, *or what he believes the truth to be.*

Ravindra resumed his story, his voice thoughtful. 'Finally, I made a breakthrough. For the first and only time that I am aware of, I was reborn in the same town where I died – although of course I had no memory of that previous life. But coincidentally, I soon met that same guru, now thirty years older and near death, when my new parents brought me, a nightmare-haunted child, to see him. I was fortunate: my new parents, being royal, were able to provide proper care for a sickly child. The guru hypnotised me and brought back those memories of that previous life – we were both amazed, for he'd never done such a thing before. He taught me his skills – how to learn from dreams, how to prevent them or induce them – and I used those techniques to recall fragments of my past lives. I began to see the patterns emerging and, finally, to make sense of it all. My name was Ravindra in that life, the place was Mandore and it was 751 AD, as we now reckon the years.'

She finished her champagne and accepted another glass. The whole world seemed to be silent, listening to this tale. 'You were a monster in that life,' she reminded him – and herself.

For the first time he flinched and he hung his head before

raising it again and meeting her eye. 'Yes, I am a monster. I have killed – I have tortured for pleasure. For a thousand years I have been unable to die, instead, drifting from body to body, possessing them like a demon of folklore. I have caused wars and misery. I feel sometimes that I am made of rage, that I am the incarnation of all Destruction – the darkest shadow of Shiva himself. Some nights I feel I am a hair's-breadth from speaking a mantra that will bring ruin upon all Creation.

'But this very year, since regaining access to Lanka, I have learned *why* – I have learned the *truth*. It does not make me less a monster, but I have learned how all of this mess has come to pass. And more than that: I have learned how to put aside my evil.'

She stared at him. 'Then do it.'

'I'm trying to,' he replied, 'but I need your help.'

Rasita put down her crystal champagne flute before she dropped it. It was too beautiful to break. She looked away. 'Do you think I'm that stupid? That I'll believe that all that's needed to heal you is my love?' She gave a brittle laugh. 'If I told you how many times Sunita has heard men tell her that—!'

'It's the truth, Rasita, and I can prove it: let me take you back to that first life, the one from where all my nightmares originate. I want you to experience the truth. Then, and only then, will you truly understand.'

Rasita swallowed. 'What do you mean, "take me back"?'

'You're afraid,' he said earnestly. 'Please, I know I am asking a lot, but until you understand this, the cycle of death is doomed to go on and on.'

'No it's not – it'll end when Vikram kills you . . .'

'No,' he said firmly, 'because I won't let that happen.'

He put his big hand on her arm and she forgot to shrug it off. 'I am no longer suicidal and I have the will, honed by centuries of suffering, to win this contest. And I am more deserving of your love than he is. Aram Dhoop – Chand Bardai, Vikram Khandavani; whichever name you choose – *he* is the villain of this tale, not I.'

She reeled. 'That's ridiculous: you're a killer, while he's *always* been a man of peace – so how can you say that?'

He stared deep into her eyes. 'Because you are my *true* wife, Rasita,' he said, his voice throbbing. '*You* are the woman whose death haunts my dreams – you are the love I lost in the cataclysm that haunted my earlier self's dreams – and *he* is the adulterous bastard who tried to steal you from me, the man who caused that cataclysm!'

'*No*,' she cried, '*that's not true*—'

She fled before he could spin more of his lies.

A few days later, a scroll appeared in her room, next to her well-thumbed copy of the *Ramayana*.

She knew what it would contain: more of his lies and manipulations as he recast the truth with himself as tragic hero and her as his only redemption.

She picked it up, ready to tear it into a million pieces and burn the shreds.

*But what if I can learn something that will give Vikram and Amanjit the edge . . . ?*

*It's not disloyal to read this if I'm helping my love win this war*, she told herself.

It still took her all day to find the courage, but eventually she picked it up and began to read.

# CHAPTER EIGHT

# I, RAVANA

*I am known in legend as Ravana. Scholars say the name is derived from a phrase meaning 'he whose words cause weeping', but they are utterly wrong. It is derived in truth from 'Ravan'; a word of my original people simply meaning 'king'. I was given the name Raias as a child until I mastered the ten aspects of the warrior-sage and so earned the name Aeshwaran, which means 'Ten-face'.*

*The place where I dwelled – where my father was king and I was one of many princes – is today an archaeological site in Pakistan called Mohenjo-Daro. That's the modern name for it, meaning 'Mound of the Dead', but to us it was Adun, which in our tongue meant 'Mother-Place'. Do not look to translate Adun to Hindi or English; that language is long lost; I and my rakshasas are the only people who now speak it. The ruined Adun is the principal site in what is now called Harappan, or the Indus Valley Civilisation, but when I as Aeshwaran lived, we called the land Sinat, meaning 'Riverland' in our tongue. Sindh, the Hindi name for the region, actually does derive from this, one of the few words of our tongue to survive in modern languages.*

*It was natural to name Sinat for those mighty rivers. Our land,*

*protected by mountains and the sea and fed by those rolling veins,*
*was truly blessed. Archaeologists and scholars now believe that we*
*were one of the first great civilisations of this world, but of course*
*we knew nothing of that. We knew only that there were primitives*
*outside our borders and order within. It was the Age of Bronze, which*
*archaeologists now date from 3000–1200 BC. I estimate that I was*
*born around 1700 BC, during this first flowering of humankind. I*
*have seen much drivel written about the Indus Valley Civilisation,*
*wishful scholars and writers imagining some kind of paradise on*
*earth, but it wasn't – we were only human, and new to civilised*
*behaviour. There was slavery, disease, wars, injustice, shortages and*
*riots. It was not even particularly advanced; Adun at its height would*
*have seemed a meagre place to a Greek or a Roman of the Classical*
*Age, or to a man of Imperial Peking in later ages. But for that period,*
*it was a wonder to behold. We built tall buildings and strong walls.*
*We diverted water into canals running through and under the streets;*
*we built the first decent drainage system mankind had known. Our*
*metalwork and agriculture was the best of its period. And we elite*
*found time for pleasure and learning.*

*Religion, such as it was, was simple, and seen by the educated as*
*a little common; we elite disdained it. To the people of Adun, gods*
*were mysterious and uncaring, embodiments of natural forces that*
*had to be placated. We had no philosophy or moral code telling us*
*how to live; we made our own rules.*

*By the time I was born, however, the good times were passing.*
*There were earthquakes in the mountains and the rivers were drying*
*up, shifting eastwards or failing completely. Despite the fertile land,*
*our farming methods had been depleting the soil, so crops were less*
*dependable. A modern scientist would have known what the prob-*
*lems were and educated us about nitrate-fixing and such techniques;*

*modern engineers might have found a way to re-divert the rivers – but all we had were priests telling us to sacrifice more to appease the angry gods. Eventually, even human lives were sacrificed – but that was later.*

*I knew little of these matters and cared less; I was young and my only concern was learning the warrior-aspects, the prime skills we considered necessary for any nobleman: weaponry, horsemanship, language, anatomy, medicine, singing, music, history, priestly ritual and astronomy.*

*I wished only to excel and best my peers. As a noble, I could aspire to be king, which was not through hereditary lineage, but acclamation, and I made it my business to be so acclaimed. I won a great following and became king – 'Ravan' – and suddenly, I had to contend personally with all of our kingdom's problems.*

*The crux of our crisis was that the rivers were dying – and therefore so were we. Everyone knew our supremacy depended upon those rivers, and primitive men from the steppes were testing our northern borders while barbarians from the east – now modern Bengal – were pushing at our defences. Our discipline and metal-working gave us an edge still, but we were weakening all the time, so much so that I began to fear that I would be the last Ravan of Sinat.*

*I changed from a vainglorious warrior to a single-minded ruler; I did everything I could for my people. I built new canals and started more excavations. I expanded the army. I even widened the powers of the priesthood, allowing them to tithe and make sacrifices.*

*As Ravan, of course I had to marry, and I adored my wife with an intensity that still frightens me. Manda was also from a well-connected family with scholarly traditions – in our land, women also learned the aspects, and in the non-martial aspects she was always my better: quick-minded and sharp-witted. Manda blazed* with self-confidence; she outshone all other women, even those others might have believed outwardly more beautiful. She had true charisma, the presence that lights up a room and draws every eye. She was passionate and glorious and we all worshipped her.

Manda shared my dedication for righting the wrongs of the kingdom; we were on a quest, she and I, to save Sinat, or to die trying. But despite everything we achieved, our quest looked doomed as each year the water table dropped further and the raids grew worse. Bandits burned border towns that were never rebuilt and the priests took to sacrificing children to placate the angry gods.

I despaired.

It was in this dark time that Dasraiyat returned. He had been my best friend, but also my greatest rival when we were learning the ways of the warrior-sage and the Ten Aspects. He'd left without taking the final tests, so no one other than I knew just how accomplished he was – at the time, I thought he'd lost his nerve and had left in shame, but he had gone all the way to Mesopotamia, in the far west, to learn secrets even we in Sinat had never dreamed of.

Dasraiyat returned with aspects we had never before seen: he could shape fire and make water dance and the winds rage. In that distant, mysterious land he'd learned what you would call 'magic'. Of course, the priests would have labelled him a demon and had him sacrificed to placate the river-gods, but he was my best friend, so when he revealed his new powers to me in private, my only thoughts were to protect him – and to use his skills for the good of the kingdom. And I wanted to learn them myself, of course; I had always believed myself to be his equal in all things.

He agreed, and I insisted Manda learn too. By day we fulfilled our royal duties, unable to stop the realm tottering towards collapse, but now our real work was in our secret chambers, where Dasraiyat *taught us all he'd learned. It took months, but we grew in knowledge, until we were ready to make a difference.*

*I must tell you something of this 'magic': it was attuned to the prime elements – Fire, Air, Earth, Water – and to reach them required mastery of Aether, the unseen linkage between mind and matter. It is the key: the nexus where gesture and word and will combine to impel an element to bend to the mind of the magician. I cannot reveal how it was done – we ingested powders and fluids that opened the aether to us, and Dasraiyat kept those ingredients secret – but Manda and I became magicians too. Even now, it humbles me to know that Manda overtook us both; her skill was truly amazing. And the bonds of friendship we three forged in that shared learning made me think that no greater friendship existed in all history.*

*We believed utterly that we were destined to save our kingdom.*

*But suddenly, the crisis was upon us: that summer the Saraswati, the easternmost of the great rivers, failed to reach the sea. The Indus River fell too, and the monsoon that followed made no impression. We didn't have enough food and water for the people. The sewage drains festered and plague swept through the poorer quarters, people developed painful sores that swelled and burst horribly just before they died. It was a ghastly time. The poor rioted after starving soldiers pillaged their farms and I had to raise taxes again to try and find imported food – but it was the sixth failed harvest in a row and the treasury was empty.*

*My time was running out; we had to barricade ourselves in the fortress.*

*But Manda, Dasraiyat and I had devised a plan, our grand design. There were no ancient texts to guide us; no sages or gods to tell us what to do, but we were aflame with determination and pride.*

*We believed that the world was balanced between the twin poles of Creation and Destruction, on a fulcrum we labelled 'Preservation' – we were in new philosophical territory, and this is before the names Brahma and Shiva and Vishnu were ever spoken in these lands. We realised that by applying these forces to the four elemental aspects, we could achieve mighty things.*

*We studied and experimented – Dasraiyat accidentally destroyed a village in the north when he inadvertently triggered an earthquake; I myself decimated a forest in error whilst manipulating fire. Only Manda never made mistakes. But we learned, and whenever we erred, we told ourselves, 'It's for the greater good.'*

*Finally, on a date selected according to the alignment of stars and planets, we tried to save the kingdom.*

*To manipulate the complex forces we intended to use, we had to, in effect, peel away a part of ourselves and join it to a magical aspect. I was strong in Fire and Air and in the destructive energies, and Dasraiyat, aligned with creativity, Water and Earth, was my ideal foil. Manda, my wondrous wife, could do all of these equally: she was the fulcrum, the Preserver.*

*Picture us in a brazier-lit chamber deep below Adun: Dasraiyat, Manda and me, naked, with protective symbols painted all over our bodies, each standing at one point of a triangle within a magical circle etched on the floor. Manda looked like a divinity to me, her body poised like a dancer, her hands pulling and weaving at the very seams of existence.*

*I stepped into the aether and invoked the aspect of destruction. My role was to clear the way, to re-carve the rivers and reshape the lands thrown awry by the earthquakes. As I did so, Dasraiyat invoked creation, Earth and Water, to cause the waters to flow back to us. His aether body was so bright, it was hard to look upon.*

*Opposite us, Manda split her soul in three, sending one into the aether to link with Dasraiyat as Creator and the second to me, in the dark hues of the Destroyer. Her third aspect, the Preserver, was a stabilising aspect in the middle, to hold us all in place and ensure the equal flow of the energies: a protective aspect. You will recognise the Trimurti in this configuration – the Creative, the Destructive, and the Protective: Brahma and Shiva, and in between them, Vishnu.*

*I raised my arms and twinned my destructive aspect to that of Manda, the male and female, while beside me, Dasraiyat twined his arms about Manda's creation aspect. Then we invoked all of the elements: I called the destructive aspects of Fire and Air and Manda the destructive aspects of Earth and Water; at the same time she worked with Dasraiyat on the creative aspects, and all the while, Manda's protective aspect controlled the flow.*

*It felt like hours, but in truth, it probably took only minutes before we were ready to unleash the powers of Ruin and Rebirth upon our beloved land.*

*It is difficult to convey how overwhelming it felt. From that dark room beneath the palace our heightened senses could perceive not just the entire valley, but the lands all around: it was how gods must see. From an eagle on the highest peak to an ant beneath a rock, it was all spread before us: incredible, majestic – so astonishing that we almost forgot why we were there.*

*I wish we had.*

*We began by finding that original earthquake, and the place where the springs that had once fed Sinat now flowed around us. Then I moved – the merest twitch of a finger – and began to carve the earth, to allow the springs to once again feed the dried-up riverbed of the Saraswati. I blasted a hill a hundred miles to the north to rubble and Dasraiyat rebuilt it a mile to the west. It was so easy.*

*We were as gods.*

*We destroyed and we created: we moved lands and razed our enemies, raining fire on the barbarians massed on our borders, listening to their screams as if we inhabited their throats. We watched our grand gestures shape the world.*

*There is a Greek word that has found its way into other tongues, including English: hubris, which signifies overweening pride leading to a fall. There is no better word for what happened.*

*We thought we were on the way to achieving our aim, but we hadn't realised that in donning the aspects of creation and destruction, our minds would be revealed to each other – and in trying to deepen my mental rapport with Dasraiyat, I realised to my horror that he had no intention of letting me live through this night. He secretly lusted after my Manda and desired my death – he saw me only as a tool, to be used to achieve his ultimate ambition: to rule with Manda at his side. That was his intention: to murder me with his powers and take my wife – who truly loved only me – in the midst of this whirlpool of magic.*

*Even as I saw his treachery, he struck – but that flash of insight had left me prepared and I countered his blow when he lashed out to destroy me.*

*But our great purpose was forgotten in the midst of this sudden battle for survival: the ritual to save the kingdom had become a war between me and him, with my Manda caught between us.*

*She tried to stop us. In her protective aspect she took the strain, struggling to hold us in place and re-channel our energies into the task. I remember her voice, pleading in our minds, trying to return us to our original focus, but she might as well have been trying to reason with a pair of volcanoes. In moments, we lost control of the forces we wielded.*

*The battle between us took seconds, but those seconds felt like eternity.*

*I saw our fires burn the whole Indus Valley, immolating our people and turning homes, businesses and farms into massive bonfires. I saw the land convulse like rippling pond water; the sea recoiled, then broke over the shorelines, sweeping away everything in its path. And all the while, the creator aspect of Dasraiyat turned and lurched across the magic circle, seeking to attack me physically, held back only by Manda.*

*It was worst for Manda, who had split herself into seven aether-forms, the three magical aspects and the four elemental ones. It was too much, even for my wondrous wife. First, the protective aspect in the middle twisted, bent and then, with a howl that haunts me still, she flew apart. One second she was whole, then for an instant I saw her writhing body in all seven aspects – and then she was gone.*

*The circle exploded and Dasraiyat and I were flung apart.*

*And yet the treacherous cur fought on! He struck out at me, but I struck back, both mad with hatred – I felt him seizing the minds of the people, intending to turn them against me, but I countered, shielding them, protecting them. I didn't see until later how he had disfigured them, my own people. We battled with cosmic forces until we were blasted apart and sent spinning out into the darkness.*

*When I woke, I was alone, and my Manda was gone without a trace.*

*So was Dasraiyat.*

*And together, we had destroyed the people and the land we had set out to save. Sinat was no more.*

Rasita put down the scroll with shaking hands. The story had moved her, but it perplexed her too, for it made no sense. It surely couldn't be true history; it was so different to what she thought she knew — what the world thought it knew. But if it *was* true, what did it mean for her and her situation — and for Vikram and Amanjit? What did it say about the *Ramayana* itself?

She thought about the source: *Ravindra is a liar and a killer, so can I believe this testimony?*

Taking a deep breath, like a diver about to plunge underwater, she went to the last section.

*You can guess the rest. When I woke I was the only one left in that chamber. Manda and Dasraiyat had both vanished without a trace. I raged at the cruelty of the gods for letting me live, wallowing in my fury at Dasraiyat for lusting after what was mine and what his treachery had caused. And I despaired at our failure.*

*When I emerged, it was to a world I scarcely recognised. Part of the city of Adun still stood, the richest parts, not the flimsier structures in the poorer quarters. The few people who had survived fire and flood were wandering in a daze; most had been driven insane by Dasraiyat's attempted invasion of their psyches and everyone who did still live had been twisted beyond recognition by his brutal infliction of bestial characteristics. Perhaps he had meant it only as a metaphor for ferocity, but it had instead become a literal truth: he had inflicted beast-like features on our people. Some were so warped and unnatural that they couldn't survive. Of the maybe three hundred thousand survivors in all of Sinat, less than ten per cent of our population, some fifty thousand, had been transformed into these half-beasts. Somehow recognising that it was I who had saved them, they held me as their protector and god and followed me like lost sheep. They named themselves 'asura', which means 'the Saved'.*

*The remainder of the survivors fled when they saw the asuras, not realising that I would never have allowed these marred people to harm them. They went east, seeking a land where they could survive.*

*My poor asuras also had to survive, so we too left ravaged Sinat. We found a new home: an island we called Lanka, and they placed me on the throne, my worshipping beast-men.*

*I was a shadow of the man I had been. Not only did I bear all of the guilt for what we had wrought, I was also damaged psychologically: it was I who had put on the destructive aspect in the ritual and it had changed me. I couldn't sit for even ten minutes without giving in to a violent outburst and my poor asuras wept at my anger and tried desperately to placate me. They loved me, but they feared me. I felt like I was going insane.*

*Soon though, my anger found a just outlet: Dasraiyat had not died in the ritual. He had pulled himself out of that inferno and he soon emerged to gather about him the surviving Sinat people, ironically, those not infected by his bestial transformations. He took them east to the Suryavansha lands and made himself king. You can guess the rest: he launched a war against me. It is still remembered, in garbled terms, this unholy war. You call it The Ramayana.*

# CHAPTER NINE

# YOU WERE BORN TO PLAY THIS ROLE

*Mumbai, Maharashtra, May 2011*

The skinny youth in the black sunglasses, denim jacket and school uniform was huddled into the darkest corner of the little Barista Café, jerking at every sound.

Deepika, wrapped in *don't look at me* charms, slid quietly through the crowd and sat opposite him. 'Hi, Lalit.'

He started. 'Sheesh – where did you come from?'

She smiled to herself. 'I just walked in, like everyone else. You were daydreaming.'

He took off his sunglasses and rubbed his eyes. 'I was? I could swear I . . . anyway . . . um, hi . . .'

'Thanks for agreeing to see me, Lalit. It means a lot to us, and especially to Vikram.'

Vikram's half-brother was small and skinny and very nervous. His soft, pampered face was almost girlish; his perfect little hands twitched constantly. 'I . . . um . . . well, I hardly know Vikram. I don't really know why I'm here. I mean, what Mum is doing is supposed to make us – well, herself, I guess – pretty rich.'

'But it's *wrong*, Lalit – she's lying to the courts, isn't she? She's breaking the law, perjuring herself. And it'll only make her rich if she gets away with it.'

'Yeah, but . . .' He bit his tongue. Deepika smiled encouragingly; he swallowed, then went on, 'I've heard them talk – Mum and Charanpreet – I *really* don't like him – and the lawyer, that Diltan Modi. They've talked about bribing officials to destroy documents, erase them from the public record, you know? And bribing people to get rid of Mum's divorce paper trail. And altering that widow's husband's will.'

'You mean Kiran?'

'Yeah, her – she'll be your mother-in-law, right? When you marry Amanjit?'

'That's right, she will.' He didn't need to know that she and Amanjit were already married. 'That's really interesting, Lalit. Thank you! Vikram is innocent. They all are – Vikram, Amanjit and Rasita. It was the drug lord, Shiv Bakli, who killed Sunita Ashoka, not your brother – I was there, so I know that's the truth, no matter what they're saying.'

She wasn't sure if he believed her, but at least he didn't call her a liar to her face.

'I heard the lawyer, Modi, say they had an insider in your camp,' he added suddenly.

*No surprise there then.* Deepika could guess who. 'Our lawyer, Meenakshi Nandita, right?'

Lalit frowned. 'They never said so openly, but I think it was her.' He looked about unhappily. 'Mum has started . . . um . . . well, *dating* that horrible Charanpreet. I *hate* him.

He's a pig, and he bullies me, but she just tells me to grow up.' He sniffed, visibly upset now. 'I just want everything to be how it was – Dad was always good to us, even though Mum was *horrible* to him. We don't need to do this – it's not like we're poor. And I'm doing well at school – I'll be able to look after us both when I graduate. We only had to hold on a few more years. But . . .'

'But what?'

Lalit looked at her helplessly. 'I don't want to go up against Mum. She's really scary, you know? Sometimes she screams at me and that's bad enough, but when she's really mad she even starts hurting herself.' His face went pale at the memory.

It was a struggle not to snap at him; she'd never had any patience with weakness. But after a moment, the protective part of her reached out and she put a comforting hand on his arm. 'All we need is for you to stand up in court and tell everyone the truth. You need to say, under oath, what you've told me: that Dinesh and Kiran were properly wed, and that you overheard Charanpreet and your mother plotting to break the law with their lawyer.' She squeezed his forearm slightly and added, 'I know you can do that, Lalit, because I know you've got the courage.'

'You don't know me at all.'

She gave him a strong smile, full of reassurance and confidence. 'I want to tell you a story – you probably already know it, but it will help, so please hear me out.' When he nodded, she began, 'A long time ago, there was a king, and he had three wives and four sons. The eldest son was the rightful heir to the throne.'

Lalit rolled his eyes slightly, recognising the beginning of the *Ramayana*, but he didn't interrupt.

Deepika grinned. 'Yeah, you're right: the eldest son was called Rama. The second son was named Bharata, and he liked his brother a lot, and he was happy to be a prince. But Bharata's mother was jealous and she wanted to see her own son advanced, especially when her wicked maid started nagging at her and filling her head with ambition and lies. And as it happened, the king owed the queen some favours, so she decided to call them in. She went to him and demanded that Rama be sent into exile and her own son be made his heir in Rama's place.'

She looked at Lalit, who was listening closely. 'Well, the king wasn't happy about this, as you can imagine, but he'd given his word to the queen and he had no choice but to do as she said. So Rama went into exile and Bharata was named heir. The whole kingdom was sad; everyone knew it was wrong to deny Prince Rama his rightful place. No one had much liked the conniving queen before this, but now they actively disliked her, and worse, many blamed Bharata, who'd had nothing to do with his mother's conniving and wanted no part in it.

Lalit was staring at his toes, so she lowered her voice a little and said gently, 'Very soon, the king died of sorrow, and although no one really wanted to, the courtiers came to Prince Bharata to make him king, as he was the named heir. But Bharata was an honourable man and he really didn't like what his mother had done, so he went to Rama in exile and begged him to take his rightful place on the throne. Rama refused, for he respected his father's promises.

So Bharata returned to the palace with Rama's sandals and he placed them on the throne as a token of his brother's eventual return. Then he refused to live in the palace and ruled only in the name of Rama.

'And so the people came to love Bharata, although they still despised his conniving mother, who lived in sad seclusion for the rest of her days. And when Rama did finally return, after slaying the demon-king Ravana, Bharata immediately made Rama king.'

Deepika patted Lalit's arm. 'Lalit, you are in just the same situation, do you see? You can live a lie, and profit from another's illegally enforced misfortune, or you can make a stand for truth and honour, and gain love and respect – including self-respect. If you do this, you will earn far more in spirit than you could *ever* gain materially from living a lie.'

At first she thought he would close his watery eyes and lower his weak chin and tell her that he was too scared to do what she asked, or that he couldn't cross his fearsome mother, and she would have understood that. But instead, he raised his face and met her gaze, and for the first time she saw something of Vikram's determination in his expression, something of Dinesh's courage and honour.

'Okay,' he said quietly. 'I'll do it. I'll be your Bharata.'

She reached out and hugged him, saying fervently, 'Thank you – *thank you*.'

'Do you think I can do it?' he added anxiously, and she thought about the power of stories to inspire – especially this one. He looked worried, but not afraid.

'Lalit, you were born to play this role,' she told him sincerely.

# CHAPTER TEN

# THE HALL OF THE DEMON-KING

*Sri Lanka, May 2011*

'Man, this place is nuts,' Amanjit whispered in Vikram's ear.

'Yeah, I know. Shh.'

All about them were demons, the vivid, toothy faces staring at them worshipfully. The interior of King Vibhis-hana's palace was as wonderfully colourful as the exterior hinted it would be. The ceilings were painted in gloriously detailed murals, the pillars were decorated with gold leaf, and graceful marble statues, so lifelike they looked like they were moving, lined the hall. One, a fish-tailed girl, winked at Amanjit as he passed. Horns blew, drums rolled and flags waved as demon-children cavorted and adults cheered, hailing the return of their saviours, Rama and Lakshmana, to Lanka. There was scarcely a dry eye in the whole court.

The demon-king was a majestic being: seven feet tall and big-chested, with a flowing silver beard, luminous purple eyes and bull-horns. He wore reptile-skin armour beneath a violet silk robe. But he hovered about Vikram and Amanjit like an anxious child after he'd sat them on the throne of Lanka and prostrated himself at their feet.

'All hail our saviours,' he thundered. 'May you reign over us for a thousand years!' The throng echoed his cry, over and over, in thunderous rolling waves of sound. There was no point talking to them. All Vikram and Amanjit got was praise, and offers of more food, more wine. Musicians played, dancers danced and poets declaimed.

They were entertained royally, for days. Vibhishana himself gave them a guided tour of the island in a flying chariot. They visited battle sites. The whole of the *Ramayana* as written by Valmiki was recited, then actors re-enacted its scenes in a performance that went on, for *days*. Each evening Vikram and Amanjit staggered back to their rooms, exhausted. They ate ravenously and drank like fish and yet they felt like they hadn't eaten for days. The only thing that filled them up was water, which they drank copiously.

'You know what this is like?' Vikram whispered one night after the servants had finally left them alone. 'It's like a video game, but the part where you've already killed the Big Boss and won the prize: it's the after-party. Everyone important has already given you their clues, all the monsters are dead, everything is done and the people are just scenery; with nothing left but a single line of computer-generated dialogue about the weather.'

Amanjit wrinkled his nose. 'I know what you mean. I reckon I could cut Vibhishana's head off and he'd just pick it up, put it back on his neck and keep telling me how wonderful we are.'

'Have you noticed how all that food and drink they're

serving us is having no effect? We've been here a week and I swear the only nourishing food we're getting are the energy bars we brought and the water from the streams. Even with all those feasts, I'm so hungry I could eat my shoes.'

'So we need to leave.' Amanjit grimaced. 'But we've still got *nothing* to go on – we don't even know where Ravindra's holding Ras. We haven't learned *anything* new at all . . . in fact, I'm beginning to feel like we've lost ground. All we've found is that we know less than we thought and we pretty much knew that from the start, if you see what I mean. And if Ravindra isn't here, then where the hell is he?'

'I don't know,' Vikram admitted. 'I've tried talking to Vibhishana about it and it's as if I'm speaking Portuguese or something. He doesn't acknowledge my words; he doesn't engage in the conversation – it's like he just switches off. And we're down to our last few energy bars, bhai. If we don't leave tomorrow, we'll be out of real food, unless we can find something that will actually sustain us here.'

'Then let's go,' Amanjit growled. 'I'm not going to starve to death while feasting on illusions in la-la-land.'

'Okay,' Vikram agreed, 'but let's try to actually *talk* to Vibhishana. We'll make this one last effort to try and find out if we're stuck in a looped tape recording, or somewhere we really do need to be.'

'Great Ones, you summoned me?' Vibhishana boomed. 'I come, I serve, O Saviours of Mankind!' He knelt in the middle of the lounge in their private quarters and waited with an enraptured expression on his face. It was increasingly looking to Vikram like idiocy rather than adoration.

Vikram gritted his teeth and launched into the speech he and Amanjit had worked out. 'King Vibhishana, please, stand, come and talk with us. We greatly need your wise counsel,' he started, cringing at how pompous he sounded, but recent experience had taught them that the king only really focused if you talked to him this way.

'I am much more comfortable kneeling before your glory,' Vibhishana answered cheerily.

Vikram sighed but gave up on that; there were other more important things to focus on than the king's immediate comfort. 'As you wish. King Vibhishana, we have come seeking clues. My wife Sita has again been abducted by Ravana and we suspect he is hiding her here.'

'Oh no, that is impossible,' Vibhishana sounded completely confident. 'Ravana, may his name be for ever accursed, is dead – you killed him yourself, my Lord, may all praise your name. And your wife has ascended to heaven in the chariot of the Earth Goddess and all Creation rejoices for her – although of course we are saddened by your loss.'

'But I am telling you, Ravana has stolen her,' Vikram snapped.

Vibhishana's serene face contorted slightly, then it smoothed over again and he said, 'It is wonderful weather we are having, my Lords. The gods bless us with your presence.'

Amanjit punched a fist into his palm and groaned. 'Bloody Ravana has stolen Sita!' he shouted.

Vibhishana cringed, then blinked, and apparently forgetting he'd been addressed at all, cried, 'It is wonderful that you are here, my Lords.'

Vikram closed his eyes and swallowed a silent scream.

'It is wonderful to be here, King Vibhishana.' He'd made up his mind. 'But we must go now, I fear: Ayodhya longs for our return.'

'No – no, my Lords, please stay– celebrate with us! Ravana is defeated and all Creation sings praises of your mighty deeds.' Tears began to roll down the king's suddenly stricken face.

It took an hour to make him leave, and only after they had agreed to stay one more night before returning to Ayodhya.

When they woke next morning, the doors and windows of their rooms had vanished.

'Hey!' Amanjit hammered on the wall where the door had been. 'Vibhishana, you donkey – let us out—'

'It's no good,' Vikram told him. 'You've been shouting for an hour. No one's answering and all you've done is given us both headaches and yourself a sore throat.'

'Damn: I *knew* it was a trap.' Amanjit looked at him. 'If they don't feed us, we'll die. I've seen it on TV: no water and you're dead in *days* . . . you can live without food for a month, but no water, no life. Those cunning bastards . . .'

Vikram scratched his head. The toilet and bathroom were outside, which meant they had no running water and no food, nor anywhere to dispose of bodily waste. Then another thought struck him. 'Damn . . . we've got no fresh air either.' He realised with alarm how warm and stale the atmosphere was already becoming.

Amanjit moaned. 'You're right.' He pummelled the wall again, then forced himself to stop. 'You'll have to take us back to our world,' he said at last.

'I know – I guess we've got no other choices, have we? So this whole thing has been nothing but a wild goose chase.'

'A total waste of time,' Amanjit agreed, 'so best we get on with it then.'

Vikram pulled out his dagger and chanted the words, exerting energy, making the sparks of air fly as he had on the beach beside the Rama Setu—

—but nothing happened. The air repaired itself instantly, seamlessly, even though he tried again and again, until he collapsed, exhausted in the now-stifling heat. They fired arrows, but they just fizzled out, smashing harmlessly against the impervious stone walls.

They were truly trapped.

Hours passed as they raged and shouted and then pleaded to the featureless walls, but nothing reacted and nothing changed, even when Amanjit changed his tune and started shouting, 'We'll stay, we'll stay – we promise . . .'

Finally, shattered and truly afraid they would die in this place, they fell asleep.

When they woke, Vibhishana was standing in the room, surrounded by a small army of asuras in medical garb. They fussed over them reverently, feeding them wine and food that never touched their stomachs; they could taste it, but it had no substance.

Vibhishana beamed down at them, his face aglow with pride. 'My Lords, my Lords, it is such an honour to have you here. May you stay with us for a thousand years.'

# CHAPTER ELEVEN

# CHAINED QUEENS

*Lanka, May 2011*

Ras reclined into the palanquin, which moved with rock-solid assurance on the back of the four massive asuras who looked like bull-headed gorillas. Embroidered silk cushions made her comfortable, and she was even becoming used to the odd owl-like appearance of her guide, a rakshasa woman called Yunikisha, Lavanasura's wife. Apart from her bird-like face and the downy feathers that spread down her neck and spine, she was shapely and graceful.

The palanquin's silk curtains were drawn back, which allowed Rasita to see – and to be seen. Heat washed over her from the streets and packed squares. Keke had suggested she seek permission to go into Lower Town as it was market day; she'd ignored the suggestion before, but she was getting curious about this place – how did the asuras live? What were they like, close up?

She was gradually becoming accustomed to the rakshasas of the court, but the Lower Town asuras were more bestial.

Their dress varied widely, from rough hides to modern attire pillaged from the real world, but they behaved pretty much like normal townsfolk: they were smoking and eating and spitting, shouting and pushing and shoving as they bought and sold and haggled and quarrelled; Ras marvelled at the weird mix of goods, both modern and primitive on offer. Half-beast children were playing or squalling about in the confusion. Glowering warriors sharpened weapons, and knuckled their foreheads in obeisance as their palanquin passed, but others leered at her, making loud comments that made each other laugh. In so many ways they were ordinary people; it was just that they hooted like birds or beasts when amused or angry.

'They are like children, you see,' Yunikisha told her with kindly condescension. 'They cannot see past their own noses. They are incapable of planning and forethought: they are caught between human and animal, the poor dears. We look after them as best we can.' She smoothed her neck feathers fussily. 'Some are brighter than others, of course – intelligent, but incapable of sorcery. They're not worthy of being rakshasas, but we give them rank in Lower Town – they keep things running.'

Once she knew what to look for, Ras could see what Yunikisha meant: the asuras might be human-like, but they had a childlike aspect to them and clearly wore their hearts on their sleeves. Whims and emotions ruled everything; there was no maturity. They squabbled and fought and courted openly and brazenly. And they obeyed the rakshasas utterly.

The sights and smells of Lower Town washed over her:

the tang of freshly butchered meat, the reek of gutted fish, the scents of fresh flowers and vegetables vying with the urine running in the gutters and dung drying in the sun. The baking of fresh bread wafted through the air, a lovely aroma.

There were lots of humans in Lower Town too, slaves, all ragged and collared. They watched her with hope, that one of their own should be crowned and carried among them; but some stared resentfully too: a traitor to her kind, a demon-lover. For the first time she realised why a squad of heavily armed guards always flanked the palanquin.

*This place will be my life forever, if Ravindra has his way.*

*Vikram will destroy it, if he has his.*

Both thoughts made her uneasy, in different ways.

'Where did you all come from?' she asked Yunikisha, trying to make the question sound offhand, but wanting to see whether she could somehow verify Ravindra's tale.

Yunikisha appeared to be expecting the question. 'Well, my dear, I've always lived here – I haven't seen the world outside, as some have, but I know the tale, from my father's mother's mother – my great-grandmother. She used to tell my sisters and me of the old times, how one day the skies turned every imaginable colour, then this dreadful storm arose and it levelled everything. Everyone was trying to get to safety or find shelter when the most terrible agony assailed them, and when she woke, her whole body was changed into something like a bird. Everyone around her was similarly afflicted, and most of them died. But my great-grandmother lived, and when the Ravan came, she followed him to safety.' Her voice had taken on a reverential tone. 'The Ravan brought us here and made us safe. But then evil men came and slew the Ravan and tried to exterminate us.' Her voice became harsh and her eyes flashed as she growled, 'They *penned* us and *slaughtered* us – they called us animals, and they treated us lower than beasts. Only those who hid survived. Our grandmother hid us.' Her voice shook with emotion.

Ras remained silent until the rakshasa had regained her composure, still wondering if she could believe everything that Ravindra had written – and surely he must have primed Yunikisha to lie?

'Where did you all hide? How did you return here?' she asked eventually.

'We hid in the wild places where men do not go,' Yunikisha replied. 'For many years we wandered in the wilderness like nomads, shunning all human contact, until eventually we rakshasas learned of a secret place where we could be safe: our Lanka, but rebuilt in a hidden place. That's when we came here.'

Ras could see Yunikisha's downy cheeks were wet with tears. She stared out at the pandemonium of Lower Town, struggling to comprehend it all. A secret place – *this* place. Vikram had told her of his adventure in Mandore, when he'd found a temple from another time, and beneath the Mehrangarh Fort, the bad guys' guns had just stopped working. And Maricha had cut a hole in the air itself and taken her . . . *elsewhere* . . . to somewhere like here: a place that was made from belief.

Her mind reeled. *Is Ravindra's tale true? Is he truly the hero and this Dasraiyat the villain? And am I really Manda reborn? No . . . Not me, but we: Deepika and me and the other five queens. Are we truly the seven aspects of Manda?*

'Are you all right, my dear?' Yunikisha asked in a concerned voice. 'Sometimes the smell here can overcome one, especially at this time of year. I can take you home if you like?'

'Yes, please take me home,' Ras said weakly.

She entered Ravindra's guest room that evening for their regular assignation with real trepidation. The longer she dwelt on it, the more disturbing were the implications of his story.

*I can't just blindly accept everything he tells me*, she told herself firmly. *All my lives he has plagued me — and not just me; he's tortured and raped and murdered his way through history. So what if I was once Manda, the last Queen of Sinat, and he was my husband and king? It doesn't make him less of a beast now.*

But did it mean he could be restored to humanity?

The tale hadn't triggered any memories or even dreams of that long-ago time: the past beyond Mandore in 769 AD remained a closed book. So she really couldn't tell if he'd lied or told the truth or mixed the two, and that was what worried her most.

*If it's true, does it change anything?* she asked herself.

*Yes*, she decided, as she entered his chambers, *if he is telling the truth, then this Dasraiyat was the villain, not him. And Dasraiyat . . . must be Vikram.*

That was the thought that utterly chilled her. Because the Vikram she knew was a true heart — or so she'd thought until she'd seen the photographs of him kissing Sue Parker. Now she didn't know who the real Vikram was. She needed to confront him. And Dusshera was only months away.

*Hurry, Vikram, find me!*

Something of her confusion must have showed in her face, because when Ravindra greeted her that evening, he spoke as if she were an equal, rather than adopting his customary courtly gallantry. 'Good evening, Rasita. Thank you for coming.'

She accepted champagne from his winged manservant and took a sip; she was learning to enjoy the taste. The heat had been steaming this last week, making even the finest silks uncomfortably close. She'd been swimming morning and afternoon, but was still sweltering; even now, she was sweating in her light sari and gauzy dupatta, struggling to preserve her modesty. Although the nights were suffocating hot, she refused to sleep naked, not in this place. There was a disturbing eroticism throughout the whole palace, which had become even headier in this sultry heat.

Ravindra, in his usual Mediterranean attire, looked almost inhumanly attractive. 'What did you make of finally learning the truth about the *Ramayana*?' he asked.

'If truth it was,' she replied curtly. 'I've only your word for any of it.'

He frowned. 'You must learn to trust me. We once shared a bond: a love towering above all others. We can renew that bond, you and I. We belong together.' He gestured in exasperation, his face pained. 'I reach out to you, and still you resist.'

'A bond, you say — all I see are *bonds*: your people are in bondage to you. Your ghost-queens are in bondage to you. You want to put me in bonds too.'

'That's just semantics, Rasita,' Ravindra said impatiently. 'There is a difference between *bonds* and *bondage*. Bonds of love and respect free us — we had such a bond once, you and I. I had hoped that reading of it might remind you . . .'

'If your story is true, then you are nothing but a shadow of the man you were — a particularly murderous, bloodthirsty husk,' she pointed out. 'Just because you're making an effort to be nice and reasonable and talk to me instead of forcing yourself on me doesn't change what sort of monster you are — or have become — if your story is true.'

His face hardened. 'Once, I was a force for good, Rasita. Once, I was accounted the greatest man alive — and I can be that man again! *You* can heal me, Rasita; you can help me re-learn myself — and in doing so, you will fully heal yourself. Don't you understand that yet?'

'I don't need your healing,' she snapped back, although she wasn't sure why she was wilfully goading him; it gave her no pleasure. 'I am whole now.'

'You reveal how little you know.' He tapped the stem of the champagne flute. 'You may be physically whole, but psychologically, you are not: you are just one part of Manda — you could become all of her.'

'Could I?' she flared. 'So why me? Why not Halika, or Jyoti or Aruna? What exactly happens to them if I do as you want? And why should I even care? I have no memory of this Manda; I don't even know if she truly existed and I certainly feel no connection to her. So why should I wish to be her?'

Her words hung in the air while Ravindra's face contorted painfully.

For an instant she thought she might have broken through his self-control, but although he grimaced, he gave her a hint of a bow, as though in acknowledgement of some cutting witticism, and then waved her to her seat.

Dinner passed with little conversation; Ravindra was simmering, clearly unwilling to talk to her, which suited her fine.

But when they'd finished eating, he stood quickly, his face full of grim purpose. 'Come with me,' he said. 'There is something you must experience.'

'What is it?' she asked. She was suddenly scared that she'd provoked him too far; that he'd use force, even violence, to get his way, as she'd feared from the start.

'You'll see. Come—' His tone brooked no denial, so she nervously pulled her dupatta about her shoulders and with her sari clinging damply to her legs, she followed him out of the room.

He led her down a long spiral staircase and she felt like they were climbing into a well. As they went deeper, the circular rooms got progressively cooler. As he passed a curved sword in a scabbard, he unhooked it from the wall and belted it about his waist. She could guess its name: Chandrahas, the Moon-blade, Ravana's weapon in the *Ramayana*.

'Where are you taking me?' she asked, trying not to let her voice break. 'What are you going to do?'

'I won't harm you,' he told her, but she could see and hear that he was still bristling with suppressed anger. 'Quite the contrary. What you see will enhance you, and further prove my sincerity.'

She followed him timidly as he strode downwards.

At the bottom of the stairs, she found herself in a bowri; the white-washed water tank was dimly lit but she could make out three shapes huddled against the walls, held in chains that gleamed brightly in the flickering torchlight. She stared in shock as three heads lifted: Halika, Jyoti and Aruna, the remaining dead queens of Mandore. They looked like reanimated ghouls now, almost bloodless, with flesh missing, tendons and bones gleaming from beneath torn skin. Their rich gowns were ragged and torn. Ras thought they must have been chewing at their wrists, gnawing on their flesh to try and escape the silver manacles. The air stank of rotting meat.

When they saw her, they hissed in hatred. Jyoti, who'd always been skinny, was now thin as a famine corpse. She snarled at Rasita, but once-plump Aruna, also an emaciated shadow of her former self, just started whimpering piteously. Even Halika looked as if her spirit had finally been broken: her haughty pride had been replaced by sullen fury and despair.

Rasita felt a wave of pity she would never have expected. 'What have you done to them?' she whispered.

'They are being punished,' Ravindra replied, his tone expressionless. 'They're jealous of you and they have plotted against you. More than that, they have harmed and endangered my people. I have imprisoned them in here for everyone's protection.' He looked pained, nevertheless. 'But you must remember, these too are pieces of my Manda. I can scarcely bear to see their suffering.'

He sounded so genuine that she found herself un-expectedly moved. 'What do you mean to do?' she asked anxiously.

'Something I should have done earlier, but for pity at their state – and concern for you – stayed my hand.' He looked at her appraisingly. 'But I can delay this no longer:

it is an unpleasant necessity, but it will help you understand your destiny.'

She still didn't understand, but watched in confusion as he walked to Halika and stroked the ghost-queen's greasy, tangled hair. She looked up at him, her eyes glowing; Ras couldn't tell if it was adoration or terror; maybe it was both.

'My love,' Halika moaned, 'please free me—'

Aruna and Jyoti begin to wail and Ras found herself backing away, but quite unable to take her eyes from the scene.

Ravindra stroked Halika's hair, then turned and walked to Jyoti. 'Ah, Jyoti, my little vixen. I will miss you,' he said in a low voice as he drew his gleaming sword.

'My king,' shrieked Jyoti, 'mercy—'

Ras felt her mouth drop open in horror as Ravindra's blade slashed through the dead queen – who dissolved into the air like dust dissipating in a breeze. There was no blood, but a wafting curl of something like steam or smoke rose from her body, coiling in unseen and unfelt breezes before flowing like a serpent towards the nearest of the other queens: Halika.

The chief wife gave an excited cry and opened her mouth. Her body arched, convulsing in pleasure, as she swallowed Jyoti's soul, and as the last remnants of the ghost queen vanished, Halika's body became rounder, softer, and her wounds began to close.

'Back in Mumbai, when Vikram contrived the death of Meena and Rakhi, their essence drained into Deepika Choudhary,' Ravindra commented. 'Their souls sustained her against the cobra poison; that, with the effects of her heart-stone, kept her alive, but it also led to her manifesting the Protective Aspect, her part of the soul of Manda, although it showed itself in a warped way, because of her distress and incomplete understanding.'

Rasita listened numbly, feeling ill, struggling to swallow the bile in her throat.

Ravindra walked to Aruna, the scimitar gleaming in his hand.

The dead queen cowered before him as Halika purred, 'Yes, Lord, kill her too. Make me whole again, for you to enjoy.'

Aruna began to cry, pleading, 'Please, Lord – remember the good times, Lord – please, Lord, remember—'

But she begged in vain: Ravindra's blade sang again and Aruna's head rolled as her body started crumbling: just like Jyoti, she faded to dust motes caught in the flickering torches as her smoky soul went coiling into Halika's eager mouth.

The last of the ghost-queens sighed in pleasure as she drank in Aruna's essence. Her body was already reclothing itself in fresh flesh as she exclaimed, 'Oh my Lord, how I *long* for you – and now I am almost whole! It has been so long . . .' Halika started moaning in anticipatory delight as Ravindra turned and walked towards her, but Ras was suspicious of the cool smile on his face – then he pulled something from under his shirt: *Deepika's heart-stone.*

He turned and gestured towards Rasita and the necklace flew like a winged snake, undulating towards her. She tried to dodge out of the way, but she found her limbs paralysed: she couldn't move a muscle. The chain wrapped itself about her brow until it sat like a tiara, with the pale crystal veined with burgundy streaks pulsing queasily against her forehead in time to her heartbeat.

Halika stared at her, and then up at Ravindra. Her face,

once again ravishingly beautiful, took on a look of total disbelief. 'Please, Ravan – you promised it would be *me* – you promised me *forever*—'

For the final time, Chandrahas the moon-blade flashed.

This time there was no soft dissipation, no drifting steam. Instead, blood fountained up the walls and covered Ravindra in gore. As Halika's body thrashed around in its death throes, her severed head fell between her thighs and wedged there, staring out. Her lips were still moving; her open eyes were round and shocked. Her lustrous coils of hair writhed and then went still, making Ras think of a dying medusa. Then thick, dark, oily crimson smoke poured out from the stump of her neck, coiling and rearing like a snake, moving as if to the beat of a dying heart.

Rasita tried in vain to scream as Halika's soul flowed towards her. She could see Ravindra was staring at her, not like a lover, more like a scientist conducting a risky experiment – and then the essence of the dead queen was upon her and enveloping her, darkness pouring into her nose, her mouth, her ears, her eyes. She even felt it flow in through her skin and she tried to deny it, but it choked her mouth and nose until she swayed, then fell, while suns and planets exploded behind her eyes.

She was dead.

She was alive.

*Her name was Halika . . .*

# CHAPTER TWELVE

## HALIKA: TAINTED LOVE

*Sinat, 1500 BC*

Her name was Halika and she was born in the Sinat town of Gholasti on the day that Sinat was devastated. Her father died, burned to nothing by the dreadful fires that rained from the skies, but her mother, giving birth indoors, was a survivor. She took her new-born daughter and joined the harrowing exodus east after the conflagration and floods. There was nothing to eat but what they could scavenge, but there were so few of them that there was little conflict. Everyone was dazed, barely able to function; those few who had managed to remain calm through the madness herded the survivors like sheep as they went seeking safety.

None of them would have survived had it not been for Dasraiyat, the king's greatest friend, who came to the aid of the refugees. He led them to springs, and some said he caused trees to grow and bring forth fruit, and roots to burgeon in the dusty soil. He even brought rain for drinking water, they said, attributing many other miracles to his name as they followed him east. They were offered sanctuary in a number of towns, but the Sinathai people had always thought of others as 'lesser men'. Gradually, as their pride was eroded, they were amalgamated into the wider population in these new lands.

The taller, fairer-skinned Sinathai survivors were of necessity forced to marry Easterners; they learned new tongues and forgot their own, until eventually they forgot that the tales of the cataclysm told of their own history in their own land.

Halika knew none of this; in her earliest memories, the exodus was already three years in the past. But she knew inside that she was different from the other children. She was pure Sinathai: taller, fairer-skinned – *better*, in her view.

And she had a secret, a *special* secret: she could make wishes come true.

She first used her wishes against another one hot day when a horrid girl pulled her hair. She glowered at the girl, wishing her ill – and that very day the girl's hair started falling out in great clumps, until she drowned herself in shame. Halika exulted. She tried her secret power on a boy who had started bullying her, and this time when she wished him dead, a snake bit him. Now she was certain, and so were the other children, who were too scared to call her a witch to her face, but avoided her as much as they could.

By the time she was ten, she knew she needed a protector, before the villagers could band against her. She found a priest, and in exchange for giving him insights about his people, even revealing the unfaithful, he taught her what learning he had, including how to read and write. She wouldn't let him do the things he wanted with her, but she found him girls who would.

Their partnership served her well for a few years, but by the time she was thirteen, she'd outgrown him. He'd been kind to her, in his own way, so she drugged him first before shutting him in his hut and burning it down with a wish.

She fled to a hermitage for women that taught ancient wisdom, presenting herself meekly to the vedavati and promising the matron a life of chastity and devotion in return for knowledge. She hated the place and despised the other girls, but she wanted to learn everything she could, afraid of what would happen to her in the greater world should they discover her secret. She buried her pride deep, far from the vedavati's sight, and learned and grew.

By the time Halika turned twenty, she was counted among the most promising of the students – and they all feared her, too, which gave her much pleasure. But she had yet to decide what her future would be . . . until a clatter of hooves announced a visitor. The man who rode into the courtyard was clearly Sinathai by birth, for he was lean and tall and golden-skinned. His fierce face looked haunted, his mouth was both sensuous and dangerous. Halika couldn't take her eyes from his well-muscled arms and thighs; when he looked down and met her eyes, in that second, she imagined everything they would do with each other, and she *wanted* him with every fibre of her being.

The man was calling upon the vedavati for advice; he gave no name, but he was clearly a lord. She made eyes at him over dinner, but he didn't notice, so she retired early to sulk in her tiny chamber.

At midnight, her door opened and the stranger slipped inside.

She didn't need to talk, not at first – not when there was so much else her mouth and tongue could be doing. But afterwards, lying naked in his arms, her mind overflowed with questions.

He was happy to answer them.

He told her he was the dreaded Aeshwaran, the man her people called 'Ravana', the cause of all weeping, but Halika didn't care, for here, finally was the man to master her. And he knew all about her – her name, her birth date, even her strange powers; he had, he said, been seeking her for the last twenty years.

Would she return with him to his homeland and become his queen?

She answered with her body.

They left before dawn, surrounded by a crowd of beast-men riders who'd been waiting in the woods for their king. When she saw them, she realised that miracles *were* possible: she'd found her destiny.

Before they left, the beast-men rounded up all the students and teachers and forced them into the courtyard, where they slaughtered them before setting fire to the place.

Halika herself set the flames blazing: with a wish.

## CHAPTER THIRTEEN

# HALIKA: SISTERS IN SPIRIT

*Ayodhya, 1500 BC*

Two years later, Halika slipped into King Dasraiyat's city of Ayodhya. She had adopted a false identity, taking the name Mandara for her mission, which was to spy upon the kingdom. It was easy enough to gain a position at court, in the household of the second queen, Kaikeyi, and very soon she was controlling every word the queen spoke. Halika was careful to keep a low profile; Aeshwaran had taught her discipline and shown her how to mask her presence from other sorcerers, which he said was vital. His parting words echoed in her mind: 'Dasraiyat is a sorcerer, just as you and I are. I suspect at least one of his sons is too, maybe more. Beware; keep your eyes open. Seek others like yourself, who were born on the day of the Conflagration — I have begun to suspect there may be at least two others, perhaps as many as seven. I want them.'

'But I'll always be your first wife, won't I?' she'd replied, feeling a trifle anxious. Although they undoubtedly shared a powerful, furious passion, there was some need in him she couldn't fill. And they had no children. which made her worry that she might be infertile.

'Of course, Halika,' he promised. 'You will always be first.'

But he said such things lightly; he would take other women to his bed while she was away, she knew that. When she found out who, they would regret it . . .

It didn't take long to find the girl she sought; as soon she heard the girl was considered fey and moon-touched she recognised her. Sita was royalty, married to Ram, the eldest of the princes, and Halika had been drawn to the girl from the start. When she'd slipped into the royal astronomer's rooms to find the girl's birth charts, she had discovered Sita had been born the same day as she had: the day of the Great Conflagration. Sita was definitely the one she had been sent to find.

One morning Halika discovered Sita in the palace gardens, fussing over a rabbit which had been mauled by cats. Sita was stroking the cowering creature and without really understanding what she did, she healed the rabbit with a touch. The girl gazed about guiltily, then started to scurry away – but Halika intercepted her.

'Oh, Mandara—' Sita exclaimed as Halika appeared in front of her.

'Good morning, Princess.' Halika curtseyed. 'I wonder if you can help me? I have a pet rabbit and he has escaped, naughty thing! Have you seen it?'

Sita's lovely eyes flashed anxiously. 'I might have.'

Halika beamed. 'Oh, that's *splendid* – where?'

'Er . . . here, in the garden . . .'

'Will you help me find it?'

Sita looked like she very much wished to refuse, but she was too guileless to conjure an excuse. Together they scoured the garden, and found the rabbit cowering beneath the bush where it had been left. Halika picked the thing up, suppressing its desire to flee with a subtle wish, and cried, 'It gashed itself on a nail when it escaped, but look – there's no sign of a wound . . . But it's definitely the same rabbit . . .'

Sita looked even more worried.

'Perhaps the presence of your Majesty has caused the wound to vanish?' Halika suggested slyly, watching the princess squirm. *What a vapid creature she is.* 'Perhaps your touch has healing powers?'

Sita turned bright red.

'Do you know what?' Halika said quietly. 'We were born on the very same day.'

'How very odd,' Sita said, her voice hollow.

'It's like being sisters,' Halika said.

'I think not,' Sita replied haughtily. 'I must go.' She fled the garden.

Halika held the frightened rabbit in her hand and as soon as they were alone, she twisted its neck. She enjoyed the way its heart thumped harder, as if desperate to prolong life, before fading into stillness.

Halika ghosted through the night-time palace like a shadow. The signal had come. It was time to strike.

The princes Ram and Lakshmana were away hunting; Sita had gone with them. Before the night was over, the two princes would be dead and Sita would be Aeshwaran's prize. Halika smiled to herself as she slipped through a richly carved doorway and into the chamber of the king.

King Dasraiyat, saviour of the Sinathai, was so beloved that he did not even have a guard standing outside his room. She hadn't seen him up close before, staying well away lest he sniff her out. He looked a little like her lord, as Aeshwaran had warned her, but where her beloved had powerful, masterful features, this man was older, *softer*. His face was lined with cares. They said he was kindly and gentle, that his politeness and courtesy were famed, that he wept at bad news.

*Pathetic*, she snarled to herself, baring the poisoned needle and lowering it to his neck. A single stab, and he'd be dead in seconds. Every sense alive with excitement, her legs trembling, she drove the needle in.

He woke, his mouth flying open. 'Manda?' he gasped as she jammed a cloth over his mouth to drown his cries, and pinned him down. His big eyes, so like Aeshwaran's, goggled up at her in total disbelief.

'My name is Halika and I am the wife of Aeshwaran,' she whispered. He tried to push her away, but the poison was already weakening him and he couldn't shift her. She felt all-powerful as she bent closer and hissed into his face, 'Tonight, my lord husband hunts in your hunting lodge. He hunts princes and princesses.'

She saw his fear and horror as he tried to rally: wishes tore at her, mental commands exhorting her to relent and let him rise; wishes that the poison be ineffective. But she countered them with wishes of her own, doubling and trebling the efficacy of the venom as she held him down with grim determination. Wind lashed her, unseen blows buffeted her, but she didn't have to hold on for long . . . just a few seconds more . . . They both rose into the air, his back arching, her own strength of body and will tested to the limit.

Then his eyes rolled backwards and he slumped onto the bed. She fell on top of him, gasping, then grabbed the cloth and forced it down over his mouth and nose again, to make doubly sure.

But he never moved again.

King Dasraiyat was dead.

Halika met her lover and his beast-men on the road to the west. Mounted on a gelding roped to his horse was Sita, who looked disbelieving, as if she were lost in a nightmare come true.

'The king is dead, my love,' Halika purred.

His eyes flared, his nostrils widened and he pulled her up onto his horse and kissed her fervently. 'Dasraiyat is dead?' He tossed his mane and roared in triumph, 'My darling Halika – my love, you are *magnificent*!'

'What of the princes?' she asked.

Aeshwaran looked suddenly angry. 'They fought off our attack – we struck as they hunted, but they had too many guards around them and we had to withdraw.' He looked furious with himself. 'Ram is a sorcerer, like us – he used Aspect arrows. He is dangerous.' He turned back and his eyes drank in the beautiful woman on the gelding. 'But we have his woman. They left her at the lodge with only a few guards.'

Sita stared at Halika, and Halika bared her teeth. 'Then this trip has been doubly blessed, my love.'

Aeshwaran raised a hand, signalling his column. 'Mount up behind me, Halika. We ride for Lanka.'

As they began to gallop, she whispered in his ear, 'Who is Manda? Dasraiyat called her name as he died — I think he thought I was her?'

He never answered that question, not then, and not ever.

# CHAPTER FOURTEEN

# HALIKA: THE SIEGE OF LANKA

*Lanka, 1500 BC*

Halika clung to her Lord's arm as she stared out over the walls of the fortress at the massive camp of the enemy. 'Have they all come, Aeshwaran? The whole East?'

For the first time in her life, she felt truly frightened.

The camp of the enemy went on for ever. It didn't matter that they were all former slaves: low-caste rabble with no breeding; they were fighting men now. Dasraiyat's sons Ram and Lakshmana had shown the people the body of their beloved king and every man and woman who had been on that awful march out of dying Sinat had rallied to their banner.

Aeshwaran had been contemptuous of the army of former slaves at first, dismissing them as less than monkeys. But he wasn't dismissing them now. Ram's army, led by a man called Hannu, had taken Aeshwaran's mocking name for themselves, calling themselves 'Hannu's Monkeys' with the kind of perverse pride that fighting men develop in war.

They threw themselves at Aeshwaran's asuras with controlled ferocity and they died by the hundreds — but there were *so many* of them.

At first Halika thought her lover would simply blast them all to nothing, but they quickly discovered that Ram and Lakshmana had magic of their own to counter his spells, and for the most part, the sorcerers on either side cancelled each other out. Now it was becoming a battle of attrition, and while the asuras were fierce, each as strong as three men, Hannu's Monkeys outnumbered them by more than ten to one.

*We're all going to die*, she thought bitterly. *Ram and his Monkeys are going to wipe us out.*

His treatment of Sita infuriated her: she'd thought Aeshwaran would bed the girl, unwilling or not; she'd been looking forward to seeing her broken. But he didn't. She was kept prisoner, a captive, but honoured and respected, and Aeshwaran visited her daily, while neglecting his other wives.

*Neglecting me* . . .

She was afraid to ask why.

Halika clung to Ravan Aeshwaran's leg, but he kicked her away, whispering, 'Do not show fear before my men.' His voice was hollow, haunted.

Then he turned and vented a theatrical roar, trying to hide the dread she knew he felt inside. Mounted on his warhorse with his curved sword at his side and his bow over his shoulder, a battle-axe slung across his back beneath his quiver, he looked indestructible — but she knew him better than anyone in all the world. She could see the despair in his eyes.

She wanted to weep, but she'd never learned how.

They had not thought the enemy princes would accept the parley, let alone the challenge; a duel to the death between Aeshwaran and Ram. It had been a desperate gambit: they were besieged within the city walls and everyone was starving. They had lost the war of attrition; this duel was their last hope.

If he killed Ram or Lakshmana, he would triumph and the balance would be restored.

She hoped it would be the younger one, Lakshmana, who accepted the challenge, but it was Ram who had taken the thrown gauntlet. She was desperately afraid of him. He had Dasraiyat's eyes.

The asura warriors bellowed encouragement, their eyes holding nothing but confidence as their king rode out through the gates amid the blare of the trumpets and thunder of the drums. 'Ravan – *Ravan*!' they chanted, believing him invincible.

She watched from among the asura captains, leaders amongst the beast-men. Thanks to the notes stolen from Dasraiyat. Meghanada, Prahasta, Meenakshi, Maricha and some two dozen others had been granted some minor sorcerous powers and elevated to her Lord's inner circle. Aeshwaran had named them *rakshasa*, a Sinathai word meaning *blessed*. They were gathered about her now, charged with her protection in the inconceivable event that the king should fall.

Ram walked out to meet Aeshwaran at the designated spot, too far from either side for the rakshasas or Lakshmana to influence the battle. She felt her knees go weak as the Ravan tethered his warhorse, dismounted and approached the young man. Ram was slender, but muscular. His prowess was legendary among the Sinathai; everyone feared him and his accursed arrows. The two paused when they were some fifty yards apart and spoke, but no one could catch the words. Both armies fell silent, wondering what was being said: challenges, taunts? All they knew was that for one of them, these were their last words.

Then Aeshwaran roared, snatched up his bow and fired, his arrow igniting in a nimbus of scarlet fire.

Ram shot it out of the air and blurred sideways, shooting back, but his arrow flared and exploded before it even reached the king. Aeshwaran waded forward, loosing another arrow as he closed in. He was easily twice the size of the young prince; if he reached him, he would rip him apart, surely—

As the arrows flew, the watchers gasped: normal men could not shoot arrows from the sky; human beings did not cause winds and fires and lightning bolts to flash across the battlefield — such wonders were surely the province of gods. But these two men could and did as they moved in barely seen blurs, making the very air crackle as they shouted their spells.

Then Aeshwaran tore the axe from his back and covered the last few yards in a sight-defying charge.

His first swing shattered Ram's bow, then the axe arced in a graceful sweep towards the young prince's neck. But Ram ducked low, even as his own sword flashed out; metal clashed as the axe met the blade and then Aeshwaran lurched sideways to avoid a counter-lunge. The whole of the asura army gasped, but their king righted himself, flinging the axe at Ram's face as he drew his sword, closing the gap again in a flash.

Ram tipped the axe aside, though its edge ripped the skin of his neck. He parried an overhand blow and a whipped slash at his side, then flashed out a lunge, scouring Aeshwaran's armour along the chest plate. Halika heard herself shriek – but long-eyed Meenakshi clutched her hand, screaming defiance.

Aeshwaran launched a flurry of blows, driving Ram backwards. His right hand pummelled the younger man's guard whilst his left hand gestured in bewitching movements, causing fires to spark, water to gush, dust to rise blindingly about his foe. But somehow, amidst all the chaos of the battle, Ram kept moving, kept his sight free and his guard up.

Then Ram's sword broke.

Halika crowed, her strength redoubling, 'Oh yes, my Lord, yes – kill him kill him KILL HIM!'

The moment seemed to slow into fragments: the sweep of Aeshwaran's sword, following through after snapping Ram's blade, which threw the king momentarily off-balance . . . the graceful spin and turn of the prince . . . the deadly whirl of her beloved as he bellowed in triumph and slashed again at the young man's wrist . . . Ram's dancing grace as he lifted the broken hilt, catching Aeshwaran's blade and locking it.

For one awful instant, his blade jammed in the hilt of the broken sword . . .

. . . and Ram's other hand pulled his last arrow from his quiver.

The arrow spun from his hand and flew—
—into her Lord's eye—
—and exploded.

Then she only knew that she was being held between Meenakshi and Maricha as she screamed and screamed at the swirling darkness.

Her last sight of her beloved, etched on her retina, was of a headless body standing like a statue, before it crashed to the ground.

## CHAPTER FIFTEEN

## I KNOW I AM A MONSTER

*Lanka, May 2011*

Rasita shook her head, still dazed. She was sprawled on the steps of the bowri with Ravindra sitting beside her, Dee's heart-stone in his hands. He was covered in Halika's gore. She could dimly make out the dusty piles of rags that had been Jyoti and Aruna, and the headless corpse of Halika.

*Halika . . .*

'She was your *wife*,' she whispered. Her voice echoed in the wispy darkness about the pool. 'Halika was your first queen – I saw it all, through her eyes.' The rest of it hit her. 'My God – the *Ramayana* – that *was* the *Ramayana* . . . Halika was the maid of the queen, the one who provoked it all – she was a spy for you – and you really are Ravana – and there really was a Rama . . . and a Sita . . . and all the rest . . . It's *all* true . . .'

She could hear the disbelieving awe in her voice. It was one thing to think that your life was somehow mirroring a legend; it was quite another to find that it had all been real. And was still changing lives.

'How can you stand to live?' she whispered.

*He's been alive three thousand years. He wiped out his own people. Everything he touches ends in death.*

'I go on,' he said simply, in as grim a voice as she'd ever heard. A voice haunted by eternity. 'I go on, until I have achieved what I must.'

'Why?'

'I have no choice. I know I am a monster – but I also know what I once was. And what we were.' He grasped her hands, bloody with Halika's death. 'Rasita, you were Sita – and you were Halika. You were all of them, in one: you were Manda. When we three, Dasraiyat, Manda and I, inadvertently caused the Great Conflagration, Manda's soul was torn into seven aspects, each reborn that same day as she tried to find me, but the births were scattered across the land. I only ever found two in that life: Halika, the Aspect of Destruction, and Sita, the Aspect of Creation. The other five – the four elements and the Protector Aspect, I could not find, not in that lifetime. I didn't know what to do, or how to restore them – I was ignorant, I was insane with grief and damaged by being trapped in the Destructive Aspect myself. And when I died, I was reborn with no memory or self-knowledge, only those awful dream-memories of what I had done.

'Everything I have tried to do since, in all my dream-racked lives before Mandore, as Ravindra and every other man I have possessed, I have done to restore Manda and to restore myself, this I swear to you. For centuries I have been a tortured soul, lashing out at everyone, ignorant of the truth. Without me, the rakshasas hid until they became legends and gradually faded into the myth-lands and I didn't see them again until one found me in my life as Ravindra of Mandore – only then did I regain any of my own memories, through the aid of that one rakshasa. I thought him my saviour then – but I've now learned he didn't tell his fellows, as he wanted all the credit for restoring me.'

'You gathered us together in Mandore to kill us,' Rasita said. 'To kill us, and to heal yourself.'

'*No!*' He sounded tortured, 'No, Rasita, to heal us *all*: that was the first time I had been able to find all seven aspects of Manda reborn, even though their birthdates were no longer aligned and none but Halika had any recollection of who they really were. With my rakshasa advisor, I devised a way to restore Manda – and yes, it did mean killing all seven of you and burning you, to release your souls into the aether. To create one single whole Queen Manda I needed a binding crystal for each, and I had to carry out certain acts appropriate to each aspect: a holy candle for Fire, a special drink for Water, and so on. The aspect of Creation would require the consensual surrender of the vessel of creation – the womb – so my consensual union in the Ether with the virginal you, Padma, as you were in Mandore was to be the final act that restored Manda to wholeness.

'But the reborn sons of Dasraiyat were present and I didn't recognise them in Aram Dhoop and Madan Shastri. They themselves were ignorant of who they were, but they instinctively acted against me. Together, they destroyed the Mandore ritual, leaving my queens and me as mere ghosts.

It took me decades to regain the power to inhabit other bodies. Only in the life of Mehtan Ali, the enemy of Chand Bardai, did I begin to remember myself, and by then my queens were scattered, their heart-stones long lost.'

'You killed us whenever you found us.'

His face looked like a wound. 'I didn't *know*,' he pleaded. 'I couldn't reason – I was compelled to lash out, *for I am Destruction*. I know this.' His eyes met hers, begging her to understand. 'Heal me, Rasita. Heal me, and in doing so, heal yourself.'

She shrank from him – because the compassionate part of her wanted to heal him, as he wanted. But there was more: Halika was now part of her soul and not only did she crave sensuality, she wanted this man beyond all reason.

'I don't know how,' she whispered.

'You do know, Rasita, in your heart. You are her: you are my Manda, whom I loved and for whom I have longed these past three thousand years. You are her Creator Aspect, the most beautiful part of her, and now you also have three other parts of the seven aspects within you. Deepika Choudhary's ghost embodies the other three. Together, you and Deepika *are* Manda. Please, I beg you, let me help you become her again. Heal me. We both need this, so very much.'

She pulled herself from his grasp, though she found herself wanting to hold him, to heal him, to turn him from monster to man: to redeem a soul lost for so many centuries.

She ran, before she could surrender to that impulse.

# CHAPTER SIXTEEN

# AN ARCHERY DISPLAY

*Sri Lanka, May 2011*

The silence was all-encompassing. Their room had doors and windows again, but the door handles were gone and although the windows were open, when Vikram tried a musafir-astra, the travelling arrow failed. The only sound they could hear was an unsettling, distressing moaning sound, as if something large and old was slowly expiring nearby, unseen and alone.

Vikram stared at the featureless white walls. 'What's that noise?' he asked for the twentieth time, and yet again, Amanjit lifted his head and sighed.

'The dying elephant sound?' he asked. 'Dunno. Maybe it's a dying elephant?'

He'd been wondering if he'd ever see Deepika again.

Vikram went back to staring out of the window in frustration, until he finally said, 'You know what, I really think we are stuck in some kind of loop. It's a logic trap.'

'I don't do logic, bhai,' Amanjit grumbled. 'I just want

to punch someone, starting with that pompous ass Vib-hishana.'

'I don't think it's his fault,' Vikram replied. 'I don't think he has any choice about what he is and what he's compelled to do. He may not be the real Vibhishana at all, just a myth-world echo.'

'That doesn't stop me wanting to hit him.'

'Me neither,' Vikram replied. 'Hey, at least they're feeding us again, even if it's not helping. I'm so hungry . . .'

Amanjit finished the turban, primped in the mirror, then flexed his fist. 'We need to get out now, before not eating real food makes us too weak to even try.'

'I know that,' Vikram replied tersely, 'and that means our next move has to work. We can't use our energy on false starts and mistakes. We've got to get this right.'

Amanjit took up a pose, brandishing an imaginary sword. 'Then *think*, Vik.' He made a few half-hearted fencing moves, then stopped and snarled in frustration. '*Think*—'

Vikram's face twisted ruefully. 'Well, either we trick our way out, sneak out or go out all guns blazing – and frankly, I'm not sure any of those will work.'

'Will *any* astras work?'

'I don't know – maybe outside, but not in here.'

'I thought that Rama could blast the world apart with an arrow – what's it called, the big shit-kicker one? The one that killed Ravana in the story?'

'You're talking about the Brahmastra. Or one of the other Trimurti arrows. Supposedly you can destroy a god with one, or wipe out an army. But you can only use each of them once in your life, according to the stories. And before you ask, no, I've never used one – I've never worked out how to make them work. I can't get a grasp on them. It's about the difference between giving and taking. All the arrows I use are limited by my own strength and endurance. They're like battlefield weapons. But the big arrows, the Trimurti ones, are more like nuclear weapons: to detonate one of those, you've got to use everything about you, and I've barely begun to learn that.'

'Would one get us out of here?'

'Maybe.' He sighed. 'But honestly? I don't know for sure.'

'Can you think of anything else?'

Vikram stood up. 'No.'

'Then get on with it, bhai.'

Vikram looked at Amanjit in frustration. 'Do you think this is easy for me? You've got the ability to do this stuff too, you know – you can use astras as well as me, so how about you do something, instead of simply heaping it all on me? If you want to help, maybe you can blast out a Brahmastra yourself?'

Amanjit grunted in mild surprise. 'Hey, chill out – I'm just making suggestions here. I don't know how to do half the stuff you can.'

'Then *learn*—' Vikram jabbed his finger accusingly. 'You just want to swan about looking cool and let the nerd do the thinking.'

*How dare you?* Amanjit stood up, properly angry now. 'Yeah? You think I don't want to get out of here as much as you? My *wife* is out there, trying to help *our* family and save *your* girl while *we're* stuck in a stupid room in La-la-land! I've got muscle you haven't and I use it – but you've got intellectual muscle and *I haven't*. Believe me, if I think of something, you'll be the first to know – but if this is a problem-solving issue, not a muscle issue, I'm *not* the go-to guy—'

'Claiming not to be clever isn't good enough,' Vikram shot back, seething. '*Anyone* can have a great idea, just like any fool with a bow can hit the target sometimes – abrogating responsibility is lazy and cowardly—'

Amanjit found his fists were clenched and he was *this close* to punching Vikram in the face . . .

Then he surprised even himself by unclenching his hands and raising them, palms outwards. 'You're right, Vik. You're right, and I'm sorry. I'm not helping and I should be – I'm just so used to you having all the answers, you know?'

They eyed each other a little warily, but the flashpoint had passed.

Amanjit reflected that some kind of confrontation had been inevitable, given the frustration of their plight: the more they pushed against their prison walls, the stronger those walls became – and they were running out of time; they had eaten their last real piece of food a day ago and they were both suffering from a gnawing hunger. He exhaled slowly and sat down again. 'Sorry, bhai. I'm just scared.'

Vikram sat facing him. 'I'm sorry too,' he admitted. 'I just can't see how to get out of this and it's driving me crazy. I don't know what to do.'

Amanjit closed his eyes, trying to focus. 'Every time you use an ordinary astra, you draw on your own energy, and that's finite, so you need to draw from elsewhere, right? So it really does come back to nailing a Trimurti arrow, yeah?'

Vikram hung his head in his hands. 'I'm not so sure — I mean, we're surrounded by spells, so maybe a Mohini is the answer, to blast the spells away. But there's something about this place: it's like there's no energy to feed on; no creation, no destruction — everything just exists in perpetuity. So there's nothing for a Trimurti astra to feed on, because it's like Creation and Destruction don't exist here.' He rubbed his aching belly.

Amanjit was struggling to understand. *If Vik is lost, then I'm doubly so . . .* 'Maybe I should just smash everything in this room and then you can use that for energy?' he suggested, only half joking.

Vikram didn't answer, lost in thought.

Hours passed and they got hungrier and more frustrated. A platter of sweets appeared on the table; they tasted divine, but like everything else they'd been served, they vanished somewhere between mouth and stomach. The water quenched their thirst, but that didn't last long.

Amanjit tried to think about Deepika, but that made him doubly miserable.

'You know, maybe there's something in that idea,' Vikram said finally.

'In what idea?'

'In smashing everything.'

'I said that?'

'Yeah, a few hours ago.'

'I'd forgotten. Sure, what should I smash first?' He looked at the pottery ornaments, his fingers twitching. It would be nice to take out his frustration on something small and breakable.

'No, no – listen,' Vikram was suddenly energised, 'I've been thinking about what you said. Whenever I've tried to draw on energy outside my own here, I run up against a big load of *nothing* – there's nothing here – no Creation, no Destruction; just a perpetual bundle of spells keeping this place intact. Master Vishwamitra thinks the myth-lands are sustained by cultural memory interacting with magical forces which creates a place where legendary people and places continue to exist. If we can somehow release that magical energy, we have something to work with.'

'I'm hearing words, but I'm not sure I understand them,' Amanjit said tiredly.

'No, it's actually quite simple,' Vikram exclaimed. 'All we have to do is get access to the magical energy that sustains this place and use it for one big destructive Trimurti astra to knock a hole in the walls, and get the hell out of here.'

Amanjit sat up. 'Now you're talking—' He stopped. 'Um . . . *how?*'

'It's got to be simultaneous – the release and drawing of the energy – otherwise this place just recaptures the energy and reweaves the spells. We've seen that in the way the walls reform instantly.'

'Simultaneous? But how will you fire two spells at once?'

'*I* won't – *we* will. You'll fire the multiple-Mohini and I'll fire the Trimurti arrow – I guess it'll have to be a Pashupatastra: as we're using destructive energy, a Shiva arrow sounds right, don't you think . . . ?' His voice trailed off. After a moment he said, 'But this place will be trying to convert it to Creative, won't it, to renew the broken spell . . . So I'm not sure . . .'

Amanjit stood up. 'So the plan is, I'll fire a mohini—'

'A multiple-mohini would be better,' Vikram put in. 'Lots at once.'

'But I've never fired even one,' Amanjit pointed out, 'and you've never used a Trimurti arrow before now.' He threw his arms wide. 'What are the odds we'll succeed?'

Vikram grinned suddenly. 'About a million to one, I reckon – which, if you think about it, happens all the time in the movies. So it's virtually a certainty we'll succeed.'

'*In the movies*,' Amanjit repeated. 'So it's happened: you've gone nuts, haven't you?'

Vikram grinned, exhilarated at finally having a plan. 'Totally insane – it's being locked up day and night with you that does it.'

A day later, they got their chance.

After a long and convoluted negotiation, King Vibhishana had agreed to allow them to perform an archery demonstration – but once he'd been convinced, the king was totally taken with the idea and pavilions appeared in the amphitheatre outside the citadel overnight.

Hunger was gnawing at their bones, but the food they were served did give the brief illusion of being satisfying as well as tasty; they were relying on that illusory sugar-rush to get them through.

'My Lords, what a wonderful idea, to demonstrate your prowess to the whole court,' Vibhishana exclaimed in his usual adulatory voice, and the court echoed his sentiments vociferously, like a Greek chorus in an ancient play.

'It's our pleasure,' Vikram said, with a bow. 'You and your

people have been so generous to us. It is only fitting that we give something back.'

'For the guests to entertain the host doesn't seem proper to me,' the warthog-faced herald muttered to Vibhishana, who started to look worried.

'Hogface gets the first arrow,' Amanjit muttered in Vikram's ear.

'No deaths, at least not among the asura,' Vikram whispered back. 'The fewer distractions the better. You've got to concentrate on nailing the mohini-and-aindra-astra combination.'

'Yeah, but the additional motivation is sure to help.'

The morning was sunny and pleasant, as always in this strange place, and every denizen of Lanka had come. Semi-circular seating housed thousands of half-beast demons clad in every colour of the rainbow. The royal family – Vibhishana and his four wives (four, because Ravana used to have three, the king explained proudly) and their many children sat apart in a special pavilion with the best view.

Vikram had spent half the night going over the intricacies of the mohini and the aindra-astras with Amanjit, then a further hour reminding himself of the theory behind the Shiva-astra, although he'd never used it before. Worry that they were not likely to get a second chance gnawed at him.

The weird wheezing sound permeated the walls and continued all night, sounding more and more like an asthmatic giant. Once Vikram called out to it, but there was no response. He slept late, but hunger woke him: it felt like a small python was inside him, writhing about and squeezing at his guts.

Amanjit said he felt the same.

*If we screw this up, will we have the strength to try anything else?*

Vikram stared out at their first test: simple archery targets for them to get a feel for the bows, although they'd been placed nearly two hundred yards away. He had negotiated the real targets with Vibhishana: flying creatures, the more magical-looking the better. There had to be *spectacle*, after all; they needed it to distract the onlookers, although the king didn't need to know that. He could see the cages filled with butterfly-winged lizards and human-headed gulls and tiny dragons and myriad other creatures: impossible beings, and therefore sustained with more potent spells – so more energy to release.

The usual fanfare and dull speeches prefigured the display, but today, unless Vikram was imagining it, these creatures, trapped in total boredom for millennia, had a greater *frisson* about them. Were they genuinely interested in something for the first time in their memories? However real or unreal they actually were, surely some remnant of independence and intellect remained?

The warthog-faced herald, still surly about this display, waved a flag, and everyone fell silent and leaned forward.

'Let's do it,' Vikram said to Amanjit.

They lifted their bows, raised them high and fired, and two arrows flew, trailing sparks, and slammed into the centre of the targets that were barely visible in the distance. These were just simple charm-assisted astras, to get themselves back into practise, but the asuras went '*Ooooo!*' and cheered riotously.

Vikram looked at Amanjit and nodded. He'd been firing

such arrows for centuries, but Amanjit hadn't – and yet the Sikh had nailed it first up. 'Good one, bhai. Naga-astra next. Think snaky thoughts.'

Amanjit grinned, his brow creased with concentration.

Two birds were released, swift swallows that shot into the sky. The bows twanged and two snakes sped through the air, catching the swooping birds in their open mouths and plunging their fangs into feathers and flesh. They tumbled to the ground, then dragged the birds away a few paces before reverting to wood. Vikram muttered an apology to the souls of the birds, though he doubted even they were real.

The asuras cheered, not apparently noticing that both were perspiring. Every astra took something from them and they were both already dangerously weak.

Vikram nodded to Amanjit. *This time . . .*

He signalled to a demon holding the door to a cage containing a pair of small dragons.

The cage door rose and the dragons arrowed upwards, flashing towards them as the crowd cheered and gasped. Vikram sighted, Amanjit in perfect sync beside him, and once again their bows sang.

Amanjit's arrow took light in a grey swirl, but it flew wide and buried itself in the ground. Vikram's failed to ignite at all – he couldn't even tell if he'd got the incantation right; there'd been no energy released for it to feed on. Amanjit cursed apologetically.

The crowd groaned, then shrugged and cheered encouragement, but the warthog-faced herald looked distinctly unhappy. He leaned forward and stared at them. Vikram met his eye, and looked away. *Does he suspect something? Is he like the others . . . or something more? What if he's real — what if he's Ravindra's spy here?*

Vikram turned quickly to the king. 'Apologies, Majesty. We weren't concentrating properly.'

Vibhishana waggled his head sympathetically. 'This time, Great Ones.'

'If I get called "Great One" one more time I'll strangle myself,' Amanjit fumed.

Vikram tightened his bowstring slightly, to release nervous energy and buy time. 'The herald suspects something. We need to nail it, okay? You got it this time?'

Amanjit nodded tensely. 'Yeah. I'll do it. You?'

Vikram raised an eyebrow. 'Of course.'

'I thought I was supposed to be the cocky one,' Amanjit observed.

Vikram winked, and signalled the next release.

Two more dragons flew; two more shots followed — and the crowd groaned as Amanjit swore. The two astras fizzled into the turf . . . and the herald began to hurry towards the king.

*He's on to us . . .* Vikram stepped forward and shouted to the servants holding the cages, 'Release them all!'

The cage-handlers stared and then glanced at King Vibhishana, who raised his hand.

'Sire,' the herald called anxiously, but the king had already gestured his assent to the servants.

'Sire—' The herald broke into a run. '*No*—'

The cages flew open.

Pandemonium was unleashed as fantastical creatures swarmed into the air: hornets the size of eagles with

stingers like tiny swords; pixies from a Lewis Carroll
dream; monsters from Stephen King's nightmares.
Dragon-headed girls swam the air like sea-snakes alongside winged nagas, some as big as crocodiles. They all
turned in mid-air, hanging aloft – and then their eyes
blazed and they swooped towards Vikram and Amanjit: a
wall of winged horror.

Amanjit felt a sudden surge of fright, then instinct took
over; he heard his voice crackle and the arrow he released
went swirling up, high above the sudden storm of wings.

The herald grabbed the king's shoulder and he turned
in affronted shock as the herald started, 'Sire, we must—'

Vikram snapped off an astra that struck the herald in
the heart and the rakshasa stared down at his chest as he
staggered backwards – then someone shrieked—

—but with a mighty crack, Amanjit's astra flew apart
like a skyrocket bursting into many, and a hundred searing
mohini-shafts fell like rain into the thickest press of the
winged monsters.

As each struck, the creature flew apart in a transparent
burst of force. There was no blood, no screams of pain, just
a roar like a tornado as creature after creature surrendered
its life force to the atmosphere.

Vikram drew in his breath, aimed another arrow and then
threw his awareness into the very air about him, pulling and
drawing, *consuming*. The released energy of the magical creatures surged into him, hammering him like physical blows,
like a current of electricity, jerking him about physically as
if he were being electrocuted. He rose into the air, battered
from all sides.

'Vik – *release!*' Amanjit shouted as from among the crowd, dozens of voices roared.

Amanjit saw a bestial shape rip through a bench of his own people like they weren't there. Another real rakshasa!

'The Lakshmana,' it bellowed, 'the Lakshmana – take him—'

But Amanjit fired, and his arrow exploded into the creature's chest, silencing him.

But still Vikram did not – or could not – fire. Caught up in the current of power flooding into him, he could barely move, although he could feel the power lessening, receding. He had only seconds before it would dissipate too much for him to use the arrow.

And still he couldn't work it out: Brahmastra or Pashupatastra? Creation or Destruction?

'Bhai – fire,' Amanjit screamed. 'FIRE!' His voice rose in desperation as he instinctively shot down an astra aimed at him, then fired back at a bow-wielding rakshasa, catching it in the eye. Behind it another came, a giant rhinoceros-thing with skin like rock and lava-eyes. '*SHOOOOOOT*—'

Suddenly Vikram realised: the forces in this place were in balance: this was the tipping place, where life – and energy – was *preserved*.

He whispered the words of the Vaishnava-astra and shot it into the sky.

All of the current suddenly reversed, pouring out of him, and he dropped like a discarded toy, hitting the ground and lying there stunned, gazing blindly upwards. But the forces unleashed by the multiple mohini-astra roared in the wake of the vivid silver arrow, caught it and exploded it like a silent bomb.

The entire arena was blown flat by the force-wave. The rakshasas and asuras and all their pavilion and buildings rippled, as if they were images reflected in a suddenly disturbed pool, and then with a shrieking tear, the entire fabric of the myth-land was ripped apart; the arena, the crowd, the entire palace, disintegrating like a torn painting.

Amanjit found himself standing over the prone Vikram in the middle of a field in a lush meadow. He caught a glimpse of King Vibhishana, looking stunned, shouting something, imploring, then he and his people were all gone in a roar of surging winds that staggered them, yet left the trees that suddenly appeared about them immobile.

A second later, they were alone in a dried-out paddy-field beneath a sultry Sri Lankan sky. The humidity hit him like a slap in the face with a wet towel. Birds sang and distant engines droned.

Amanjit bent over Vikram, who moaned, barely conscious. 'We did it, bhai – we did it . . . what a team!'

Then he heard a noise, the sucking sound of a foot rising from a muddy puddle and the faint exhalation of breath over jagged teeth. He whirled, and saw the rock-skinned rhinoceros-rakshasa he had glimpsed before the Vaishnava-astra flew. It was standing at the edge of the paddy-field, glowering at them with molten eyes. Roaring in fury, it lowered its head, aiming its single curved horn at them, and charged.

# CHAPTER SEVENTEEN

# COURTROOM DRAMA, OLD SCHOOL

*Mumbai, Maharashtra, May 2011*

Deepika Choudhary waited beneath an old banyan tree outside the civil courts in East Bandra. The towering banyan was slowly being wrapped in a strangler fig, which made her think of a great wooden squid, reaching out from the earth to pull the tree down and swallow it whole, but the shade was a blessing in the stifling hot mid-afternoon air. It looked like half the city's auto-rickshaw drivers were sleeping here, sprawled in their passenger seats on the side of the road, oblivious to the roar of the traffic going by. She fought the stink of petrol fumes and the waves of heat from the road making a nauseous swirl about her with spells that cooled and cleansed the air.

*How much more manageable life is now that Vishwamitra's taught me how to use my powers*, she thought, a little smugly. She was squatting on her haunches, wrapped in a headscarf and hidden behind big round sunglasses, muttering charms against being noticed – the old man at the paan-stand beside her hadn't even noticed she was there. She hunched over a tiny indentation she had dug into the dirt and filled with water, watching the tiny images playing there; the words carried to her ears alone. The scrying spell allowed her to watch Lalit giving his testimony.

Deepika had smiled to herself when Tripti had introduced their witness, dryly observing to the judge, 'It's a surprise witness, your Honour: some old-school courtroom drama, for the purists.'

The looks on their faces were priceless as Tanita, Charanpreet and Diltan Modi watched the innocuous-looking witness take the stand.

Lalit, soft-spoken but defiant, had done even better than Deepika could have hoped for, not only publicly denouncing her lies, but producing a great sheaf of documents that his mother had believed he'd shredded, including lots of correspondence between Tanita and Charanpreet that proved conspiracy without any shred of doubt. And while he was busy single-handedly destroying his mother and Amanjit's uncle from seizing all of both families' money, he even made an impassioned plea statement of his half-brother Vikram's innocence. He looked pale but determined, and it was clear the judge was impressed with the young man who'd decided that the truth was what mattered.

Deepika smiled with satisfaction, and thankfully released the spell, which had started to make her feel a little dizzy.

It was another half an hour before they emerged. Tanita Khandavani, Dinesh's *lawfully divorced* first wife, wore a mask of pure, cold fury. Charanpreet Singh Bajaj, Amanjit and Ras' uncle, tried to put a hand on her arm, but she shook it off and when he persisted, she whirled on him, shrieking abuse, and stomped away. Then Diltan Modi, Tanita's *extremely* expensive lawyer, appeared: he spat deliberately on the footpath at Charanpreet's feet before stalking past without even looking at him.

Charanpreet lingered, flexing his shoulders and muttering to himself, until Kiran Khandavani emerged with her eldest son Bishin, her lawyer Tripti and young Lalit, her stepson. Then Charanpreet snarled and started storming towards them, a big ex-soldier with the heft and aggression and know-how to hurt someone badly. Deepika rose as Bishin straightened and went to meet his uncle head-on. He looked as if he'd realised for the first time that he was no longer the boy his uncle had bullied mercilessly; he was as big as his uncle in stature, and he was younger and fitter.

In seconds they were pushing and shoving each other, while onlookers whirled to see what the disturbance was. Charanpreet began to spew out abuse, screaming in his nephew's face, spraying spittle as he ranted and swore, while Bishin shouted back, telling him to shut his damned mouth, and how dared he do such a thing to *family*?

'Stop this, please,' a suddenly tearful Kiran shouted, and Charanpreet whirled on her, calling her a whore and a treacherous bitch – and suddenly punches were flying, Charanpreet and then Bishin reeling as blows connected.

Deepika began to move, hurrying toward the scene, torn between revealing herself and stopping this before it got completely out of hand, but Tripti was taking matters in hand, screaming for Security.

The guards outside the courthouse peered at her curiously,

but their faces hardened as they realised what was happening and they reached for truncheons and rifles. Two of them shouldered forward and Bishin, seeing them coming, tried to back up. Charanpreet threw a wild punch and missed – and then realised that the security men were closing in and paused, panting and red-faced.

'This is *not* over—' he started.

'I think you'll find it is, Mr Bajaj,' Tripti retorted firmly, taking Bishin by the arm.

Faced by men with guns, Charanpreet swore virulently, then turned on his heel and marched off past Deepika, not even noticing her, his face like thunder. Deepika stopped where she was, still thirty yards away, hoping the danger was over.

Kiran's face was still ashen from the tension and the violence. She hugged her eldest son, sobbing, and then turned and went to Lalit, embracing the shy young man before sobbing on his shoulder too. Deepika lip-read, 'Thank you, thank, thank you!' repeated over and over again.

Lalit was still pale himself, but he looked immensely relieved and proud. Everyone was now embracing, and Deepika wished she could risk joining them, but she was still a danger to them, and anyone could be watching. So she just shadowed them as they walked to the car park, wondering if the court had made any provision for Lalit; she was quite sure he'd be in physical danger if he went home with Tanita. Even if his mother could manage to restrain herself, which was no given thing, she doubted Charanpreet would be able to keep his hands off the boy who'd lost him a fortune.

Tripti had promised she would arrange something and Deepika hoped she'd kept her word. She moved closer——

——and so did others. As the family reached Tripti's car, Deepika saw movement out of the corner of her eye: a tall man with a sinister goatee and tied-back long hair, dressed in a black silk shirt and slim-fitting black trousers and a tailored jacket, despite the heat. She'd seen the man before: this wasn't his true face, just the illusory form he favoured. She focused her gaze as the sage had taught her and penetrated the illusion, revealing the hulking goat-faced rakshasa called Prahasta, the rakshasa to whom Ravindra had promised her body. She felt her shoulders tense as anger stirred inside her.

Lurking near the rakshasa was a woman in green salwar kameez, her face wrapped in a dupatta. She moved awkwardly, as if she was in pain. Although only her bewitching green eyes were showing, Deepika recognised Meenakshi Nandita . . . *Surpanakha*.

She began to run as Prahasta strolled towards Kiran. Tripti turned to see the handsome stranger just as his hand slid inside his jacket and he said coolly, 'Just in time for some retribution, old-school, you snotty-nosed bitch.'

Deepika cried, 'Watch out!' as he pulled out a gun; Surpanakha turned, startled, but Deepika had to focus on Prahasta: her hand shot out as the rakshasa's finger tightened on the trigger and a blast of force erupted from her fingers just as the gun roared.

Tripti staggered, doubled over and crashed to the ground as Kiran started screaming. Bishin grabbed his mother and pushed her down, but Lalit stood paralysed, staring in horror as Prahasta aimed the gun at the young man.

Then Deepika's blast struck the rakshasa in the chest, hammering him backwards into a parked car. The door buckled and he sat down hard, dazed, his nose trickling blood. But he was still holding the gun.

Deepika hadn't stopped running; she was weaving her way between the parked cars while everyone else scattered, running for cover, even the security men had dropped their rifles and were pounding away towards the nearest building. The carpark emptied in a flash as people ran, screaming in terror.

Surpanakha's hand emerged, revealing a pistol, which she pointed Deepika, snarling, '*You!*' in the same breath as she started firing.

The first bullet ripped past Deepika as she dropped to the ground. Bishin was huddled over his mother, who was staring wildly at Deepika, while Tripti, keening in agony, had her hands clasped to her bleeding stomach.

But Lalit was *still* just standing there in dazed shock, unable to take his eyes from the gun Prahasta was pointing at him.

She knew Surpanakha was just waiting for her to break cover, but Lalit had sacrificed everything for them. The rakshasa was perhaps thirty yards away – and she needed a clear sightline. She leaped to her feet and zigzagged through the cars as fast as she could move while Surpanakha's pistol spat bullets at her – and as his gun came up, she shouted, 'BURN!'

Flames blazed from her hand and enveloped the rakshasa, but she was an instant too late; even as he was losing his grip on the melting metal he managed to fire, and she heard Lalit cry out in pain.

A sword materialised in her hands as she closed on the demon, who rose, fighting the flames with spells of his own – then his eyes went wide as he saw her blade flash towards him. He twisted awkwardly, but swayed away from her blow and instead of shearing through his flesh, the blade smashed the window of the car behind him – and then he was lunging under her guard and throwing himself at her.

Crisped fur and the iron reek of blood filled her nostrils as he slammed her to the road, smacking the back of her head against the ground. His face loomed above her as the air whooshed from her lungs and stars burst through her skull. His left hand found her throat, pinning her down, his right hand bunched above her face and he snarled, 'At last . . .'

Deepika realised in fright that the car park was fading, trees appearing where there had been only broken concrete and crumbling bollards.

*He's dragging me into the myth-lands!*

She fought his control, keeping them both in the real world. He growled and spat on her, his eyes throbbing, as he promised, 'My Queen – I'm going to—'

'Nooo!' Lalit launched himself at them, his face full of foolish, youthful invincibility, but turning almost lazily, Prahasta backhanded him, an effortless slap that sent Lalit flying backwards. He hit a parked Maruti and slid bonelessly to the ground, where he sprawled, unmoving.

Prahasta's eyes had left Deepika for half a second – and in that instant, she called his gun to her hands. He turned his attention back to her, his mouth open to finish his taunt – and she fired straight into his mouth at point-blank range.

The back of Prahasta's head exploded outwards, the force

of it lifting his body away from her. He crashed down beside her, limbs twitching.

*Finally got you, you bastard*, she thought as she sat up, wolfing down air. She fired twice more into his chest, just to be on the safe side. He jerked and convulsed, his legs kicking, then, at last, he went completely still.

The trees had faded, the car park solidified back to normal—

—and all her instincts screaming, Deepika twisted and rolled – just as a bullet gouged the exact place she'd been lying. A second hit her, searing a furrow down her shoulder as she rolled again, firing blindly towards the muzzle flashes. She heard metal rip and glass shatter as she fetched up against Lalit's body. She could feel blood welling from her shoulder, but she was certain it was just a graze, horribly painful, but not fatal.

She suddenly realised that she was hearing all-too-human screams; clearly not everyone had found cover when the shooting started, and bullets had been flying in all directions. As she bent over Lalit, she muttered, 'I hope someone has had the sense to call an ambulance.' She was horribly afraid he'd died for his chivalrous behaviour, but with a huge sigh of relief she heard a shallow hiss as he managed a breath. She put her fingers on his wrist: his heart was beating – it wasn't strong, but it was there. He'd definitely been hit, though; there was blood all over his sleeve – the bullet had gone through his forearm. She looked around, seeking signs of a response: this was a court; surely there had to be more guards? But the only two she'd seen had vanished. She snarled in anger at them, before reflecting that they'd probably had no training, and were on minimum wages.

*No wonder they ran . . .*

Somewhere alarms were screeching. She could only hope some real policemen were on their way. She lifted her head and looked around until she saw Tripti. Her eyes were open and her mouth was still emitting a high-pitched howling sound, even while blood pooled about her. Bishin was next to her, holding his mother close. Then he spotted Deepika and stared at her with desperate hope.

She wondered what she looked like right now. Had her skin turned black? Were her eyes glowing? She could feel that familiar rage bubbling up inside her . . .

'Bishin,' she shouted, 'call for help – there's at least one more gunman – I'm going after them!'

Without waiting to check that he'd understood, she began to move – just as a green-clad woman darted from behind a row of cars, sprinting for the far side of the carpark: Surpanakha was trying to make her getaway.

*In a few minutes, she'll be in contact with Ravindra, and he'll know to check out my heart-stone – and as soon as he realises I'm alive, he'll use it to turn me to jelly. If I don't get to her before that, I'm lost forever.*

She leaped to her feet and stormed after the fleeing demoness.

*The Darya is alive!* Surpanakha's limbs were still twisted and broken from her last encounter with Deepika, so she conjured shadowy wings that blurred on her back, allowing her to bound in long floating strides. She'd never been able to fully fly, but she was moving faster than any ordinary human could, tearing from the parking lot and into the first alley she passed. A boy on a bicycle got in her way; with a grunt, she flung him against the wall, dashed aside a water-seller and a motorbike and leaped a fence. All she needed was thirty seconds' respite, just a brief pause so she could open a gateway out of this wretched world—

—but three seconds later, someone vaulted the fence behind her.

Swearing, she spun around and snapped off a shot, though she couldn't pause to aim and in any case, she doubted the bullets would matter: the thing behind her was no longer human, but an ebony mass with wild hair and many arms, like a huge bipedal spider, and it was matching her stride for stride.

Surpanakha ripped through another fence and into a rubbish-strewn garden, bowling aside someone hanging out clothes; she heard the washerwoman's ribs snap and hoped against hope that her pitiless pursuer might still be human enough to stop to help the stricken woman. As she leaped the next fence a child looked up at her and screamed.

*This is my only chance.* She scooped up the brat and turned, pressing her vicious nails into the child's throat, just as the wooden fence behind her shattered in a hail of splinters and a black shape burst through it.

'Stop,' she shrieked, 'or the human child dies—'

A face carved in ebony with blazing eyes and almost lumi-nous white teeth contemplated her savagely – the features were akin to Deepika's, but there was something else as well. A nimbus of fiery hair glowed about her like a halo.

She didn't speak, but roared like a great cat, a snarl with no words in it.

'I mean it!' Surpanakha shouted, although she was trembling with terror herself. 'Another step and I'll rip the brat's throat out.' Her voice sounded shrill and desperate to her ears. 'Do you hear me, you insane bitch?'

That ghastly, gorgeous face spat at her – but Deepika stopped advancing.

'Deepika Choudhary,' Surpanakha called, trying to reach the girl behind the goddess, 'you have to control that monster inside you. I can show you – you and I, we can work together, you know we can – we're so alike—'

At her words, the darkness drained from Deepika's face.

*Yes, loosen your grip on that hideous energy and I can escape you*, Surpanakha thought with glee. *I can even take you down ...* 'Remember your humanity, Deepika – for the sake of this innocent child's life. You must learn control . . .' Surpanakha readied herself, still trying to decide: *fight or flee?*

From behind her came a deep, throaty coughing sound—

—and a tiger the size of a horse effortlessly leaped the fence. It growled, making the ground tremble, and fixed its amber eyes on her. Its glorious coat rippling in the sunlight, it bared six-inch teeth and pawed the earth. The intelligence in its eyes shone out – but the menace in its stance stole the strength from her limbs.

*This isn't possible—*

But when she turned back to Deepika Choudhary, the woman had changed again – into something else, another being. The madness was gone, clearly, but neither humanity nor pity had returned.

There would be no escape.

Surpanakha felt her knees wobble and had to hold on to her hostage for support.

Then she remembered who she was: *I am sister of the Ravan himself* . . .

The child in her grasp looked up at her and she looked down, contemplating its innocent, frightened face, and the poverty-stricken future it was doubtless facing. *Pathetic*. She flung it against the wall and roared defiantly, 'Kill me if you can!'

## CHAPTER EIGHTEEN

# DANCING IN THE RAIN

*Lanka, May-June 2011*

As April turned into May, the temperatures soared. The stone palace was searing hot in the sun and even in the shade the heat lingered oppressively. Rasita asked for a ceiling fan and instead was sent a muscular asura with a punkah. She sent him away when she could no longer bear to stare at the servant's muscles rippling as he plied his huge fan.

Some nights she couldn't get to sleep for hours, lying in her sweat and trying not to melt in the raging summer heat. Above her, the painted couples on her ceiling mural played out their passions. The painting, in the eighteenth-century style of the Hamzanana, changed moment to moment like an animated cartoon. The painted people on her ceiling had been decorous and courtly when she'd first arrived, but ever since she'd taken in the essence of the dead queens, they'd changed; the current theme appeared to be the *Kama Sutra*.

The first night after that tumultuous evening when she'd absorbed Halika, Aruna and Jyoti, she'd had a steamy dream of herself as Sunita Ashoka, cavorting with one of her men – and when she woke, her ceiling was covered with painted lovers entwined about each other in dreamlike motion. Now every night was the same as Halika took her through centuries of lovers while the mural tormented her with its lewd imagery.

When she complained, Kaineskeya gave a throaty laugh and said, 'You're the one they take inspiration from, mistress.'

Ras blushed scarlet, to the rakshasa maid's huge amusement.

She couldn't make them go away or stop them and she began to dread looking up. Nor would her dreams give her any respite; apparently in her past lives – her own Gauran lives, and Halika's dark past – she'd been anything but chaste. Now Rasita felt like she was drowning in old passions.

*This is torturing me.*

She was sure Ravindra knew, for he demanded her companionship every day now as she was his only queen, taking every opportunity to touch her, kissing her cheek in greeting, letting his fingers drift over her hand whilst guiding her to a seat. His clothing became looser and more revealing, just like the outfits he sent to her rooms.

She could no longer deny that she was craving the things she dreamed of, wanting to experience them herself in this life.

But somehow, she restrained herself.

It wasn't that she was waiting for Vikram any more; the hope that he would save her was receding daily. Increasingly she began to believe that even if Dasraiyat wasn't as evil as Ravindra told her, he'd been no saint, so by extension, Vikram was no better than Ravindra. And she was still seething about that kiss – he might even have slept with Sue Parker; she wouldn't have been at all surprised. *It's all right for men*, she thought bitterly. *For a man to be experienced is good – but for a woman it's wrong. That's so unfair.*

Nor did she hold herself back for lack of desire; she couldn't look at Ravindra without aching to reach out, to feel his strong arms around her, his lips on hers. Halika had *always* desired the Ravan, and had revelled in fully sating those desires – and those memories were Rasita's now. She caught herself allowing him to stroke her arm, to press a hand on her shoulder, or run his fingers down her back. He was charming, and knowledgeable and dangerous, she knew that, but she began to believe she could tame him, and that was weirdly exciting. She drank more, some nights weaving back to her chambers feeling distinctly tipsy.

There was only one thing stopping her from flinging herself into Ravindra's arms and crying out like the best romantic heroines, 'Take me, I'm yours' – and that was the increasingly strong conviction that Deepika was still alive.

She had watched as Ravindra had badly wounded Deepika, and then seen the earth swallow her up in Panchavati, but Ras had awakened one morning with a feeling that Dee was not just alive, but actively looking for her. At first she'd been certain it was just wishful thinking, but now she believed she was right – and she wasn't going to give up until she was proven wrong.

Because if Ravindra's tale and Halika's memories were true, then between them, she and Dee contained the fractured soul of the sorceress-queen Manda. They were more than sisters: they were parts of the same being: Manda – Queen Mandodari of the *Ramayana*. So if she succumbed to Ravindra, there would be implications for Deepika. She didn't fully understand what they might be, but felt that she could be risking the destruction of her brother's true love. That was a line she would *not* cross.

But for all this place was timeless, the days and weeks were wearing on. It was early June, the monsoon season would come soon and Dusshera was fast approaching. Keke was already excited: there were going to be huge celebrations, apparently.

'You'll have such fun, mistress,' she cried, clapping her hands. 'We must make you radiantly beautiful, so that you will truly win the heart of the king.'

Rasita couldn't tell whether Keke was a wicked demon or an innocent girl. She reminded her of a loveable but naughty child who wouldn't stop licking the honey spoon, despite being told she couldn't. She was feral yet girlish – and she was Rasita's only friend here.

Except for Ravindra.

That morning she woke from another raunchy dream, tangled naked in the damp sheets – somehow she'd lost her resolve to remain clad when she slept – and heard the sound of falling rain. Then Keke danced into her chamber and seized her hands, singing, 'Mistress, mistress, get up – the monsoon has begun—'

Rasita threw on a kameez, then let Keke pull her out on to their balcony. The little rakshasa maid's honey eyes were glowing, her horns gleaming on her brow. All about the palace, half-naked rakshasas were pouring out into the courtyards, dancing, hooting, prancing and laughing. Below in the city horns were blowing as thousands of asuras thronged the streets and squares, tossing coloured powder around as if it were the Holi festival, while above them, brooding clouds rumbled as they sent down torrents of rain.

Keke cupped her hands, filling them with rain, then laughed and tossed both handfuls into the air. Rasita gasped as the water, glowing from inside, remained formed, then she stared in amazement as the maid juggled the two balls, giggling mischievously. She added two more, her tongue stuck sideways from her mouth as she concentrated, and Rasita backed away, entranced and amazed.

Then Keke threw her a ball of glowing water and she caught it, more by instinct than thought. It felt like jelly. She tossed it in the air, then Keke flung her another and another, and before she knew it, her hands were a blur of movement. Her mouth fell open and she felt suddenly giddy, frightened and joyous at once, not quite believing what was happening.

'How are you doing this?' Ras squealed.

'I'm not, not any more,' Keke laughed. 'You are.'

She froze, and all four balls fell to the wet slate floor and splashed back into ordinary water. She stared at the puddles, a feeling of elation in her heart. *I just did something magical . . .*

Then Ravindra stepped on to the balcony and sat down opposite her. He was naked to the waist and his golden skin was stained a rainbow of vivid dyes. He'd evidently been dancing with his people and he looked damnably, dangerously good. Ras stood petrified, not knowing what to do with herself as he ran his eye down the wet kameez clinging to her skin. She was wearing nothing underneath.

'You look lovely, my dear,' he purred.

*I refuse to blush like a little girl*, she thought imperiously, instead turning her back, because this was something new and incredible: *I did magic!*

Recalling how it had felt, she gestured, flicking her hand so that droplets sprayed about her, and then with the slightest mental exertion, made the droplets hang in the air. She looked at them, pictured a circle and they began to spin lazily about each other, glowing from within.

Keke jumped up and down, clapping excitedly.

'Ah,' said Ravindra. 'I wondered when this would happen.'

Ras paused and let the droplets plink to the wet floor. 'What do you mean, *when* this would happen?'

'Your soul-sister Deepika was manifesting such abilities already, and you have absorbed the essences of three other queens, and Halika was a very powerful sorceress. It was only a matter of time.' His voice contained a rich thread of hope. 'You are regaining yourself, my Manda, a little more every day.'

She pulled the wet tangle of hair from her face and asked, 'How is that possible? It's never happened before.'

'In the past *your* soul has been too divided for such things, but I have had reports down the ages of the Darya-soul manifesting such powers on occasions, although always in an untutored and uncontrolled way.'

Rasita remembered Deepika as she'd last seen her: a ferocious force akin to the goddess Kali. 'Why did Deepika manifest that . . . that Kali-thing? You said she was the Protective Aspect?'

'The Protective Aspect stands at the tipping point: it is the fulcrum between Creation and Destruction. When these are in harmony, life is preserved and maintained. Too much destruction and they fall apart; too much creation and nothing changes. In either case, the result is stasis. But Deepika's internal harmony has been destroyed by her soul's suffering through the ages, and so she started manifesting Destruction more keenly. Her power resembles Kali because in this life she is a Hindu. If she believed in other gods, you would have seen a very different manifestation.'

'You're the one who made her lives miserable,' Rasita reminded him sharply.

'I do acknowledge that it was I who made her suffer; you already know why. Together, we can end *all* of our suffering. Believe me, she was no more whole than you are – and now she is a ghost. I've called to her and she will come – and then we can *all* be made whole.'

Rasita bowed her head miserably. Her belief that Deepika was still alive felt like a childish hope. *It's her ghost I'm sensing, that's all*. She bit her lip, then voiced the fear she'd been harbouring ever since Ravindra began to speak of his hopes of recreating his mythic love, Queen Manda.

'If we're made whole, will I still be me? Or will some other being erase me?'

Ravindra paused, watching her carefully, before saying, 'Once Deepika's spirit arrives here, it can be reunited with you. Ideally, I need your heart-stone, but perhaps we can make do without. We must . . . achieve consummation; this is what will make you whole: a new Manda who is *all of you*, will emerge. You will still be you, Rasita, but better in every way.'

She thought about that: absorbing Sunita had been easy and gentle; but the dead queens had been harder. She looked up at him, and asked, 'And you?'

He tilted his head curiously. 'What are you asking?'

She leaned forward. 'If Manda is made whole, need you and Vikram still fight? And what of my brother, who has lost his fiancée? What of him?'

Ravindra looked beyond her, then admitted, 'The restoration of Manda will mean that the victor will live forever, but the other will perish forever – at least, that is what my research leads me to believe. As for your brother, I am sorry. It's too late: Deepika is already dead. Her ghost will come here soon – any day now – and she will be as demanding as the Padma ghost, but you are promised to me and so she will join with you as one, as the Padma ghost did. And remember this, lady: Manda was my eternal love. We worshipped each other. Dasraiyat was a would-be-adulterer with whom Manda worked, but never loved.'

'I have only your word on that,' Rasita pointed out. 'What if she loved him, and not you?'

He clenched his fists and his breath went short. 'I did not lie.' Abruptly he got up and strode away.

She sat, shivering, on the chair, mourning Deepika anew.

The whole day long, the entire city danced, and in the evening there was a feast to celebrate the monsoon's arrival. Rasita, seated at Ravindra's right hand, was treated as a queen. The rakshasa minstrels sang new songs, adaptations of Bollywood film songs, she was sure, and she found herself enjoying the spectacle. She had maybe a little too much wine, but she still had the strength of will to go back to her own rooms that night. She was wide awake still, and not at all tempted by Ravindra's hungry looks. Well, not too much. She had other things on her mind.

She stared up at the ceiling. The mural on the ceiling was no longer cavorting lovers.

Now it depicted magicians.

The next day, Keke took her to a tower she had never been to before, guarded by a baital. The bat-winged man the size of a small child watched from a perch hung from the ceiling. Old books were piled in corners and a dusty crystal ball glowed on a tall stand; tarot cards were scattered about the huge oak desk.

A cobra-headed rakshasa in loose robes crept slowly from the shadows.

'Hail, my Queen,' Lavanasura lisped. 'Ravan Aeshwaran has decreed it is time for your training to begin.'

# CHAPTER NINETEEN

# MY LEAST SIGNIFICANT LIFE

*Sri Lanka, June 2011*

If Amanjit stood his ground he would be flattened. If he didn't, the rhinoceros rakshasa would run right over Vikram – then an idea flashed through his mind. He couldn't say whether it was from an action movie or some residue of a past life, but the image and the idea were clear. He knelt and jammed an arrow fletching-first into the ground and said, '*Spear.*'

It wasn't an incantation, but the vocalisation of his will – and it worked a treat: the arrow instantly became a thick-hafted, eight-foot hunting spear. He knelt and gripped it, lowered the point towards the charging demon-beast and braced himself. The stone-skinned creature thundered towards him, nose down, the rhinoceros horn jutting wickedly; Amanjit adjusted the spear slightly, aligning it with the creature's right shoulder and jammed his right foot into the ground behind the butt of the weapon.

The rakshasa steamed towards him, his eyes fixed as if

this were a deadly game of Chicken. Resisting the almost overwhelming urge to hurl himself aside, Amanjit gritted his teeth and prepared for impact — but at the very last instant, it was the demon who jerked away. Amanjit pulled the spear from the ground and lunged, catching the thing inside the right shoulder, punching through the heavy skin until a screech told him he'd found flesh. The demon wrenched sideways, ripping the spear from Amanjit's grasp, and started thrashing about, roaring in pain.

Amanjit drew his bow and cautiously stalked the wounded demon, which rose on hind legs, standing shakily, and with an agonised effort, broke off the spear shaft, leaving the point still embedded in the shoulder.

Breathing laboured, swaying, the rakshasa hissed wetly, 'I will kill you before I die.'

'Sure you will.' Amanjit glanced about. This was the only demon who had followed them through the disintegration of the Sri Lankan myth-land. *We can't have anyone warning Ravindra that we're free.* He circled warily, trying to assess the remaining threat.

'You could have killed us when we passed out back in Vibhishana's palace,' he commented.

The stone rhino spat blood. 'We would have, if we could. But we couldn't get close enough. The myth-creatures wouldn't let us get closer, even though they didn't know our intention.'

'Vibhishana didn't know you were there?'

'That *imbecile* was not Vibhishana,' the rakshasa said scathingly, 'or not the real Vibhishana. That travesty you met was just a folk-memory, a construct of the myth-lands.' The rakshasa blew a bloody bubble from its mouth and staggered. 'Your spearhead has pierced my lungs. I'm doomed.' He eyed the bow. 'Draw your sword: kill me cleanly.'

'Too risky,' Amanjit said. 'I'm not coming within reach, buddy.' He raised the bow.

'Wait, wait – don't you want to know the name of he whom you have slain?'

'Why, are you famous?' Amanjit searched his conscience, but he could summon up no sympathy for the creature. He took aim at where the stone-beast's heart might be. 'Are you a rock star?' he asked harshly. 'One of the Rolling Stones, maybe? Or should I just call you "Pebbles" – you know, from *The Flintstones*?'

The rakshasa growled weakly. 'Mock me not, human. I am of a nobler kind than thou! My name is—'

Amanjit buried an arrow in the rakshasa's chest, and the demon collapsed, gasping desperately. Amanjit nocked another arrow. 'I don't care what your "noble" name is, you bastard,' Amanjit told him. 'You've spent far too long killing "ignoble" little nobodies like us for me to want to know. If being forgotten means you'll never return to life in the myth-lands, then I hope you're forgotten for ever.'

Murmuring the words for the parvata-astra, he loosed the arrow, which struck the rakshasa like a boulder, shattering him into chunks of broken stone-flesh.

He turned and ran back to Vikram, who was returning to consciousness. 'Come on, bhai, we've got to get going,' he said urgently.

'Did it work?' Vikram asked, still looking dazed. 'Are we actually free?'

Amanjit squatted beside him. 'It worked.' He checked about them, but the fields were empty and the corpse of the rhino-rakshasa was already disintegrating into a pile of mud, as he'd seen them do before. 'There were a few real demons in there and one got through on our tail, but I nailed him.'

'Well done, bhai.'

Amanjit put a hand on Vikram's shoulder, keeping him where he was to give him a chance to regain some of his strength. 'I guess that Trimurti astra really took it out of you.'

'You've no idea.' He held up a trembling hand. 'I'm shaking like a leaf.'

A rasping sound came, the sound of something large struggling to fill its lungs, followed by soft exhalations from a leathery throat. It was coming from the landward side, where the trees were thickest and the shadows deepest. Amanjit stood up slowly. 'It's that dying elephant sound again. I'll go and check it out, Vik – you stay here, okay?'

Vikram smiled weakly. 'I'm not going anywhere right now. Be careful.'

'Sure thing.' Amanjit nocked an arrow and stalked into the thicket, following the breathing, but it didn't take long to find the source of the sound: a dark mound was lying sprawled in the undergrowth. At first sight it was like a beached whale, but as his eyes grew accustomed to the gloom, he realised that it was actually man-shaped. The earth around it was broken, as if it had fallen there from a great height. Black steaming blood was running from its mouth and nose and soaking into the dark earth.

Amanjit stepped closer, then slowly let his breath out as

he recognised the ravaged features. The prone demon had once been immense and majestic, bearded in silver with purple eyes and sharp bull-horns – but now he was a ruin, emaciated and barely breathing. There was so little flesh on him that in some places the bones were poking through the worn-out, papery skin.

'King Vibhishana?' Amanjit slowly lowered the bow, his mind reeling. *This* was the real Vibhishana. In the *Ramayana*, Vibhishana had loved Rama and justice so much that he had betrayed his fellow demons; he had fought against his own people, and had been installed as King of Lanka upon Ravana's death.

*So if this is this the real Vibhishana ... then it's all real, isn't it? The whole thing—*

Amanjit dropped the bow and ran to the fallen king's side, begging, 'Stay with me – I can help you, King Vibhishana . . .'

*And you can tell us where the real Lanka is – you can maybe help us in the fight, and tell us what we face ... My God, this is the breakthrough we need—*

But the king closed his eyes and lost consciousness, leaving Amanjit pummelling the earth in frustration. Here he was, stuck in Sri Lanka, with Vikram almost catatonic and a dying demon – if he wasn't dead already. *What the hell can we do? I need a bloody doctor, not magic arrows . . .*

Then he stopped and his eyes went wide. He leaped to his feet and ran back to Vikram, shouting, 'Vik – Vik, wake up! Have you still got that doctor's phone number? That guy we met in Madurai, the one with the LTTE contacts—?'

*

It took Kasun half a day to get there. He was with his older brother, a tough-looking man named Tyag, who'd volunteered his battered old truck for the journey. Vikram climbed unsteadily to his feet as Amanjit waved them down, still worrying about exactly what they were going to say. It felt insane to be seriously thinking of betraying their deepest secrets to a Sri Lankan graduate doctor they'd met once for a couple of hours, and then immediately presenting him with the strangest patient he would ever deal with in his whole life . . . but what choice did they have?

Kasun shook Amanjit's hand firmly, then hurried towards Vikram. 'Namaste, my friend – but what are you doing out here? This is bad country.' He gripped Vikram's hand in both of his and stared at him, looking concerned. 'Are you all right?'

'I'm fine,' Vikram murmured as the world folded slowly sideways and the lights went out.

Vikram woke to find himself lying on a low flax mattress with a drip stuck in his arm in a small room that smelled of cooking spices and cleaning fluids. Kasun was sitting beside him, biting his nails furiously, a panicked look on his face. When he tried to sit up, Kasun jerked in alarm and bent over him.

'Vikram? My God— What is happening to the world? I have an actual *rakshasa* in my recovery room . . .'

He knew it was going to be a long and deeply weird conversation, one he couldn't avoid now. But he found it helped order his thoughts, trying to explain the whole story to someone new and – until now, at least – not involved; it crystallised some of his own thinking about Lanka, Ravindra and especially about Rasita.

When they'd finished talking, he watched Kasun carefully, half expecting the young doctor to declare him incurably crazy and try to section him – but then, with King Vibhishana as 'Exhibit A', even the most Doubting Thomas could hardly call Vikram's tale impossible.

He'd sensed a friend in Kasun the first time he'd met him: someone he'd wanted to get to know better – and Kasun didn't let him down. Far from dismissing the tale, he accepted it totally, and before Vikram had even asked, he was promising to look after Vibhishana, and Vikram too, for as long as they needed.

It only took eight days; even Vikram was surprised to see how quickly he mended. But he and Amanjit were both frightened at how much time this failed journey south had taken; they had no idea where the real Lanka might be and Vibhishana, the only person who might be able to help them, remained in a coma, unresponsive to anything.

At last, deciding they were fast running out of time, they agreed they must return to India. Kasun promised to look after the fallen rakshasa and to contact them if he recovered consciousness, but he wasn't holding out much hope. They parted warmly, then Vikram led Amanjit into the trees, seeking a private place to invoke the traveller arrows.

As the moon rose over the steaming jungle, two arrows shot into the air, each with a young warrior balanced on them like two surfers riding the night skies.

They landed on the same deserted beach they had left weeks ago. It felt like forever.

Amanjit theatrically kissed the sand and declaimed, 'Mother India: I'll never leave you again.'

Vikram slumped to the ground beside him. He felt weak still, but was gradually getting his strength back. He picked up a handful of sand and let it run through his fingers, thinking of all the time they'd lost. Weeks, maybe months? For nothing.

*Where's Ras? Has she——? No, she would never . . .*

'What now, bhai?' Amanjit asked. His voice sounded hollow, and Vikram knew how he felt. 'Where do we go now? How can we find them if our only clue is the *Ramayana*, and even that isn't working any more?'

Vikram slowly stood, struggling to contain his sense of hopelessness. The heart-stone in his pocket felt distant and inert; he'd stopped sensing Rasita through it when she'd been taken. 'I don't know,' he admitted. 'It makes no sense – Sri Lanka *is* Lanka, in every version of the story. Believe me, in the last year I've checked out all of them: the *Reamker* of Cambodia and the *Yama Zatdaw* of Burma and Thailand's *Ramakien* and all the other regional variants, looking for clues. Sometimes a bit of the geography of the story varies, but Lanka is *always* Sri Lanka.'

'Then Ravindra is double-bluffing us: he knows we know that, so he's got her somewhere else. He's tricked us.'

Vikram said slowly, 'You might be spot-on, but if this is all tied up with the *Ramayana*, I would have thought he would need to take her to the real Lanka to fulfil everything properly. To *win*.'

Amanjit exhaled wearily and slowly stood up. 'This whole thing is really making my head hurt. Vik, there *must* be some clue in your past lives, maybe? Or in a history book or something? There *must* be. It can't end like this – after all, he's got to kill you to win, hasn't he? So eventually he's going to have to come and get you, if we can't find him.'

Vikram rubbed his chin. 'But what if it's too late? What if us going to the wrong place gave him the time to . . . you know . . . have his way with Rasita?'

Amanjit gripped his shoulders and growled, 'No: that's my sister you're talking about. She's as tough as old boots – she didn't die when all the doctors were sure she would, don't forget. She and Dee are the most determined people I know.' He fumbled in his pocket. 'Speaking of which – I'll call her, tell her we're back.'

He turned away, leaving Vikram swaying slightly, clinging to the last of his energy.

After a minute, Amanjit scowled. 'Damn telecom company. No connection – typical.'

Vikram sank back down. The musafir-astras had taken much of his strength, so he let the noise fade and lying on his side in the warm sand, he simply closed his eyes.


Amanjit got Vikram to the guesthouse they'd used last time, a shabby but serviceable place where not too many questions were asked. Vikram was asleep again in minutes, but Amanjit stayed up trying in vain to call Deepika all day till dusk.

*If something's happened to her, I'll never forgive myself for leaving her alone . . .*

Finally he had to take the risk, police wire-taps or whatever notwithstanding, and phone home. To his enormous relief, Bishin picked up. 'Hey bhai,' he started.

Bishin squawked in surprise. 'Amanjit? What's happening? Where are you?'

'Can't say, bhai: I have to keep this brief. Is Mum okay? Has the court stuff happened yet?'

'Yes – and get this: *we won* – Lalit testified for us. He brought up a whole lot of paperwork, stuff that really helped us. *We really did it: we won!*'

Amanjit wondered why Bishin still didn't sound happy, when this was the best news possible.

After a moment, Bishin told him. 'But brother, things aren't good. We were attacked in the car park afterwards – this slimy dude pulled a gun and shot Tripti, our lawyer. She's still in hospital, but the doctors say she'll live. Lalit took a shot in his arm – it broke the bone, but otherwise he's fine. The rest of us are okay.'

'Was Dee there?' Amanjit asked, suddenly afraid.

'Yeah – soon as it happened, she came charging across the car park like a mad thing – swear to God, she took down the gunman! Scariest thing I've ever seen. She just ran at him while he was shooting, grabbed his gun off him and blew his brains out. Then she ran off after the second shooter – I never even saw that one – but the weirdest thing was, by the time the cops finally got there, all that was left of the dead guy was a pile of stinking mud and ash.'

*Rakshasas!* Amanjit found his hands were shaking. 'Did Deepika get the second shooter?' he asked carefully.

There was a pause that felt like it went on for months, then Bishin said softly, 'I don't know, bhai. She never came back.'

Amanjit sat down slowly, his brother's words echoing in his skull.

*She never came back . . .*

Vikram stared at his hands, fighting down his fears, then looked across at Amanjit, lying on his bed. Apart from limping into the toilet every few hours, he hadn't moved for days. He looked borderline suicidal, all his native strength shredded by Deepika's disappearance.

*We need a plan*, Vikram told himself. *We need a purpose, before we both go mad.*

There had to be *something* – some tiny clue, something obvious they had missed – but no matter how hard he tried, if it was there he kept missing it.

Eventually Amanjit revived enough to ask, 'Tell me about my past lives. Even the least significant one you know of. I need to *know*.'

'I thought you didn't want to know about such things,' Vikram replied, although he was relieved that Amanjit was showing an interest in life again.

'I don't. But if you can't think of anything, bhai, then maybe the clue is in *my* lives, not yours.'

*It was possible*, Vikram decided, but before he could reply, Amanjit rolled over and went back to sleep. Vikram sat by him all through the night, thinking about his own past lives, especially the ones he seldom considered, what Amanjit had called 'the least significant of them', just in case there might be something useful.

At dawn, he shook Amanjit's shoulder. 'Amanjit, wake up.'

The Sikh came awake slowly, muttering, 'Wassup?'

'I had a thought – I need to do some research. I'll be at that internet place on the next block.'

Amanjit groaned and clutched his head. 'Sure, whatever. Bring me back a coffee. No, two. Or three.' He rolled over and closed his eyes. 'And shut the bloody door.'

It was Amanjit's words that triggered it: *the least significant life*.

It was one Vikram hadn't thought of as having any bearing on anything. It had been brief, for a start: he'd never even reached puberty or recovered his past-life memories. He'd been murdered when he was just eleven, hanged by a homicidal Pakistani zealot, just before Partition.

*But perhaps it wasn't my most insignificant life; perhaps it's the most important clue of all . . .*

He still wasn't sure until he saw the photograph, an old sepia print from an archaeological dig in the western Punjab that the Historical Society had helpfully posted on their website. The site hadn't been in Pakistan then; the excavations had started before Pakistan even existed. The picture showed ancient towers being unearthed, sun-blackened figures with shovels and wheelbarrows, delving amidst the dust and rocks.

But the name of the photographer was Timothy Southby. *Tim-sahib*.

Vikram spent hours in the internet café, alternately sipping chai and bottled water, following leads in obscure archaeological journals to trace a man whose life had been spent in the pursuit of knowledge. Birth, death and marriage certificates led to him to the telephone directories, and, *finally*, to a number worth trying. He paid up and went in search of food – it was afternoon already and he dimly realised he'd not gone back to check on Amanjit, or taken him a coffee. But he had the scent in his nostrils. He couldn't stop now.

He ordered a beer and a thali and while he waited, he thumbed his telephone and heard it connect.

A phone rang, thousands of miles away.

'Hello?' A woman's voice: English, middle-aged perhaps. She sounded bleary – it was only eight o'clock in the morning in England, he realised guiltily.

He tried his best to keep his accent neutral. 'Hello, madam,' he said in his best schoolboy English, although he'd not been back to Britain for some years. 'Is this the house of Timothy Alexander Southby, please?'

He could picture the woman blinking slowly. 'Mister Southby is my grandfather-in-law,' the woman responded eventually, her voice a trifle wary. 'What's this about, please?'

*She said 'is', not 'was'*, he thought with a flare of hope. 'Mrs Southby? Mrs June Southby?'

'Yes. What is it you want, please?' she repeated, sounding worried.

'Madam, may I speak to Mister Timothy Southby, please.'

'I'm sorry, that's impossible.'

*Oh no – he's dead after all. Or in a coma, or . . .* 'How is that, madam?'

'He is away on holiday,' she replied. 'In India.'

Vikram's eyes flew open. *Thank you, every god, thank you!* 'I am calling from India, madam.'

'I could tell by your voice that was where you were calling from,' she said, more warmly. 'I was worried when I heard your accent that you were phoning with bad news. We didn't want him to travel, but the old duffer insisted. So Mike – that's his grandson, my husband, went with him.'

'No, there is no problem, madam. I'm related to someone who knew him when he was a photographer in the Indus Valley. I was hoping to talk with him. But maybe I can even meet with him?'

'I can't see any problem with that. Tim loves to talk about the old days. I'll get you the number.'

'Hello? This is Timothy Southby.' The voice was quivery, frail.

*He must be in his eighties, at least*, Vikram thought, *but it's definitely him*. He felt a sudden glow and his eyes stung. *Timothy-sahib*.

He felt his voice begin to break and struggled to speak. The boy from his least significant life was weeping inside him. 'Mister Southby, sir – you don't know me. But I'm related to someone who knew you, a long, long time ago. His name was Ramesh, and he was a chai-wallah at the archaeological dig in Harappa, in the spring of 1947.'

# CHAPTER TWENTY

# TIM-SAHIB

*Ayodhya, Uttar Pradesh, June 2011*

They met in the north a week later. Vikram and Amanjit retraced their journey back, veering eastwards and crossing Uttar Pradesh, sleeping in cheap hotels and eating at roadside joints to avoid attention, although the media frenzy over the murder of Sunita Ashoka was dying away. Everyone believed Vikram had fled the country.

The new story currently filling the papers was of the latest ambush of the military in the northeast. More soldiers dead: isolated patrols wiped out and their weaponry taken. What was puzzling everyone was that none of the known insurgent factions were claiming responsibility, which they were seldom slow to do – oddly, they were completely denying involvement. Was a new terror organisation emerging?

Trains were guarded and military checkpoints proliferated as Vikram and Amanjit got closer to Ayodhya, in Uttar Pradesh: the legendary city where Rama was born;

the place where Valmiki was said to have begun composing the *Ramayana*. Tim Southby was staying there with an old friend, he'd told Vikram.

Modern Ayodhya wasn't very modern: a sleepy place on the banks of the wide Saryu River, *lost in the past*, Vikram thought as he walked the streets, trying to reconcile it with anything at all in his mind. He'd been here before, in past lives, seeking clues and finding nothing.

There were Jain temples and a Muslim masjid, but this was primarily a Hindu town. Long ago, Muslims had constructed a mosque over a Hindu mandir. It was an inflammatory enough move following conquest, but more recently, Hindu scholars had claimed that the site was the site of Rama's birth and the mosque had been wrecked in 1992, replaced by a makeshift Hindu shrine. Then in 2005, Muslim fundamentalists had retaliated by attacking that shrine, and been gunned down after setting off a bomb. Now it was guarded by soldiers and a maze of barbed wire – all to protect a tiny idol visitors couldn't get within twenty yards of.

It was an embodiment of all that was wrong with the world, Vikram decided, thinking of all the religious wars he has seen down the years and wishing most devoutly for impossible things like peace and fellowship.

Timothy Southby and his grandson Michael were staying at the house of one Varun Kapoor, a historian from the Historical Society of India. The house was behind Naya Ghat, near the river, surrounded by a stone wall topped with jagged glass and barbed wire; there were guards at the gates.

Varun Kapoor was apologetic about his security. 'I have

been outspoken at times,' he said as he greeted Amanjit and Vikram. 'I make enemies just by opening my mouth.'

'Then you must be related to Amanjit,' Vikram grinned.

Amanjit punched him on the arm gently. 'Vikram lets his mouth get him into trouble too, as you can see,' he laughed. He'd been in a better humour since Vikram's memory had rekindled hope.

Varun Kapoor chuckled gently. He was a tiny man with white hair sprouting from the back and sides of his skull, in stark contrast to his bald pate that was darkly tanned and spotted with age. He walked with a limp. 'Come, come. This way. Timothy awaits you.'

Vikram felt a small *frisson* of remembrance, hearing the name.

Varun led them through an untidy house full of mementoes from all over the world. 'So much junk, eh?' The historian waved a negligent hand about him. 'My "dust collectors", I call them.' He paused in front of a crude bronze piece: a dancing girl. 'This is from Harappa,' he remarked, picking it up tenderly and handing it to Vikram. 'No, it's not the famous dancing girl statue that everyone studies, but a lesser version we found. I kept this one secretly – a little naughty, I know, but there wasn't much goodwill at the dig when they finally reopened it. Too many memories.'

Then he opened the door and Vikram followed him into a room where an ancient European man was seated on a cane chair, staring out of the window, through the trees towards where the river gleamed. He wore an old-fashioned tie, a plaid jacket and flannel trousers, despite the heat. Vikram glimpsed aluminium where the ankle should be, the only visible evidence of the Englishman's missing leg.

'Timothy-sahib?' he blurted, the years washing away in an instant.

Southby blinked. 'I've not been called that since . . .' He swallowed, then extended a sun-blistered, finely wrinkled hand. His face was leathery, his thin hair white. 'I'm Tim Southby. You must be Vikram?'

'Yes, sir. And this is my friend Amanjit.'

Southby shook their hands, then introduced a sporty-looking thirty-something Englishman, who'd been sitting in the corner reading a newspaper. 'This is my grandson, Michael. He has no interest in history or archaeology at all, do you, Mike?'

He grinned. 'If it doesn't involve a ball and a bat, it's not worth knowing, is it?'

The two old historians rolled their eyes at each other. 'The younger generation, eh? A lost cause.' Varun winked at Vikram. 'Excepting yourselves, my young sirs.'

'Absolutely, sir. I am a keen student of history and—'

'—and I'm a keen student of cricket,' Amanjit put in. 'This is more Vikram's scene than mine.' He bobbed his heads towards the two old men and backed away, then turned to Michael. 'Do you follow the IPL?' he asked.

Michael Southby grinned. 'Of course, although I'm more a Test man myself.' He shook Amanjit's hand solemnly and suggested, 'Shall we go into the lounge? It's the third day of the Australian Test; we can leave the old-at-heart in peace.'

They exited, already chatting cricket, and as they pulled

the door shut behind them, Vikram took a deep breath and tried to order his thoughts.

Tim Southby smiled at Vikram. '"Old-at-heart". Is that what you are, young Vikram?'

*Older than you could ever realise.* 'I don't mind the phrase, sir. In fact, I rather like it.'

'You don't mind us speaking in English? My Hindi is very rusty these days.'

He hid a smile. *It was never really that good anyway, Tim-sahib.* 'I grew up in England, sir, although I was born here in India. We only returned a couple of years ago.'

'And how are you related to poor young Ramesh?' Tim Southby asked.

Vikram gave him the fiction he'd invented on the journey here: that Ramesh's family, cousins of his father's, had fled Pakistan after the raids by the Muslim National Guard and settled in Rajasthan. 'What happened at the site, sir, when the Muslim National Guard came?'

Tim Southby related in hushed tones what he recalled of that awful day, and when he was done, they sat in silence for some minutes. Vikram had to fight down a rush of nausea. His own memories were very shaky, but he could still remember Mehtan Ali – Ravindra, of course – driving in those spears, first piercing poor Kamila, while they made him watch, and then into him . . .

'I wish I could give you some comfort, young man,' Tim Southby said softly, 'but your cousin Ramesh and his friend, that poor little girl, died horribly.'

*Kamila must have been Kamla reborn,* Vikram thought sadly, which made him wonder where Sue Parker was. He brought his mind back to the matter at hand. 'Sir, I knew that Ramesh was killed that day. I thank you for the details.'

'Don't be carrying anger in your heart, young man,' Varun Kapoor put in. 'It was long ago. There are many such stories, too many, but gradually they are laid aside. Prolonging a vendetta solves nothing.'

Vikram thought about Ravindra and vendettas that last for millennia, but he shook his head dutifully and promised, 'I'm not here seeking fuel for a fire. All I seek is knowledge.'

'Then it is my privilege to be of assistance.' Tim Southby's voice was filled with emotion; he looked as if those dangling, impaled bodies haunted him still.

Vikram took a deep breath and turned to Varun. 'Sir, one of my studies in university is the *Ramayana*. What do you think about the epic? Is it a true history? Or something else?'

Varun blinked owlishly. 'No small question that one,' he chuckled. 'How much time do you have?'

'I've wondered whether the epic is linked to the Indus Valley civilisation,' Vikram responded, wanting to narrow the discussion down to Tim Southby's specialist subject. If his brief life in Harappa had any significance at all, then surely Southby's recollections were the key.

Varun glanced at Southby, who was still staring into space. 'Tim, that would be your area, I fancy.'

Despite appearances, the Englishman had heard every word. 'Of course, Ramesh. I'll be happy to tell you what I know and surmise on the subject.'

*Ramesh* . . . Vikram didn't interrupt to correct the name.

Varun offered tea, and while Southby sipped his, collecting his thoughts, Vikram waited patiently until he was ready. Somewhere in the house, a cricket commentator was making terse observations, and he could dimly hear Amanjit and Mike Southby chatting.

Then the old man began to speak. 'The *Ramayana* was probably written around 300BC and no earlier than 400BC. It is said that Valmiki began it right here in Ayodhya, and as Hinduism spread throughout Southeast Asia, so the legends did too, changing as they travelled, although the core of the story always remained the same. Obviously, it looked back to an earlier period – but the problem with mythology is that it is never pure history. Myths usually contain elements of allegory – for example, an elephant can symbolise all manner of things, or it can simply be an elephant. Myths can tell convenient lies: they can convey a claim to territory by pretending that a certain tribe had always held those lands, or justify the imposition of a law or a ruler or a religion. And phrases can mean many things. How literally do we take phrases like "son of God", for example? All myths contain such problems. But raising questions about them can be dangerous, as myths also encapsulate things that are important to the people that propagated them. Varun here is a good example – his article about the history of Ayodhya has brought threats upon his life from all sides – because he told too many truths and questioned too many vested interests.'

'No one likes the truth,' Varun put in wryly. 'We only want stories we agree with.'

Vikram rested his chin on his hand, thinking about that, but Southby went on in his dry, conversational tone, 'Just to complicate things further, myth can also contain aspects of ritual – a myth about a man killing his father and sleeping with his mother might be taken literally, or it might be conveying some moral message, or be referring to a ritual of inheritance – or all three. That's why any interpretation of mythology is a minefield.

'So, on to the *Ramayana*: was it real, you ask? Was Rama born a few yards away here in Ayodhya? Was there really even a Rama at all? Well, I can tell you that *no one* can claim categorical knowledge – they can choose only to believe or disbelieve. What *I* have come to believe is that there may have been, which is a limp kind of answer, I grant you, but there's so little reliable evidence. Those who say that all the evidence is in the sacred text are blinding themselves to what these texts are: I call them collective cultural memory repositories.

'So what would Valmiki have had to look back on, in 400BC? Well, the earliest civilisation in India was the Harappan or Indus Valley culture, which existed from approximately 3000-1500BC. It was quite advanced, certainly for its time – and for later times too. It ended when the Indus Valley lost the capacity to support life in the numbers it had, probably due to a combination of over-farming and the rivers drying up – we now think localised earthquakes may have changed the river courses. For years we reckoned there was some "Aryan invasion", but the archaeology doesn't support this theory; it's more likely the people gave up the now arid lands and instead were absorbed into the more backward Suryavansha tribes to the east who inhabited the Ganges river plains. It's possible that the *Ramayana* chronicles this fall-out from natural disaster, and perhaps some undocumented military actions that took place during this late Harappan period. Perhaps "Ravana" was the last King of the Harappans. But it's no more than speculation.'

*Damned good speculation, perhaps,* Vikram thought excitedly.

'Others place the *Ramayana* in the later, post-Harappan, "Vedic" period,' Southby went on. 'After the fall of Harappa, new kingdoms were founded, wars were fought, alliances made and broken. The kidnapping of Sita may be a romanticised "Helen of Troy" story used to justify a campaign in South India – at the time, the south drew its influences – and possibly its bloodlines – from East Africa, not the north. You'll remember the *Ramayana*'s subhuman race of "monkeys" – that's describing the people of the south, and a hint that the northern inhabitants of the sub-continent did not believe that they shared ancestry with the southern peoples.'

'So Lanka was Sri Lanka then?' Vikram asked, as the old man paused.

'Here we go,' Varun laughed. 'You shouldn't ask old heretics like us such questions, young man.'

Tim Southby turned back to Vikram, clearly animated by the topic, which made him look years younger. 'Harappan culture didn't spread into the south, Vikram. Even the Vedic period barely touched the south; really, we have to wait until the Mauryan Empire to see northern influences in south India. But unless Valmiki wrote the *Ramayana* a lot later than we think, the Mauryan Empire came afterwards.'

'So you're saying that the *Ramayana* could be relating events of the Harappan *or* the Vedic periods?' Vikram wanted to be certain he'd understood what the historians were suggesting.

'Or it may be entirely fable,' Varun interjected.

'But if it concerns the Harappan period,' Tim Southby went on, overriding his friend with a smile, 'then it's likely to have taken place entirely in that region. Only if it relates to the Vedic period would "Lanka" be Sri Lanka, even though that's traditionally what's believed.'

Vikram remembered the power of the myths that had ensnared them at Vibhishana's court. 'But you don't think so, do you, sir?'

'A perceptive fellow, this,' Varun said to Southby. 'He can read you like a book, Tim.'

'Varun thinks that because I'm obsessed with Harappan culture, I want to site everything within its bounds. It's true we scholars are prone to this – we want everything important to fall within our sphere of expertise. Of course, Varun has the same fault,' he added slyly.

Varun slapped his thigh, grinning merrily, as if this were an old joke they both enjoyed.

Vikram waited patiently, and was rewarded as Tim Southby grew serious again. 'Well, young man, if you want my view, the *Ramayana* is based entirely within the Indus Valley, and it is concerned with the end phase of that civ- ilisation. Ravana is associated strongly with the area – he wed his wife Mandodari in Mandore, which is in modern Jodhpur, and he is still worshipped there. Virtually all of the early parts of the tale are based in that region, barring those set here in Ayodhya, which are, when you think about it, the parts pertaining to the victors, not the vanquished. So, if the *Ramayana* is about the fall of Harappa, then I believe we can look at the Harappan sites for our alternate "Lanka". To suit the role, it would need to be an island with a large Harappan site on it.'

Vikram stared at him. 'Is there such a place?'

'As it happens, there's a place called Khadir Island, in the Rann of Kutch. It's surrounded by salt-flats in summer which then flood during the monsoon. There's an ancient causeway which still services it, and a large Harappan site was discovered in 1967. Excavations suggest the place was occupied on and off until the late Harappan period, right through to 1200 BC, though it looks like its large-scale population abandoned it in the fifteenth century BC. If I were a betting man, and if such a place exists, that's where I would place my "historic" Lanka.'

*An island. A causeway. An ancient settlement.*

'Where is it, sir?' Vikram blurted. 'What's it called?'

'The locals call it Kotara,' Tim Southby replied. 'The archaeologists called it Dholavira.'

# INTERLUDE

# THE AMBUSH

*Jharkhand, North India, June 2011*

From where he huddled, the soldier could see little except the slash of cloudy sky above. The platoon was working its way northwest along a ravine towards a village reported to have had insurgents looting food and killing wantonly as they'd been passing through. He'd seen the misery these terrorists left behind and he sorely hoped they would still be in the village when his platoon arrived.

Private Suresh Goel, Rifleman of the 3rd Platoon, 2nd Battalion of the Mahar Regiment, was twenty-two years old. A second son with no interest in his father's tailoring business and little formal education – having frittered his schooldays away on cricket and truancy – he had few prospects. He knew he wasn't considered a good catch and he didn't like the girl his father wanted him to marry, so he'd left home at eighteen and joined the army.

They'd been the best four years of Suresh's life. He'd made friends and seen something of India – and he'd even been abroad, thanks to a brief peace-keeping stint in Timor. Sure, it could be boring, but he didn't have to worry about how to earn a living or what to do next when there was always someone to give an order and make up his mind for him. He had money in the bank, two uniforms and his INSAS rifle; the Indian-made variant of the Russian AK-47 was his constant companion. He didn't need much else. He might be small, but he was wiry, fit and strong enough to lug his gear all day and still be up for an evening run. He'd never thought to grow up as a soldier, but now he couldn't imagine anything else.

His platoon consisted of twenty-eight men: three sections of eight riflemen plus a second lieutenant in charge, a sergeant, a radioman and a medic. The undulations of the ravine meant they'd got strung out a little; there was easy walking on a larger path just nine hundred yards to the west, but it would be under observation. The insurgents were accomplished at leaving traps and ambushes and this landscape, with its sheer cliffs and rough hillocks, was a lethal maze. The air was damp and the rains had come early, pouring life into the vegetation, which burst from every nook and cranny and covered the uneven ground. The air was laden with the scent of frangipani and rotting leaves, but despite the rains, the heat was still oppressive, weighing on the air.

Suresh's skin tingled suddenly, as if he'd just received a mild electrical shock. It felt like it had gone pulsing through him and earthed in the mossy boulder he was working his way past. His lungs tightened and for an instant it was hard to breathe. In that same instant the birds fell silent, then lifted into the air in an unnerving whoosh of wings.

He hit the dirt and flicked off the safety on his rifle, calling softly to the man in front, 'Ajit?' Behind him, Altaf, one of that summer's new recruits, was looking about him nervously. Suresh gestured for him to go to ground, then crawled around the boulder.

A repeated clicking noise met his ears and he spotted Ajit, huddled in the undergrowth a few yards ahead, cursing fluently. 'Did you feel that?' he asked Suresh.

'Like electricity?'

Ajit held up the platoon's radio. 'This bloody thing's shorted out.' He screwed up his nose. 'Now the whole thing is dead, like there's no battery.' He reached into a pocket and withdrew a heavy black cartridge. 'Lucky I've got the spare.'

Suresh waved Altaf forward. The young recruit was still edgy, but he started breathing easier as he joined them.

Then they heard a sound like a swooping bird, Ajit gave a strange cough and Suresh turned to see the big man clutching at a long arrow that was jutting from the back of his left shoulder. His pudgy face looked bewildered – he rolled his eyes, and then lost all expression as he slumped over his radio set. The replacement battery fell from his limp grip.

'*Ajit—?*'

More arrows were whipping down from the forested slopes above and Suresh's brain at last caught up with his eyes. He threw himself flat as the big radioman was impaled several times over, and when he took a moment to look back, he could see Altaf was pressed against the boulder while shafts rattled and snapped on the stone. He could hear screams of pain and fear all down the line, and someone shouting orders: '*Return fire: shoot, damn you, shoot!*'

All down the line, the air was filled with battlefield noise, shouts and crying and orders . . . but no actual gunfire, just that terrifying *whoosh* of air and the *thud* of arrows striking flesh.

Suresh wormed into the lee of the boulder beside Altaf, trying to make out targets. He grabbed Altaf's shoulder, about to tell him to retreat and find the next squad, but his frantic instructions fell on deaf ears: the boy slid down the boulder and hit the ground, two arrows in his back.

*They're on both sides!*

Suresh wriggled deeper into the undergrowth as deep, throaty calls, sounding more like hunting tigers than men, echoed from high above. He peered between two boulders to see fantastical shapes detaching themselves from the deep green foliage: big men in some kind of costume, with horned helmets and demonic face-masks . . . one appeared clearly, forty yards above him, making no effort to conceal himself, as if he held the soldiers below in complete contempt.

Army discipline took over: Suresh lifted his rifle, locked it on single shot and sighted through the telescopic lens. The face mask was hideously real-looking, all craggy leathery jowls and curling ram horns; even the teeth looked life-like, long and yellowed rows of jagged malice. As if it weren't a mask at all.

He pulled the trigger.

The gun clicked impotently.

The masked insurgent heard, and its bestial face turned his way.

*New Delhi, June 2011*

The general acknowledged the young secretary who was holding open the door and entered the office beyond. It was smaller than most people expected, as was the figure behind the desk: a little Sikh man with a gentle face.

'General, thank you for coming,' the Sikh said politely.

'Prime Minister,' the general said, reaching for more but finding no words. He was no politician, full of slick phrases and platitudes; he was an old bear, a veteran who'd seen real service, real combat against Pakistan in '71. He'd been young then, and had risen far.

He'd never been this frightened.

'What's the news, General?' the Prime Minister asked as he motioned him to a small couch against a wall full of photographs of world leaders and diplomats. What would great men like Gandhi and Nehru make of his news?

'Another company completely destroyed, Prime Minister – wiped out to the last man.'

The Prime Minister closed his eyes, wincing in pain. 'Where?'

'In Jharkhand. We've lost more than sixty men in seven different incidents over the last two months, but this is the worst.'

'And it's the same people?'

'We presume so: everyone was slain by primitive weapons and not one of our men fired a shot. We've had the science boys in; they're pretty sure both weapons and radios were rendered inert prior to contact.'

'And no survivors at all?'

'None, sir. They've all been shot with arrows or hacked apart with bladed weapons and there's been no trace left of the perpetrators except their spent arrows.' In despair, he said, 'We're under attack, Prime Minister. India is under attack.'

The Prime Minister stared past him, trembling visibly, but his voice remained composed. 'Has anyone claimed responsibility? The Maoists? The Naxalites? Islamic extremists? My God, is it *Hindu* extremists?'

'There's been nothing, sir. Nothing, except . . .' His voice trailed off miserably.

'Except?'

He leaned forward. 'Sir, we have kept this fact from the media, although it has not been easy. Every corpse has been branded – after death.'

'What sort of brand?' His face was ashen.

'Ancient symbols, sir, burned into the flesh of our dead soldiers. We've contacted the archaeological departments of the university for a translation. Sir, the brands use an alphabet that predates India itself; the scholars think it might translate as "Sons of Ravan".'

The old man put a hand to his own throat. 'Sons of Ravan?'

The general bowed his head apologetically. 'Yes, Prime Minister.' He tugged on his moustache. 'Sir, I don't know what we are dealing with. They can destroy us at will. We cannot appear to even *hurt* them, let alone stop them. If some demand is received . . .'

The old man bowed his head, considering that. Then slowly he straightened and rose. Coming around the table, he said, 'We'll deal with that if and when it happens,

General. Until that time, we go on. Investigate every lead: this is the age of forensics and digital surveillance – they'll have left some trace. And stay strong – tell your staff that. We're under attack, but we remain strong, General.'

'Prime Minister, they're attacking us with impunity. We don't even know who they are. I – we – feel so helpless.'

The Prime Minister laid his hand on the general's shoulder. 'A way will be found, General. We are India. We have endured all manner of crises before. We'll endure this one as well.'

# PART TWO
# TO REIGN IN LANKA

# CHAPTER TWENTY-ONE

## FALLING

*Lanka, July 2011*

Rasita faced Lavanasura, raised her hands and made an elaborate flowing gesture, a lot like dancing. But she wasn't dancing: she was marking out the three-dimensional space in which she would perform her next task. Faint vapour-trails of light streamed from her hands, leaving a large transparent sphere in the air before her, pulsing in time to her heartbeat.

'That is good, Rani,' lisped the reptilian rakshasa. 'My Rani is skilled, yes.' His multifaceted eyes reflected dozens of tiny images of her. His tail flicked about restlessly. 'Now the next step, please.'

Frowning, she pulled everything she had been doing that morning into her mind – the hours spent caressing the stem of the frangipani tree, letting her consciousness feel the way the roots and stem were created, how it existed, pumping its water, processing the light and heat, feeding its growth. She still could not have named the parts of the plant, nor said how it functioned . . . but somehow she just *knew*: she'd *experienced* it. And now, within the sphere, she called it back into being.

It was a month since Lavanasura had begun to formally teach her how to use the powers she'd manifested. It was intense, demanding all of her being, the outpourings of energy leaving her shaking. But it was also easy; it seemed to come naturally. Nothing that Lavanasura had demanded had proved beyond her – provided she gave it her all.

Within the hollow sphere, the skin of the bubble began to slowly flow into the middle in long arcing flows, like a galaxy forming, or a spray of surf on the wave of a beach. It swirled into the heart of the sphere, and began to metamorphose into a delicate structure: spindling branches and fraying roots that grew imperceptibly yet inexorably into the recognisable shape of a tree.

With a faint smile, she made it flower. The heady scent flowed outwards through the bubble and into the garden. With her free hand she made a digging gesture – only realising partway through that this was indeed an arm, made of spirit flesh, which startled her. The whole sphere wobbled, then somehow she rallied and went on using the spirit hand – no, *hands*; there were *two* of them – to dig a hole. She conjured water into the hole, and then gently lowered the sphere.

With a final contortion of arms and hands, she laid the plant into the ground, packed the earth about it and released the sphere. Her skin was slick, her lip swollen and painful where she had bitten it, and her limbs felt hollow. The extra pair of arms she'd manifested dissipated, and she gazed up at what she'd done.

The newly grown frangipani tree was about twenty feet tall. It was covered in flowers, and looked like it had been there for years. It was a thrill to see it, despite the sudden weakness that overcame her after the task.

Lavanasura clapped his hands. His reptile face didn't really do expressions, at least not ones she could recognise, but his neck-ruff had gone pinkish, a sure sign of pleasure. 'Splendid, Rani! Superb!'

Another pair of hands joined the applause and she turned to see Ravindra leaning against the wall. She wondered how long he'd been there and was suddenly conscious of the way her sari clung to her sweating body. He was clad in pantaloons and an open shirt and looked barbarically magnificent.

'Well done,' he said in his musical voice. It held something of longing, almost envy. His own powers were caught in the aspect of Destruction, she reminded herself, so everything she could do was beyond him, and all his rakshasas: they'd all been imbued with power by Aeshwaran and Halika, so except for a rare few like Lavanasura, Destruction was all they knew.

'You steadied me, just at the end,' she acknowledged, caught between annoyance and gratitude.

'I saw you realise that you'd manifested spirit flesh unknowingly and that it had thrown you off-balance. It was a small thing – you will know to expect it in future.' He stepped towards her, a handkerchief appearing in his hand, and wiped blood from her cut lip. He sniffed it with a small shudder, a gesture that made her shiver. Just at times, he revealed his nature, frightening her just when she was beginning to feel at ease.

*I relax too much around him now. He is not my friend, he is my Enemy. I forget that too easily.*

He looked up at the tree, nodding appreciatively. 'It is always humbling to see someone do something that I cannot,' he said eventually. 'You make rapid progress, Rasita.'

His praise made her uneasy, because she enjoyed it. 'It feels natural,' she admitted.

'In all of your past lives, you've been less than whole. Now you're nearly complete.'

'I feel whole already.' She thought about that. 'Almost.'

'Almost.' The word meant different things in his mouth.

She faced him, hands on hips. 'I won't let you kill Deepika, even if it makes me what you call whole.'

'She's already dead, Rasita. When her ghost returns, you will drink it in, as you did the other queens, and then you will finally be Manda again – and Deepika will be alive inside you.' He put a hand on hers and she forgot to pull away, she was listening so hard. 'Do you remember what it felt like, when your souls were reunited: Sunita Ashoka and Rasita Kaur Bajaj? Are you truly now one or other of those women? No, you are someone new. A fractured soul partially heals, like a lizard grows a new tail to replace the old, but it's never perfect – not the way you will be. When your last two souls unite and you are Manda complete again, then you will know what it means to truly be alive.'

Rasita remembered that shuddering, dying-alive feeling as Sunita and she became one – and he was right: she was neither Sunita nor Rasita any more, but someone new – someone who also had Halika, Aruna and Jyoti inside her, with all their lusts and desires for this man. That joining had been like waking up after spending her life half-asleep; like recovering from a dreadful sickness. It had been revelation and enlightenment, and now she was finding herself saying or doing something the old Rasita would *never* have done.

'You said that you summoned her months ago,' she mused aloud.

'Yes, these things take time. Deepika's spirit will be moving at walking pace. I sense her vaguely at times.' He frowned. 'But it is still taking too long.' He touched her swollen lip. 'Lavanasura will tend your mouth.'

She flinched at his touch, although it was gentle. His face filled her vision and she felt herself overcome by a sudden desire to have those hands touch her more intimately still. She fought the urge down with difficulty, and he saw.

'You know, there's now enough of Manda in you that I see her reaching for me,' he said. 'Do you remember any of your life as her?'

She felt a quiver of fright at the thought. *Not more memories – I can scarcely deal with those I have.* She stepped away before she lost control and fell into him. Putting on her mask of defiance again, she said, 'You're taking a risk, Ravan. You're training me, but I'm not your ally. I'm *not* your Manda.'

'No, not yet,' he agreed. 'Not yet.'

Someone knocked, and at Ravindra's summons, the hunch-backed, tiger-headed Syhajeet entered. 'My Lord, your sister has returned.' He gave Ras a surly look; he still didn't trust her.

Ravindra looked grim. 'About time. Rasita, I must attend upon her,' he apologised, as if she would miss his presence.

*Surpanakha* . . . Keke had told her Ravindra's sister had

returned to Mumbai to monitor her mother's court cases. 'May I come with you?' she asked, hoping to glean news of her family.

Ravindra hesitated, then shrugged. 'My sister isn't a pretty sight these days, not after what Deepika Choudhary did to her. But if you wish it, you may accompany me.'

He led her down yet more corridors she'd never seen, past armed guards and into a suite of rooms that she thought must be his private domain. The room of green marble overlooked a small garden filled with ivy-covered trellises. The lighting was poor, but it was refreshingly cool. A single long table was set with a dozen chairs, with a throne at the window-end. Ravindra walked past it to the window, where there was a small seat, and indicated Rasita should sit there – then lowered himself beside her, an imposition of intimacy that made her skin prickle.

A moment later, Surpanakha was shown in.

The demoness was in the guise of Meenakshi Nandita, the lawyer who'd betrayed Rasita's mother. She was wrapped in a thick sari, with a blanket over that, as if she were suffering from the cold, and walked as if she were crippled. Surpanakha was Ravana's sister in the legends, and maybe she really was a blood relative – it wasn't clear from Ravindra's tales or Halika's memories how rakshasa kinship actually worked.

Surpanakha was clearly not pleased to see Rasita. 'What's *she* doing here?'

'Rasita is my queen,' Ravindra replied simply. 'Rejoice, sister.'

The rakshasa looked as much horrified as stunned. 'Then she has . . . ? Have you—?'

'I would have thought you would be pleased that my queen was whole,' Ravindra observed coldly. 'But no, we have not yet reached that stage.' He raised his hand and the blanket and sari flew apart, leaving Surpanakha wrapped only in a thin undergarment. She buried her face in a curtain of hair.

Rasita gasped. Surpanakha's left leg had been bent brutally, and she could see blood and pus still oozing from a dozen gashes on her thighs and arms. The rest of the illusions surrounding her dissolved, revealing her true form: a battered hag with bestial ears and hands and ape-like arms trailing to the ground. Most horribly, her nose had been cut off right down to the bones of her skull. The loose skin at the edge of the holes flapped wetly as she breathed.

Rasita turned her face away, fighting the urge to vomit.

'The Darya made a mess of you, sister,' Ravindra commented.

'Please, brother,' Surpanakha begged, 'do not shame me like this.' She jabbed a finger at Ras. 'Especially not before her.' She conjured her Meenakshi guise again, humiliation clear on her face.

Ravindra leaned forward. 'Report. How did the court case fare?'

Surpanakha cowered. 'Badly, brother. The Bharata betrayed us, as you feared. The case fell apart.'

Rasita had to quell the urge to punch the air in joy.

'Good,' Ravindra said, surprising her. 'It wasn't necessary that Charanpreet and Tanita were victorious. This victory is a further sign that the epic is asserting itself in our favour.'

He put his hand on top of Rasita's. 'I'm pleased that your mother has this comfort, Rasita.'

Surpanakha eyed her brother's hand sourly and Ras wondered why. *Is she jealous of his affections?*

The demoness bowed her head. 'Lord, I have further bad news. Your son Prahasta is dead.' Rasita heard a touch of malice in her voice. 'He became cocky, exposed himself and was shot.'

Ravindra bowed his head abruptly and Rasita had to stop herself squeezing his hand in comfort.

*What am I thinking? I should be rejoicing — I should be taunting him . . . But this place isn't like I thought it would be . . . and neither is he . . .*

Ravindra seemed to her to be a tragic lost soul, compelled to act in violence first, constantly left to pick up his own wreckages and try to repair them. The old tale slipped into her mind, of the monster who could be healed only by true love's kiss . . .

*Dear Gods, is that my destiny?*

'His body?' Ravindra asked eventually.

'I couldn't recover it,' Surpanakha replied. 'He was my favourite. I mourn for him, and for you.'

Ravindra's face hardened. 'Your relationship with him never won my approval, sister. You led him down paths he should never have walked. Now leave us — find Lavanasura and see if he can ease your wounds.'

Surpanakha glared back at him, then she looked at Ras. 'Yes, my Lord Brother — but allow me to escort the rani back to her rooms.' Her eyes conveyed something, but Ras had no idea what.

'Rasita can find her own way,' Ravindra told her. 'I'm sure she doesn't want *you* for company.'

They exchanged sour looks, then Surpanakha limped away, wheezing painfully.

'Deepika Choudhary wielded pure destructive energy,' Ravindra said. 'It may be that Surpanakha's wounds can never be healed. Lavanasura is a creator, but his powers are weak. He may offer some temporary alleviation at best, but frankly, the only person capable of healing her is you.'

'Are you asking that of me?' she asked, surprised. She loathed Surpanakha, but it hurt her to see someone in such pain, even such a monster who'd tried to kill her friends and destroy her family.

He placed his hand over hers. 'You are a good spirit, Rasita, but stay away from her: she means you ill.'

His face was painfully close to hers and her whole body felt dangerously hollow and unsteady. 'I have to go,' she whispered. *Before . . .*

She went to rise, but his eyes followed hers. The shoulder fold of her sari slipped down her arm. Her breasts felt full and painful, straining at the fabric of her bodice. Her stomach clenched, her legs were hollow and trembling. He leaned in and kissed her parted lips, then locked onto her, breathing through her. Almost without volition, her arms wrapped about him as his hands explored her bare shoulder and drifted down to her bodice. His mouth tasted sweet, with a lingering hint of tobacco. He smelled of tension and desire.

'Mmm,' she heard herself groan, deep in her throat. '*Uh . . .*'

One hand slid down her back, fingering the lacing, and she sighed, accepting the inevitable as she felt her whole body surrender in his arms. His tongue invaded her mouth, probing and coiling slickly about hers.

'Brother,' Surpanakha's voice wheedled across the shadowy room—

—and Ravindra *erupted* in fury, throwing Rasita against the wall as he rose and crossed the room in a heartbeat. He struck his sister's pulverised face, a ringing backhanded blow, sending her reeling to the floor.

'How *dare* you!' he stormed, looking as if he was about to lash out again.

'I'm sorry, brother,' Surpanakha whined, 'I'm sorry. I didn't think—'

Suddenly Ravindra must have realised what this violence would look like to Rasita. In an instant, he was kneeling at Rasita's feet and pleading, 'My Queen, I'm sorry – I'm so sorry. The shock, my need . . . I lost control. I swear it won't happen again – I *swear* it!'

Rasita looked down at him, her heart palpitating, her skin still quivering at the touch of his hands, her mouth still alive to his taste. She pulled her hand from his grip and stood unsteadily.

*I came so close.*

'Don't go,' he begged her. 'Stay – please—'

'I can't,' she whispered.

'*See how I am,*' he said. 'I am a wounded thing, wounded more deeply than even my sister – and you can heal me with your love!'

'I can't — it's too much,' Rasita whispered. 'You want too much.'

He grabbed her knees. 'Not too much, my love — not to you.'

*I could stay — and I want to. I could give him everything he wants, and take what I want. No one would ever know . . . Vikram has already betrayed me, so why should I hold back? I will be his Manda, and have power like a goddess and a throne to sit upon and a kingdom of wonders to rule . . .*

But she remembered that glimpse of his inner rage and it quelled any desire she felt.

For now.

*I could love him. When he kissed me I could see him as his Manda must have seen him. I felt her memories queuing up inside my head.*

She pushed these thoughts away. *But not now . . . His violence is too great and it scares me. There's too much going on.*

'I'm sorry,' she breathed, although she wasn't sure what she meant by the words, and fled the room. The crawling Surpanakha whimpered something after her, but she couldn't tell what. She thought Ravindra would attack his sister again and almost longed to see this vicious creature get what she deserved . . . but then she was relieved when he didn't.

She was glad to regain the relative safety of her own room, to close it all out.

*Dear Gods*, she pleaded, *please give me a sign! What is it you want from me?*

Dusshera was only weeks away and she could scarcely remember Vikram's face.

# CHAPTER TWENTY-TWO

# HEMANT'S PEOPLE

*The Rann of Kutch, Gujarat, late July 2011*

They rode their motorbikes cautiously through marshland on a rutted gravel road that gradually started to rise. Vikram's whole body ached; these roads required total concentration. He was longing for the journey's end – and a wash; he'd spent the day riding in a fug of Amanjit's dust.

He suddenly realised that Amanjit was braking at the top of the rise; as he skidded to a halt, Vikram slowed and drew up alongside him.

Amanjit removed his helmet, revealing a sweaty bandanna; his normal full turban was too bulky for a helmet. 'I think we're getting close,' he called above the rumbling engines. He'd trimmed his beard and his regrowing hair was spiky now, recovering from the indignity of being shaved off. He looked full of grim purpose as he added, 'We'd better be in the right place this time, bhai,'

Vikram removed his own helmet. His lank, damp hair was

caught in a topknot. 'No guarantees, man,' he said, adding, 'but I'm sure – totally sure.'

They'd been winding westwards through north India for days until they'd crossed Rajasthan and into Gujarat. The journey was nearly complete; the final confrontation awaited them.

'That guest house should be about another mile on,' Amanjit said, looking at his mobile GPS. He pulled off his bandanna and wiped his brow, then peered ahead at the long dirt road carving through the empty coastal plains of Gujarat. 'That last place was Rapar, so as long as we took the right road out, we're nearly there.'

Indian sign-posting was notoriously bad and they'd already lost at least a day to wrongly marked turn-offs. 'Let's hope so,' Vikram breathed.

The Rann of Kutch, the salt desert on the Pakistan border that descended to marsh and occasionally water during the monsoon, as it was right now, spread about them in every direction. They'd been warned that if they strayed off the main road, the military would show up – running into a tank and getting blown up wasn't the end of the quest that Vikram had in mind.

They were about to remount when Amanjit, who'd been looking around, pointed back over his shoulder and exclaimed, 'Hey, look at that!'

Vikram saw a small lake covered with vivid pink birds. *Flamingos*. There were hundreds of them, some swirling elegantly above while others swooped into graceless landings, making the rest turn their heads in withering disapproval.

'Wow,' Amanjit breathed eventually. 'Did we bring a decent camera?'

'Nope. We're going to war, not a National Geographic photoshoot,' Vikram replied dryly. 'But we'll come back some time as tourists.'

They could almost pretend they were the only people in the world. The land undulated, rocky outcroppings giving way to rough soil, then turning marshy again. Thorn bushes clung tenaciously to cracks and crevices and sheltered the occasional fox, peering from the shade they provided. From time to time they spotted distant herds of the native wild asses, and Amanjit thought he'd glimpsed a tiny antelope at one point.

The air was hot and humid, with only a few impotent clouds above. They had left Ayodhya three weeks ago. The main roads were teeming with military, apparently hunting for a terrorist group called 'The Sons of Ravana'. The papers were all over this new radical Hindu group, although their aims remained unknown. Surprise checkpoints had been set up everywhere, which might have made clandestine travel difficult, but no one was really interested in Vikram Khandavani right now and so far they'd managed to avoid recognition. Now those should be behind them; the Rann of Kutch was one of the most isolated and sparsely populated regions in all of India.

There were still villages, of course, peopled as much by Muslim drovers as Hindu small businessmen and their families. A devastating earthquake a few years ago had left many ruined buildings on the fringes of the tiny settlements. The people were Meghwal, descendants of ancient bloodlines, small-built, wearing traditional vibrant colours. The married women sported nose-rings of gold and silver necklets.

Vikram wondered whether they had their own *Ramayana* stories, but he didn't stop to enquire. 'Let's go. I want to get there before dark so we can settle in and look around. We shouldn't be far from the causeway to Khadir Island.'

'Which may or may not have been built by Hanuman and his monkeys,' Amanjit commented. He was still gazing at the swirling flock of flamingos. 'Dee would love this,' he murmured. The worry in his voice was plain; they'd heard nothing further from her since the gunfight in Mumbai.

*If she's even alive* ... The thought came unbidden, and Vikram didn't voice it.

They rode on until they found themselves quite suddenly at the eastern end of a long causeway fenced with a low barrier of modern concrete dividing land from water. In the distance they could see the island. There was no one in sight except for an old man on a bicycle that looked like it was made of rust.

As they stopped for water, Vikram said, 'This is pure white salt in the dry season. Dead flat, goes on for ever. You can drive on it – I saw a documentary a few years ago.'

Amanjit was staring at the island. 'Lanka,' he breathed.

Vikram yawned wearily. 'It'd better be. I feel like we're running out of time,' he admitted.

'We've got all the time it takes, Vik. Ras is strong: she won't let you down.'

They crossed the causeway and onto the island, a rough landscape, drier than any they'd yet seen other than the heart of the Thar Desert. Tiny farmsteads struggled against the pitiless elements, but at least early monsoon rainfall had settled the dust and there were flashes of green here and there.

They found the government tourist resort, the Torun, and a well-paved, clean-looking motel with cylindrical Kutch-style huts of concrete, but thatched in the traditional style. The owner, happy to have any guests out-of-season, didn't look at their papers, so there was no need for Vikram's subtle manipulations. His wife cooked them a chicken biryani and as they didn't have the required permit to drink alcohol – Gujarat was a dry state – she brought cold nimbu-pani; the lime soda was the perfect quencher after hours of road dust. They reasoned it was good for them to stay sober if they were going into battle.

'Cheers, bhai,' Amanjit toasted, when the tired-faced woman had gone. 'To Dee and Ras,' he added as they clinked glasses. 'Hey, I was meaning to ask: did you have a snoop around the mythic side of Ayodhya when we were there?'

Vikram shook his head. 'After Sri Lanka, I didn't want to risk it. Sri Lanka and Ayodhya are the two known sites most connected to the *Ramayana* and Sri Lanka turned out to be a death trap. I think in Ayodhya I might have run the risk of meeting some myth-land version of myself who might have seen me as an interloper and tried to kill me. You'd have likely had the same problem.'

'Yikes,' Amanjit said, with a low whistle. 'Of course, I could thrash a low-rent version of myself any day, but I could see you might have a problem.' He grinned and gulped down his soda.

Vikram glanced towards the motel gates – and stared.

There was a small man there, studying them intently. He seemed to have something on his shoulders – but he scampered away as soon as he realised he'd been seen.

*Someone was looking out for us . . . and now they know we're here . . .*

They rode out to the old Dholavira archaeological site at dawn, hoping to look it over while no one else was around. They slipped through the fence at the edges of the site and walked through sparse woodland to the diggings.

The ruins weren't overly impressive to their eyes: just some ancient stepped reservoirs thirty to fifty feet deep, ducted and channelled. The little water that had collected was already green and slimy and covered with clouds of midges and mosquitoes. But the site was half a mile long and nearly as wide, and with a little imagination they could picture a sizable ancient keep and town. A faded information board told them there had been a citadel on the south side with a middle town, and a lower one beneath.

They found a high point in what had been the old citadel. As they stared out at a reservoir, Amanjit asked, 'Hope it's bringing back some of your memories, 'cos it's not doing anything for me.'

Vikram sat and looked across the rough terrain. He'd been prodding with his senses; he knew there was a pocket of myth-land but it was barred to him somehow – the same sort of forbidding that had prevented them from escaping the false Lanka down south. He took that as an encouraging sign: perhaps Ravindra had built in protections to prevent enemies from opening gates into his citadel.

He looked about him, trying to picture the citadel as it had been. Fragments of stone buildings lay half buried, like disturbed graves. The site extended five hundred yards north of where they were sitting, and to either side. 'It must have been a big place.' He peered around, then said, 'This is the highest point, so I reckon the map's right, it's the palace. Then there would have been housing for the regular folks below us, to the north.'

'Correct, more or less,' rasped a strange voice and they both whirled around, Amanjit's hand going straight for his sports bag, where his sword was stashed.

'Peace,' said the voice, and a middle-aged man stepped from the lee of a bush, where he'd been hidden from sight. His skin was almost black, his hands like tooled leather, but his eyes were bright. He was dressed like a labourer, in rags, but his back was straight and his hair was thick and black.

'What are you doing here?' Amanjit asked harshly.

'I could ask you the same,' the man replied dryly. 'I was just enjoying the sunrise. I live over there.' He pointed northeast. 'My people have dwelt on the island for many centuries.'

From the shadows behind him a Langur monkey with sleek grey fur and an inquisitive black face crept out to huddle at his feet, making an almost conversational *chee-chee* sound.

Vikram realised this was the man who'd been spying on them last night. 'Then you would know this place well?' he asked carefully.

'I know it very well indeed.' He sat beside them on a mound of earth and stared out at the sunrise. 'My name is

Hemant. I come here every day, keeping watch.' He ran a curious eye over them. 'The site is not open to tourists until eleven a.m.,' he added.

'This was a Harappan site,' Vikram stated, ignoring the reference to their illegal entry.

'Yes, the old people: the Sinathai.'

'Sindh?'

'No, *Sinathai*: the people of Sinat. Our elders remember. They lived in the city before my people arrived and we served them. Then when the masters went, we remained, while the waters dried up.'

Tim Southby had told him the villagers had moved back into the ruins after the original occupants had abandoned them centuries before. *Is this man and his people descended from those?* 'You must have many stories of this place,' he started. 'And the, um . . . Sinathai?'

'Many. But which tale interests you most, young masters?' He looked pointedly at Amanjit's bag, where the sword hilt was just visible. 'Tales of battle, perhaps?'

They felt a chill, as if destiny had touched them.

'Sure,' Amanjit said. 'Do you know any?'

Hemant met his gaze and stroked the head of the monkey. He had the air of someone who didn't quite believe what was happening to him; Amanjit knew what that was like.

Finally he said, 'The elders say that this place was the last refuge of the Sinathai. They came here, fleeing a great catastrophe – fires in the sky, floods and earthquakes, much devastation – and they were changed into beast-men – demons. *Asura*. Their king led them here. So my people remember.'

Vikram felt as if his heart would stop. 'What happened then?' he asked.

'Men came from the east, years later, hunting the beast-men. They made war on the asura and their king and killed them all. They freed the slaves and a few of those stayed on, although there was no good land for farming. They wanted to keep watch, lest the demon-king ever return.'

'Wasn't he dead?'

'So it was thought, for a long time. But not now. Demons don't die for ever. He has returned.'

Vikram looked carefully at Amanjit. 'What do you mean?'

'The soldiers are trying to conceal it, but they can't. *We* understand, *we* know: the killings that the papers speak of.' Hemant looked pained. 'Many soldiers have now died, slain with arrows and spears and swords while their guns fail. The bodies are branded.'

'Branded?' asked Amanjit, outraged. He came from a family of soldiers, and to dishonour the corpses of the fallen struck home. 'Branded how?'

'With old symbols. I have seen them. They say these words: *Sons of Ravan*.'

The words hung in the air, echoing as if spoken into a well. Vikram looked at Amanjit, his throat tightening. The stakes were rising all the time. Ravindra was flexing his muscles. He could almost picture the scenes – asuras and rakshasas paralysing modern equipment with surges of magical energy and then moving in on soldiers suddenly rendered helpless. 'How many have died?'

Hemant shrugged, although there was no nonchalance

in the gesture. 'We do not know, but the whisper is that it is nearing a hundred,' he replied. 'The media is blaming fanatics, but they know of less than a quarter of the attacks, and little of the detail. We know better. It is the asuras – they are active again. The mightiest rakshasas have returned and they're becoming bolder. They have a new urgency.' He turned to Vikram. 'They sense your approach, perhaps.'

Vikram bit his lower lip, then stopped. Now was not the time to show doubt. He looked about them. 'And this place was the home of the asuras?'

'Yes, lord.' Hemant waved a hand about. 'For many years, long before my birth, people have come here that do not . . . *feel* right. You will know what I mean: their reflections are strange. They come up here and vanish as if into the air. And some mornings, when I look up at this place from my home, I think I can see it as it once was, in all its glory.'

'What did they call this place?' Vikram asked softly.

'The Island,' Hemant replied.

'Lanka?' Amanjit asked. 'That means "Island", doesn't it?'

The man said slowly, 'They called it Lanka.'

Hemant took them to his home on the northeast side of the ruins, a simple Kutch thatched hut, jammed with a loom, leather-working tools and utensils. There was no electricity; the cooking was done over a fire. The langur stole a shrivelled mango and vanished.

Hemant's short, skinny wife fussed curiously over them, while their tiny children gawked. There were seven of them, all ragged and dirty and all below ten years of age. They were too shy to speak, but the youngest tugged at Amanjit's sleeve and then climbed on to his lap and nestled there like a king on his throne.

Three of the Meghwal elders came after breakfast. The woman and two men were uniformly stooped and white-haired. They stared intently at Vikram and Amanjit while Hemant's wife herded the children outside.

'So, this must be where you reveal that there is an ancient prophecy that two heroes will come and you must help them,' Amanjit said, into the awkward silence.

None of them laughed, or even smiled. 'We do not have such a prophecy,' Hemant said.

'My friend watches too many movies,' Vikram commented. 'But you must have some reason for taking an interest in us?'

The elders looked at each other, and then at Hemant. 'Several weeks ago a man came among us. He told us that if two young men came – one a Sikh, the other from Maharashtra – we were to contact him. There would be a rich reward, he said: *many* lakhs. He told us names, but said these fugitives – that was his word – may use aliases. He said they are wanted for murder, of a famous actress.'

'Have you gone to the police?' Amanjit asked.

'No. We did not like this stranger. The dogs feared him. His shadow was strange in the firelight. But we thanked him politely and let him go on his way.'

'He was a demon,' the woman added emphatically, 'a rakshasa.' The others nodded, as if such things were a commonplace part of their world. Perhaps they were.

'You are the young men he spoke of,' Hemant stated.

'We have committed no murder,' Vikram replied firmly, 'but we are being blamed for it.'

The three elders went quiet and Hemant picked at his fingernails. Finally he spoke again. 'We say of ourselves that we are the descendants of the slaves of the old people, the Sinathai. That name is not known outside our people any more. They were the first people of Kotara, what you call "Dholavira". We rebelled against our masters when they turned to evil and helped the men of the east, the Suryavanshi, to kill the Sinathai king. Many of us settled here afterwards. We have watched the ruins a long time. We know the signs. The evil ones have returned. They raid our cattle, when we cannot afford to lose even one. They take our children. Seven have disappeared this year already. Sixteen were stolen last year.'

It felt to Vikram as if they were awaiting some sign, some portent that would confirm their loyalty. He sighed softly, took out an arrow from his bag and spun it gently on his fingertip. 'I am hunting asuras and so is my brother-in-law,' he added, indicating Amanjit. 'Will you show us the way?'

The Meghwal elders looked at each other intently, then Hemant bent at the waist.

'My Lord,' he breathed, tears in his eyes. Then he grinned, just like his pet langur. 'This is the part where we say that even though we have no prophecy about this, nor a movie to guide us, we will help you as best we can. We are the sons of slaves. "Monkeys", the demon-king called our forebears. For that insult, and for your sakes, we will aid you, even unto death.'

\*

Two days later, Vikram led Hemant and the Meghwal men to a gateway he'd constructed about a mile north of the ruins in an otherwise empty wasteland. The Meghwal were all labourers, but they'd brought weapons, and Hemant had told them that more would come in the following days, as word spread.

The gate Vikram had made was just the door of a ruined barn, at least at first glance, but the posts were carved with symbols to hold the energy he had poured into it to open a path from the real world to the myth-lands. Amanjit herded the men armed with machetes and rifles towards the ruin, where they peered curiously through the doorway, which looked as if it led into the barn as normal.

Vikram touched the posts and as he exerted his will, the symbols he had carved crackled and the men gave a collective gasp. Through the gateway they could suddenly see a wooded glade, with trees pressing up against the opening.

The men made frightened noises, but Hemant calmed them, saying, 'Be calm. These are good men, come to free us from the asuras.'

One of the Meghwal came forward. His voice dropping to an awed whisper, he asked, 'Who are you? Rama and Lakshmana?'

'Just Vikram and Amanjit,' Amanjit replied. 'We hunt asuras. Are you with us?'

Some of the men knew their names and murmured slightly: news of the manhunt for the killers of Sunita Ashoka had reached even here.

Hemant spoke up immediately. 'Yes, we will aid you. The asuras have our children.'

Vikram and Amanjit led the way through the gate and into a wet forest freshly doused in rain; dark clouds were swirling above. One of the villagers looked up and gasped, swearing he could see the Sun God in his chariot in the midst of the sun, but they fell silent at Hemant's command.

After half an hour or more clambering through the thinly wooded terrain, they emerged at the edge of green pastureland and paddy fields. Crook-backed beast-men waved whips over the head of bent, scurrying slaves. And beyond, presiding over it all, was a walled city. They all stopped and stared in silence and wonder.

There was an outer wall and within, the roofs of housing; the orderly layout of the city was evident even at this distance. The stone caught the sunlight and glowed in shades of honey. Towering above it was a thirty-foot-high curtain wall and beyond was the citadel, crouching in the morning light. Towers rose from within. Smoke arose from cooking fires within the city, and armoured asuras strode the battlements. It looked as solid as the earth beneath their feet, this place of legend.

Vikram and Amanjit shared an awed look.

They'd actually found Lanka.

# CHAPTER TWENTY-THREE

## LET US BE MARRIED

*Lanka, 29 July 2011*

Rasita lay on silken sheets beneath the weight of her lord's chest. Their bodies touched, filling them with mutual need, igniting their passions. He kissed her, and she returned his kiss with hunger and worship, moulding herself to him as—

'Mistress? Wake up! Wake up!' Keke bustled into the room, her face pale and scared. 'Mistress, you must get up, *now*. The Ravan asks to see you.'

Rasita, her face flushed red, unpeeled herself from the damp sheets. The dream lingered in her senses, while on her ceiling the painted characters continued to kiss. She looked away sharply. In the dream, she'd been Halika, in bed with Ravan Aeshwaran, and the images were like cobwebs, tangling her thoughts.

'Keke, what is it?' she asked, her cheeks still burning.

'Mistress, there has been an attack – people have been killed. The king asks for you.'

Rasita blinked dazedly. *An attack?* Here? *That makes no sense—*

Then it hit her in the pit of her stomach. *Vikram and Amanjit have come for me at last!*

Only a few days ago, she had come so close to giving herself to Ravindra. Her dreams were intensifying, no longer just fantasies of her overwrought imagination, but Halika's memories and she couldn't suppress them. She was frightened that she might be going insane.

The fact that she was not complete and never would be unless Deepika came to Lanka was beginning to hit her. And now she could feel those others inside her – Halika, Jyoti and Aruna – battling for supremacy, feeding on her doubts, trying to rise up and possess her. It terrified her that one day she might lose control of her own body to these other presences. She had to complete this process if only to save her sanity.

And now the boys were here to rescue her. Their quest now felt absurd – a side issue, a petty rivalry. She didn't want to be rescued; she just needed to find the ghost of Darya and be made whole. To become who she was destined to be: Manda of Lanka! There was nowhere on Earth she wanted to be but here, the one place where that could happen. There was nowhere else where could she unravel these twisted, knotted threads and heal herself.

She entered the Ivy Room, glancing with guilty longing at the bench where she had almost surrendered to him. Ravindra's expression was ambiguous as he greeted her. 'My Queen, thank you for coming.'

The leaders of the rakshasas, gathered around the table, were watching her suspiciously. Lavanasura, his faceted eyes as always unreadable, bobbed his reptilian head. Surpanakha, her ruined face like a weeping sore, stared at her stonily. Meghanada Indrajit, huge and bull-like, and the hunchbacked tiger-man Syhajeet, both glowered. Atikaya with the eagle-head chirruped aggressively. Ravindra's Uncle Khumb, normally jovial, blinked at her unhappily. Others she didn't know watched her silently.

*They all think I'm endangering them. They would all rather kill me than risk defeat.*

She turned, wanting to take Ravindra's hands and kiss them, soothe away his anxiety over this attack. *Look at me: can you see? I'm turning into your Manda. And I don't care . . .*

'What's happened?' she asked.

'The Rama and the Lakshmana have come again,' growled Meghanada before Ravindra could speak. 'They're here for you,' he added accusingly.

'Raiders with astras attacked the supervisors in the fields,' Lavanasura put in. 'They killed five asuras and stole many slaves.'

'The fields are worked by captives,' Khumb rumbled, 'as it has always been. Meghanada is right: they're here for the queen. Because she withholds herself from the king, they feel they have licence to come and plague us for your return.'

Ravindra slapped the table. 'What lies between Rasita and me is my business and hers, not the business of this council,' he said sternly.

'It is all of our business if we are to be attacked because of it,' Khumb boomed. 'The attackers used astras, my Lord. They're deadly, even to us. Our soldiers are frightened. A king would—'

Surpanakha interrupted in a harsh voice, '*A king* would not be so preoccupied with his manhood and some woman,' she spat. '*A king* would have hunted down these men and slaughtered them by now. Instead, this one wastes his time pushing Valentine's Day cards under his reluctant queen's door.'

Ravindra's eyes blazed. 'You ignorant sow: you know *nothing* of the forces in play here.'

'I know enough to see that this woman has rejected you, and she continues to do so. Her life now endangers us all. We're not blind. We can see what is happening – the *Ramayana* itself is conspiring against us – and if you die at the hands of the Rama, we all perish, and this time it will be *forever*.' She hammered the table. 'The girl rejects you: you must give her back or kill her, so that the *Ramayana* cannot be fulfilled—'

'Aye,' Meghanada Indrajit growled, 'send her hence, or kill her now.'

The call was taken up around the table.

Ravindra gripped Rasita's hand. 'She is under my protection,' he warned.

'Which means *what*, precisely? That you're prepared to let her mock and reject you and risk all our lives?' Khumb snarled. 'Where is the king I have awaited all these centuries? Has he become a weakling in his absence from here?'

Ravindra stood. 'I have power beyond all of you,' he roared. 'Your arguments are the ignorant yapping of dogs, got by feeding on scraps of information dropped from my table. You know nothing – *nothing*. Any resemblance to the *Ramayana* is illusory. The only thing that matters is this: that we slay the Rama and the Lakshmana – naught else matters to you, including my relations with this woman.'

'Then take her, Lord, claim her,' Atikaya snapped, his shrill voice threaded through with desire for a spectacle. 'Take what you want from her – or give her to us and we'll do it.'

Meghanada Indrajit coughed and leaned towards her. 'Give her to me, Father,' he growled. 'I'll have her mewling for mercy in short measure.'

Ras looked up at Ravindra, her mouth dry, her heart pumping almost painfully. *No, he wouldn't . . .*

*Or would he? Was Surpanakha right? If he is convinced that I'll never sleep with him, then perhaps he'll simply despoil or kill me, just to prevent Vikram from claiming victory. It would be like sweeping a hand over the chessboard and scattering the pieces on the floor . . . It's a logical strategy . . .*

'Manda,' he said, turning to her. 'You've heard them, my darling. What do you have to say?'

*Manda.*

Conflicting thoughts welled up inside her, a clamour of arguments and counters that gradually resolved into a stream of decisions: *Deepika is already dead: I know this in my heart. Her ghost is coming home to me, and then I will be whole: we will be as one. Aeshwaran was my husband and Dasraiyat the usurper. Vikram has Sue Parker: his Kamla. He doesn't want me – he doesn't even know me. I will never be the one he wants.*

*And Ravindra . . . with one act, I can heal him – and maybe save the world in doing so.*

She found herself standing. 'My Lord Ravan,' she said in a quavering voice, 'this situation endangers your soul, when redemption is so close at hand.' She heard the rakshasa lords suck in their breath. 'Your soul is precious, Lord. Let me save it. I will give myself in love to you. To end this state of eternal war and restore you and I to all we once were, let us be married, and united as one.'

Ravindra's eyes filled with sudden wonder. He looked like a child at Diwali, watching sky rockets fill the night sky with enchantment. First he smiled like a teenage boy, then he became as grave as a millennia-old king.

'*Manda. My love,*' was all he said.

The rakshasas let out their breath, then they hollered with triumphant joy – all except one.

Surpanakha climbed to her feet, her ruined face livid. 'She's lying – can't you see? She's lying to buy time!' She stamped her foot. 'You know her love is reserved for Vikram Khandavani – we all know it.'

Rasita shook her head in denial. 'No. Vikram is nothing to me now.'

The other rakshasas turned on Surpanakha and hissed, shouting her down, before resuming their backslapping and congratulations.

Ravindra clasped Rasita to him as Surpanakha shuffled from the room. 'My Manda,' he whispered, 'I will give you eternity.'

# CHAPTER TWENTY-FOUR

## DEATH FROM ABOVE

*Lanka, 29 July 2011*

Vikram crawled behind Hemant towards the wall of the citadel as the twilight deepened. There was a vantage point about a hundred yards from the walls they could get to without being observed. He heard Amanjit slithering behind him as they reached the place, the intersection of three fields, and stood beneath a banyan tree and peered about them.

After their predawn raid, the asuras had pulled back to their walls. The raid had been a success – the Meghwal had freed eighteen slaves, some of whom they soon realised had been taken *centuries* before. They were all adult and mostly male; for now, they were being kept in a staging camp near the gate, but still in the myth-lands. They spoke the local dialect, and had revealed a lot about the layout of the city and citadel and the nature of the asuras: the beast-men were more violent and childlike than evil.

*Not precisely what we'd expected*, thought Vikram.

They had wanted to keep the element of surprise, but they had to find out what lay within the walls, and what manner of beings they faced, which was why the morning raid had been necessary, even though it had put the citadel on high alert. Now they had to decide how to proceed. They had quickly found that modern weaponry didn't work in the myth-lands, becoming inert as it passed the gate. This was a huge problem for them: an asura soldier was stronger and faster than a normal man, formidable even against elite soldiers – but the Meghwal men, who were mostly small and malnourished, hadn't any training in warfare at all. Without guns they'd be no match for the enemy. Only surprise and the astras had enabled this morning's success. In a straight-up fight against the asuras, the Meghwal would be slaughtered.

And the rakshasas were something else altogether. The magic-wielding demon captains could mesmerise their opponents or fire their own astras, deadlier then bullets, which meant only Vikram and Amanjit had any chance of facing them.

So rushing the walls would just get them all killed. They needed a better strategy, and for that, some scouting was required. Hemant had joined them on a circuit around the fortified town and citadel, seeking weak points, but they hadn't found many.

'Let's face it,' Amanjit said as he came up beside him, continuing the argument they'd been having all afternoon, '*we're* outnumbered – and *we* need to be the ones outnumbering the people in a stronghold, right? Even I know that! We've got fifty guys against several thousand asuras and two dozen or more rakshasas – and *we* can't use guns. We're going to get slaughtered, Vik. The rakshasas have spent the last few months killing fully trained regular army *for fun*—'

'The army was surprised and disarmed, and they didn't know what they were facing. Here, Ravindra's on the defensive and we know what we're up against.' Vikram pulled a face. 'Beyond that, you're totally right.'

'I mean, with *tactics*,' the Sikh went on, 'like sniping at them and penning them in, we might force them into a rash charge, unleash a few astras, maybe bring down some of the big boys. But if they knew how few we are, they'd overrun us in minutes. And if we try a rush, we'll get minced.'

'I know. Shush.' He indicated Hemant ahead of him. 'Not in front of the troops.'

'Him? He knows, he isn't dumb.' Amanjit tapped his nose, then called softly, 'What do you think, Hemant?'

The Meghwal chief grinned. 'That we'll get "minced" if we rush them,' he said, mimicking Amanjit's words and tone. He tapped his ear. 'Neither deaf *nor* dumb, my friend!'

Amanjit rolled his eyes. 'So what do you think?'

'I think when your enemy is stronger, but tied to one place, then you hit and run.'

'That's my man!'

Vikram cupped hands over his eyes. 'I'm not sure. We've got no idea what's happening in there. There are too many other balls in play. We don't know how Rasita is doing. I want to arrange a parley and talk to Ravindra – at least that way I might be able to get some understanding of what the situation really is.'

'Like he's going to tell you anything but lies and what

he wants you to think,' Amanjit objected. 'Truces are so last-century — we should just unleash hell, like that guy in *Gladiator* says.'

'I don't know. It sounds too American — just nuking a problem doesn't solve it.'

'I thought you liked Americans,' Amanjit laughed, then cursed himself; Sue Parker was still missing, and while she meant nothing to him, she evidently did mean something to Vikram. 'Sorry — bad joke. Really bad.' He reached out an arm, and winced as Vikram batted it away. 'Sorry.'

'You're an idiot, Amanjit.'

'Yeah. I know.' He exhaled heavily. 'So, what do we do?'

Vikram felt nauseous at the thought of the killing to come, recalling all the bloody battles of his past lives. 'Ravindra's protective spells only encompass the main citadel. Everyone outside is vulnerable. Most of the asuras are in the lower town. That's nearly ten thousand souls . . .'

Amanjit put a hand on his shoulder. 'Vik, they're demons. They don't have souls.'

'Are they? Don't they?'

Amanjit said impatiently, 'You can't pity your enemy — think about what they did to Uma and Tanvir. Think about your father. And where's Sue? Where's Dee, for God's sake? You've looked Ravindra in the eye: you *know* what he's like.'

Vikram's head slumped. 'You've seen war in other lives but you don't remember. I do. There's no glory in it, no right or wrong: it's just large-scale butchery.'

'We have to get past these asuras to get to Ravindra, Vik. What choice do we have?'

'I don't know,' Vikram whispered, 'but I do know we

have to think of one, if we can. Before it's too late and the killing turns us all into devils.'

Amanjit scowled glumly. 'Then if we can't "unleash hell", what can we unleash?'

Vikram stared into space, then slowly turned, his face clearing. 'How about we unleash pandemonium instead?'

That night, Vikram went to the east side, below the citadel, while Amanjit went to the west and Hemant took his men north. Only the citadel, where the rakshasa surely resided, was not pinpointed for attack. They had to even the odds on the softer targets first.

Some kind of celebration was going on within the palace, but Vikram blanked it from his mind, instead picturing Rasita's strained, sickly face when he last saw her in Udaipur, the night he lost her. Deepika was missing, perhaps a prisoner here, maybe dead. Sue Parker was missing too —was she also inside? Poor Uma and Tanvir, and his father, whose death had never been fully explained to his satisfaction. And so many others, in so many past lives.

He felt his anger growing; that would fuel his first astra.

At midnight, Hemant's men kicked up a racket on the north side, firing makeshift bows and generally making a lot of noise. As they saw asuras appear and start streaming along the walls, looking for the battle, Vikram sighted along his arrow and fired the biggest, most juiced-up twashtar-astra he could summon, combined with an aindra-astra, to multiply the shafts fired. The confusion arrow soared, breaking into many as it curved in the night sky – then as ten thousand pale shafts of light rained down upon the fortress, he followed it with another, then broke cover and ran towards the lower-city gates.

He'd never used the twashtar before. The arrow of confusion and panic required victims who were ill-disciplined and lacking focus for it to work. Surely the asuras, with their childlike minds and animal volatility, were the ideal subjects?

A wave of shouting erupted from within the walls as he blasted down the doors, Amanjit beside him shot down those guards who had not been panicked by the fiery astras. Hemant and his men followed, hammering upon drums and blasting horns into the midnight stillness.

To the asuras, it was as if all hell were descending upon them. When Vikram smashed the gates with a parvata-astra, the whole mass of beast-men erupted into the streets, hooting with fear, calling madly for the king or the moon or their mothers. They recoiled from the advancing men in utter dread, breaking in seconds as Amanjit fired vivid aindra-astras into their midst, bringing down those who tried to resist. The riot that ensued became a rout in seconds, the asuras fleeing the sound and thunder of the invaders, running hither and thither, anywhere – as long as it was *away* from Vikram and Amanjit.

Arrows flew down at the boys from the citadel walls, but the darkness made the aim erratic. Vikram shot down one astra that flew from above, and then fired back at the rakshasa archer, but his shot broke on some protection woven into the citadel. Mostly though, they were unopposed as they drove the panicked asuras before them.

The party sounds in the citadel had ceased, to be replaced

by wails of despair and hatred. Fiery astras flew from the walls, but by then Hemant's men were already in Lower Town, emptying the slave pens. Hemant led a stream of human slaves out of the eastern gate, past dead asura guards and into the welcoming arms of the waiting tribesmen. Children were among them, including the missing Meghwals, and Vikram heard fathers crying out in relief as they recognised the faces of missing sons and daughters.

The tide of asuras fleeing the city dispersed in all directions. Some found refuge in the citadel, but most surged out into the night and kept running, scattering for miles across the island, even trampling each other to death or turning on their own kin in their need to escape from the twashtar-induced panic. Any who turned on Vikram and Amanjit were shot down.

Ten chaotic minutes later, the city was almost empty: hundreds of slaves had been freed and the asuras were scattered, with dozens dead.

Then the rakshasas and their guards finally got themselves into ranks on the citadel battlements. Hemant kept his men clear of arrow-fire, but Vikram and Amanjit were forced to withdraw swiftly from the growing barrage of astras from above.

Finally they rejoined the Meghwal near the gates to the real world. The tribal warriors were exultant, naming them heroes, saviours, and maybe they were. Around them were the freed slaves, confused but excited, and some already armed.

But when Vikram met Amanjit's eyes, they were dark, his need for vengeance unassuaged.

'We've bought maybe a day before the asuras re-form and return in force, with ten times our numbers,' Amanjit said in a low voice. 'What will you think of this mercy of yours then, bhai?'

# CHAPTER TWENTY-FIVE

## I NEED MY HEART

*Lanka, 30 July 2011*

Rasita could not reconcile her laughing brother or serious, compassionate Vikram with the devastation in the city below. From her windows, between the pre-wedding rituals and bathing and pampering, she scanned the smoking ruins. At midnight the city below had burst into chaotic panic. Fires had been started by panicked asuras, and hundreds had been trampled to death. The people of Lower Town were scattered to the winds, apart from those few who had kept their heads and got inside the citadel. The blazes were still raging below, Keke reported, the little maid so enraged she could barely speak. Blackened corpses were lying everywhere, in plain sight.

It reinforced her feeling that she was right to reject Vikram in favour of Ravindra.

*The sooner I am wed to Ravan Aeshwaran, the sooner this horror can end,* she told herself firmly.

'Let me speak to Vikram,' she begged Ravindra when

he came to her, his face grim and drawn. It was the middle of the night, but no one was sleeping. His people had been decimated in the city below. The Ravan had warded the citadel to prevent similar catastrophe within, but at great personal cost – sorcery was draining, even to him.

He shook his head. 'What could be said? Do not fear, Rasita. His attack was clever, as the asuras were unprepared and vulnerable to the twashtar, but the effects are brief. Within a day or two those who live will return, and then we will overwhelm him. It need not delay our plans.'

'Then let us be wed now,' she pressed, putting her hand on his chest. 'I am ready.'

Ravindra smiled. 'I wish we could. But there are preparations that must be made, even in such a situation.'

'You were willing enough to proceed, that afternoon in the Ivy Room,' she whispered.

He gave a throaty chuckle. 'Indeed, but I would have held back, my love. Credit me with some strength.' He smiled, kissing her hands. 'Have the maids been pampering you? Has Lavanasura performed the prayers?'

'Yes, Lord.' It had felt a travesty, to be washed and perfumed and blessed while outside his people – *my people too, now* – were dead and dying. 'But I was thinking: my heart-stone – won't you need it?'

'No,' he replied. 'Its function is primarily to sustain you through death. The Ravindra who devised the ritual of Mandore thought death was needed, but I have learned better. In fact, the heart-stone only represents danger to us now: it could be used against you.'

She couldn't conceive of Vikram harming her, despite his faults. 'Is there no way of regaining it?

He went to shake his head, then suddenly smiled. 'Actually, now that you're so close to whole, there is.'

Just before dawn, Vikram stirred in his sleep. He dreamed Rasita was calling his name. Her face was sad. He woke to find himself in a fogbound room, where high-backed antique furniture loomed mysteriously out of swirling mists.

She stood beside the bed, clothed in a beautiful sari, more lovely than he had ever seen her, radiant as an expectant bride. 'Vikram, I need my heart,' she whispered.

'Here it is,' he answered eagerly, fishing under his pillow for the heart-stone, then holding the pulsing gem on its chain necklace out to her.

She took it and put it inside her bodice, where it pulsed once and faded. There was a solemnity and distance in her face that scared him.

Then she spoke, not in the warm tones he had expected, but with cold dismissal. 'Go home, Vikram. This war is wrong. You don't understand what is happening. Leave me alone and go home. I know who you are – I know what you did!'

'What do you mean?' he asked, suddenly feeling that he was in a nightmare. 'Who am I?'

Her face went utterly cold. 'You are Dasraiyat, an adulterous traitor, and I reject you!'

'*What?*'

Vishwamitra's training took over and he forced himself to wake, finding himself in the Meghwal encampment, with Amanjit snoring softly nearby.

He clutched at his top pocket and realised it was empty. Rasita's heart-stone was gone.

Ravindra stood alone in the highest tower of the citadel, staring out at Lower Town and the plains beyond to the edge of the woods, trying to determine how many foes they actually faced. Not many, he was sure – apart from Vikram and Amanjit Singh, they'd seen only small squads of other men, rough little tribesmen; a paltry force.

Every hour brought more returning asuras as the panic started wearing off. By the day's end most should have returned, and then he would take the fight to his foe. The asuras might fear him; they might still spoke of Vibhishana with affection, but *he* was their king. They would return to him and he would triumph. And after that, he could tighten his grip on the real world, where he had three squads harassing the Indian army, laying the groundwork for his eventual 'negotiations' with the government. By year-end, he would control India from the shadows.

He lifted the Rasita heart-stone to his lips and kissed it silently, then laid it aside and took up the Deepika heart-stone, staring into it thoughtfully. It was shadowy, inert, and yet . . . where was the ghost? Why had Deepika Choudhary's spectre not come crawling over the walls or hammering on the gates? The final piece of this jigsaw still eluded him and he scowled silently.

There was a knock, then the bulky shape of Khumb lumbered in and bowed. 'My Lord,' the rakshasa rumbled. Khumb really was his uncle, from when both were mere mortal humans in Adun, just as Meenakshi was his real sister. 'More asuras return. The enemy did not assault the citadel, even though we had lost most of our defenders — are they fools?'

Ravindra gave a taut smile. 'Not fools, but weak. They have only a peasant rabble at their command. The attack on Lower Town was the most they could achieve. In their place, I would have used far more lethal astras and slaughtered the asuras. Their lack of ruthlessness is revealing. They're still boys at heart.'

'What are your plans, Lord?' Khumb rumbled.

'We will attack,' Ravindra replied. 'Arm all the asuras we have and mass them before the gates. Keep them protected from astras. Let us show the enemy our might.'

Khumb bowed, eager for battle. Then he straightened and looked pensive. 'Preparations for the wedding are complete, Nephew — why must we wait?'

'For the Darya,' Ravindra replied, eyeing the gem as it caught the light.

'Then where is she?'

'That, Uncle, is a good question. If she were truly dead, she should be here. Which means she may have survived after all, and be hiding from me.' He twisted the gem in his fingers so that refracted light danced about the room. He smiled grimly. 'In which case, all the better.'

'What will you do?'

'Something I should have done earlier: I will assume she is alive. I will use this gem to channel my powers to find her and bring her here.'

As he spoke, he reached inside himself and sent a blast of mental energy into the gem.

His blow struck home and his face lit with satisfaction. Somewhere — somewhere close! — Deepika Choudhary shrieked in sudden pain, and then pulled down shields against him: mental shields he began to hammer against, blows she might hold off a while, but not for long . . .

# CHAPTER TWENTY-SIX

# A PARLEY AT THE GATES

*Lanka, 30 July 2011*

Vikram told no one of his strange dream and the loss of Rasita's heart-stone, not even Amanjit, in case it drove his friend to do something rash. Amanjit was already suffering too much from Deepika's absence. The loss of the Rasita-stone had shaken Vikram to the core, as had Ras' cold attitude towards him.

*I don't understand – why would she be so hostile?* It almost paralysed him. *I'm here to rescue you*, he whispered inside, *so why do you turn away?*

He resolved to press on with the struggle. Dawn brought another cloudless sky, the monsoon still holding off. The air was thick, the heat oppressive as the humidity grew. And as the sun speared the darkness, worse was revealed.

A horde of asuras was growing before the citadel gates. Hundreds of them had been streaming back into the city from the surrounding forests as the effects of the twashtar wore off, and now more than three thousand were being armed and forming into lines.

Vikram watched from the eaves of the forest, Amanjit glowering beside him.

*Maybe you were right. Perhaps we should have used deadlier astras when we had the chance.*

All morning they watched the enemy army massing. The fires in Lower Town had been extinguished, the bodies pulled clear. Now the rakshasa lords strode among them, poised to deal with any astras that might fly from the forests, but Vikram could see no point. He'd miscalculated; he'd shown mercy when war allowed none. He was failing yet again.

Before midday, trumpets blew and the asuras tramped out of Lower Town, the rakshasas driving them on, until they faced the forests in thick ranks. The armoured beast-men were almost throbbing with fury, especially when they caught sight of Vikram and Amanjit on the low rise from where they watched. They hooted and jabbered, shrieking for vengeance for the damage and loss caused the night before.

Hemant touched Vikram's shoulder. 'Lord, we must fall back through the gate. If they attack, only you can stop them.'

Vikram wavered, wondering whether falling back now was to fail forever.

'Let's take a few down first,' Amanjit growled, picking up his bow. 'They can't block every arrow.'

Vikram shook his head. 'To what end? We can't win today.'

*We threw away our chance. It's my fault.*

He turned to Hemant to order the withdrawal when he saw something away to his left that made his jaw drop.

At the edge of the forest, clad in a robe so thickly embroidered with gold thread that it shone, was a massive figure clinging to a tall stick. Although bent, it was clear he was still powerful. The head bore huge bull horns. One hand was raised in solemn greeting – then the inhuman skull turned back to the advancing asuras.

'Vibhishana?' Amanjit gasped, while Vikram just stared. The last time they'd seen the erstwhile King of Lanka, he'd been under Kasun's care in Sri Lanka.

*The real Vibhishana – here? How?*

A skinny man stepped out of the trees beside the rakshasa and raised a tentative hand, and Vikram yelped in disbelieving excitement. 'Kasun?' He almost fell over himself as he hurried towards the newcomers. 'King Vibhishana – but how are you here?'

Amanjit ran beside him, his expression lifting as he began to hope again.

'My lords,' Vibhishana bowed, clinging to his staff with white knuckles, 'I believe that I owe you my life.' His voice was thin and wheezing, and the closer the two boys got, the more they could see the strain the giant rakshasa was under to just remain standing.

Kasun was hovering like an anxious parent. He clasped Vikram and Amanjit's hands, speaking fast. 'It's incredible – he woke a few weeks after I took him into care, then he said he had to come here . . .' His eyes went back to the hordes of asura. 'He told me this is a place that appears on no maps.'

'He's right on that count,' Amanjit drawled. 'So how'd you get here?'

'My brother knows people – he got us to Tamil Nadu by boat, then I hired a truck – Vibhishana told me where to come. I tried calling you, but I could never get any connection. We drove through the whole of India and no one noticed! Mind you, I think he can play tricks with people's eyes and minds.'

Vibhishana smirked. 'Humans are easy to manage. Unlike not my own kind.' His eyes were on the ranked beast-men currently being worked up into a charge by the rakshasas marshalling them.

'Why are you here, Lord?' Vikram asked.

'I sensed you both in the false Lanka. I am here to help you. You and your doctor friend saved me; I owe you my life.'

Trumpets blared and they suddenly realised the asuras were streaming towards them, already less than a hundred yards and closing fast. Hemant shouted an order and the remaining Meghwal began to pull away, but he himself lingered, his pet langur monkey on his back snarling at the oncoming hordes.

Amanjit lifted his bow. 'Either we get out now or we fight,' he growled.

Then Vibhishana stepped forward, into full view of the oncoming asuras.

The blasting trumpets were drowned by the sudden howls and clamour from the first to see their lost king, and the charge broke into a stumbling morass of wide-eyed and disbelieving beast-men.

Kasun took a step towards the rakshasa king, but Vikram caught his shoulder.

'Stay out of it,' he whispered, his own eyes locked on the unfolding scene as he pulled himself away.

Vibhishana stood like a stick planted in the sand against the oncoming tide, but the asuras washed harmlessly over him and around him, pulling and touching and crying while Vikram, Amanjit and Kasun backed away, ignored and forgotten. They climbed the small knoll again and watched the old rakshasa as he was welcomed back by his people. For a time, all looked to be going well. The joy on the asuras' faces was palpable.

Then a rakshasa strode through the masses and tried to lay hands on Vibhishana – but the asuras pulled the assailant down, tearing him apart when he tried to invoke sorcery – and things turned bloody. Those rakshasas loyal to Ravindra tried to drive into the asuras at the fringes to reach Vibhishana, shouting that he was a traitor and ordering them to seize him. In the middle were a mix of loyalties: weapons had already been drawn for the charge. It was no big step to put them to use.

Amanjit saw another rakshasa move against Vibhishana and shot an agniyastra. Blades lifted and fell and suddenly they were in the middle of a bloodbath. Rakshasas sent their own astras from the edges of the press and Vikram couldn't shoot them all down; they watched as the masses below them convulsed, the bestial cries grew louder and Vibhishana visibly stumbled – but a hard core of loyal asuras had formed about him and they began to cut down everyone they perceived as enemies.

Trumpets blared again, but whatever they were signalling

was lost in the confusion and the cacophony. The noise throbbed about them, deafening and terrifying.

Vikram looked up at the citadel, where he could see the rakshasa leadership clustered like ants about a central figure who must be Ravindra. He wondered if Rasita was watching.

He wondered what on earth he should do.

Then Vibhishana roared above the entire battlefield, 'Ravindra – I am returned! You who betrayed me, beware, for I have returned to reclaim my throne!'

The entire field fell silent for a few stunned seconds, and then all discipline collapsed as asuras turned on each other. Ravindra's rakshasas were being pulled down and torn to pieces; some managed to flee, screaming, while other asuras and rakshasas fell to their knees in disbelief as a seething mass bristling with sharp steel and bared teeth formed about the exiled king. Anyone trying to reach Vibhishana, whether to kill him or to simply fall before him and give their homage, were forced away. The bloody fallen were everywhere.

Bugles on the citadel walls sounded the retreat and maybe a third of the asuras remaining obeyed. The trumpets brayed again, calling imperiously, demanding obedience, and the asuras, conditioned by centuries of rakshasa rule, wavered.

Then from the ruins of the Lower Town, a hum arose, like nothing Vikram had ever heard: the musical thrum of a beehive, or perhaps distantly heard cattle, or wolves calling to the rising moon. Over the low walls of Lower Town, distant figures swarmed. It was from their inhuman throats that the strange sound issued. The women and children of the asuras, come to see for themselves if it were true that their lost beloved King Vibhishana had returned. At first they walked – then they ran, stampeding through the men-folk, a weird horde of half-beast and near-human that had a strangeness somewhere between beauty and hideousness to human eyes, but in this moment of wonder and joy, all had some element of loveliness.

With their arrival, half of those who had been retreating to the citadel deserted, leaving only a few hundred of the most hardened of Ravindra's asura subjects, those he had favoured and given dominance, to return to him inside the fortress.

The rest remained outside to bask in the glow of their beloved returned king.

'This is incredible,' Amanjit exulted. He hammered Vikram on the back. 'You *knew*, didn't you? That's why you only used the twashtar against them – you knew eventually they'd be on our side—'

Vikram, who'd known no such thing, shook his head. 'We just got very, *very* lucky, that's all.' But the relief he was feeling felt sent from above. 'Look at them,' he grinned.

It was indeed a sight to see. The centuries-ago reign of Vibhishana had taken on a mythic Golden Age glamour after the asuras had found their freedoms sharply curtailed when the rakshasas loyal to Ravindra had overthrown their king. Now they sensed that perhaps those past days could return. Several hours passed as the old king, still ravaged by centuries of imprisonment in Sri Lanka, received the homage of his former subjects, which appeared to involve a lot of kneeling and kissing of the hand.

Tears were streaming down most faces and even Vikram found his eyes wet.

The Meghwal gradually crept back, staying at the fringes as they cradled their own freed children and watched with wide eyes. The two groups remained carefully apart, but no hostile movements were made.

Then a vast cry erupted from the citadel and Vikram saw a bolt of light arc from the battlements above the gate and stream towards the massed asuras. He reached for his bow, but Amanjit had already nocked his arrow and fired, muttering the words to a mohini, the magic-destroying astra, as if he'd been doing such things all his life. His shot blasted apart the incoming astra and it exploded across the sky like a skyrocket. For a second the whole plain fell silent, and then the asuras hooted and brayed as they realised what had happened.

Ravindra, their king, had fired on his own people – and they'd been *protected* by the humans. Vikram could not have asked for a more eloquent way to break down the barriers between the two groups.

From then on the asuras went among the humans, finding former slaves and gifting them with weapons and food. The Meghwal brought up their own supplies, which were deployed in a clearing in the forest, and Hemant established a watch on the Citadel while the new-found allies gathered about Vibhishana, sitting on an improvised throne. The old king looked exhausted, but transcendentally happy.

'My people will aid you,' he told Vikram. 'The usurper must fall.'

Whatever Vikram might have said was drowned by the clamour of a thousand sword hilts being hammered on shields.

All he could do was bow and wonder if this time, at last, the cosmos was on his side.

That afternoon, they attacked. The asura archers, under cover in Lower Town, sleeted arrows over the citadel walls while Vikram and Amanjit moved among them, swatting aside the returning astras. Between them, they slew six rakshasas with astras that flew like sniper bullets, then struck at the citadel with parvata-astras, hammering at the ramparts. The walls were woven with spells; although they cracked in places, they stayed strong.

Hemant's people were also deployed in Lower Town, the crowded buildings offering thousands of vantages for archery. They were joined by hundreds of the released slaves, those strong enough, or strengthened by hatred of their captors, to fight. Creeping among the ruins, they poured arrows over the citadel walls until they ran out of shafts around mid-afternoon. Vibhishana had set the asura women-folk to making more, using branches and sharpened stones.

The Meghwal men fighting alongside the asuras appeared to be impervious to the insanity all around them. Their tales were filled with demons and astras, so perhaps to them, asuras were just another known species, and an astra no stranger than a battle-tank or a jet-fighter. In the staging camp, the women of both races set up first-aid stations and tents for the exhausted warriors, and they cooked con-stantly. And more people came to their aid through the real world via Vikram's gate – not just Meghwal, but many other tribes too, all with a secret past linked to the old Sinathai. Hemant and his fellow Elders were everywhere, ordering the camp, generating the renewed flow of arrows and bows, ensuring meals were ready for those returning. Once these newcomers had looked over the citadel and expressed their wonder, the tribal warriors became as matter-of-fact about it all as any soldier stuck in a stand-off.

Suddenly Vikram and Amanjit realised they had *thousands* under their command. Both human and asura cheered them whenever they saw them, and the responsibility of keeping their new army alive felt heavy on their shoulders. If they were to protect them, they'd have to shoot down all the rakshasas' astras, which was an impossible task.

As casualties mounted, they knew they had to do something *more*, and soon. They still hadn't gained a foothold on the walls and this effort was not sustainable. Something had to give.

Then, with sunset an hour or so away, a white flag appeared at the main gates of the citadel. A nervous-looking rakshasa boy with snakes for hair and colourful scaled skin brought the request for a parley, to take place at sundown.

'Just your leader and our king,' the messenger said, his mature demeanour belying his youthful appearance.

Vikram agreed, and hostilities paused as both sides made ready.

'Let's just shoot Ravindra when he comes outside the gates,' Amanjit suggested, with cheerful disregard for the etiquette of warfare. 'You know he'll try something of the sort.'

'I think I'd rather talk to him,' Vikram replied. 'We're supposed to be the good guys here.'

'Good, bad, what's the difference? It's results that count.'

The Sikh appeared to be able to accept the casualties as nothing more than a hazard of conflict. Vikram was less callous, even when it came to their enemies' deaths.

'Don't you care that real lives are being lost here?' Vikram snapped. 'Even these asuras are thinking, feeling creatures – you can see that, surely?'

'That's war,' Amanjit said, matter-of-factly. 'I'll care later. For now, they're just casualties: *enemy* casualties.' He turned and walked away, refusing to discuss the matter further.

Vikram waited for Ravindra in front of the broken north gate to the city. He wrapped himself in protective wards, but he didn't think Ravindra would try anything, despite his reputation and Amanjit's misgivings. It would be out of character. He remembered the parley between Mehtan Ali and Chand Bardai before the Second Battle of Tarain and stiffened his spine. *I will not be humbled as I was that day.*

He waited in the cooling dusk. As the gates opened, he saw blackened, ruined buildings, and carrion birds everywhere. No one had cleared away the bodies, which suggested that Ravindra's resources were now stretched to breaking point. For the ravens, this was a feast-day.

A man appeared at the north gate with the snake-haired boy who was holding his white flag. He walked towards Vikram, displaying empty hands: Ravindra in Majid Khan's body, wearing kingly robes, unarmed, but exuding danger. The boy stopped short, but Ravindra walked on.

'Stop right there, Ravindra!' Vikram called when the demon-king was thirty paces away.

Ravindra halted. The air about him prickled with wards and protective charms – difficult to maintain for long, but effective in the short term, just like the ones Vikram wore. They would both want this talk to be brief.

'Here, I'm known as Ravan Aeshwaran,' Ravindra answered. 'Ravan is "king" in my people's tongue.'

Vikram licked his dry lips. '"Ravindra" will do for me.'

Ravindra stared levelly at Vikram. 'Yet I am the Ravan, the king of this place. And you've murdered many of my peaceful subjects. Are you proud?'

Vikram fought down his guilt. *It's an act . . . he doesn't really care.* 'I hardly believe they were peaceful. I think those who would desire peace are currently with Vibhishana, the rightful king.'

'Vibhishana the usurper. Vibhishana the ancient. I marvel he can still stand unaided,' Ravindra sneered. 'My rakshasas burn to take vengeance upon you, *murderer*.'

'Then lead them out to fight us,' Vikram retorted.

They glared at each other until Ravindra made a show of shaking his head wearily. 'When did you become a killer, Aram Dhoop? Even I was moved by your verses, all those years ago in Mandore. I was so blinded by your gentleness that I didn't recognise you for who you were.'

Vikram fought a surge of anger. Seeing Ravindra playing at sadness and regret after all the evil he'd done in so many lives was nauseating. 'I've been persecuted by you in every life I have ever led. I've been killed by you, directly or indirectly, in every life. I have seen you murder my friends and family and loved ones in every life – and in this one also! Don't try out your twisted morality on me, Ravindra. I know what is at stake.'

'Do you indeed, Aram Dhoop? Tell me, what are the stakes?'

'That I must live and you must die. That I must save Rasita. That the *Ramayana* must be fulfilled.'

Ravindra looked at Vikram as if he'd failed a test and in doing so confirmed his suspicions. 'Aram Dhoop, I didn't realise you were so ignorant of what is really happening. I thought you might understand fully, at last.' He made a gesture towards the ruined Lower Town. 'However, I see you won't be swayed. You have powers – hugely destructive powers; the evidence lies behind me. Another week like this and only you and I will still be alive. So let's prevent all that bloodshed so one of us at least is left with a kingdom to rule. Let's settle this between us, just you and me.'

Vikram stared. *Why would he offer this?*

The obvious answer was that Ravindra was losing: cornered in a citadel that offered only temporary shelter from all the terrible things Amanjit and he could do.

*But it's also fulfilling the* Ramayana *... in which he loses ... So why?*

'Where's Rasita?' he asked, buying time. 'If you've harmed her, you'll pay.'

Ravindra smiled blandly. 'Queen Rasita is well. She has all my care lavished upon her, the best of all things, and she has never looked lovelier.' He winked theatrically. 'I rather think she's falling for me.'

Vikram felt like he'd been punched in the throat. His mind went back to that dream of Rasita, and her words to him: *Dasraiyat, I reject you!* He still didn't know what that meant.

'She is *not* yours,' he snapped, although all his fears were returning. He was suddenly sick of this parley and wishing he'd never agreed to it. 'She never will be—'

'She's blossoming into a loveliness worthy of Sita herself,' Ravindra gloated. 'And her kiss is so *very* sweet.'

'Save it, Ravindra.' Vikram found himself trembling. 'You murdered Sue Parker—'

'I have never laid eyes on *your wife*, Chand – not in this life, at least.'

Vikram felt rage swell inside him until he thought he would belch fire when he spoke. 'All right, let's settle this, you scum: you can have your duel, right here and now—'

Ravindra gave a half-bow, chuckling. 'Tomorrow, at midday.'

'Why not now?'

'I have other matters to attend to, and I am sure you have farewells to make,' he said loftily. 'Tomorrow, here, at midday.' He turned on his heel. 'Sleep well, Aram Dhoop. If you can.'

Vikram tried to find a caustic reply, but couldn't. Finally he whirled and stomped back to his camp, feeling like an utter fool, his mind a churning morass of fury and fear.

Amanjit pushed through the dense foliage of the forest that only existed in this world, trying to find Vikram before the sun went down. The heat and light of the day were locked outside these verdant halls pillared with massive tree-trunks.

Vikram had come back from the parley, stated the terms of the agreed duel and then walked into the forest, wanting to be alone – but it was getting dark now, and if he really was going to take on Ravindra, he needed to eat and rest. Amanjit had taken it upon himself to find his friend, but it wasn't proving easy.

Finally he stopped, mentally cursing himself, and pulled out an arrow. He spoke his name, just as Vikram had done so often, and the arrow spun, then pointed to the right. *I've got to get used to this weird stuff*, he told himself as he returned the shaft to its quiver and started trudging in the direction it had pointed. In a few minutes, he spotted a slight figure sitting motionless in a clearing.

'Vik? There you are!'

Vikram was sitting cross-legged on the ground, his face an agony of frustration and indecision.

'Vik? What's happened?' Amanjit hurried to his side, knelt and put a hand on his shoulder. 'What's happened? Is it Ras?'

Vikram shook his head helplessly and angrily brushed at his face, leaving dirty streaks. 'No, she's fine, as far as I can tell.' He bunched his fists. 'I just don't know what's going on and Ravindra *does* – he knows everything, and I – I feel like I'm falling into a trap.'

Amanjit gripped his friend's shoulder. 'Vik, kill him, rescue Ras. It really is that simple. Everything else is just mind games. Keep focused.' He squeezed. 'I'll take care of the others; you get Ravindra. We're going to win.'

'But there's something else happening, Amanjit: something we know nothing about. Ravindra is totally confident: somehow, he *knows* he'll win – but *why?* What are we missing? How can he be so damned confident?'

'It's all a front,' Amanjit said. 'He's losing – he knows we'll crack his castle open in a day or two, so he's gambling on a one-on-one duel, that's all. If you'd declined the combat — and I'm not saying you should have — we'd win anyway.'

Vikram shook his head. 'No, trust me: it's more than a front. He knows something we don't, something crucial . . . and he's still got the strongest of the rakshasas, and loads of asuras too. It could take us weeks to get inside, but he wants to settle it tomorrow. So *why*?'

As he pondered Vikram's words, Amanjit started to look worried too. 'I don't know,' he said slowly. 'You're right, it makes no sense. Well, unless he's bluffing, or delusional.'

'I saw the look in his eyes when he spoke. There was neither doubt nor fear. He *knows* he'll win.' Vikram looked pained. 'And there's only be one thing it can be: he's seduced Rasita and captured Deepika, so he knows the *Ramayana* won't ever be fulfilled — *that's* how he knows he'll win.'

Amanjit shook his head violently. 'No, you must be wrong — Ras would *never* choose him—'

Vikram hung his head. 'Amanjit, I failed her. I never included her, even when my memories returned last year. I courted Sunita Ashoka when I should have been courting her. I almost fell in love with Sue — with Kamla — all over again. The truth is, I barely know Ras in this life. I've given her no reason to love me — and then I left her alone so that Ravindra could kidnap her at Panchavati, unopposed by me. It's a repeating pattern: Aram Dhoop never even noticed Padma because he was so obsessed with Darya. Rasita has no reason to believe in me. No reason at all.'

Amanjit grabbed Vikram's shoulders. 'But that's just not true. Have you forgotten how seriously ill she was? Even if we'd wanted to, we *couldn't* have included her, could we? And it was only because of *Swayamvara Live!* that she got healed. And it was *you* who made her whole again, by pursuing that. And let's not forget, I spent *months* with her in Delhi when we were hiding out. Trust me, she's *totally* in love with you – she went on and on and on about you all the time! She *knows* Sue Parker was just a past-life thing; I'm sure she doesn't hold that against you. She believes in *you*. And anyway, Ras would *never* fall in love with Ravindra.'

Despite Amanjit's enthusiastic defence, Vikram's expression barely changed. 'You're wrong, Amanjit. I've let her down, and she knows it.'

Amanjit wanted to shake him until his fighting spirit returned. 'She loves you, Vikram,' he repeated. 'She's my sister, and I know she loves you—'

'Then she's wrong to: you see, I let her down. Fidelity is a two-way street, and I betrayed her with Sue.'

Amanjit froze. 'You *what?* When?'

Vikram hung his head. 'The night before you arrived in Udaipur last year.'

Amanjit closed his eyes, trying to push down a rising tide of nausea. *Oh no . . . So under the terms of the* Ramayana, *we've already lost*. He balled his fists. 'How *could* you? All you had to do was stay strong! How could you? You've doomed us all! *How could you?*'

Vikram hunched lower. 'I didn't—'

Amanjit bent over and screamed in his face, 'I hope you had fun screwing her, because you were screwing us all when you did it!'

He couldn't look at Vikram any longer. He spun on his heel and stormed blindly through the trees.

Vikram knew he should have gone after Amanjit, but his legs felt too weak to move.

*I've messed this up so badly . . .*

He thought about Amanjit, so completely straightforward, with his feet on the ground, all life black and white. He thought of Deepika, her fiery temper and passionate nature; of Rasita, enquiring and tenacious. He'd failed them all in life after life, and now to stand so close, only to have let them down again . . . it was heart-breaking.

*But that night with Sue . . . she was Kamla, my wife of so many lives, and we were both so frightened, needing each other to go on, even if it wasn't together . . .*

Then with an effort he pushed all that aside, and tried to just *think*, letting unconscious disciplines take over, using meditation mantras to calm the mind, to soothe away dread and confusion. To let the mind fulfil its function and reason things out.

*I've been a fool. My understanding is too shallow. How has Ravindra got so far ahead of me? He always wins . . . and this time, even though I've got so close, I still don't know why I'm losing, only that I am . . .*

*What do I even know, any more? What can I state is certainly true? Beyond doubt . . .*

Fact: Ravindra has spent centuries killing us all, but getting nowhere. In some lives, there were hints that the *Ramayana* was significant, but nothing concrete. Ravindra is always hunting the women, but without the heart-stones, all he ends up doing is killing us. Ever since Mandore . . .

. . . *Mandore* . . . it all began in Mandore, with Ravin-dra-Raj and his ritual. Seven heart-stones, seven wives, each to die so that Ravindra could become Ravana.

*But why seven?* Was it any seven, or did it have to be *those* seven? *Fact: Rasita is Padma, my destined lover, but she has rejected me — and she called me* Dasraiyat . . .

*So* who *was Dasraiyat?*

*What did Ravindra say? That in Mandore, 'I was so blinded by your gentleness that I didn't recognise you for who you were.'*

*Not* 'what', *but* 'who' . . .

But he'd never met me until Mandore — or had he? And I'd never met him before Mandore either . . .

*Or had I?*

Vikram opened his eyes and the words tumbled aloud from his mouth into the shadowed glade. '*There were earlier lives, before Mandore!*'

'Yes, Lord. There were.' Hemant's voice carried on the still air from the edge of the clearing.

Vikram turned his head, shocked that he wasn't alone, but he felt no threat. Hemant's grey-furred shadow, the langur monkey, crept forward and hunched in front of Vikram, its eyes preternaturally bright.

'There was Lanka,' the Meghwal elder said as he joined him, gathering the big monkey in his arms and sitting. 'I thought you already knew this.'

'Knew *what*?' Vikram stared. *What does he know?* 'Who was I?'

'Ram, the prince of Ayodhya.'

Vikram blanched. 'No, I am not – I am no god – and that is blasphemy—'

'No, Lord, it is so. When the evil king Ravan Aeshwaran settled in Lanka with his beast-men, Ram and Lakshmana, the princes of Ayodhya, came with an army of men, former Sinathai. There is no question that you and Amanjit are the sons of Dasraiyat returned. My people see this clearly.'

Vikram rocked back on his haunches, his face pale. 'The sons of *who*—?'

'Dasraiyat, my Lord.' Hemant stared at him curiously. 'Dasraiyat of Ayodhya.'

*Ram . . . Ravan Aeshwaran . . . Lakshmana . . . Sinathai . . . Dasraiyat . . .*

The names . . . these were the keys to unlocking the final mysteries of that past life . . . Vikram reached back into the deepest recesses of his mind, seeking, reasoning, moving fragments and pieces . . .

Then darkness rose about him and coughing, he sprawled on to his back as memories washed over him like a tide.

# CHAPTER TWENTY-SEVEN

# WEDDING PREPARATIONS

*Lanka, 31 July 2011, morning*

Rasita woke trembling with anxiety and anticipation. The night had been harrowing. So many asuras had deserted in the afternoon to this Vibhishana, this false king, as Ravindra named him. Keke was beside herself with grief and rage, more like a feral cat than a person, and Rasita had to soothe her as if she were a child, until eventually the rakshasa girl fell asleep in her arms. She couldn't bear to wake her, so she just lay there, frightened at what her life had become, until eventually sleep claimed her too.

As Rasita stirred, Keke woke, and squealed in embarrassment at having fallen asleep on her mistress' bed.

'I'm so sorry,' she exclaimed, but Ras forgave her easily. She'd grown to love the little maid, and anyway, it was her wedding day.

They bathed, and then began a morning of further ritual bathing and yet more purifications, which felt like nonsense until she realised that Lavanasura was weaving charms and incantations into the prayers: slow, forceful words, binding her soul with Ravindra's. She accepted it with equanimity; the events of the last few days had removed her doubts.

The attacks on the citadel had ended after Ravindra went to parley with Vikram, Keke reported. It tore at her, to think of these two meeting. Despite Ravindra revealing Vikram as the reincarnation of the villainous Dasraiyat, she still felt something for him; she didn't wish him ill.

*Just go away, Vikram*, she thought, *and end this stupid war.*

She was convinced she was doing the right thing. *I'm healing Evil. I'm bringing his Destructive soul back into balance. I am Manda, healing my Lord Aeshwaran and restoring myself. I am healing the wounds of the world.*

It was just after sunrise. In four hours, at ten a.m., she would be wed.

As they went through the rituals of make-up, hair and dressing, Keke kept squeezing her hand. 'Oh Mistress, I'm so happy for you.'

The next hours almost vanished as Ras was beautified. Jewellery was tried and discarded until a set so delicate and lovely it looked priceless was selected. Beautiful wedding saris worth a fortune in the real world were paraded until she chose one in red silk and gold thread. They wrapped her inside it: the king's present, his alone to unwrap.

'The king's sister has gone missing,' Keke whispered to her. 'The soldiers are hunting Surpanakha, but no one will say why. Perhaps she's been killed.'

Rasita wouldn't be sorry if she had, not after all the awful things the sorceress had done. 'She hates me – she'd have tried to ruin everything,' she sighed.

As the appointed hour approached, she grew more and more serene, secure in the knowledge that she was doing the right thing. Within an hour, she would be wed, and so many good things would flow from that ceremony: the healing of Ravindra and herself would resolve centuries of pain.

The guests were already arriving. She was learning to know her new subjects, who were all anxious to show honour and obedience to their new queen. She greeted Lavanasura, her tutor and fellow Creator-magician, with fondness. Others still made her nervous, they looked so frightening and alien, but she took their obeisance with dignity, even from tiger-headed Syhajeet.

Then some distraction, movement outside the walls, maybe, caused many of the guests to leave, but she couldn't hear anything outside, and she refused to look from her balcony.

*I am done with those people and that life*, she told herself.

At last all the guests had finished greeting her and she sat alone with Keke in her room, her maid holding her hands and calming her. It all felt so sudden – her change of heart, her realisation that Ravindra was hers to heal – although it also felt like the culmination of everything that had happened to her in every life. And now it was so close . . .

A dark shape limped through the door and she thrilled at the sudden thought that this would be a messenger, come to summon her to begin the ceremony. *It's time* . . .

Then she saw who it was: Surpanakha, stalking into the room, cowled and misshapen.

'What are you doing here?' Rasita demanded.

'Surp—' Keke leapt to her feet and tried to dash for the door, opening her mouth to call the guards.

Surpanakha's fist cracked across the girl's jaw, felling her, and she collapsed in a crumpled heap. Rasita gasped, about to scream, but the demoness wrapped a hand about her mouth and a knife dug into her throat.

*'What the hell do you think you're doing, Rasita?'*

The demoness pulled down her cowl to reveal her face. Rasita's eyes bulged.

*'Deepika?'*

# CHAPTER TWENTY-EIGHT

# THE FINAL REVELATION

*Lanka, 31 July 2011*

'You must forgive your brother,' Hemant told Amanjit as they shared a morning chai. The dawn had come, red and sullen. Hemant was affectionately stroking his pet langur's head and feeding it biscuits. The impending monsoon hung heavily in the air, but although there was lightning on the horizon, still the rains didn't come.

Amanjit spat. 'He's not my brother, not any more. The marriage that brought us together ended when his father died. He was supposed to be my sister's guy, but he's wrecked that. He's not my brother.'

'He is your brother: he is your soul's brother. You need each other.'

Amanjit looked away, unwilling to acknowledge the truth in the man's words.

'He's meditating,' Hemant went on. 'My men are watching over him. He is safe. I'm not concerned for him.' Hemant lit a cigarette. 'I'm concerned for you. The sons of Dasraiyat must be whole and united to be victorious.'

*The sons of who?*

Amanjit looked at him. 'My wife is missing and I don't even know if she's alive. And Vikram has pretty much ensured that we'll all be killed today, and him first. With all that's happened, I think it's final. All those lives spent chasing a goal – and today it'll end. That bastard Ravindra will have won and who knows what he'll do then?' Amanjit hung his head. 'And I couldn't even spend my last night alive with my wife.'

Hemant listened impassively, stroking the coat of the monkey.

'What happens to a failed soul, do you think?' Amanjit asked. 'All our lives we're told that we are reincarnated until we achieve moksha, and once we've got spiritual perfection, then we're ready to ascend to Paradise. But what happens to the failed souls?' He tipped out the dregs of his chai. 'I guess I'll find out first-hand.'

'Faith, son of Dasraiyat,' Hemant said. 'Have faith.'

'In what?'

Hemant poked a solitary finger skywards.

Amanjit grunted disconsolately. 'Is that the best you can give me?' He rose and slouched away.

He found a vantage on a hillock at edge of the forest and watched the citadel. For some reason, it was lit up like a party was about to break out. But there was no music, not yet at least. The air was utterly still.

It was as if the whole world was holding its breath.

*

Vikram woke – or rather resurfaced – from the deepest of meditative trances. He had no idea how much time had passed; it might have been millennia, or a few minutes . . . but now he knew the truth. Finally, for the first time in millennia, he knew *everything*.

He got up slowly and stretched his back and his limbs, then slowly lifted one leg, extended it and then completed a slow dance, like a cross between tai chi and yoga, to limber his body. As he slowly turned and lunged, lifted and stretched, he felt life return. His mind was clear.

*I've made mistakes, but past mistakes can't be healed by regret, only by right deeds. And the right words.*

Now he had to act. It wasn't too late.

*Ironically, after all this time, the one person I'm not is Ram or Rama. I'm not a god, just a man. One with strange powers and skills, but just a man.*

That was an inexpressible relief: he'd never had any desire to be otherwise.

He gathered his weapons, realising that it was morning, the day of his duel. But he knew that there was much to do before then. And he knew who he was, finally.

*I am Dasraiyat.*

Amanjit didn't turn his face, but he knew who'd jogged up and joined him. They stared together at the citadel, from whence music had begun to gently carry on the still morning air.

'Well?' he asked gruffly.

Vikram took a few seconds to answer. 'I'm sorry.'

'Are you still my brother?' Amanjit asked. The words felt sticky and difficult in his mouth.

'Always. Please forgive me. I'm not perfect, but I'm trying hard to be. I was wrong – I was weak. But I won't be weak again. Will you let me earn your forgiveness?'

Amanjit exhaled. He'd never held a grudge in his life and he wouldn't start now. He turned and bear-hugged Vikram until his face went red.

'You already have,' he told him, cuffing him gently about the ear. He wiped his eyes surreptitiously and pushed Vikram away. *It feels good, this reconciliation thing.* 'So, what's the plan? Win the duel, rescue the girl?'

Vikram waggled his head ambiguously. 'Sort of. I've remembered something: something I've never known before – and it's a game-changer. New data; new rules.'

'I'm sick of all this bloody remembering stuff.'

Vikram smiled grimly. 'So am I. But this was the last revelation and now I know it all.'

'You always were a know-it-all,' Amanjit exhaled, and with trepidation in his voice asked, 'So, what's happening?'

'I've worked out why Ravindra was so cocky about the duel last night, but still insisted on doing it today. It's because he's planning to marry Rasita beforehand. She's been holding out, but now she's cracked. She's fallen for his story – and it's a damned good one, so no blame to her. She thinks she's doing the right thing, that she's healing a damaged but virtuous man, and she won't realise the truth until it's too late. If I hadn't reached the key memory just now, I'd have shown up at midday, seen Ras on his arm, fallen into total despair and lost the duel: forever.'

Amanjit bit his lip, trying to understand. 'What about Deepika?' he asked. 'Any revelations about her?'

Vikram's face went still. 'I'm sorry, nothing – well, except that if I'm right, Ravindra's going to either kill her today, or she's already dead and her ghost is his prisoner. Either way, her soul will be obliterated unless we do something.'

Amanjit felt hope and despair well inside his chest. He struggled for calmness. 'Damned if I'll let that happen. So, what do we do?'

Vikram put his hand on his shoulder. 'We can't wait until the duel – it'll be too late for the girls by then. We have to stop the wedding.'

Amanjit said grimly, 'Good plan.' He pointed towards the citadel, where music was now swelling out like an overflowing fountain. 'But if we're about to become the stars of *Wedding Crashers II*, we've got to hurry. It sounds like they're about to start the party.'

'Then there's no time to lose: let's find Vibhishana and get this battle started.'

Inside half an hour, Vikram was leading the tribesmen through the deserted, fire-ravaged Lower Town and winding towards the citadel. Every man they had; Meghwal, asura and freed slave, was waiting in Lower Town, ready to open fire with every shaft they had made or salvaged.

Lower Town hadn't yet been cleared of the dead and the festering asura corpses stank. Everyone wrapped noses and mouths in scarves, but the stench still permeated. Vikram couldn't help but stare at the bodies lying twisted and burned beneath the morning sun, most of them now purple and discoloured, bloated by the internal gases of their decaying bodies. Horrible images, ones he'd hoped never to see again, but all too familiar, in too many lives.

*We did this: Amanjit and I . . . We brought fire and war. May we be forgiven . . .*

Somewhere behind them, Vibhishana was moving the asuras stealthily into the ruined town in support of the Meghwal. Once a breach was effected, they would all move forward together.

Vikram and Amanjit crawled behind a low wall and into position. Around them, Hemant's people crept into whatever cover they could find and checked their weapons. 'We're going to take a lot of hits, Vik,' Amanjit commented in a low voice. 'Those walls are still strong, and they've got protection from our astras. As soon as our guys break cover, their archers are going to mow them down.'

His face serious, Vikram said quietly, 'I know. Hemant says his people are willing. I've told them to stay under cover as long as possible, but it's up to us to minimise their losses. We've got to make a breach and get Vibhishana's people inside as quickly as possible.'

'Yeah. I keep thinking I'm going to hear a wedding march any minute.'

Beyond their position was seventy yards of clear ground. Hemant slid into place beside them, the langur as always clinging to his back. 'My men are in position, Vikram-ji.'

'No one shoots until my first astra strikes,' he reminded Hemant.

'And no one advances until there's a breach,' Amanjit put in.

'No hole, no go,' Hemant agreed in a sing-song voice.

'Give us two minutes,' Vikram said. 'We just need to set ourselves up.'

Hemant scurried away to pass on the deadline to the Meghwal and Vibhishana's asuras, hiding all through the ruins. Vikram and Amanjit quietly sorted through their arrows, leaning a few against the wall in easy range, pre-aligning them to certain spells so that their efficacy would be improved. Amanjit removed his turban, replacing it with a steel helm.

There was nothing left to say. The plan was simple and flexible: blast a hole, get in, find Ras. They clasped hands, then turned to the wall, looking for a weak point.

'There, where it's already cracked after last night,' Vikram pointed. He raised his first arrow, sighted it and waited while Amanjit did the same. They both took a deep breath, as if about to plunge into deep waters.

Vikram clasped his hand. 'Good luck, brother!'

'Yeah, see you inside, bhai,' Amanjit replied.

Music welled up and flowed over the walls, filling the air about them.

Wedding music.

They aimed, muttered their spells and fired.

# CHAPTER TWENTY-NINE

## LOVE AND FIDELITY

*Lanka, 31 July 2011*

'Ravan Aeshwaran, I give you my love and fidelity, forever.'

Ravindra bowed over the hand of the woman before him and kissed it, accepting the reverence in her eyes as his due. Her upturned face was filled with hope.

'Unataka, I accept your renewal of fealty on this, my day of marriage.' He stepped forward and kissed the sunken skull-like face of the rakshasa known as the Naga Queen. Her leathery green skin ran down her almost naked torso to blend with the giant serpent trunk that began at her hips. She bobbed in a serpentine approximation of a curtsey while her snake-body wove rapid patterns on the tiles as she backed away.

She was the last of the rakshasa queued before him to renew fealty. It was more than just a ritual, when so many asuras had gone over to Vibhishana. But there had been one notable absentee, and now muttering sounds ran through the court. His sister Surpanakha hadn't come to renew fealty and it had been noted. It troubled him too: she'd gone missing overnight and he couldn't believe she'd defected or died – she was more bloodthirsty in his own cause than anyone. So where was she? He'd had people looking, but she wasn't to be found, even using magical means.

But the time had come. He put his sister from his mind and turned to the giant Meghanada Indrajit, who was obviously relieved that the tedious waiting was ended. The giant warrior made a drinking gesture.

Ravindra nodded, forcing a smile; he was also weary from spending the night trying to batter down Deepika's defences. She felt close, very close, but he couldn't break her, which worried him that something might be going badly wrong. He needed to begin Rasita's final transformation as soon as possible.

'Ensure the walls are secure, Meghanada, then join us.' He looked to see Lavanasura, lisping into the ear of the eagle-headed Atikaya. 'Lord Lavanasura, bring the bride to the mandir.' He clapped his hands. 'It is time!'

There was a sudden blast and the floor quivered. It came from the thick north wall, a hundred yards from where they stood. The distant shudder of power released suggested earth-shattering parvata-astras hammering against the northern walls.

He realised what was happening immediately: Vikram hadn't honoured the truce until their midday duel. His rakshasas started howling in fury, snatching out weapons and beginning to move willy-nilly.

He made his voice cut above the din. 'My Lords, hold – *hold!*'

He waited until their initial alarm had subsided, then spoke again, projecting confidence. 'My Lords, we have strengthened the walls. Real-world artillery couldn't breach those wards in a day of constant firing. Our warriors are well armed. Meghanada will inspect the assault point. The rest of us have a celebration to attend – so let our enemies pound us all they like. We'll not even hear them in the wedding chamber.'

The rakshasas murmured at their king's composed demeanour and bowed respectfully. He raised a calming hand, reflecting on how close it all was now. So long, so much suffering – but now everything was falling into place. He thought hungrily of his bride.

*Oh, sweet Manda, how will you feel when you realise that you are mine once more . . . and this time, for all eternity?*

He turned his attention back to the here and now. 'Meghanada, go to the walls. Take those we know would rather fight than feast. The enemy might have realised what's happening and be planning an interruption.'

'But the duel is not until midday.' Indrajit frowned. For all that he was a heavy-handed killer, he had a very strict sense of protocol and honour. 'We have a truce that must stand until after you and the Rama have fought,' he rumbled indignantly.

'Our enemies are not so noble as we might imagine,' Ravindra told him. 'Secure the walls!'

The huge warrior bowed, his armour clanking. 'My King!' he roared, and shouldered his way through the crowd, picking warriors to accompany him as he went. The uproar diminished as those rakshasas scattered, going first to seek their weapons of choice. Ravindra watched them, steeling himself for the day to come.

*Meghanada, you were always the most competent of these monsters, apart from Maricha and Surpanakha.*

*Surpanakha . . . why did you not come, my sister?*

*And where is Deepika Choudhary? How is she resisting me? Has someone trained her?*

He felt like a climber, precariously placed above a precipice, watching his footholds crumble in slow motion.

*I must move, right now . . .*

But he stopped, his brow creasing, as he made the connection: Surpanakha . . . Deepika . . .

*She's here — she's been here all along—*

Roaring in fury, Ravindra threw up his hands and began to conjure.

# CHAPTER THIRTY

## PASHUPATASTRA

*Lanka, 31 July 2011*

Glowing astras hammered and shattered against the walls of the city. Every impact was like a bullet hitting glass, sending a spiderweb of cracks radiating out, but almost at once those glowing cracks would fade, cut short and disarmed by the protections woven into the structure, leaving only small pits in the stonework.

Hemant's men and Vibhishana's asuras ensured the heavy fire continuously swept the walls, but the defenders were keeping their heads down, apart from the occasional pot-shots that whistled harmlessly over the rubble. Every so often Amanjit broke off pounding the walls to launch aindra-astras, raining shafts from the sky, but they hit an invisible shield that flared at each impact in a glorious technicolour flash, dissolving the astras. It was an incredible light show, but they were getting nowhere. Vikram and Amanjit called upon greater reserves, and increasingly heavy blows hammered into the structure, causing ever-brighter explosions, more dust and shaking ground, as they kept pounding and pounding . . .

And it was all to no avail.

'It's not working, Vik,' Amanjit panted. 'We're not even making a dent.' He glanced up. 'Do we attack?'

Vikram cursed. 'Without a breach, there's no point.' He swallowed, then set his jaw. 'It's clear this citadel, unlike Lower Town, has centuries of accrued enchantments protecting it. I think we've only got one option.' He nocked an arrow, one he had kept carefully aside. 'We need the Pashupatastra.'

Amanjit blinked. 'The *Shiva-astra*? That'll half-kill you, Vik – you were laid out for a week after that Vaishnava-astra in Sri Lanka – and then Ravindra will slaughter us.' He held out a hand. 'Let me try it. You know I'm handling astras I never managed in Sri Lanka.'

'But you've never used a Great Arrow, Amanjit. Miscast it and you'll kill yourself – and then Dee will kill me.'

'It's too risky. And even if it does work, I'll still have to take on Ravindra alone.'

Vikram gritted his teeth. 'I'll manage. We have no choice.'

Amanjit groaned. 'This is so not good.'

'I think we're pretty much out of choices at this point.' Vikram stood up; this arrow required a classic open-chested, upright stance. An asura on the battlements saw him and took aim, but ducking wasn't an option; he had to focus. As he sank into the trance, he wasn't even aware that Amanjit had loosed his own astra and blasted the asura in the chest before he could fire.

Vikram focused, throwing all of himself into the mantra

Vishwamitra had taught him so long ago, bringing all his concentration to bear upon this great task: gathering the forces of Destruction, the Shiva aspect, and loosing them on the wall.

*We have to keep him safe until he can shoot*, Amanjit thought as Vikram immersed himself in his impossible task.

He shouted at Hemant, 'We have to protect Vik, okay? So anyone who appears on the walls, don't take chances, just shoot them down.' Then he added, 'And when Vik does shoot, keep your bloody head down!'

The tribe's chief waved, then bent and muttered something into the ear of the man next to him. Seconds later, the man lifted a wooden pipe and sent out a complex pattern of high-pitched, carrying peeps and at once, the arrow-fire along the line intensified.

Amanjit could already see that the forces Vikram was drawing on were beginning to affect the natural world. Winds had started to rise and swirl, sending stinging dust into eyes and noses. Through the haze he dimly glimpsed a red figure at a window high above, held by another dark shape, and thought, *Red is the bridal colour* . . . But then he saw the winged rakshasas circling lower and had to shift his gaze – and his aim – to them, as beside him, Vikram's mantra took on even greater force. The air crackled as dust and smoke swirled in towards the darkly glowing arrow. Amanjit felt his hair lift; static electricity crackled.

Vikram went rigid. His bowstring taut, lightning crackling along the shaft, he shouted one word, both invocation and spell, '*Shiva!*'

The Pashupatastra arrow roared. Winds whipped at the attackers as the slipstream formed behind the arrow, which had become a trident glowing livid violet – and with an ear-splitting concussion, it *crashed* into the ensorcelled stonework.

Amanjit was already pulling Vikram to the ground as the citadel erupted before them and a wall of force threw them backwards. As Amanjit hunched over Vikram's limp form, the air pulsed and throbbed, dozens of attackers, both human and asura, hurled around as if they weighed nothing, while stone shrapnel tore the air above their heads.

Amanjit's ears throbbed, his eardrums pulsing – and then the daylight vanished as the shockwave washed all of the dust and debris right over them. The oxygen was sucked from the air and he found himself gasping, trying to breathe.

Vikram looked stunned. 'Hold on,' Amanjit shouted at him. 'Stay with me—'

'Air,' Vikram gasped, 'we need air, for Hemant's men and our asuras . . .'

Amanjit nodded, bent close to the ground and sucked in a mouthful of air, then blindly fired straight up into the sky, shouting 'Vayu—' to invoke the vavayastra of the wind god.

He hit the dirt again, covered Vikram's slumped body and clung on as a gale ripped through the battlefield, The air was like sandpaper, scouring the ruined town and ripping painful swathes across exposed skin. Anyone who hadn't managed to hunker down in a hole or cling on to something was thrown hundreds of yards.

Then it was gone.

For several seconds, utter silence prevailed.

Then a woman screamed.

*Rasita*—

His sister's voice was unmistakable: Amanjit shouted her name as he leaped to his feet, his heart in his mouth. The wall before him was shattered, a massive breach torn by the destructive power of Vikram's Pashupatastra, and behind it, the main buildings of the citadel had been broken open; the place looked like it had been pounded by a massive fist. Towers lay in ruins, the rooftop gardens were gone and inner rooms had been torn open to the skies.

There were no enemies in sight and nothing moved.

The only sound was the echo of Rasita's voice.

Without waiting for Vikram, Amanjit drew his sword and ran for the breach, shouting, '*Ras*—'

Deepika slowly released her iron grip, but she didn't remove the dagger from Rasita's throat; the tip had gouged the skin, leaving a shallow, bloody track.

'Well?' Deepika demanded, wondering, *Do I actually have to kill you to stop this wedding?* 'What the hell do you think you're doing?'

'Dee? Is it really you?' Rasita's voice was disbelieving. 'But I saw you—'

'You saw me fall down a hole. I climbed out again. I met the boys. We set out to rescue you from the Big Bad Demon-King. And now I find you about to *marry* him? So I ask again: HAVE YOU LOST YOUR FUCKING MIND?'

'But how? Surpanakha—'

Deepika looked over her shoulder. There really wasn't time for this, not with the stunned guard outside and the maid on the floor . . . *But somehow, I have to try and talk her round . . .*

'Surpanakha tried to kill your family in Mumbai, but I got her instead. I ransacked her mind, looking for clues – then her ride home showed up, so I used some skills Vishwamitra taught me and I took on her shape. It was a spur-of-the-moment thing. Shape-changing is easy once you know how.' She tried not to look smug, and failed. 'So here I am. And now the boys have shown up too. But slutty Rasita can't keep her hands off Ravindra,' she added with a snarl.

She saw Ras' face twist miserably. 'It's not like that.'

'Isn't it? Gods, if I hadn't interrupted you before, you'd have been lost already. He nearly unmasked me then – do you have any idea how *hard* it is to keep a false shape together when an evil, all-powerful demon-king is kicking you in the guts? And on top of that, I've been holding off Ravindra's attacks through the heart-stone all night – but I can't keep it up. I'm pretty sure he knows who I am now.'

'I'm sorry,' Rasita said miserably, 'but you don't understand—'

'No, *you* don't understand, Rasita. He's got you thinking you're saving the universe, but you're not: you're just damning us all.'

Ras blanched. 'What do you mean?'

Deepika clutched Rasita's head and stared into her eyes. 'When I was in Surpanakha's mind, I saw the *true* history – I know it all, now: the destruction of Sinathai, the seven fractured souls of Manda, the sons of Dasraiyat and their war on Lanka.'

'Then you know how Dasraiyat wronged him and—'

'You *idiot*! Do you really not get it? *Dasraiyat* was the one who was wronged, not Aeshwaran! Ravindra's told you the story, right? About how King Aeshwaran and his best friend and the king's wife engaged in this ritual to save their land, and in the middle of the ritual, one betrayed the other? Well, I'll bet he didn't tell you the *true* version: how all that Aeshwaran – that's Ravindra, as he is now – ever wanted was to destroy his rivals, *all* his rivals, and Dasraiyat especially. Once he was inside the ritual, he didn't need his so-called "best friend" any more, nor his poor, benighted Manda, his exceptionally clever and talented wife who was virtually his slave. He'd always *hated* that she surpassed him. There was no way he was going to let her survive once they'd completed the ritual.'

She shook Rasita gently, willing her to understand. 'Ras, I've been in Ravindra's study – I've seen the notes for his Mandore ritual. If you saw the things he did to those poor dead queens once he had them bound by those heart-stones in the Ether – then you'd realise what he's *really* like. My God, he really *is* a monster – he's not been human for a very long time.' She shuddered. 'And I've been inside Sur-panakha's head: she was truly his sister, you know, and she knew the truth. Her attempts to kill Kiran and Tripti were on Ravindra's orders. He's a cold-hearted bastard.'

Rasita shut her eyes and moaned, 'Nooooo . . .' She started shaking her head side to side.

'Yep, 'fraid so, sister. He's lied to you at every step. *He* was the one who disrupted the attempt to save Sinathai in a jealous rage, not Dasraiyat. He wanted no rivals in sorcerous power. He intended to kill Dasraiyat and enslave Manda. He abused her like the monster he is, but he still needed her. And *that* is what this has been about, ever since: Aeshwaran trying to restore Manda as his puppet, and Dasraiyat – Aram Dhoop, Chand, Vikram and all the rest – trying to save her.'

Rasita burst into convulsive sobs and Deepika found her fury dissolving in those tears. She sheathed the knife and pulled Ras to her chest, stroking her back and repeating softly, 'There, there. It's going to be all right, now that you understand. We'll get you out of here. We'll make it right.' She let the girl cry for a few more seconds, then dabbed at her face with a corner of her bridal veil.

'Rasita, listen, you've got to pull yourself together now. I know it's been a shock, but we can't afford to wait. We've got to go.'

'You kept telling Ravindra that he should kill me,' Ras whimpered. 'In that council meeting . . .'

'That's because I thought you were so far gone that killing you was the only option. When I came in just now I was all ready to slit your throat right then and there, without even giving you a chance to speak – I'd lost hope of ever getting through to you.'

Ras looked as if she wanted to curl up in a ball and die.

The hour of the wedding was upon them. Deepika looked around, wondering how to get Ras moving. Then the stunned rakshasa maid groaned and raised her head.

*Shit. I'll have to deal with her more permanently . . .* She drew the dagger again.

'No,' Ras gasped, suddenly animated. 'No, she's my friend.'

Deepika stared. 'She's a *rakshasa*, Ras. She's *no one's* friend.'

'She's *my* friend,' she repeated. 'Please, don't hurt her.'

Deepika rolled her eyes. 'For God's sake – we'll probably end up having to kill her later,' she grumbled, but she pulled Ras to the window. 'Let's fly out of here before the wedding party arrives.'

Suddenly the door curtains parted behind them and a slender figure stepped through: a cobra-headed reptilian thing with insect eyes, long robes flapping about him. Behind him, other shapes peered, and a bell began to ring.

Rasita exclaimed, 'Lavanasura—'

'Go, Ras.' Deepika pushed her towards the window, calling on her powers.

The rakshasa made a hurling gesture and conjured a spear that flew straight at her.

'*No.*' She gestured and the spear splintered and flew aside, but the rakshasa was already conjuring another. She took a step forward and hurled fire at him, which he doused in a wet curtain of droplets he sprayed about him, almost vanishing in a cloud of steam.

*Nice trick, bastard*, she thought, and realised: *He's not like a normal rakshasa: he's using Creative, not Destructive energy.*

Then her conscious thought gave way to anger, she balled her fists and shrieked a bolt of lightning at him, right into the droplets screening him. Electricity flashed through the droplets, straight to his flesh, and he howled, dancing in her lethal grip—

—until a hulking shape roared through the doorway behind him and pulled the reptilian rakshasa back before leaping towards her.

Deepika blasted him with another lightning bolt, smiling

grimly as he too howled in pain . . . but only for a moment, for he did something that arced the electricity into the stone, earthing it. Sparks rippled around the doorway. She inhaled, released the lightning and *punched*, her fist becoming a ball of force that hammered into the new enemy and slammed him into the wall. He hit with a wet splat and slid to the ground.

An arrow crackled into the room, an agniyastra. She stopped it in mid-air and spun it so it flew back to its starting point. Fire bloomed and someone cried out: another one to her. But more enemies were coming. They had to get out.

Striding to the window, she made wings spring from her own back, wincing at the discomfort. Ras was already on the ledge. Her arms were shimmering, surrounded by spirit-flesh in the shape of her own wings: she'd obviously learned something of sorcery. 'Good girl,' Dee said encouragingly. 'Let's get the hell out of here.'

Outside the window, it looked like a cross between Diwali and an artillery duel. The defensive wards of the citadel were crackling and dancing as showers of astras and normal arrows continually attacked the bubble-like membrane of enchantment holding the walls together. Coruscating light danced, dazzling and captivating.

They both hesitated, wondering if it would be safe to fly into such a storm—

—when it suddenly went quiet.

'Go high,' Deepika shouted, 'up and over.' As they readied themselves to jump, she cried, 'On my count—'

—suddenly the curtain wall *disintegrated*. It looked for all the world as if a god had punched his way through the stone and out the other side. Then a wave of soundless force rolled over them, sending them flying backwards, and they fell sprawling to the floor where they lay winded and gasping. A mighty roaring made the very air quiver, then everything fell into a ghostly silence. There were great clouds of dust and detritus everywhere.

Deepika crawled to Rasita and helped her back to the windowsill, where they clung teetering to each other, awe-struck and frightened.

'It's Vikram – it has to be,' she shouted, or thought she did; her ears were ringing and she could barely hear herself. 'We've got to get out of here, sister.'

But great sweeping clouds of dust and smoke washed over them and all they could do was cling blindly to the window frame. Then a great gale buffeted them, and only after that could she see that the citadel looked like a broken toy. Some of the towers were down and theirs had cracks running all through it.

All had fallen silent.

'Come on.' She pulled on Ras' arm encouragingly and they both re-conjured wings.

They launched themselves into the air, beating their magical pinions towards freedom.

Ravindra turned his attention from his subjects and his mind sought Deepika Choudhary . . . and found her at last, in Rasita's chambers. He roared in rage and ran for the balcony, his eyes raking the tower that housed his queen. Two women stood at the window, wings on their backs, poised for flight. He felt his blood boil in his veins. He was dimly aware that the enemy outside had stopped firing, but his mind was consumed with the two young women on the tower.

*NO, YOU CANNOT*— He raised a hand again, to trap them both and finally claim—

—as the curtain wall disintegrated with a roar, a shockwave lifted him from his feet as easily as if he were a doll and flung him across the room. For an instant, the whole of Creation teetered on the verge of implosion. He lay dazed, his courtiers strewn around him like toys, wreathed in dust and smoke and choking for breath, as stunned as he was.

And then there was silence.

His brain struggled to process what had happened. He felt like a runaway train had missed him by a fraction of an inch. He could barely think.

Some of his courtiers started groaning, but many more were not moving at all.

He clambered to his feet and staggered back to the window. He barely had time to register the breached walls, the inner buildings flattened in one dreadful blow, when he saw the two winged shapes launch themselves from a window of Rasita's tower.

*No*—*!* Raising a hand to the Darya heart-stone and extending the other towards the two fugitives, he snarled a word and a bolt of energy throbbed through the air towards the fleeing queens.

# CHAPTER THIRTY-ONE

# BRONZE AGE DRAINAGE

*Lanka, 31 July 2011*

Deepika felt like a giant fly-swatter had struck her, thwacking her sideways into the stone tower. Black stars exploded inside her skull, then, too dazed to resist, she was falling, and an explosion of agony nearly knocked her unconscious as she smashed into the paving stones below. She bounced like a thrown doll and lay sprawled on the cracked stones.

Then the pain stopped and she went utterly numb.

She couldn't feel anything at all, nor could she move a muscle below her neck.

*It's broken . . . My spine is broken . . .*

She couldn't see Rasita anywhere.

Then . . .

*No . . . Ras—*

Ravindra spiralled gracefully through the air towards her. He held a jewel in his hand.

*A heart-stone.* My *heart-stone.*

She could feel it beating in his fist.

Out of the corner of her eye she could see blood pooling around her. The silence was deafening. His lips were moving as he descended, but she could hear nothing.

*This is what death feels like . . . this fading feeling . . .*

Rasita leaped into the air, her wings bearing her away from her tower window and above the broken walls. *I'm free*, she thought gleefully – until a deep voice spoke, then she heard a shriek behind her.

*Deepika?* She spun, losing height, losing control, and cried aloud in shock as she saw Deepika bounce into the tower, then plummet into the pavement before Rasita could even raise a hand.

Blood spread from the motionless body.

Then she saw Ravindra, gliding as if walking on the air, descending upon Deepika with a gloating smile.

In that instant all confusion vanished. Her nascent love for him died and she was able to truly accept, in her very core, that everything Deepika had told her about this – this *creature* – was true. He'd played her emotions as masterfully as a concert pianist.

Her senses racing, she pictured everything around her, and took the only path that could save them.

Even as Ravindra touched down beside Deepika, his head turning to look upwards, only just starting to register her presence, she howled words of command and dropped onto her sister-in-law's body . . .

. . . as the paving opened to her shrieked command . . .

. . . and they plummeted, wrapped in each other, into the stream of water flowing through the drains below the footpath.

And above, the pavement instantly slammed shut over them.

Water swallowed them, pulling them along, and following Lavanasura's lessons, she inhaled it and extracted the oxygen she needed. She dragged Deepika behind her, frantically seeking another way out before the earth reopened behind her, and all the while, her mind was working at her sister's broken body, holding on desperately to the tiny spark of her life-force.

*Stay with me, Dee*, she begged silently.

Then she felt the pulling upon the strings of her own heart-stone.

Ravindra stared at the cracked pavement in stunned disbelief. One instant, the dying Deepika Choudhary had been at his feet and he'd been about to suck her soul into her heart-stone. He'd not become aware of Rasita, swooping down upon them at a fatal speed, until too late.

Then both were gone, and it took him precious seconds to realise what Rasita had done: instead of splattering herself across the stone, she'd somehow opened the paving stones like a door and borne the broken Darya down with her into the drains — and closed the ground behind her, too.

He admired the audacity and quickness of thought even as he cursed it.

Around him, his rakshasas floated down to join him, some landing heavily, others gliding to a light-footed halt and all jabbering inarticulately: something had been stripped from their psyche when he'd warped them so long ago so that they reverted to animal intellect under stress.

'Calm yourselves,' he told them. He raised his sword and

pointed it at the breach. 'The Rama has fired a Trimurti astra.'

He let that thought chill them. It frightened him too, but it also enraged him.

*The Trimurti astras . . .* He thought about the Pashupatastra, remembering. *Yes . . . that was how it went . . .*

He raised his hand to quell their nervousness. 'Yes, he fired a Great Arrow, so he is weakened now, weak as a child, and only the Lakshmana guards him.'

The rakshasas growled savagely, regaining their ferocity as the thought of their enemy's vulnerability sunk in.

'The man who destroyed our city now lies helpless as a babe,' he told them. 'Go, my children. Go, rip the Rama and the Lakshmana apart. Tear out their hearts and feast upon their flesh. *Go!*'

Meghanada bellowed a war cry. Beside him Atikaya opened his beak and shrieked, and as the rest joined in, Ravindra commanded, 'Kill them all – bring me their heads.'

Howling their bloodlust to the swirling skies, they thundered towards the breach.

*Should I join them?* He thought about how good it would feel to put an end to Dasraiyat, perhaps forever, then wavered. *No, I cannot let my queens get away. The risks are too great.*

*I have always been able to defeat Dasraiyat – but a freed Manda? That, I cannot risk.*

With a gesture, he opened up the cracked stone pavement and leaped down into the flowing water. He let his eyes adjust to the total darkness before conjuring a small light in his blackened hands. Peering into the drainage canal, he pondered his next move. *The Darya was near death . . . so they would have gone with the direction of the flow . . .*

He clutched at the Darya-stone and found only a very faint pulse. She was still alive, but barely. Then he tried the Padma-stone . . . *Ah, there you are, Rasita* . . .

All doubt disappeared. He had needed to woo Rasita because he hadn't got her heart-stone, and by the time she gave it to him herself, she was already emotionally his, so he'd decided to enjoy himself and continue reeling her in.

But the Darya must have persuaded her of the truth. Now that ruse was up, he would need the heart-stone to subdue her after all . . . He grinned lasciviously as he made his plan: he would kill the Darya first and consume her soul, then take the Padma's virginity, completing the last step of the Mandore rite. And when he did, Manda would reform, super-powerful, but utterly enslaved to him: his own personal djinn, at his command, forever.

He altered his form to swim better. Part man, part shark, Ravindra swept into the darkness, following the trail of blood in the water.

Boring history lectures echoed dimly in Rasita's mind as she navigated the lightless drainage system of Dholavira. She could almost hear her teacher saying, 'The Harappans had extensive water drainage systems, the first in the world, which ran beneath the city, carrying drinking water in and sewage away. They were a truly advanced people. *Blah blah blah* . . .'

She remembered thinking that there could be no more irrelevant subject to study. Now it felt like the most valuable life-lesson she could have learned. And she'd barely listened . . .

*Just let there be a way out.* She conjured bubbles of air about their faces. The strain of keeping Deepika alive was tearing her mind apart slowly. *Mouth: breathe. Heart: contract; release. Wounds: mend! Stay with me, Dee. Don't you* dare *die.*

She had to get them to a safe place and stop moving. This journey was placing too great a strain on Deepika's precarious hold on life, and the strain of conjuring fresh air from the water was wearing Ras down; there was no way she was going to be able to sustain this.

Suddenly there was light ahead. Muttering a prayer of thanks to whoever was listening, she pulled Deepika along as fast as she dared. She turned the metal grille before her to paper with a thought, then pushed through. As an afterthought, she sealed the hole with porous stone, trying to disguise their path, before looking around.

She recognised where she was instantly: they were in the women's bathing pool. *Perfect.*

She tugged Deepika, aware she was now having to strain even harder to keep her soul-sister alive.

An insistent, insidious thought surfaced in her mind: *If I let her die, I would be whole . . . I would be Manda . . .*

She refused to listen, just kept pulling her sister through the water to the steps, where she could try to heal her, if that was even possible. She had no plan beyond that.

She struggled to the foot of the steps, wondering how she was going to find the strength to lift Deepika out of the bathing pool. Then a shadow fell over her.

She groaned and looked up. *Please, no . . .*

A slender figure, horns jutting from its brows, and pale glowing eyes, loomed over her at the top of the stairs.

'Mistress?' said Keke in a tremulous voice. 'What's happening to us?'

# CHAPTER THIRTY-TWO

# HEALING HERBS

*Lanka, 31 July 2011*

Amanjit stopped before the breach as a huge shape with massive horns jutting from its temples and shoulders strode towards him. The rakshasa hefted a war-axe in one hand and a massive curved scimitar in the other. There were others behind him, more rakshasas than he'd ever seen in one place, and too many blades to keep track of, all hooting and growling like animals as they slowly advanced, eyeing his blade fearfully.

Amanjit called energy to his sword to make it more potent and it glimmered menacingly as he raised it. He slashed about him, establishing his reach. They stayed away, pushing at each other.

*One rush and I'm dead ...*

He grinned about him fiercely. 'Tell you what: you know me. I won't go easy. I promise you I'll cut in half the first three of you to attack,' he told them. 'Which raises the question: who's going to wait to be fourth?' He slashed again, and they backed off a few more steps.

Then they came at him in a wave—

—and instinct took over as he started ducking and spinning, arching his back to avoid spear-thrusts. His sword slashed out, cutting through armour, flesh and bone like butter. An arm was lopped from one while another fell, disembowelled and screaming as entrails snaked from a split belly. He caught an axe in his right hand and struck the left eye of the wielder, darting sideways as the rakshasa fell stone-dead, parrying a sword-blow and then leaping over three slicing blades in a spinning cartwheel that left another rakshasa cut almost in half.

They fell back, staring at him, and then at the four bodies strewn on the broken ground.

He panted, 'Sorry, I was too modest. Next time, who wants to be the fifth?'

They backed away, keening softly.

Behind him, coming up through the rubble of Lower Town, he could hear the horns of Vibhishana's asuras braying a challenge as their battle cries rose into the air.

Ravindra's rakshasas milled about, clearly uncertain, then the largest one, the bull-headed giant, stepped forward.

'I am Meghanada, known as Indrajit,' the rakshasa rumbled. 'Well met, Lakshmana.' He gestured with his axe to the rakshasas behind him, barring them from joining his attack, and told them, 'The Lakshmana is mine.'

'Is that right?' Amanjit leaped forward, his blade flashing low, then he altered the angle to slash at the rakshasa. Their blades met and he had to throw himself backwards as Meghanada's war-axe split the air, barely missing his chest.

The rakshasa snarled at him warily.

'Well, do you still fancy it?' Amanjit snarled. 'Because I have to tell you, I'm in a bit of a hurry right now.'

He attacked again, this time coming in low and slashing at Meghanada's feet, but roaring in indignation, the rakshasa leaped over the blow. Amanjit rolled and parried as Indrajit tried to cut him in half. Metal clanged torturously, then he whipped his blade up to his enemy's throat, the war-axe rose to block and with a sharp *snick*, the sabre swept through the haft, and the half-moon axe head fell to the ground beneath them.

They staggered apart and Meghanada Indrajit snarled, 'What true warrior attacks the *feet*? I see you are still a snivelling cheat with no sense of honour or battle etiquette.'

'Oh yeah, that's right: didn't Lakshmana beat Indrajit by making sure his morning prayers were interrupted or something?' Amanjit panted. 'Learn anything?'

'Yes, it taught me a valuable lesson,' the rakshasa growled. 'Cheats prosper.' He gestured, the axe-head lifted and spun like a discus at Amanjit's belly.

Amanjit yelped, flailing to one side, and the whirling blade spun in the air and flew back onto the axe-haft.

Meghanada roared at his warriors, '*Let's* all *kill him* . . .'

And the wall of rakshasas swarmed forward again.

Vikram lay on his back, barely conscious that Amanjit had left him. His ears were ringing, his vision coming and going and he felt sucked empty. Amanjit had been right: the Trimurti astra had taken too much. The Destructive Aspect was not his strength and his Pashupatastra had been weak and poorly executed, taking too much from him and not enough from the world about him.

*Ravindra won't need to fight me. I couldn't hurt him now if I tried.*

*I need help . . .*

A small figure appeared at his head: a langur monkey, its grey coat covered in dust. It made a concerned noise, and then Hemant's face, for once not smiling, appeared behind it. 'Vikram-ji,' he said, 'what's wrong?'

'I . . . I . . . can't . . .'

Kasun crawled up beside Hemant. The doctor was covered in blood. They both considered him gravely, then Hemant cocked his head. 'I am thinking you need a pick-me-up, Vikram-ji.'

*That's the biggest understatement I've ever heard . . .*

Hemant patted Kasun on the shoulder. 'You have the things I recommended?'

Kasun smiled doubtfully and pulled out a syringe. Without preamble he slammed the needle into Vikram's shoulder and depressed the pump. Vikram felt a numbing that filled his bones in seconds.

'Uhhh . . . ?'

Hemant leaned close. 'You are expecting perhaps Sanjeevani herbs from the Himalayas, like in the *Ramayana*, I suppose?'

'Ehhh . . .'

'Sadly, the mountain is too far away and we have no time. Instead, your friend here has this concoction of opiates, mixed with pseudoephedrine and a dangerous quantity of adrenalin.'

Vikram stared from one man to the other.

Kasun looked apologetic. 'As your doctor I should warn

you that you have maybe a quarter of an hour of energy before you collapse and perhaps die.' He swallowed. 'I'm sorry.'

'There is much at stake, Kasun-ji,' Hemant pointed out, pouring something sweet and syrupy down Vikram's throat.

Vikram's mind reeled, but suddenly nothing hurt any more. 'What's the drink?'

'Caffeine, guarana, ginseng and cola. And some other things.'

Vikram winced, but everything *was* feeling better. 'If you're thinking of selling it, you really need to work on the flavour,' he managed to gasp, somewhat deliriously.

'I am thinking the World Health Authority might be a bigger obstacle,' Kasun replied.

Vikram found he could sit up because nothing actually weighed anything now. His vision had become tunnelled and oddly discoloured, as if he were living in an out-of-focus three-dimensional movie, but still there was no pain. His body rose of its own volition. 'Where's Amanjit?' His voice was echoing strangely in his ears and his words were slightly slurred.

Hemant pointed to the breach in the walls and Vikram stared: the middle section of the citadel had been smashed open and in the breach, two figures were exchanging words and fierce blows.

*Amanjit . . .*

Vikram swept towards them, his limbs pumped with power and life. An incredibly seductive feeling of invulnerability swept over him as he accelerated, his hands going to his weapons again.

Behind him, Vibhishana's asuras were flooding through Lower Town, howling war cries. Their king, carried on a palanquin in their midst, was waving them on.

Hemant's Meghwal emerged from their hiding places and they too streamed towards the breach.

It was now or never.

## CHAPTER THIRTY-THREE

## KEKE'S CHOICE

*Lanka, 31 July 2011*

Rasita looked up at the rakshasa maid, whose face was swollen from Deepika's earlier blow. 'Keke? What are you doing here?'

Keke came down the steps, her hooves clicking on the stone paving. She was wrapped in a thin shift and looked frightened. 'Mistress, when I recovered, our tower was damaged and you were gone. I was frightened – I thought Surpanakha had taken you. There was a dreadful noise outside – the walls are breached; did you know that? I ran down here to hide.' She looked back over her shoulder. 'We all did.'

Ras looked over the lip of the pool and realised there were more than three dozen rakshasa and asura women, including young children and the aged. Rakshasa ladies and asura servants were holding each other tightly, cowering at every noise from above. Dust filled the air, lending the torchlight a glowering haze.

'Mistress, who is this?' Keke descended the steps, the fur on her thin legs floating out like bristles on a bottlebrush as she joined Rasita in the water. She peered at Deepika's unconscious face.

Rasita tensed, but when Keke showed no recognition, she realised Keke had only seen Deepika disguised as Surpanakha, not her real form. 'This is my friend, Deepika.'

'Is she a queen too?' the maid asked innocently as she put her arms beneath Deepika to help lift her out of the water.

'Yes, Keke, she's also a queen, just like me.' Ras cradled Dee's upper body and let Keke take her legs. 'Come on, let's get her out of the water.'

Together, awkwardly, they lifted Deepika up the stairs and laid her on her back on the paving. The wound on the back of her skull had closed over during the journey, thanks to Ras' ministrations, but she was still unconscious, and limp as a corpse.

Keke cupped Dee's face. 'She is very beautiful, Mistress.' Then she suddenly cried, 'Oh, Mistress, this has ruined your wedding – and your poor sari.' She peered at the silk that was miraculously still tightly wrapped about her, although it was torn and soaking. 'Mistress, this is awful. We must pray the Ravan will protect us.'

Rasita bent over Dee, dipped deep into her last reservoir of energy and opened up her mind to find the thin spark that was still Deepika. She called, *Sister.*

Dee's breathing rasped. *Ras?*

*I'm going to save you, I swear it – just hold on, and don't let go. Talk to me.*

*I'll try . . . It's like I'm swimming, Ras. I could just float away and sleep . . .*

*DEE. STAY.*

*I read that note he left you, Ras: the one you kept beside your bed? About Aeshwaran and Dasraiyat. And Manda. The Ritual . . . We're her, Ras . . . you and me . . . we're what's left of Manda . . . so if I die, you could take me up and you'd be whole . . .*

*No: you're going to live, and when this is done, Amanjit will look after you and you'll walk again and have children and you'll—*

*I don't mind dying . . . not if through that you can be Manda and end this nightmare.*

*No, I won't let you, so stop that nonsense. You're going to be okay. You just have to hold on. The boys are coming.*

Suddenly the walls of the bathhouse shook: Someone was battering the stone plug she'd used to seal the inflow shut. The whole wall blasted open and the rakshasas and asuras shrank back, whimpering.

Ravindra – no, this was *Ravan Aeshwaran* – entered the chamber. He was massive, at least eight foot tall in this guise, and his coppery face was cruel and hard, his eyes blazing.

'ENOUGH OF THIS CHARADE,' he roared. 'I'M GOING TO RIP YOU BOTH APART. THIS TIME I WILL *NOT* BE THWARTED.'

He held aloft two glittering heart-stones in his left fist. Chandrahas, his beautiful curved moon-blade, gleamed in his right hand as he ploughed through the water towards her.

Rasita gripped Deepika's hand. There was nothing they could do – but they had to try. She extended her other hand, with some vague idea of pushing the demon-king away, but he saw the movement.

'FREEZE.' The demon-king lifted the heart-stones and she felt her whole body lock rigid. Beside her, Deepika's mouth went still, her face contorted.

*Sister.* The part of them that was still free, their exhausted, battered souls, clasped together, and they felt something stir inside, something that had been waiting a millennia to happen. Something *pure*.

But it was happening too late.

Ravan Aeshwaran towered above them, holding aloft the heart-stones, and aligned his sword with Deepika's heart. 'Farewell, Darya. The end has come, at long last,' he purred. 'When I cut you open, you will reach inside yourself and pull out your own heart, which you will give to me, to fulfil your role in the Rite of Mandore.'

Deepika's eyes went wide, but her arms, which a moment ago had been lying useless at her side, rose to her chest as if to receive the sacrament of his blade.

Ravan Aeshwaran looked at Rasita. 'And then I think you know the rest, my *lover*.'

Vikram didn't think; he didn't need to. He just fired the arrow. 'Vavayastra,' he shouted, which felt like the thing to use: a hurricane to rip through the enemy.

The shaft roared over Amanjit's shoulder and sent a Force Ten gust radiating from the tip. The first rakshasa it struck, a bull-headed monstrosity, was tossed aside like a stuffed toy, then the force flattened the horde of rakshasas behind the bull-headed warrior like wind-blown rubbish in a gale.

Vikram could barely focus on anything from one moment to the next; his mind was flip-flopping about crazily. He kept wanting to stop and admire the way the sparks trailed from his arrows, or admire the ineffable and fleeting beauty of the patterns of smoke in the air.

Amanjit peered at him dazedly. 'Vik?'

'Hey – what's happening?' Vikram slurred, as he sought some kind of control. He felt flushed and incredibly hot, as if raindrops would sizzle if they hit his skin. But shooting arrows helped, so he fired another one, which exploded into an eagle-headed thing, blowing it apart in a gorgeous spray of red liquids that caught his fascinated gaze . . . 'Hey, freaky . . .'

Amanjit stared. 'Are you okay?'

'What? Huh . . . Um, no time, bhai. I have about ten minutes to save the universe before my head explodes.'

'*You what*—?'

'Really. No time.' His eyes wild, Vikram pushed himself into a run, clearing the rubble and the cordon of dead or dying asuras with an effortless leap. 'Come on,' he called over his shoulder, but Amanjit was already behind, with . . . *Thingy, and Whatever* . . .

Then some central core part of him caught the scent of his quarry and with a gesture, he tore open the earth.

'Ravan,' he shouted. Dark water swirled past, some part of the citadel's ancient drains – but there was no time. He ran at a wall, and exploded through it.

'RAVAN—!'

Amanjit started to follow Vikram, but a massive shaggy form in dented armour, covered in dust and blood, lurched creakily to its feet and blocked his way.

Meghanada Indrajit staggered, caught himself and turned. But his eyes flashed in sudden eagerness and the weariness fell from his stance. 'Lakshmana,' he snarled, 'this is our day of destiny, at long last. Let us renew our ancient duel and finally see who is the better man.' He straightened and a sword appeared in either hand. 'Let us see who among us, we who live in the shadow of great men, is the mightier.'

Amanjit groaned. 'Bloody hell, you oaf, I really don't have time for this.'

Vikram had already disappeared into the tangle of broken stonework and Hemant's men, surging towards them, would be here in seconds, unless this bull-headed monster managed to rally his warriors and stopped them.

*I've got to finish this.* He picked up an arrow and, not even bothering to find a bow, yelled something and pointed. It flew like a rocket from his hand at the towering rakshasa, hitting him in the middle of the chest and blasting him away.

Meghanada jerked, staggered and collapsed.

'I'd have won anyway,' Amanjit told the dying monster as he broke into a sprint. 'It's just that was quicker.'

*Now, where the hell is Vikram?*

Rasita gripped Dee's hands, screaming her name, and energy flowed through their hands, coalescing until something formed; it felt like jigsaw pieces slamming together.

But they were too late.

The moon-blade glittered and began to fall.

'NOOOO—' A small feral thing detached from the shadows and hurled itself at the arm of the demon-king, ripping and tearing, spitting and shrieking, dashing the blow aside. Slashing wounds ripped along Ravan Aeshwaran's arm, shredded skin splattering blood as he roared, let go of the heart-stones and seized the shape that was fighting him.

*Keke?*

The little maid struggled valiantly in Ravindra's grasp, flailing and screaming – then the mighty arm drew back, and threw her. She struck the wall with hideous force, bounced and fell. Her limp body did not move again.

Ravindra roared in fury, howling in the face of his rebellious subjects, and raised his sword again—

—as a wall of female flesh struck him, every single one of the women present, and he went down in a churning tide of bestial forms, vanishing in the rushing waters.

But with a ghastly roar, Ravan Aeshwaran erupted from the crowd, tearing apart Rasita's protectors and turning the waters red. His shining blade whirled and another beast-woman was carved in half; her lifeless body fell to pieces and disappeared into the bloody depths.

The remainder fell back in a semi-circle, terrified, but spitting fury at him.

'Stay away from our queen,' one snarled, and the others hissed in agreement.

His voice filled the chamber. 'I AM YOUR KING: SHE BELONGS TO *ME*.'

'You promised us *healing*,' a grotesque beast-woman howled at him. 'You promised us *redemption. You promised you would make us whole.*' They bared their claws again at the master who had promised them everything and given them nothing, for centuries. '*You told us you would learn to love, and through love, you would heal us all.*'

He spat blood and growled, 'Foolish wretches – you are nothing but *animals*. I AM YOUR KING AND YOU BELONG TO ME!'

He took a step towards Rasita and Deepika – and the women fell on him again, prepared to give their lives to protect their queen.

All the while, Ras was fighting to hold onto Deepika's failing consciousness, barely aware of the nimbus of light forming over them. Tears streamed from her eyes at the strain, and every muscle clenched with the effort. She trembled, on the brink of motion—

There was a dreadful scream from behind them, and Ravan Aeshwaran strode from the slaughter, Chandrahas dripping with gore. Then even he paused and stared at the light above them.

At last Rasita looked up and realised that it wasn't just a shapeless glow: it had the form of a woman, who was shimmering brighter and brighter: a woman she almost knew . . .

Then the roof of the bathing chamber disintegrated and the dust went howling away in a sudden blast of hot air that scoured the chamber.

'AESHWARAN,' shouted Vikram, hovering in the air above. 'COME OUT AND DIE.'

The demon-king spun, his expression changing from anticipation to thwarted fury, but his body sprouted another set of arms and he walked up the air as if it were solid stone steps. He threw one last glance at Rasita, then he lifted his sword aloft and turned away to deal with Vikram. Chandrahas shone in the moonlight and his blood-wet flesh rippled in the silver sheen as he erupted into the air above, where Vikram awaited him.

'DASRAIYAT,' he howled, his voice resonant with hate.

With a brilliant flash, both fired arrows that exploded halfway between them as they met. And then, amidst bursts of fire and light, they passed from Ras' sight.

Ras fell onto Deepika's chest as the spell immobilising them fell apart, but even freed to move, she found she still couldn't. The pale ghost standing above them reached down, unseen hands clasped them both and something left her and instead flowed into that beautiful glowing form, which began to drift into the sky, growing more and more distinct all the time.

A woman.

A queen.

A being who was part of her . . .

No, *she* was part of that being.

A woman named Manda.

# CHAPTER THIRTY-FOUR

# MOKSHA

*Lanka, 31 July 2011*

Amanjit started to follow Vikram, but he immediately found himself in the middle of a firefight. Hemant's men, streaming behind him through the breach, were being bombarded by deadly astras from the last desperate defenders. Without him, he knew they would be slaughtered.

'Find cover,' he shouted at them, and Hemant followed up with whistled orders. Once relatively safe behind a half-destroyed wall, Amanjit assessed their position. At least half a dozen of their men already lay wounded or dead around them. He fired off an aindra-astra to keep the enemy heads down, then as Hemant's people rained arrows down on the rakshasas, he dragged one of the wounded men under cover. Hemant's monkey bent over the fallen man, cooing sadly — but astras from above started ripping into them again and cursing, Amanjit changed mental gears.

*You're on your own for now, Vik. If I don't help these guys out, they're all dead.*

Perhaps it was destiny, if such a thing existed.

Behind the enemy position, another part of the broken fortress exploded and two dark figures flew upwards into the sky, the air between them crackling with pulsating light.

For a moment, the enemy fire stopped, and Amanjit tensed his legs, ready to go to Vikram's aid after all – but the hidden rakshasa archers weren't done yet; once again the air was filled with lethal shafts. All Amanjit's energies went into protecting the men around him; his hands blurred as he fired again and again, shooting down astras he barely saw.

Suddenly, there was a mighty cry and Vibhishana's palanquin was borne into the breach on the back of his asura horde. The courtyard filled with warriors cheering their beloved king, then the advance swept forward again.

Amanjit ran with them.


Legends told of duels between heroes that lasted for hours, sometimes even days.

Vikram knew from centuries of deadly experience that real fights were generally over and done in seconds.

He shot an agniyastra from the sky with a mohini and tried to counter with a naga-astra, but Aeshwaran was just too damned fast, and before he'd even finished casting his spell, a vavayastra was blasting him backwards. Then he had to contort his body wildly to avoid being crushed by a parvata-astra that sent a boulder whistling down on him like a train.

His own vajra lightning arrow was countered effortlessly by his Enemy's mohini – but he had no time to react before he found himself enveloped in a wall of writhing snakes. He shouted in sudden agony as a dozen pairs of fangs buried themselves in his flesh and clung desperately to his bow as he felt the lethal venom began to numb him, his false, drug-induced energy beginning to waver. All the while, his eyes were following Aeshwaran as the sorcerer-king floated languidly to a better vantage point and raised his bow.

Vikram shouted in terror and sent out a pulse of energy from his core that blasted the snakes from him. His flesh was torn and bloody, burning where broken fangs were still embedded, but he was hanging on to his bow, and although Aeshwaran contemptuously swatted aside his next astra, at least it interrupted the spell he'd been attempting to cast.

Below them, Vikram could feel the surge of battle, but up here where they circled each other, walking the air as if it were earth, it was just the two of them. There was nowhere to hide any more.

Vikram was being forced to dodge and block, to keep moving, and he knew his Enemy was wearing him down and setting him up for the kill.

The last few yards between them vanished in a heartbeat and now Aeshwaran was on him, brandishing Chandrahas, the moon-blade, in his hand.

Vikram yanked out a dagger and blocked, but his blade was instantly blasted apart and Chandrahas slashed his shoulder as he dived away. He leaped onto a blasted tower, only to spin aside as fire billowed from Aeshwaran's hand. He sucked in the smoky air as despair and exhaustion overpowered him. He could feel the drugs Kasun and Hemant had pumped into him waning; his movements were slowing, his shoulder was bleeding badly, radiating pain, and the venom was coursing deeper into his arteries.

In his heart and his mind, Vikram felt the bitter truth emerge, reinforced by centuries of failure: he was losing. But he pulled out his sword, gritted his teeth and tried to close in, determined to go down fighting.

Amanjit caught a glimpse of the incoming astra, but it was just one of so many. The mohini he fired in retaliation had become a cluster and taken down much of the incoming fire, but that one shaft had flashed through his defences – and it struck Vibhishana dead centre in the chest, blowing the rakshasa's enormous ribcage apart.

Vibhishana's asuras shrieked, and above them, while the enemy crowed, they faltered, turning this way and that as if looking for a miracle. For an instant Amanjit was frightened that they would give up, or fold, or even change sides.

He jabbed a hand, pointing up at the rakshasa archers above them. 'Look upon them,' he roared, 'there they are: there are your *slave masters*. There are the bullies who have made your lives a misery for *centuries*. There are the killers of your true king!'

A mass of arrows flew down at him—

—and with no real idea what he was doing, he raised a hand and somehow *willed* the shafts to stop . . .

*And they did.*

The flight of arrows was frozen in the air: a torrent of death held in abeyance as rakshasas, asuras and Meghwal alike stared.

Then the arrows fell straight to earth, impaling the ground and surrounding him like a mini forest.

A giant goat-headed asura rebel screamed a war-cry, then thousands of mouths opened and thousands of throats gave vent to the fury and hatred of centuries as men and beast-men flooded past him and up the stairs towards their oppressors.

The moment of indecision was gone. The king was dead. Long live the next one.

Amanjit nocked another arrow and joined the assault.

Vikram flew at Aeshwaran, but he was no match for the Ravan at swordplay. A neat thrust neatly skewered his wrist and his blade fell from the air as he reeled away. Ravindra could have followed him and cut him down with ease, but for some reason, he didn't.

Vikram worked it out: death wasn't enough, not this time. The demon-king intended to end this for ever. Aeshwaran had drawn his bow once more and as he trained the arrow, Vikram could see it exuded all the tell-tale signs of a burgeoning spell: the Pashupatastra, the Trimurti astra of Destruction.

*This is it* . . .

All of his past failures replayed in his mind, a blinding flash that broke apart the last vestiges of his battle-fury. The venom had finally overcome the drugs in his system and now he felt the exhaustion from casting his own Pashupatastra drag him down. Swirling violet light surrounded Ravan Aeshwaran as he muttered the final phrase, pulled a fraction further, then released.

Vikram had nothing left. Hanging there in the sky, beaten,

he was the perfect target. Gravity began to tug, but too late; the Pashupatastra was already flaring as it seared towards his exposed heart.

*I have failed again. For the last time . . .*

He closed his eyes.


And nothing happened.

He opened his eyes again to find himself still hanging in the air. The Pashupatastra had stopped dead an inch from his chest – and a woman's hand was wrapped around the shaft.

He *knew* her, although he'd never seen her before: she was Rasita and Deepika, and she was whole and perfect and she burned so bright it hurt to look at her.

'Manda?' he stammered.

She smiled at him. 'Dasraiyat, my love.'

The Pashupatastra in her grasp bucked, like a rocket trying to fly. All along its length purple light danced. The universe had gone utterly still.

He stared at her. She was transparent, a spirit-thing only, but she held the astra in her hand with strength beyond any mere mortal.

He looked up at Aeshwaran, who was also suspended in the sky; his face was so contorted with emotions ranging from hatred to fury to despair to twisted adoration that he looked barely human. His eyes were locked on Manda.

She turned to face him and Aeshwaran reached out to her. In his left hand he grasped the heart-stones, but as he lifted them, they crumpled to ash. Vikram could see faint skeins, like spiderwebs, running from Manda's left hand, which was holding the Ravan motionless in the air.

'Manda,' Aeshwaran pleaded, 'I loved you.'

'What you called love wasn't love at all,' she replied, her musical voice cold. 'Love does not imprison, it frees. Love does not take, it gives. You have no idea what love is, and you never will.' Her eyes blazed. 'All those years ago I endured your cruelty, thinking I had to sacrifice myself to preserve the kingdom. No more.'

Vikram suddenly found he could move. He raised his bow. Only one astra would work, and although he had no energy left, there was an energy source beside him that would provide all he needed. He drew on Aeshwaran's own Pashupatastra, seized its flow and started reshaping the energy as swiftly as he could. From it he made a Brahmastra.

*Just like in the Ramayana*, he realised: the Creator's astra, the antithesis of Destruction.

Ravindra hung in the sky, helpless, his eyes pleading, but his wife's expression held no pity at all. 'Shoot, Dasraiyat,' Manda said in a voice of aching sorrow. 'End this now.'

As the arrow in her hand faded and crumbled to ash, its energy flowing into his own astra, her face turned slowly towards him and she spoke in his ear. 'Goodbye, Dasraiyat, forever. For me, there are no more lives. There is just one thing more I must do, and then . . . *moksha*. I shall at last be released.'

The Brahmastra flew true, but Vikram couldn't watch as his ages-old Enemy finally perished. Aeshwaran-Ravindra wouldn't just die. *He would cease to be.*

Instead, he watched Manda, whose face held such a look of transcendent joy and sadness he could scarcely bear to see it.

Then she was gone, his arrow struck Ravindra in the chest
and a burst of light sent the world spinning away.

Through the jagged hole in the roof of the bathing pool
chamber, a searing flash lit up the sky. A pulse of energy
shocked through Rasita and Deepika, and Ras embraced it,
cherishing the extraordinary feeling of well-being; it felt
like being immersed in warm scented water, caressed by
loving hands, kissed by a lover, held by a mother. All her
pain fell away and when she looked down, she saw her own
body, lying on the stone, with a look of ecstatic wonder on
her face.

Deepika was lying beside her, with exactly the same look
on her face. Then Ras fell back into her body and found
herself staring up at the brilliant figure above her.

A goddess knelt over them, clothed in light and joy, and
she held Fire and Water and Earth and Air in her hands.
She bore three faces: on the left, she was stern and dark,
her right was shining and celestial, and in the middle was a
balance between the two; the face that was the most human.

'Mandodari?' Rasita and Deepika croaked together.

'Just Manda,' the shining being replied. 'I am whole now.
The Ravan is dead. I can go on now.'

Rasita felt a surge of panic and loss. '*Go on?*'

'But what about us?' Deepika asked fearfully.

Manda reached down a hand to them both, and smiling,
said, 'You will remain behind. In joining your essence, you
have remade me, but only for a short time. Had you surrendered yourselves to Aeshwaran, I would have been chained
spiritually, a source of overwhelming power for him, and

there would have been no limits to what he could do, in this world or in yours. But you held out, and so I was free to help Vikram destroy Aeshwaran – forever. Now I can use my power to repay you both.

'After I was broken apart, my seven little soul fragments remained separate, weak, dying young, time and again. But souls are composed of life and they can regrow – and every one of the seven Aspects I broke into have been trying to do so. The four elemental ones were the weakest, but the Destructive Aspect, Halika, was able to function as a normal human, albeit one twisted towards evil.

'You, Darya, were the Protector Aspect, and you were more resilient than Halika. You were always reaching for the light, although in times of peril, the darkness overwhelmed you.

'And you, poor Padma, were broken again: an already fractured soul sundering into three, ensuring that your lives were always brief. But now, through your courage, you two have restored me and I have mastery of all Aspects once more. I have the power to make you whole in yourselves, so you need not think of yourselves as fragments of a broken whole any more. I will make you both complete, whole individuals, forever after. You have already brought yourselves a long way along that road.'

'Will we die?' they asked simultaneously, and Manda smiled.

'No, no, my dears, for the first time in millennia, you will *truly* live. This is my last life, but it will be your first.'

Then she bent over them, and despite the fear and wonder, they dimly felt her prise apart their clasped hands, then each spun away, floating, falling headlong into a beautiful sleep.

# CHAPTER THIRTY-FIVE

## TEMPLE OF LOVE

*Agra, Uttar Pradesh, September 2011*

'Excusing me, sir,' said the T-shirt seller in affected English, 'would you like to be buying a very fine T-shirt?' He held up a thin white shirt with bad stitching, dirty hand smears over the hem. A poorly realised drawing of the Taj Mahal, surmounted by the phrase *Temple of Love*, was written on the front in garish orange. 'Only three hundred rupees, sir, a bargain.'

Amanjit raised a hand and pointed towards the shimmering marble dome in the distance. 'This is not a "Temple of Love",' he snapped. 'The guy who built this? He bankrupted his kingdom, got overthrown and locked away by his own son and died in prison. So don't give me your bullshit.'

'Yes sir.' The T-shirt vendor blinked. 'How about two hundred rupees? Very nice T-shirt.'

Amanjit rolled his eyes and turned away. Deepika took his hand and they gazed up at the Taj Mahal, shining in the glorious September sunshine. There were thousands of tourists, but they were alone, wrapped in solitude and sadness.

Or they had been, until the vendor approached again. 'One hundred and fifty rupees, sir: you are my first customer today, so I give you special price.'

'It's four o'clock in the afternoon,' Amanjit pointed out. 'How can I be your first customer?'

'I slept late, sir. And it has been a very slow day. One hundred and twenty, maybe?'

Deepika dragged Amanjit away before he hit someone. They found a bench and sat in the sunshine, wrapped in their own personal gloom. 'I don't understand,' Amanjit whispered. 'I don't know why we can't *all* be happy.'

Deepika sighed. 'I don't know either.'

It wasn't them. They were as deeply in love as they had always been; or more as Deepika no longer flared at the slightest misunderstanding and Amanjit reacted to mishaps like a man, not an overgrown child. They laughed easily and were playful as kittens at times, but they shared a dignity that was almost regal.

She brushed at his uniform. He'd been accepted into the Air Force; he'd had few qualifications when he applied, but his aptitude in the initial tests had startled the recruitment officers. Amanjit had always hated exams, but incredibly, when this one started, he found he knew all the answers. They were telling him now that the sky was the limit, without any hint of a jest: he'd been accepted as a trainee fighter-pilot. What had once felt like a futile ambition now looked not just possible but probable.

The two months since Aeshwaran-Ravindra had been

defeated had been like a dream. They'd left Hemant and his people sifting through the wreckage of Lanka while the grieving asuras buried Vibhishana with all the pomp and ceremony they could muster. Those remaining beast-men loyal to Ravindra had surrendered or fled. They'd started trying to repair the castle, but Amanjit suspected they might end up having to abandon the place.

They'd returned together to the real world in a state of stunned wonder. Conversations petered out, for Vikram, Ras and Deepika were almost beyond words, so intense had those last moments been.

But human needs remained.

The girls were both whole, not just uninjured but transfigured. Deepika felt like she could dance on water if she wanted, and her reunion with Amanjit was the most wonderful night of her life, even better than her wedding day.

But in the morning, Ras and Vikram were both gone, leaving separately. They'd exchanged barely a word, let alone looked at each other.

'It makes no sense,' Deepika said. 'It's like the worst tragedy ever – they're Rama and Sita if anyone is, so how can they not be in love? How can they not want to be together?'

Amanjit said helplessly, 'I don't know either.' He repeated, 'It makes no sense.'

At first they were cautious, concealing their identities as they returned to their rented hideaway in Delhi, but within a few days, sensational news hit the television, the papers and every other form of media: all the charges against 'India's Most Wanted' – Vikram, Amanjit and Rasita – had been dropped. The police had issued a statement proclaiming that their interest in the whereabouts of Vikram, Amanjit and Rasita was over.

They could return home.

According to the world's press, two mysterious strangers – no one had recognised Amanjit and Deepika – had slipped into the Mumbai Police Headquarters with enough documentary and video evidence, recovered by Deepika from Ravindra's rooms in Lanka, to prove beyond a shadow of a doubt that Majid Khan had murdered Sunita Ashoka.

For a few days the media had gone mad, and then again when Amanjit came out of hiding. He'd been a minor celebrity for a while, but told the press only that he'd been hiding in Assam. After a few weeks he'd been largely forgotten again.

The only questions he couldn't answer, even if he'd wanted to, were: *Where's Vikram? And where's Rasita?*

Lalit had moved in with Amanjit's family, and when he and Deepika had visited them in Jodhpur, they found a letter from Ras, telling them she needed time and space to think. They'd heard nothing more.

Then the Air Force recruitment took Amanjit and Deepika back to Delhi. After a proper homecoming with Deepika's family, they moved into married quarters on the Willingdon Air Force base. Deepika had immediately joined the Air Force Wives' Association and was already helping run one of their high class shops in Santushti Market.

This trip to Agra was his first leave and they'd really been looking forward to it, but the glaring brightness of the white marble was too much; the so-called 'Temple of Love' was more oppressive than uplifting, as if it were mocking them and their friends.

Without a word, they rose and walked away, hand in hand.

Deepika suddenly grinned. 'Hey, I didn't know all that stuff about the Taj Mahal – did you make it up?'

'Nah. I've just spent eighteen months trailing after Vikram; droning on and on about historical stuff is what he considers a "fun chat". I guess some of it must have stuck.' He laughed. 'Let's go, shall we? I'm so over this ancient crap.'

'I love you: you know that, don't you?' Deepika asked softly, as she did every hour or two.

He smiled. 'Yeah, I'm picking that up.' He tweaked her nose playfully. 'But if you feel an overwhelming need to prove it to me, I know just the place.' He dangled the hotel key.

She smiled and put her arm about his waist and they drifted through the crowds of tourists and sightseers and guides, seeing only each other.

# CHAPTER THIRTY-SIX

# DUSSHERA

*Rishikesh, Uttarakhand, late September 2011*

Vikram wandered aimlessly among the small groups of tourists. It was late for the summer crowd escaping the heat, early for the winter visitors seeking snow in Rishikesh, so the hotels were half-empty and not much interested, more focused on taking a break and doing running repairs than servicing guests.

He was still travelling under a false name, which suited him fine.

The *Ramayana* said that Rama had come here to Rishikesh in the aftermath of victory, seeking penance for the killing of Ravana; despite being evil, he'd been a great man and a follower of Shiva. So propitiation of the god was apparently required.

Vikram had no such attacks of conscience – Ravan Aeshwaran had been evil personified, as far as he could see, and he'd resisted coming here at all, instead spending several weeks on his motorbike drifting through Jammu and Kashmir, telling himself he needed to be alone. But somehow, he'd ended up here anyway.

There was a big grey Shiva statue beside the river. The foothills of the Himalayas loomed all around him, swathed in pine with mists clinging like a comforting blanket. He bathed in the cold headwaters of Mother Ganges, but felt no better for it.

He'd seen the newspapers. The charges against him had been dropped, the police had announced, so he was free to come out of hiding – but he didn't want to. He hated the idea of being chased and harassed by the media all over again, and the thought of the lies he'd have to tell nauseated him, not to mention the tiresome fuss that would be made. And then he would be forgotten again: a no one, just as he'd started. So it was better to just stay a no one and leave out all that bullshit in between.

He felt like a drained bucket, dumped and forgotten.

India rolled on as normal as the weeks passed, with cricket tours and Bollywood blockbusters, economic deals and political scandals. No one knew or cared what he'd really done. Oh, sure, the mysterious ambushes of the military had ceased; he could take some pride in that, but little else. His duel with Ravindra had consumed sixteen lifetimes, but now it felt like two madmen killing each other for the right to be king of somewhere long since forgotten. He felt horribly alone as he drifted from town to town, but he couldn't face going back.

*Dad is dead. Amanjit and Deepika are happy. And Rasita . . .*

He was afraid even to think of her . . .

. . . The morning after the death of Ravan Aeshwaran, he'd woken whole, the drugs and the venoms burned from his system. He knew Manda had saved him. He was surrounded by cheering Meghwal, asura and rakshasa warriors, all dancing like they'd won an international cricket match.

When they all came together, the four of them, in the aftermath of Ravan Aeshwaran's final death, he'd thought for a fleeting moment that he would die of happiness. He'd hugged Amanjit, held Deepika, and then turned to Rasita, standing shyly in the corner, waiting for him . . .

. . . and then they'd just looked at each other . . .

The moment their eyes locked, they both knew how false their triumph was.

She'd fallen for Ravindra, beguiled by his lies and his beauty – if Deepika hadn't got there, and if he hadn't realised in time, she would have married him, gladly and of her own free will, giving the Ravan the final key. With the power of an enslaved Manda, Ravindra would have slain Vikram, and after that, who could ever have stopped him?

And in that same instant, she'd looked at him and known what had passed between him and Sue . . .

They'd stared at each other while Deepika and Amanjit kissed, oblivious to anything else, then vanished inside their room.

Then he and Rasita had turned away from each other.

He didn't want to see her ever again.

## *Khadir Island, Rann of Kutch, late September 2011*

Rasita sat cross-legged across the fire from the small man with the monkey on his shoulder.

Hemant puffed a pungent marijuana chillum and said sympathetically, 'We are safe now, lady. The remaining asuras have returned, but with most of the rakshasas dead, they have sworn they will no longer raid our world, only trade.'

A large number of the rescued slaves of Lanka had refused to come to the real world, terrified of leaving the only place they'd ever known. Most of them had been born centuries before anyway, and everything they had once known was long gone. Only the youngest had been happy to be reunited with their distant relatives; the rest decided to stay in myth-land and rebuild Lanka as free citizens, working alongside the remaining beast-men. They had no king: neither Ravindra nor Vibhishana had left an heir, and all of Ravindra's remaining rakshasas had been imprisoned, because no one trusted any of them on the throne.

Lavanasura was the only rakshasa permitted to come and go freely, for he was a healer.

September was waning, the nights slowly cooling, and the country erupted into wedding fervour. In every town and city the length and breadth of the sub-continent the streets were filled with dancing and singing grooms and their parties, riding to their marriages.

After weeks of aimless wandering, Rasita had found it all unbearable and had returned to Dholavira.

She was alone in the Meghwal settlement, but they

all knew her; she was safer here than anywhere, except maybe her home. She missed her mother and her brothers, but she felt a restless stirring that kept her from stepping back into that life. Unlike Deepika and Amanjit, who had ambitions and purpose as well as each other, she felt haunted and adrift, stuck in a backwater eddy instead of negotiating life's currents. She did write a letter home, but she knew if she went back, it would be impossible to leave again.

'I am sad, lady, that you are not with Vikram-ji,' Hemant said, puffing on his chillum.

Rasita didn't really want to talk about that. 'So is there peace now?' she asked instead.

Hemant let the subject be changed. 'Messages have been left with your military authorities, advising them that the "Sons of Ravan" have forsaken their terror campaign. There is talk of anonymous payments to the families of the dead soldiers.'

'Has there been any change with Keke?'

Hemant shook his head slowly. 'No, lady. I am sorry.' He'd heard of the fatal heroism of the rakshasa girl and the other women in the bathing pool. 'She sleeps still.'

Ras bowed her head. Keke might not have woken from her coma, but she was still clinging to life. She was just one sad story among many; Lavanasura had dozens of patients in his hospital. Kasun was working alongside him, using his modern medical learning to wondrous effect in Lanka.

Hemant leaned forward. 'In the *Ramayana*, after he has rescued Sita, Lord Rama made her walk through a fire to prove her fidelity to him. I am thinking that there are fires you must both walk through, to find peace.' He opened his hand, in a pleading gesture. 'Go to him, lady. For all of us.'

She swallowed a lump in her throat as she slowly shook her head. Those cursed photographs replayed in her mind, as did her own folly.

*I nearly cost us everything . . .*

'I can't,' she whispered. 'I just can't.'

## Rishikesh, Uttarakhand, late September 2011

Fireworks exploded over the river, wave upon wave of explosions like an artillery bombardment, sending smoke rolling over the water and booming rockets echoing about the mist-clad hills. Swarg Ashram, with all its yoga centres and meditation schools and tourist lodges, was overflowing with life, the music filling the streets interspersed with blaring car horns. Children waving sparklers danced between the laughing people spilling out into the lanes and alleys: rich and poor, old and young, Indians and Westerners, in couples and large groups, all set on having a good time. The Ram Jhula and Lakshman Jhula suspension bridges were thronging with pedestrians watching the fireworks.

Vikram sat near the river, beside a time-stained old shrine hung with flowers that had almost vanished beneath a smog of taper-smoke, the incense rolling from it in clouds. His hair was long again, tied back in a loose knot. That morning, thinking he might move on, he'd remembered to shave, but as he packed he'd realised it was Dusshera and attempting to travel anywhere would be futile. Across the river, a massive papier-mâché effigy of Ravana was being readied for burning, part of the traditional celebration, the festival of the victory of good over evil that had been commemorated since time immemorial.

*Except that I remember — and I know how close Evil came to being victorious.*

All day he sat by the river, shutting out the noise and the music and the crowds, ignoring everything around him. He did text Amanjit, wishing him well, then shut off his phone so he wouldn't have to read the reply.

Then he closed his eyes and let the hours float away.

As darkness fell and he began to feel hungry, he opened his eyes.

There was a young woman sitting cross-legged beside him, mirroring his posture, waiting.

'Hello, Vikram.'

He swallowed a lump in his throat. 'Ras,' he whispered.

'I thought I'd find you here.' She looked out at the river. 'I've read the *Ramayana* so often I can just about quote it line for line. So when it said that Rama came here for penance, well . . .'

'I didn't mean to. It just happened.' He felt awkward as a child. 'You know, I was thinking about something. When I was Dasraiyat, and I died, my son Ram called my spirit to him, to be his guide. When he killed Ravan Aeshwaran that first time, it was with my guidance. Except neither of us knew that we needed to use a more potent arrow, so we failed. The storytellers added the detail of Rama using the Brahmastra later. My spirit watched unseen, then left him. I'd done my work. Aeshwaran had left Sita untouched — he had to for his ritual, I presume. But she was tarnished goods. Any other man would have put her aside. But my son took her back.' He bowed his head. 'I was proud of him for that act more than any other.'

'Was he a god?'

Vikram shrugged. 'I don't know. He was my son, and that made him divine to me.'

Her face was expressionless, her eyes unreadable. When she did finally speak, he knew what she would ask before the words came out of her mouth.

'He showed me photographs, of you and her. You and Sue.' Her mouth twisted painfully as she said the American girl's name.

Having thought about little else since Lanka didn't make the words come any easier. 'I was alone,' he said at last. 'We were both frightened, *terrified*. And she was my ex-wife or – no, she wasn't even just that: she was the soul of my beloved wife of numerous lives. These are reasons, and they are also excuses. I'm sorry. I needed comfort that night because I was scared and because I had lost any faith that we could be victorious. Everything I've done since this journey began has been for you, *except* that. I was wrong.'

Ras made no response, but fat tears were rolling down her face. Vikram ached to hold her, to wipe them away, but instead, he steeled himself and went on, 'You were true to me in this life, but I wasn't true to you. I don't deserve it, but I am begging you to *please*, forgive me. I will walk through fires for you, if that's what you ask. I will do *anything* to win your forgiveness.'

She was silent for so long he thought she would turn him

away, but at last she reached out slowly and took his hands in hers. 'I was about to marry him,' she whispered. 'I am not without shame.'

'You were misled,' he said. 'I can't blame you for what happened. There is nothing to forgive.' She looked about to demur, but he raised a hand to stop her before she could say anything. 'I was weak,' he repeated. 'The greater sin is mine.'

She met his gaze. 'I forgive it. Freely, totally and utterly.'

He sighed. 'Thank you. *Thank you*. But I cannot forgive myself.'

'Then you should, you fool.' She leaned towards him until they were almost touching. 'Forgive yourself: *that's* the fire you must walk through.'

He swallowed, hard, then as if strings had been severed, releasing him, he collapsed, sobbing, into her arms. Rasita wiped her own cheeks, lifted his face and kissed his lips. They tasted of salty tears and warm spice.

'If you forgive me, then I must do likewise.'

'Do you forgive me too?' she whispered.

'I do,' he said, meaning it from the depths of his heart. Drawing her to him again, he lay back and let her snuggle into him. The fireworks exploded above them, and inside their hearts and minds.

Afterwards they walked into a night made safe that belonged to them alone. Behind them, already forgotten, the burning effigy of Ravana crumbled into the bonfire.

The next morning they walked hand in hand along the river.

'What do we do now?' he asked in a hollow voice. 'The story is over.'

She stared out over the Ganges if there might be an answer there somewhere in the rippling water and dancing light. 'I want to go home,' she said softly. 'I just don't know where that is any more.'

'My home is where you are,' Vikram replied.

## Jodhpur, Rajasthan, Diwali, 26 October 2011

Amanjit and Deepika danced around the bonfire in Clock-tower Square, alongside what looked to be the entire population of Jodhpur, including chittering monkeys over-head and bewildered-looking cows meandering wherever they wanted. Even Lalit was there, with Bishin and their mother; Kiran was laughing and singing the old songs with a group of women. Everyone was high on music and drink and laughter.

Diwali, the celebration of the return of Rama and Sita from Lanka, had been a day of mixed joy and sadness: there were so many happy faces about them, so many beloved family and friends, but two faces were missing and their absence made everything else feel hollow.

Some local boys carried effigies of blue-skinned Rama and white-skinned Sita, hand in hand, through the throng. As Amanjit saw the benevolent smiles on their faces, he fought back a tear. *Namaskar, Vikram, Ras. Wherever you are*.

A reply came instantly, spoken right into his skull: *Namaskar yourself, bhai*.

The soundless greeting resonating in his mind brought him up short. He turned and stared at Deepika, then whirled as a thin young man with long hair, clad in a hoodie and jeans, slipped through the crowd.

'*Vik!*' He leaped on his best friend, his brother, and bear-hugged him, pounding him on the back – then he saw his sister, hovering in Vikram's wake, and thrusting Vikram at Deepika, he pulled Rasita into his arms. '*Didi, you're home*—'

Suddenly, the world was perfect.

Bishin had clocked Amanjit's roar and was pushing his way through the crowds, his mother on his arm. Kirin's smile was wide, but her cheeks were wet and she was shaking as she held her lost daughter as if she would never let her go. Amanjit whooped again and hugged them both as Vikram drew Lalit in an embrace and Deepika threw herself at Ras.

The crowd about them parted, as if sensing something profound was happening, and finally he heard the murmurs of recognition: '*Look! It's Vikram and Rasita.*'

Tomorrow, the media would go mad all over again; there would be one last burst of Vikram-fever; one more excuse to wallow in Sunita Ashoka's tragic life and death – then someone else would come along to shock and stun the nation, and they could fade into the background forever.

But that was for tomorrow.

Tonight was for family and for love.

# THE KING AND QUEEN OF LANKA

*Lanka, December 2011*

Two young people, a man and a woman, walked out of the world on a cold December evening. It was the hour before dusk and the sun was a pink-orange disc in the sky. But when they crossed the threshold of the gate they cut in the air, the setting sun changed into something else: a chariot of gold drawn by glowing horses.

They didn't look back as the gate in the air closed behind them. Their farewells were done, and anyway, it wouldn't be forever. These two worlds were not so far apart.

Beyond the gate was a forest, and a small knoll where invaders from another world had once stood. Beneath it a king had been welcomed home by his people on the day before he died. Before them a damaged city waited, hung with lights that shone like fallen stars.

The gates of the citadel were open and five figures waited there beneath the arched gate.

A small man holding a monkey waved his hand and the animal, its eyes bright, mirrored the gesture.

Beside him, a hunched figure in a robe smiled. His strange eyes in his cobra-like face glittered in the light glimmering in his hands and dancing in solemn merriment.

Between them, a young woman with goat legs and deer horns waved merrily. She was holding the hand of a Tamil doctor, whose expression was somewhere between bliss and bewilderment.

On the walls, trumpets blasted out a welcome. The prophesied king and queen had come, to rebuild and repair and to heal. Asura, rakshasa and human danced in the streets, waving banners and torches as they thanked their gods.

King Vikram and Queen Rasita had come home, to where they were most needed.

# GLOSSARY

| | |
|---|---|
| Agniyastra: | The fire-arrow. |
| *Agni*: | Fire. |
| Aindra-astra: | An astra (magical arrow) that splits into many shafts. |
| Ardas: | A traditional thanksgiving prayer. |
| Astra: | A magic arrow. |
| Asura: | A demon of Hindu mythology, usually portrayed as being a blend of man and beast. |
| Baital: | Batlike demons. |
| Bhai/bhaiya: | Brother (used between male siblings and sometimes by friends). |
| Bhoot: | A ghost. |
| *Bhumi*: | Earth. |
| Bowri: | A step-well: an old underground well with stairs descending to the water surface, often used for bathing by the well-to-do in summer in past times. |
| Brahma: | One of the Trimurti, the three supreme male deities of Hinduism. Brahma is the |

Creator. Despite this his worship is secondary, as he is considered to have fulfilled his immediate purpose by creating the world, and to be asleep, resting from his labours until he is woken again to create a new world.

Brahmastra:      One of the three Trimurti astras: the Brahma-astra will never miss; it is said to be able to kill a god or destroy an army.

Chai:            Indian tea.

Chai-wallah:     Wallah means (more or less) 'fellow' or 'boy'; chai-wallah is a tea-boy or tea-seller.

Dhaba:           A small family restaurant/road-house.

Dhimayastra:     The slow arrow.

Djinn:           An evil spirit of Middle Eastern and Indian folklore.

Dupatta:         A long scarf used to cover a woman's face for modesty and protection from the sun.

Ghat:            A stepped bathing area on the banks of a lake or river.

Gurdwara:        A Sikh temple.

Guru:            A sage-teacher.

Gurukul:         A residential school, usually with a guru (a sage-teacher) living alongside the students.

Haveli:          A guest house.

Ji:              A form of address approximately meaning 'revered one' or 'sir'. It has a connotation of holiness.

Mandir:          A Hindu temple.

Masjid:          A mosque, an Islamic place of worship.

Mohini-astra:      A magic-dispelling astra.

Moksha:            In Hinduism, moksha is when a soul is released: it attains ultimate holiness and is able to transcend the cycle of reincarnation and ascend to Paradise.

Musafir-astra:     The 'travelling arrow'.

Naga-astra:        A magical arrow that turns into venomous snakes.

Paan:              A concoction of betel nuts, betel leaves and spices, chewed as a stimulant by many Indians.

Pandit:            A Hindu priest.

Pashupatastra:     One of the three Trimurti astras, the Big Three magic arrows; this is the astra of Shiva; it will never miss, and is said to be able to kill a god or destroy an army.

Punkah:            A large fan wielded by a servant (a punkah-wallah) to keep their employer cool.

Rakshasa:          An asura with magical powers. They are not necessarily evil.

*Ramayana*, the:   An ancient epic poem describing Rama's efforts with his brother Lakshmana to rescue his wife Sita from the demon-king Ravana; one of India's great mythic cycles.

Sahib:             A Hindi form of address, equivalent to 'sir'.

Salwar kameez:     A traditional outfit of a long overshirt (kameez) and baggy trousers (salwar).

Sammohana:         A sleep arrow.

| | |
|---|---|
| *Shabd bhedi baan vidya*: | The art of shooting blind. |
| Sherwani: | A highly ornate long Indian coat, like a frock-coat. |
| Shiva: | God of death and rebirth, lord of dance, a guide for one who searches. |
| Suryastra: | The light astra. |
| Swayamvara: | A bridal challenge, in which men compete for a bride. |
| Trimurti: | The three principal Hindu dieties, Brahma, Shiva and Vishnu. |
| Trimurti astra: | The special astras of the Trimurti. The Brahmastra, Pashupatastra and Vaishnava-astra, from Brahma, Shiva and Vishnu. |
| Twashtar-astra: | The confusion arrow. |
| Vaishnava-astra: | The astra of Vishnu: it will never miss, and is said to be able to kill a god or destroy an army. |
| Vajra-astra: | The lightning arrow. |
| *Varuna*: | Water. |
| Varuna-astra: | The water arrow. |
| *Vayu*: | Wind. |
| Vavaya-astra: | The wind arrow. |
| Vedavati: | In the *Ramayana*, Vedavati was a holy woman, an avatar of the goddess Laxmi. In this novel, I've used the name as a title for the head of an Indus Valley holy order. |
| Vishnu: | One of the Trimurti, the three primary male deities of Hinduism. Vishnu is the law-bringer, protector and warrior, and mankind's champion. |

# AUTHOR'S NOTE

The decision I have taken in this series to site Lanka at Dholavira in the Rann of Kutch rather than the more conventional site of Sri Lanka, was not taken lightly; these are my reasons.

First and foremost, it was driven by story-telling needs: *The Return of Ravana* is about fictional modern young adults who find their lives mirroring the *Ramayana*. However, having your novels follow the plot of such a well-known tale can tend to make things predictable, unless some surprises are thrown in, and the location of Lanka is one of those, designed to ambush the reader a little. But after researching the subject extensively, I think using Dholavira as the real Lanka, if such a place ever did (or does) exist, does have genuine merit, for the reasons Tim Southby so passionately expresses in *The King*.

First, it is very possible that the *Ramayana* does look back to the time of the Indus Valley culture, which never extended far beyond that area — and if the *Ramayana* is talking about the Vedic period, the same argument holds true.

It was also fortuitous for me that Dholavira's quasi-island location lends itself so well to both the *Ramayana* and my story.

Of course, I'm still flying in the face of tradition, and while I don't exactly apologise for that, I do acknowledge that I'm writing fantasy, not trying to change millennia of tradition.

I'm a New Zealander who has had the privilege to live in India from 2007 to 2010. I'm now back in colder South Sea climes, and missing Incredible India and the wonderful people we met there. These books are a gift in return for the privilege of being able to live there for a time, and I hope you enjoy them for what they are: entertainment, and a little insight into the things that I found most striking about this rich and intoxicating country.

This series was first published by Penguin India, for which I am very grateful. I would also like to express my thanks to Jo Fletcher Books for green-lighting these revised editions: it's not often a writer gets the chance to go back and rewrite their own published work, and while the shape of the story is still the same, it's been nice revisiting the world, and making some improvements.

I've had a great time writing this series and I hope you have enjoyed them too. And if it has made you a little curious about the historical periods and the *Ramayana*, well, that's good too.

Thank you for your company these past four books.

David Hair
Whakatane, New Zealand, 2018

# A Brief Introduction to the Ramayana

## The Story of the Ramayana

The Indian epic known as the *Ramayana* forms the core mythic background for the four books of *The Return of Ravana* series. For readers unfamiliar with the *Ramayana*, here is a very basic summary.

In ancient India, Dasaratha, King of the northern Indian kingdom of Ayodhya, is childless. He makes an offering to the gods and is rewarded with a bowl of magical food called kheer. His three wives each eat a portion and become pregnant; they give birth to four sons: Rama and Bharata and the twins Lakshmana and Shatrughna.

The children grow up under the tutelage of the sage Vishwamitra, and learn the skills required of the warrior-prince. Rama is the most gifted, and the heir apparent to the throne. He kills demons plaguing the land and like all the brothers, is beloved by the people. When a neighbouring king announces a swayamvara, a bridal challenge, for the hand of his daughter Sita, the loveliest maiden in the land, Rama competes, and by breaking the supposedly undrawable bow of Shiva, wins Sita's hand in marriage.

He returns to Ayodhya with his bride, but Queen Kaikeyi, mother of Bharata, his brother, is goaded by her maid (who in some versions of the tale is really a rakshasa in disguise). The maid plays on the queen's jealousies and insecurities, convincing her that if Rama ascends the throne, he will ill-treat her son. The king had granted Kaikeyi a boon years before, for saving his life, and she uses it now to prevent this perceived threat. She demands that Rama is banished for fourteen years and her own son Bharata made heir. The king, honour-bound to grant her the wish, reluctantly banishes Rama.

Rama goes into exile in the forest with his wife Sita and his devoted brother Lakshmana, settling in a cottage there. King Dasaratha dies of sorrow, making Bharata king, but in defiance of his conniving mother, Bharata goes to Rama and begs for his return. When Rama refuses – for this would compromise his father's honour – Bharata takes Rama's sandals and places them on the throne, in token that one day Rama will return and take his rightful place as king. Kaikeyi and her conniving maid are ostracised, and eventually the queen pines away and dies.

In the forest, Rama, Sita and Lakshmana lead an idyllic lifestyle for twelve years, troubled only by the occa-sional demon, which the two princes destroy. In one such encounter, they dismiss the advances of a female demon, Surpanakha, who has taken a fancy to the two brothers. Rama spurns her attempts at seduction, as does Lakshmana, who mocks her. When she attacks Lakshmana, he wounds her, cutting off her nose and driving her away – but Surpanakha is actually the sister of Ravana, the demon king. In a fury, she goes to her brother and tells him of these men who so insulted her, and of the beautiful Sita. Ravana, who is not just mighty in war and magic, but very proud, resolves to have revenge for his sister's injury. He sends a shapeshifter demon, his uncle; Maricha takes the form of a deer and succeeds in luring Rama and Lakshmana away, although he is hunted down and killed for his trouble. While the princes are distracted, Ravana kidnaps Sita, killing Jatayu, the giant eagle sworn to protect her. He takes her to his island kingdom of Lanka and sets about trying to seduce her, but Sita resists his advances.

Increasingly frustrated and obsessed, Ravana ignores all his wives, even his chief wife Mandodari, daughter of a celestial sage and, before Sita appeared, accounted the world's most desirable woman.

Meanwhile, Rama and Lakshmana are hunting for the missing Sita, following clues and encountering numerous perils. They fall in with Hanuman, the monkey god; he is the son of the wind god and can fly, and is able to locate Sita in Lanka. Hanuman is advisor to the Monkey King Sugriva, who agrees to help Rama. He assembles a monkey army to invade Lanka – normally the monkeys would have little chance against the asuras, but with Rama and Lakshmana both masters of archery and using astras, arrows with magical powers, the odds are tilted. In the battles that follow, despite various setbacks and crises, the princes and their allies gain the upper hand, killing many of the rakshasa, the demon-lords, who surround Ravana.

Finally Ravana has no choice but to come out and fight in person. In an epic duel, he is slain by Rama, the demons flee or surrender and Sita is recovered. However, knowing that his people will suspect Sita of infidelity during her captivity, Rama asks that Sita undergo a test of fidelity. Though insulted to be doubted, Sita is determined to prove her loyalty to him and invokes the fire-god, asking that she be consumed, should she have been unfaithful. She is surrounded by flames but isn't burned: having proved her fidelity and chastity, the couple are reunited.

With this accomplished, they are free to return home triumphantly, reclaim the throne of Ayodhya and live happy lives. At his eventual death Rama learns that all along he has been Vishnu, the Protector God, in human form, sent to save the world from Ravana.

## Holy Book, History or Myth? Or all three?

There is considerable debate on how much of the *Ramayana* is history and how much is mythology. It is also a religious text as the hero Rama is seen as an incarnation of the god Vishnu, who in Hindu mythology is the Protector of Mankind.

Some Indians have described the text to me as a sacred holy book and therefore one hundred per cent fact; others as a history and others as a fairy tale for kids. By and large, consensus tends to place the *Ramayana* on a similar level to the *Iliad* or *Odyssey* and other mythic epics: it contains divine characters whose actions can be studied to provide a moral example, but primarily it is seen as a heroic myth with some possible basis in history.

Putting aside this issue (because everyone will have their own opinion and I'm sure no mere fantasy writer is going to change yours), the next question is: if some of it relates to real events, when did these take place? The *Ramayana* was composed around 400 BC (Valmiki, its composer, is believed to have taught poetry to Rama's sons). How far it looks back is the question.

Discounting many extravagant claims and seeking a historical period, one possibility is that it looks back to the first great civilisation of the Indian subcontinent, now known as the Indus Valley Civilisation, which at its time was possibly the most advanced in the world, flourished between 3000–1200 BC in and around the Indus River valleys, the modern India/Pakistan borderlands. The people of that time had sophisticated mathematics, science, trade and art, and predated Hinduism. The civilisation failed when climatic and tectonic changes caused the rivers to dry up and the land to become arid, leaving the major cities without water. The people largely abandoned the region as it turned to desert and migrated south and west across the Indian subcontinent in what is known as the Vedic period. So perhaps the *Ramayana* is a fanciful reimagining of the fall of India's first great civilisation, written with a religious slant.

A second possibility is that the *Ramayana* looks back on the battles and rivalries of the north Indian kingdoms during the Vedic period (1500–500 BC), during which Hinduism was codified. This option isn't entirely satisfactory, as the historical tie-ins to known events are tenuous. I don't pretend to know which is right, but I have taken a stance in the story, as you'll find in Book 4.

It is probably fair to say that the *Ramayana* is regarded by educated Indians today more as a legend and quasi-historical tract than a purely religious document, but the religious aspects cannot be ignored. The reign of Rama was seen as an exemplary model for all rulers, and his role as Protector mirrors that of Vishnu in Indian cosmology. Gandhi invoked Rama during the creation of the Indian Republic. The tale remains as much a part of the fabric of Indian culture, society and religion as Old Testament tales do in Christian countries.

As the origins and meaning of the *Ramayana* are hugely contentious, and I don't claim any expertise, I've incorporated conventional truths if they suited the story and ignored others that don't. *The Return of Ravana* is an adventure series written to entertain, first and last. If this all sounds like a plea to not be hounded by historians and scholars — it is.

## Hinduism at a Glance

Hinduism is arguably the oldest surviving religious tradition in the world, and the third largest, after Christianity and Islam. However, most of its adherents live in one country, India, with the remainder primarily in Southeast Asia. It has a plethora of holy texts, including the *Vedas*, *Upanishads*, *Puranas* and the epics *Ramayana* and *Mahabharata*.

Hinduism was not even treated as one religion until the nineteenth century; it still has huge regional diversity.

Outsiders think of it as having many gods, but this isn't entirely the case: each of the gods (and there are *millions* of Hindu gods if you take into account local deities and ancestor worship) are seen as part of one supreme being, so taking one set of rules and saying, *this is Hinduism*, is never entirely correct. Nevertheless, taking a broad consensus approach:

The supreme being (known as Ishvara, Om, Bhagavan and many other names) created and maintains life. The goal of existence is to merge in eternal bliss with the supreme being. Attaining this state requires purifying oneself spiritually by the pathway of dharma (righteousness), artha (livelihood/wealth), kama (sensual pleasure) and moksha (release). A person must experience what the world has to offer and learn from it before setting life aside in favour of the spiritual and divine. Hindus believe that a person reincarnates, living many lives, until they attain moksha.

To guide mankind, the supreme being manifests in many different forms, which enables different people to find moksha in their own way, which is why there are many gods and goddesses in Hinduism.

Nowadays, the three primary male gods are known collectively as the Trimurti: Brahma, the creator who made the universe, is usually seen as having done his work, so he is seldom actively worshipped. He is portrayed as resting, until he is needed again. Hindus believe the universe has been created and destroyed several times already.

Vishnu the Preserver protects and champions mankind, especially against forces of evil like asuras and rakshasas. Vishnu as a deity embodies the manly virtues and has become an avatar – a god embodied in flesh – many times, including in the god-heroes Rama and Krishna, always to guide and protect mankind.

Shiva represents destruction and rebirth. Unlike Vishnu, Shiva teaches the putting-aside of worldly concerns and the seeking of moksha, and he is said to have invented yoga to facilitate this. He is normally portrayed in furs and a loincloth, dancing or practising yoga. He is also, with his consort Parvati, the prime fertility deity.

Each of these gods has a female consort. Saraswati, Brahma's lover, is the goddess of music and learning, and a favourite of schoolchildren. Laxmi is the goddess of wealth, Vishnu's consort. Her image is to be found in most business premises. Parvati, Shiva's wife, is the example of the good wife and beautiful woman, the most sensuous and loving of the female deities. She is also the most dangerous: when roused she is warlike, becoming Durga, who embodies the female warrior spirit, and when pushed to the limits, she becomes Kali, a bloodthirsty force of destruction.

Other important Hindu deities include Hanuman, the monkey god, a spirit of fidelity, cleverness and courage and devoted to Vishnu. Ganesh, the elephant god, is lucky and provides good fortune.

There are also beings akin to angels and demons, called devas and asuras respectively. Asuras are not always evil: both sets of beings co-operated with Brahma in the creation of the world, but devas are celestial and asuras are baser and more malicious. Rakshasa are also demons, but more powerful than asuras.

In the Hindu cosmology we live over and again, seeking

release and the divine. The gods help with their wisdom and interventions as we make our way in the world, becoming wiser until we eventually turn to the divine.

## A Quick Note on Sikhism

Sikhism was founded in the fifteenth century in the Punjab in northern India. It teaches of a universal god without form, and that salvation comes from merging with that god. The Five Evils – ego, lust, greed, attachment and anger – are seen as the main obstacles to oneness with God.

There are a number of behavioural tenets (wearing turbans, bearing knives, etc.) by which traditional Sikhs may be recognised. The religion is guided by teachers called gurus, and worship is carried out at a gurdwara, where the holy texts are read and there is traditionally a bathing pool and a kitchen dispensing free food. Sikhism, the fifth largest organised religion in the world, has most of its followers in the Punjab.

# ACKNOWLEDGEMENTS

This series was first published by Penguin India, for which I am very grateful, especially to Mike Bryan and Heather Adams (who are now my agents) for opening those doors, and to Sudeshna Shome Ghosh for her terrific editorial work and vision in the original editions.

I am also very grateful to Jo Fletcher Books for green-lighting these revised editions: it's not often a writer gets the chance to go back and revise their own published work, and while the shape of the story is still the same, it's been a great experience revisiting it. And many thanks to the JFB art team, especially Rory Kee, for the great new covers on these revised editions.